MW00799554

Praise for
Floats the Dark Shadow

"Yves Fey writes with the eye of an artist, the nose of a perfumer and the nerves of a hardened gendarme in this chilling tale of love and love's perversion. Not for the faint of heart!" — Cuyler Overholt, award-winning author of *A Deadly Affection*

"This dark, gothic tale will delight fans of decadent, sensuous, fin-de-siècle Paris." — Kenneth Wishnia, award-winning author of *23 Shades of Black* and *The Fifth Servant*

"Yves Fey delves into the dark well of occult, violence and eroticism lying just beneath the surface of fin-de-siècle Paris. The valiant heroine, American artist Theo Faraday, confronts the ultimate evils of child torture and murder as the serpentine page-turning plot unfolds. Beware! It's strong stuff." — Barbara Corrado Pope, author of *Cézanne's Quarry* and *The Blood of Lorraine*

"Fey not only captures the last decadent decade of nineteenth century Paris, but she does so decadently...." — Tyler R. Tichelaar, Ph.D. and award-winning author of *Spirit of the North: a paranormal*

"Yves Fey recreates the haunting world of absinthe, of the Symbolist poets, of Salomé, of the Golden Dawn, and of darker, more unfathomable forces, that was Paris in 1897. This well-researched thriller offers satisfyingly complex characters. Powerful, violent, elegant." —Beth Tashery Shannon, *Pushcart Prize* winner, author of *Tanglevine*

Library of Congress Control Number 2012934486
Casebound: 978-1-937356-20-0
Trade: 978-1-937356-21-7
Kindle: 978-1-937356-22-4
EPUB: 978-1-937356-23-1

Publisher's Cataloging-in-Publication Data

Fey, Yves.
Floats the dark shadow / Yves Fey.
p. cm.
ISBN: 978-1-937356-20-0
1. Murder—Fiction. 2. Paris (France)—History—1870-1940—Fiction. 3.
Satanism—Fiction. 4. Blood accusation—Fiction. 5. Historical mystery
novels.   I. Title.
PS3606.E99 F56 2012
813.6—dc22
        2012933526

Book design by Frogtown Bookmaker.

Front cover photograph by Michel Colson
Back cover photograph by Eugène Atget (1913)

Refugiatta Std.font copyright © 2012 by Juan Casco.
Horst font copyright © 1990 by David Rakowski.
WW Floral Corner font copyright © 1999 by Wind Walker.
Title page Art Nouveau font copyright © 1998 by Scriptorium.

Published by BearCat Press: www.BearCatPress.com

Floats the Dark Shadow

by

Yves Fey

BearCat PRESS

For Judith, this time.

For Richard. always

France, 1897

When your heart is in horror lost,
And over your present like a ghost
Floats the dark shadow of the past...
                    Charles Baudelaire

Chapter One

Some perfumes are as fragrant as a child,
Sweet as the sound of hautboys, meadow-green;
Others, corrupted, rich, exultant, wild….
                    Charles Baudelaire

Gilles unlocked the scorched oak door and raised his lantern, illumi-
nating the staircase that coiled down to the dungeons of the chateau.
Underneath the smell of ashes, of damp stone and lantern oil, he inhaled
traces of other odors. Mold, urine, and feces. Clotted gore. Fear. The fetid
bouquet blossomed in his nostrils. Repugnance entwined with anticipation.

In his ancient castle, opulent perfumes would have dizzied his senses.
The wine rich scent of hippocras would have spilled from a goblet set
with jewels, mingling with the crushed almond aroma of honeyed
marzipan. Luscious red roses would have shed petals bright as virgin's
blood on pure white linen. Over all, plumes of incense would have drifted,
saturating the night with a scent at once sacred and lasciviously profane.

But that was another place.

Another century.

Another life.

And there was a pleasing austerity in these simpler smells. A perverse
purity.

Gilles closed the door and descended the winding staircase, his
leather soles scuffing on the limestone. No other sound—but the mortal
odors intensified with each step. When he reached the bottom, the stench
clogged his nostrils. The lantern cast a sickly light on the stone walls
surrounding him. A barred gate stood ajar. He saw nothing but his own
flickering shadow. He heard nothing. No, there, a faint noise, like a breath
caught. A sob. He moved forward quickly, stepping through the iron
gateway into a large chamber.

In the center of the room the boy hung from the rafters. Ropes bound
him tightly and an iron hook and chain held him suspended. He revolved
slowly in the air, not struggling, silent but for his weeping. His eyes were

swollen, and runnels of tears slid down his cheeks to drip off his chin. Letting out a cry of outrage, Gilles rushed forward. He set aside the lantern and lifted the boy down.

"Don't be afraid," he whispered as he tugged at the knot on the ropes. They came loose in his hands and he tossed them aside. The child threw his arms around him, weeping more fiercely with relief. Gilles drew him into his arms, comforting him. "What is your name, boy?"

"Denis," he choked out, fighting to stifle his sobs. Though old enough to grasp at manly courage, the boy clung to him. His chilled limbs felt deliciously fragile.

Gilles held him for a moment, then drew back to look into his eyes. Gently he stroked the sweat-soaked fringe of hair plastered to Denis' forehead. "Who did this to you?"

The boy clutched him more tightly, tears and snot smearing Gilles' velvet-clad shoulder. "A man in Paris promised me a job as a stable boy," he blurted. "He said we would ask my mother—but then he covered my face with a rag. He brought me to this awful place. He dragged me down to this wine cellar!"

"Dungeon," Gilles murmured, but too low for Denis to hear. From what he knew of the boy, he had expected more imagination.

Denis looked over to where a thin trail of smoke drifted over pieces of charred wood. "He lit a fire—I thought he would burn me."

"Terrible!"

"He put it out when he left. I thought I would freeze!" The boy's gaze darted around the walls. "He will come back."

"I will take you somewhere else," Gilles promised him, bringing another spasm of sobs from Denis. He stood, taking up the lantern with one hand, beckoning with the other.

"Back to Paris?" Bright with hope, he looked up at Gilles.

"Come now, you must be brave." Gilles smiled a little. "St. Denis was brave, wasn't he?" Swallowing back a sob, the boy made a small choking sound. Was he imagining his martyred namesake carrying his head through the streets of Paris? Was he imagining his own head severed from his body? Lovely.

Denis frowned. "I know you sir, don't I?"

"Do you? Yes, I believe you do."

Denis looked confused. He rubbed his eyes with the heels of his hands, wiped his nose on his sleeve. He rubbed his sore arms, shivering with the winter cold as he glanced anxiously at the barred doorway. Gilles clasped the boy's shoulder protectively, stroking it to warm him. "There's another way." He hurried him across the chamber to another iron gate, opened it, urged Denis into the passage beyond. "Through here."

"You know this place, sir?" Denis asked.

"I own it." When he felt the boy tense, Gilles shook his head and frowned in concern. "There were rumors about my stable master. At first I did not believe them, but finally I came to investigate." A few feet, and they stopped at another door, strapped with decayed leather and studded with iron. Gilles reached up and took the key from the lintel.

"He told me I would work in a beautiful chateau." Denis' voice was hesitant. Tears still glistened on his cheeks. "But this place is in ruins."

"So it is." Gilles unlocked the door. It opened into darkness lit only by the lantern light falling across the threshold. The odor of fleshy rot enveloped Gilles as he stepped through, coaxing Denis to follow. Would he resist? That might be amusing. But no…the boy crossed over. Gilles' heart gave a lovely shudder, as if struck like a bell. He locked the door behind them, then led the way to the center of the chamber. Lifting the lantern high, he smiled.

When the boy saw the others, he began to scream.

Chapter Two

Seductive evening, friend of the criminal,
Enters like an accomplice, a stalking wolf....
                    Charles Baudelaire

Leaving the Palais de Justice, Inspecteur Michel Devaux, detective of the Sûreté, inhaled deeply, clearing away the stink of the jail with the scent of incipient rain. Cold, moist air prickled his skin. Above the glare of the arc lamps, lowering clouds swallowed the stars, the waning moon thin as a fingernail paring. He glanced up at the corner of the Conciergerie, where the oldest clock in Paris told him it was just after midnight. The adrenaline of the hunt and arrest had drained away during the questioning of his prisoner. His body ached for home and sleep but his mind remained watchful. He could spend an hour playing his guitar instead of staring at the ceiling, unreeling horrors. The axe murders had been particularly gruesome, the killer's grandmother and her equally ancient maid hacked into pieces.

Yet the hunt for the killer had served as distraction from even uglier childhood memories. Twenty-six years ago yesterday, the Paris Commune had claimed rulership of the city. Two months later their reign ended in slaughter. His own life ended then.

Ended and began again.

Music might ward off all kinds of blood-drenched nightmares.

The March wind gusted and the rain came down cold and sharp as needles. Michel turned up the collar of his jacket and set out across the Île de la Cité. The pale limestone of the city looked ghostly in the night. The Right Bank was all but silent, but looking over to the Left he caught glimpses of the activity always brewing in the *cafés* of the student quarter. He made his way past Notre Dame, where the illuminated carvings of kings and saints glistened with rain. Soon its rooftop gargoyles would be gushing. He crossed the small bridge to the tiny Île Saint Louis, and turned to follow the slant of the quai down toward his apartment.

A man stood under the trees at the far point of the island, his shape dark against the lamp-lit shimmer of the inky water. Michel knew no one had followed him from the detectives' bureau, but any detective could have enemies lying in wait. On guard, he continued to approach, listening for other movements to the side or behind. No one else. The shadowed figure struck a match, cupping it against the rain as he lit a thinly rolled cigarette. The quiver of light revealed one of Blaise Dancier's henchmen, his *âme damnée,* Jacques le Rouge. For a damned soul he had an oddly angelic face, though his hair was red as hellfire. "Le Rouge" was not for the hair, but for the throats he cut. The red scarf around his neck was deliberately provocative. Michel stopped, waited. Jacques gave a brusque nod toward the Right Bank. Moving forward, Michel saw a carriage waiting just across the Pont Louis-Philippe.

Intrigued but not apprehensive, Michel followed Le Rouge over the bridge to the waiting carriage and climbed inside. With a sharp snap of the whip, the coachman set off through the narrow cobbled streets of the sleeping Marais district, where the lavish abodes of sixteenth century aristocrats were now the crowded homes of poor Jews. The road smoothed as they moved into increasingly fashionable areas. Rain drumming on the roof was the only sound. The street lamps sent stray slices of light through the carriage windows, showing Michel his companion watching him with ice blue eyes. Normally, he tried to bribe someone like Jacques le Rouge to give up tidbits of information about his employer, but Dancier tossed gifts to beggars bigger than Michel's bribes. And a bribe wouldn't have worked with the taciturn Le Rouge. Michel already knew he was utterly loyal. Blaise Dancier could inspire that.

Criminel extraordinaire, Dancier had done it all—thief, pimp, assassin. Michel could not bring himself to call such a man a friend. Neither would he deny that he enjoyed Dancier's company and valued their odd alliance. Still, Michel was surprised when the coachman entered the courtyard of Dancier's home on the far side of L'Opéra Garnier. Usually any exchange of information took place somewhere neutral. He understood that a meeting at Dancier's townhouse was intended as a compliment. He felt extremely curious and slightly annoyed at the unwanted intimacy. Also, very slightly, complimented. No doubt, Dancier was equally ambivalent about him.

Michel descended from the carriage and crossed to the door. It opened before he knocked. The man who admitted him was an impressive combination of muscle and *maître d'hôtel* manners. He took Michel's wet jacket, then led him to the salon. Dancier was waiting, deliberately casual, perched on the edge of his desk, brandy snifter in hand. He waited till the butler departed, then lifted the Baccarat decanter on the tray beside him. "Cognac?"

Michel recognized the bottle as Napoléon's favorite. One taste could be counted as a most extravagant bribe. He smiled a little—after all, courtesy was important. "Thank you."

As Dancier poured the amber liquid, Michel idly wondered if the decanter was stolen or perhaps actually purchased from some fine shop on the grand boulevards. Dancier handed him the other snifter. Michel inhaled the rich aroma, letting it tease his senses as he silently thanked his lover for her tutelage in such matters. Lilias' skills went far beyond the erotic. He took a small sip. As expected, the cognac was as sumptuous, fruit melted into amber fire. Michel nodded his compliments, relishing hints of apricot and honey, a tinge of cinnamon.

"Courvoisier. Only the best." Dancier gestured with the snifter, indicating the brandy, the glass, the whole room.

"Of course." Rather fantastically, Michel had imagined Dancier surrounded by a vast piratical treasure trove of stolen booty. Not so. The salon was elegant in the most modern style, paneled and furnished with fluid and rhythmic woodwork that looked almost alive. The velvety wallpaper was a riot of autumn leaves, vivid as splashes of flame. A strange chandelier of crimson lilies coiled overhead, a multi-headed hydra, beautiful yet sinister.

"You missed a good *savate* session tonight," Dancier told him.

"It was worth it and I made good use of my skills."

"I hear you kicked the chopper in the throat—sent him ass over ears down the stairs."

"It seemed expedient. He came at me with an axe."

"A louse who cuts up old ladies—why not just shoot him between the eyes?" When Michel refused to respond to that, Dancier shrugged and went on, "What kick?"

"*Fouetté.*"

They'd met through their *savate* teacher, an acknowledged master, a student of the man who had taught Dumas. Michel had taken several classes, Dancier private lessons. The master suggested the two meet and spar. Reluctantly, they'd agreed and found he was right. Physically they were well matched. Michel had an advantage of height and weight, and had trained himself to an implacable calm. Dancier was thirty-seven, five years older than Michel, but possessed whipcord strength, lightning reflexes, and a dynamic, almost manic energy. He claimed fire flowed in his veins instead of blood and scoffed that Michel might as well have ice water. They had become sparring partners in life as well, always *en garde* against a false step, a hard kick, a dirty trick that might shatter their tentative alliance.

"At first I just wanted cane fencing lessons, figuring I could learn a new trick or two. But *la savate*—I thought I already knew all there was to know about the old shoe." Dancier displayed a highly polished pair of boots, their gleam mocking the old sailor's shoes that gave the sport its name. "One demonstration taught me I was wrong. The man put me on my ass." His eyes narrowed slightly at the memory and he adjusted his jacket with a sharp tug. Vain and prickly as a cat, Dancier kept himself perfectly groomed, dark hair in artful curls, mustache in perfect twists. His clothes were impeccably cut, ostentatiously expensive, and blatantly gaudy. Catching the dubious glance at his magenta waistcoat, Dancier lifted his eyebrows in a delicate shrug. "I make fashion. When they copy me, they tone it down. No testicles."

Michel considered Dancier might need an extra helping to defend his sartorial choices. Blaise scanned Michel's clothes in turn. "And you— just how do you do it, Devaux? You make a *flic's* salary suit look like *haute couture.*" He added an almost lascivious wink.

"I'll introduce you to my tailor." The conversation, however amusing, seemed pointless. Michel went to the heart of the matter. "Why am I here?"

Dancier began to prowl the room. For all its richness and innovative ornament, the space was not cluttered, allowing Dancier's movement free rein. Michel was used to the restless energy, but surprised at Dancier's hesitation in voicing his request. Was it something Michel would have to refuse?

"You weren't supposed to catch the axe man on your own," he complained. "I had my men on it."

"You wanted to dispatch him yourself?" It made no sense to Michel. Nothing in the case should interest Dancier, only a man who slaughtered two harmless old women in hopes of claiming an inheritance. "Did you know one of the victims?"

Dancier swiveled, impatient. "No. I wanted to make you a gift."

Michel understood instantly. "A bargaining chip?"

Dancier paused and leaned back against the desk, examined his manicure. "Give a gift, get a gift."

"And what gift did you want in return?"

"I'm missing a couple of kids," Dancier said. "I want you to investigate."

Michel felt a cold sinking in his gut. Cases involving children were the most disheartening. He was surprised that Dancier would engender a debt for what was likely to be a futile task. There would be a reason. "Tell me."

"Jamet was a great little pickpocket. Smart kid. Funny. A couple of weeks ago, I sent him to get me some tobacco. He didn't come back. Broad daylight yet no one sees him vanish."

A hundred things might have happened. Especially to a boy caught picking pockets. "You looked at the morgue?"

"Right off. He wasn't there."

Michel waited. There must be more.

"I'm a better boss, true?" Dancier asked, his eyebrows stabbing upward.

Michel nodded, watching the other man resume his prowl. Dancier had a personal code of honor. He took good care of the people who worked for him as long as they didn't cross him. Like any crook, he was greedy to the core, but unlike most, he was greedy for admiration, for affection, as well as money. Like Machiavelli's Prince, he knew it was better to be feared than loved, better still if you could manage both.

"The boy's got no reason to leave. He stays with me, he knows he can work his way up—like Jacques did. The good life." He paused. "I checked. No rival tried some cheap ploy to eat into what I control."

"Few would dare." Michel knew of a couple, but they'd have paid the boy to spy.

"Jamet was a pretty boy, so I even asked at a few of the houses. Most of the madams, they wouldn't try anything like that. Not with any kid that works for me."

Michel was six when the Commune fell. Children that young had been shot by the government troops. Orphans were taken into the workhouses of the Daughters of Charity. Michel had escaped those fates, but might as easily been snatched off the street and trained in crime. Trained by someone far crueler than this man. Dancier did not put his kids in brothels. "You said a couple of boys?"

Dancier paused again. There was a flash of something in his eyes. Guilt? "About six months ago, there was another kid. His trainer's in the ragpicker racket. One day the kid is just gone. The trainer is in fits—this kid is so good at looking pathetic it brings in extra. I searched, but not much. I didn't like the kid, you know? A whiner. Good riddance." He grimaced.

"So, you think two?" Michel asked.

Again Dancier hesitated. "Just two of mine."

"There are others." Michel didn't bother to make it a question. He felt a sudden frisson, an intuition that Dancier was right. Their eyes met.

Dancier squared his shoulders, a typically belligerent gesture, yet Michel suspected it was from the same sort of chill that trickled along his own spine.

"When I started asking around the neighborhood, I heard of some other poor kids gone nobody knows where. Some were young girls—less likely to just run off."

"But probably not related?"

"Maybe not. But another boy—some laundress' kid named Denis— disappeared into thin air a couple of months ago." Dancier tapped his nose. "I smell a rat."

"Your nose is keen." Michel frowned. "I will ask questions, Dancier. But surely, in this situation, your resources are better than mine?"

"You've got a sharp eye. Maybe you'll learn something we missed." Dancier shifted, aware the situation was tenuous. "Even if you find nothing, I thought you should know. I thought you should spread the word."

"I promise I will investigate on my own," Michel assured him. "If I find any evidence to confirm your suspicions, I will inform Cochefert. He is sympathetic to any situation involving children. Something may strike him from other cases."

"Yeah, tell the chief." Dancier smiled at Michel. "He picked my pockets once, just to prove he could."

Michel smiled briefly. It was a favorite trick of Cochefert's, and neither criminal nor gendarme was safe. Michel had caught him trying it but he didn't tell Dancier that. "Do any of these children have parents, friends, trainers? Tell me where to begin." Dancier gave him some names, some dates, and Michel wrote them down. He would see if these cases had any elements in common, perhaps cross-check them with other unsolved disappearances. He could also ask Lilias to inquire but only if something proved to be amiss. Dancier said he'd spoken to some of the madams, but Lilias was a courtesan of the upper echelons, with a more rarefied clientele.

"I'll see you get a gift of equal value, Devaux. Meanwhile—" Dancier rummaged through a desk drawer and extracted two tickets. "The Grand Guignol opens soon. These are for opening night if you want them. Take a pretty girl." He gave a theatrical shiver. "Nothing like a scare to get them excited."

Michel had heard that Dancier was investing in the new theatre. He had also heard that his main interest was a certain blonde actress. But he did not accept this sort of favor. "No thank you."

"Your loss." Dancier shrugged off the snub. "It's raining. My carriage is at your disposal."

Michel didn't refuse again. He finished his cognac and bade Dancier good night. "I will let you know what I learn, though I do not expect it to be much."

Dancier looked up, his eyes glinting darkly. "Too little might be better than too much."

Chapter Three

I'll rush at life so swiftly and so hard,
With a fierce embrace and an iron grasp,
That before the day's sweetness can be torn from me
It will warm itself in my winding arms.
                              Anna, Comtesse de Noailles

Branches swayed overhead as Theodora Faraday cantered along the bridle path in the Bois de Boulogne. Shafts of light broke through the massed storm clouds, and the bright chartreuse of the lime tree leaves gleamed, eerily vivid against the ominous charcoal grey. To either side, lush meadows glittered with a king's ransom of golden dandelions. Feeling the mare's impulse to gallop ripple through her own muscles, Theo shifted forward, merging with the lengthening stride of her horse. Elfe had a lovely gallop, smooth and supple beneath Theo, her hooves drumming an eager rhythm on the ground. The March wind whipped the little mare's mane, and scattered raindrops sparkled chill against Theo's skin as she rode. Laughing, she urged Elfe to go faster. "*Va, chérie, va!*"

One dark rain cloud swept over them and passed on, leaving them wet but cheerful in an expanse of dappled sunlight. Theo eased Elfe back to a canter, then to a sprightly trot. They followed the Route de la Grande Cascade to the picturesque waterfall then rode back along the lake toward the stables. Elfe pranced, wanting to return to her waiting hay, but Theo kept her to a walk so she could savor the gorgeous afternoon light. She found a long pathway where the cherry trees were bursting into bloom and guided the mare into the glorious universe of pink. Theo hadn't planned to sketch, but she never went anywhere without pencil and paper. There was a small sketchbook wrapped in oilcloth safe inside the pocket of her jacket. She let Elfe roam along the trail while she looked about for the best composition. She loved the wide horizontals of pink blossoms above and fallen petals below, the stormy sky looming behind and the path curving through. Even more, she was enticed by the elegant branching of one particular tree, asymmetric like a Japanese print, the bark flat black against the glowing grey clouds. Then a patch of azure opened behind one corner of the blossoms, making Theo giddy with delight. But the blue sky was to the east, and now the clouds overhead began to spatter her with rain. There was no point in making sodden drawings. If tomorrow brought sunshine, she would come back with her pastels. With luck, the rain would spare most of the blooms. If not, she could sketch the beautiful form of the tree.

Theo loved working *en plein air*. Painting with the ardent Impressionists in Mill Valley had shaped her technique with oils and taught her to see an infinity of color amid the gold and green of California hillsides and the cool, ever-changing expanses of bay and ocean. But she often felt it was a kind of madness to try to capture the truth of the light when it shifted so quickly. She'd heard that Monet took a wheelbarrow of canvases with him to whatever place he had chosen to paint. Depending on the light, he plucked out whichever one was most like the current moment. Theo laughed at the thought of wheeling a dozen canvases about Montmartre in search of yesterday's perfect vision. It was not the evanescent glimmer of light that she wanted to capture but the emotion the landscape evoked.

Laughter came easily now that the misery of the last months in California had faded. She'd lived in Paris a little over a year, lived as a participant, not a voyeur. When the century turned, she wanted to be established here in the center of the world for an artist—a world that Impressionism had exploded into a million glittering pieces. Each new piece another shining world to explore.

Before leaving the row of cherry trees behind, she broke off a spray of blossoms and tucked it into her jacket so she could capture the details of the flowers and the nuances of color. Cherry time…everyone in Montmartre was singing *Le Temps des cerises*. Theo warbled what she remembered and filled in the rest with humming as she set Elfe back on the road to the stable abutting the Longchamps racecourse.

> *When we gather in the cherry season*
> *gay nightingale and blackbird mocking*
> *will both be rollicking*
> *the pretty girls will grow all giddy*
> *and lovers' hearts all sunny*
> *when we sing the cherry season*
> *the mocking blackbird piping all the more….*

In the stable, Theo dismounted and handed the mare over to a young groom. "She's a lovely ride," Theo said, stroking Elfe's soft nose.

"Your ride home will be wet," the boy answered, nodding toward the bicycle she'd left resting against a wall.

"Very, very wet." Theo gave what she hoped was a truly Gallic shrug, collected her mechanical mount and wheeled it out into the rain. Despite the weather, there were still fancy carriages rolling through the Bois de Boulogne, filled with fashionable Parisians determined to show off their costly garments and extravagant *chapeaux*. Theo relished weaving her bicycle in and out between them. After that diversion it was indeed a long and very wet ride back to the bottom of the Butte Montmartre. Tired and dripping, she pushed her bicycle to the top of the rue Lepic and, finally, through the entrance of her landlady's enclosed garden.

As she approached, Averill Charron opened the door and leaned against the doorjamb, smiling. Theo was elated to see him cheerful rather than melancholy, but a burr of disquiet snagged her bright surge of happiness. Her cousin had promised to pose yesterday. Once again, he'd vanished mysteriously. The memory rankled, but she ignored it and smiled a welcome.

Stepping into the entryway, Theo felt, as always, the shock of recognition. His features were almost twin to hers, high cheekbones, short straight nose, and full lips. At a ridiculous five foot ten, she matched his height, and his pale blue eyes regarded her as if in a mirror—but his thick tumble of black hair made it a dark mirror.

Averill held something small and golden. A cookie. He sketched tantalizing circles in the air, then tapped her nose before popping it into her mouth. "Madame Masson let me in from the rain. She fed me hot chocolate and *macarons* while I waited for you."

Theo smelled the luscious fragrance of chocolate clinging to him and felt a swell of relief. She had expected the licorice undertone of absinthe. Greedily, she finished the *macaron* before she chided, "I hope you left some for Matthieu."

"One or two."

Once Averill had realized his father's elegant prison was suffocating Theo, he'd found this place for her, complete with chaperone landlady, and loaned her the funds to move. His father, her Uncle Urbain, was livid. Her own father had been displeased to find her living in racy Montmartre but reassured by Madame Masson's respectability. Matthieu was the widow's only child, and Theo often had him assist her after school to earn pocket money. He would far rather carry canvases than pose, but always made a valiant effort not to squirm.

"Come upstairs," she said to Averill. He hesitated, then picked up her bicycle and carried it to her top-floor apartment—a large studio, a tiny bedroom, and a miniscule kitchen. Entering, Theo instantly went to the painting on the easel and covered it. Her second painting of Matthieu was no more successful than her first. She felt a pang of dismay.

Before her father left for Italy, he'd seen her working on the first portrait. He'd urged her to submit it to the Salon, claiming it was certain to be accepted. But the longer she worked, the less she'd liked its bland pastel prettiness. Theo had taken the finished portrait all the way to the door—and stopped. She'd worked hard to please her father. Acceptance by the Salon would have been proof she was worth the upkeep of her studio and her lessons at the Académie Julian. And it had not been only for her father that she had struggled with the portrait. She wanted her work displayed. At the Salon de Champs de Mars, her painting would be viewed by twenty thousand people a day.

Not this painting. Theo had carried it back and scraped it down.

She waited tensely for some probing question from Averill and was grateful that he said nothing. Turning around, she found him still leaning in her open doorway, artfully insouciant, a wicked little smile hovering about the corners of his lips. "I have an invitation for you."

"An invitation?" she prompted.

He sauntered over. "To the Gates of Hell…and beyond."

A riddle. *La Barrière d'Enfer.* Theo knew Hell's Gate was what they called the old southern toll gate out of Paris. And beyond? The guillotine had once stood nearby, but no longer. Then, beneath? "The catacombs."

"*Exactement.*"

Theo smiled, feeling a shiver race along her spine—apprehension, but anticipation too. Wandering through a labyrinth of ancient bones wasn't her first choice for an evening out in Paris, yet Averill made the darkness alluring. Life was more vivid when contrasted with death. Theo had been promising to go to the catacombs ever since Averill said he was writing a poem about them. To illustrate it she would need to see the beauty in their desolation, as he did.

"Casimir is playing his violin in a midnight concert tomorrow—at midnight on April 1st. We are all invited."

Casimir Estarlian, baron de la Veillée sur Oise, was Averill's oldest and closest friend among the Revenants, the group of poets—and one California artist—who'd joined together last year after the performance of Oscar Wilde's *Salomé.* Their magazine, *Le Revenant,* had created quite a stir in the literary world. "A revenant is a ghost that is not only visible but tactile," Averill had explained to her that night. "Sometimes even a corpse risen from the grave. A ghost that feeds upon emotion. Upon desire." Averill had written four poems, all highly praised. Theo had illustrated them for him in the intricately twisted style he favored. Those illustrations had won her praise as well.

"A midnight concert in the catacombs?" She tilted her head, considering. "How can I resist?"

Averill smiled with such boyish delight that this time her answering smile was unforced. He had challenged her. She had accepted. It would be an adventure, and however forbidding the territory, she would be with him.

"It will be unique." He looked at her intently, frowning slightly now.

"What?"

Reaching out, Averill smoothed back a strand of wet hair sticking to her cheek. Then he broke off a cherry blossom from the branch she'd put inside her jacket and tucked it behind her ear. He nodded toward the easel. "You should do a self-portrait—*The Bedraggled Amazon.*"

Theo sputtered with laughter, amused and embarrassed. The Revenants had dubbed her their *Amazone blonde.* She was skilled with horses and weapons. Her nickname was masculine and she often wore trousers instead of skirts. That choice was daring. Illegal. They applauded her for it, their bold American. But sometimes she felt she was permitted her brashness because she was from California, a name they pronounced with the same exotic savor as Trinidad or Madagascar. She was something not quite tame. At times, Theo felt more like a mascot than a person. But never with Averill. "Beware the bedraggled Amazon doesn't skewer you for the insult."

"The Amazon is far too merciful to inflict pain." Even in shadow, his blue eyes had a luminous glow she knew her own did not possess. "Theo," he said hesitantly, "I must apologize. I promised to pose."

"Yes?"

"There were arguments at home…exams for which to study…."

"Or not?" Theo hated the acid in her tone.

"Or not." Averill shrugged elaborately, but did not look away. "Sometimes I am tempted to fail again just to aggravate my father."

Theo did not look away either, though she was sorry for her cut. "But you are succeeding. For yourself."

"Yes. The new school of psychology fascinates me—almost as much as a new poem." He smiled ironically. "I was distracted this past week, but that is not why I avoided posing."

"Then why?"

He hesitated. "I think I fear what you will see if you paint me."

"Fear?" The resentment melted. Of all the reasons she had imagined, that was never one.

"You see very clearly."

"I thought…" She had suspected him of gallivanting about the city with Casimir, drinking champagne and seducing actresses. But that had never been the most probable reason. "I thought you were remembering Jeanette."

For a moment Averill looked utterly stricken. An instant later, he smiled ruefully but his gaze was shuttered. "I can never forget Jeanette."

When Theo first met Averill, they were both coming out of mourning. Averill's beloved younger sister had died a year before. His father had told the world her death was caused by a freakish carriage accident, but Averill had wormed a different truth from him—a truth Averill confided not to his mother, nor to his other sister, but to Theo. Jeanette had committed suicide. Last week was the anniversary of her death.

There was a painful silence. Theo knew she had overstepped some boundary, even though it was one he had opened for her to cross. Of late, the special rapport they shared seemed to have faded. When she chased after it, it only eluded her more. "I'm sorry," she whispered, which covered both her sympathy for him and her own hurt.

He shook his head, then abruptly returned to their earlier conversation. "The fiacre will come for you at ten. That will give us time to tour the catacombs before the concert."

She smiled valiantly. "I'll be ready."

He turned to go, then swiveled around. "I will keep my promise. Soon."

"When you can," Theo answered. Despite her yearning to paint him, she could not bear to push him.

Cupping her face tenderly, he kissed her on both cheeks. The first kiss was barely more than breath, the second warm, soft, and faintly moist against her skin. At each touch of his lips, a thrilling vibration played along her nerves. Drawing back, Averill smiled at her—that smile so full of secrets.

"I will see you tomorrow night," he said, and then went dashing down the stairs.

Feeling dazed, Theo wandered back inside. "Tomorrow," she murmured.

A sudden rush of sunshine poured into the studio. All around her, the walls she had painted wine red glowed in the afternoon light. She crossed to the windows, watching the grey rain clouds scudding across the eastern expanse of Paris, leaving pure cerulean sky behind. Montmartre fell away beneath her in a cascade of steep roofs, chimney tops, and trees frothy in their new spring finery of green leaves and creamy blossoms. Theo raised a hand to her cheek. The vibration of her nerves spread until her skin tingled everywhere. Her heart was thrumming from the softest brush of his lips. Each beat sounded a different emotion. Excitement. Apprehension. Sorrow. Hope.

She was in love.

How infinitely stupid.

Theo had been sure she was *en garde*. Safe from further hurt. Safe from broken promises and disillusion.

In California, with a dowry of money and horses promised her, there had been suitors. She'd known since she was little that she was a bastard. John Faraday, the man who'd raised her, the man she'd believed was her father, had called her a Faraday but never adopted her. His wife was concerned for her own two sons' inheritance, so he put nothing for Theo in his will, not even her favorite horse. Then they were all dead in a train wreck, except for the wastrel youngest son who tossed her out on her ear. Theo had nothing left but the clothes in her closet, her paints, and her grief.

The suitor who had seemed most ardent came to see her after the funeral. She remembered her rush of gratitude when he appeared. Her world had been shattered. Emotional comfort and financial security would help mend that world, and Theo felt the promise of love like a rosebud ready to unfurl and open the tight clutch of her heart. But the ardent suitor did not offer marriage. Instead, he suggested a nice little house in San Francisco, where he would visit occasionally.

It was a hard lesson, being jilted and tossed on the rubbish heap. Nothing she had believed in was real. There was death, and after death, betrayal. Coldly, Theo decided she would never marry. A husband would believe he owned her. Intolerable. Nor would she make the daring leap of taking a lover—she might as well sell her heart into slavery. Loving her art would be enough.

But she had found art was an expensive *amour*, one she could barely afford. She'd developed her skill with pencil, with pen and ink, because tubes of paint were too dear. Sometimes she'd felt all the color had faded from her world. It was a miracle that she wasn't still slaving at the Louvre Bar in the rough end of Mill Valley, thinking that was the closest to Paris she would ever come. But the miracle had happened. A lawyer climbed the rickety stairs to her room to tell her Phillipe Charron was her true father—an elegant French portrait painter who had seduced an American society girl. The lawyer adamantly refused to name her mother. But her father would bring Theo to Paris, if she wished. *Yes.* Theo wished.

So she sailed to Paris—and in Paris she once again had family. There was the new father she seldom saw, an invalid grandmother who spent all her time with her ancient poodle, an uncle she loathed, an aunt she pitied, an insipid female cousin she liked too little—and the male cousin she liked far too much.

Loved.

From the first, Averill had captivated her. His compassion had soothed her lingering pain and eased her still raw anger. Ignoring the turmoil churning inside her, Theo set about glossing her rough surface. She'd struggled to reclaim the finishing school polish that had become so tarnished, to transform her haphazard schoolgirl French to something approaching Parisian fluidity and her raggedy wardrobe into Bohemian chic. Averill had helped her with it all. Fellow artists, they quickly became fellow conspirators, fellow rebels, dearest friends. His morbid moods made her frightened for him, sometimes even frightened of him. But always she was fascinated. Averill was everything mysterious and seductive that was Paris to her—challenging, enticing, and forever elusive.

Bathing in the sunshine, Theo lifted her hands to cup her face, fingertips curved to her cheeks, where the sensation of Averill's kisses still lingered. The throb of excitement pulsed through her once again, hot and sweet. Her heart and her body were at war with her mind.

There was knocking at the door. She spun around eagerly, even as she realized the quick barrage of taps wasn't Averill's. She went and opened the door. "*Bonjour*, Matthieu."

"*Bonjour*, Mlle. Faraday," he said politely.

He was a beautiful boy, with curling light brown hair, and large expressive hazel eyes. But not just beautiful. Her first painting had not captured his energy or his impish curiosity, his secret seriousness. The portrait now on her easel overcompensated, gaining vitality but forcing a hard look onto his face. That tough little urchin wasn't Matthieu any more than the dreamy pastel princeling had been. He was everything she'd tried to capture in both paintings, but everything all at once. She determined to do a portrait worthy of him.

"Maman saw you return, mademoiselle, and she would like to invite you for dinner this evening, at seven." He lowered his voice and confided, "She is making her *cassoulet*."

"Delicious," Theo said with a smile. "Thank her and tell her I will bring wine. Is there something you would like?"

"*Éclairs?*" he asked, almost breathless at the thought.

"Oh yes, I love *éclairs*, too!" Theo exclaimed.

"At seven then, Mlle. Faraday." He waved and dashed off, rather like Averill had earlier.

Alone again, Theo took out her old sketches of Averill and spent more than an hour sifting through them. Remembering what they had talked about as he posed, she was filled with a sweet nostalgia, but none conjured the lovely surge of creative passion that would send her rushing to her easel and stop her brooding.

They did not capture what she felt now.

Theo sighed with frustration. It was growing late. If she left now, there would be time to explore the streets for a possible landscape as well as for tonight's dinner offering. She would return to the cherry trees in the Bois de Boulogne, but she wanted to find something closer to hand as well. After locking her door, she descended the stairs and went outside, setting off up the street toward the Place du Tertre.

There was a man in the rue de la Mire—not really a street, but a long set of stairs descending the hillside, narrow as an alleyway. Theo watched him for a moment, not sure why he had captured her attention. He didn't look at all like a bum or a ruffian, but neither was he a workman or businessman going about an errand. He was exploring. But why? She liked his attentiveness, however mysterious, and the way he moved, with economy and grace.

Almost instantly, he was aware of her watching and turned. He paused, then climbed the steps toward her. "*Bonjour*, mademoiselle." His manner was serious, his voice low and quiet. "I'm Inspecteur Devaux of the Sûreté."

"What are you investigating?"

"The disappearance of Denis Armand."

"Ah, yes," she said, feeling sadness take hold of her again. She remembered how sweet the little boy was and how grief-stricken his mother. Theo had helped organize one of the many searches for him. "Is there any news?"

"No. I am looking at his neighborhood again. He would have passed this way on the night he disappeared."

The other policeman she'd talked with hadn't told her that. Theo was appalled that Denis might have been taken right beside where she lived. There were bushes to one side where a kidnapper might lurk. Chills trickled down her back.

The detective perused a list. "You are Mlle. Theodora Faraday, the American?"

Theo nodded. "Is it so apparent?"

"Your French is excellent," he answered in careful English. Surprised, she smiled encouragement, but he returned to French. "I saw the drawing you gave the police. It was skillful."

"But not much of a likeness—so small. His mother was the centerpiece."

He nodded. "Still, it is good to have anything like that during an investigation."

"He has been missing over a month."

"I do not expect to find him alive," the detective said bluntly.

"Do you expect to find him at all?" Theo prickled, but she did not think Denis was alive, either. There was a kind of emptiness around his name now.

He shook his head. "I doubt it."

Theo felt a chill of premonition. "Has another child disappeared?"

His face became more expressionless. He didn't answer her question, but instead asked, "What can you tell me about Denis?"

"Very little. He used to come with Jeanne to collect the laundry." Theo was disturbed. The detective's refusal was an admission. She must warn Matthieu to be careful. "Sometimes, his mother would send Denis alone to fetch small bundles."

"What about his mother? Her character?"

"Jeanne is extremely devout. She named Denis for a saint and told stories about them—and about Jeanne d'Arc, her namesake." Theo paused, remembering how avidly the little boy had listened to those tales. "Denis was very impressionable. I think he might be more susceptible than other Montmartre boys to being led astray by some romantic story."

"Do you remember what you were doing that evening?"

"Yes, I went to tea with a friend at Ladurée." Casimir had taken her there for a treat—her favorite chic spot when she felt like being elegant.

"Would you give me her name—or his?" he asked.

"Surely he can't be a suspect?" Theo heard her voice growing sharp. The police intruded everywhere.

He did not react, simply said, "I do not even know if I will question him, mademoiselle, but perhaps he glimpsed something, or someone, that evening."

The detective was only doing his job, and perhaps some small piece of information would lead to Denis being found. "Casimir Estarlian, baron de la Veillée sur Oise," Theo said, a bit smugly. The whole title sounded so elegant. Suddenly, she wondered if the detective would assume she was Casimir's mistress. It was just the sort of thing a policeman would think. Blushing did not help, nor did staring at him defiantly. Nor did fighting off laughter at the ridiculousness of her response.

"He is just a friend," she said, as if that would convince a *flic*. Despite Casimir's handsomeness, she was not attracted to him. He was Averill's good friend, so she wanted him to like her, and supposed he felt the same. She had been suitably charmed when he treated her to the ballet or the opera. Once they'd gone to the races. He flirted artfully without being seductive. He was flattering, amusing, informative—but they were both more lively when they were with Averill and the others. Alone together, they were always on their best behavior. "We went to tea," she repeated, feeling foolish.

The Inspecteur nodded and scribbled.

As he wrote, Theo's gaze swept down the walls of the alleyway. Obscene graffiti chalked the stone. Here and there were smudged religious symbols. Jeanne would probably have seen the black cross and blessed herself. The arms were long, with something like wings swooping out from the top. Theo was aware of the other graphic words and images and suddenly felt uncomfortable with this man she didn't know. But it was the crude drawings that made her fidgety, not anything he had done. She realized that he had detached himself from their conversation almost completely. It was deliberate, she thought. He was able to withdraw into himself, almost vanish.

She studied him again. The quiet he had put on like a mask was intriguing, even a little sinister. How could you capture those layers in a portrait? First, she had seen a hunter, prowling. Next he was the public official, respectful, but expecting respect as well. The tension, the intentness, were well hidden, but there. He had an interesting face, wedge-shaped with high cheekbones. A strong nose and chin framed refined lips. His ash brown hair revealed chestnut when the sun touched it. Under straight brows, cool grey eyes were tinted with warm green. He was handsome in a severe way. She wondered what he looked like when he smiled.

He was regarding her just as directly now, and she felt like squirming. The artist in her was always studying people too closely. Curious to think how similar, yet how different, it must be to look at the world through a detective's eyes.

"I have an errand—chocolate *éclairs*." She smiled, apologetic, flustered. "There's really nothing more I can tell you. If I don't hurry, the bakery will close."

"*Merci beaucoup*, Mlle. Faraday," he said, then resumed his exploration of the passage.

At her favorite *patisserie* near the Place du Tertre, Theo bought three *éclairs*, plump with custard and shimmering with chocolate glaze. Afterward, she wandered through Montmartre seeking the perfect view. Storm clouds were gathering again, a glowering darkness on the horizon, but the late sun was bright, the shadows sharp. Theo savored the wet, saturated colors of the spring growth, the new leaves on the trees and the scrambling tendrils of the vines making their way across the limestone walls. Coming back laden with olives, baguette, and wine as well as her parcel of *éclairs*, she glanced at the Moulin de la Galette, the windmill turned dance hall that every artist in Montmartre had painted a dozen times, including herself. She had a warm affection for the building. It was sturdy enough, but still had a sort of rumpled, tumbledown air. Usually. Today the sun struck the blades and pinioned them against the smudged purple of the clouds. The windmill became strangely menacing, like some sorcerer's machine. Even as she stared, transfixed, the light flared then began to fade. Theo drank in the image, because the old *moulin* might never look this way again.

And a painting of it would be hers alone.

Chapter Four

I am a cradle
Swung in a cavern
Of sadness and night….
                    Paul Verlaine

A thousand candles burned in the darkness of the catacombs. A thousand flames wavered, golden lights bending and rising with the doleful ebb and flow of the music.

Repelled and fascinated, Theo watched their flickering glow caress the curved domes of the skulls. Tinted by candlelight, the naked bones took on a sepia patina like sacred reliquaries carved from amber. A shiver swept her. Nothing—not her delight in the outrageous, nor the wickedly delicious thrill of the forbidden, not even the inspiration the images would bring to her art—nothing overcame her sense of oppression. They were deep in the earth. Room after endless room of bones surrounded them.

The black hollows of the eye sockets seemed to watch the concert as attentively as the audience of chic Parisians still clothed in mortal flesh and fancy silks, still breathing the dank, stifling air of the chamber. As the last notes of Chopin's *Marche Funèbre* echoed, the gathering applauded with fervent solemnity, saluting the musicians' skill and their own daring in coming here. Elegant in their tuxedos, the orchestra lowered their instruments with a flourish and rose, first bowing to their guests, then once again to their skeletal hosts. Theo smiled and clapped with them, fighting off her apprehension.

"They call this the Empire of Death." Averill leaned close and Theo bent to meet him. In the eerie light, the smile hovering at the corners of his mouth shifted from sweet to sinister and back again. His breath caressed her face and she caught a hint of absinthe. The scent churned up a chaos of emotion—concern, frustration, anger, yearning.

A pang of jealousy.

How perfectly Parisian, she thought, *to be jealous of a liqueur.*

When had his flirtation with the green fairy become a love affair? Two months ago, four? He called absinthe his muse, but she stole as much as she gave. Under her influence, Averill's moods grew ever more erratic and his exquisite, fantastical poems ever more bizarre.

A fierce impulse surged through Theo's turmoil—to paint Averill as he looked now, bitter and sweet, taunting and tender. She envisioned him almost emerging from the canvas. Strands of dark hair tumbled over his eyes, pale blue flames glowing too bright within the shadows. Patches of rose madder made a fever flush on both cheeks. Her fingers twitched eager to render mustache and beard in quick, narrow strokes of lamp black touched with indigo, a frame for the quick twist of a smile that mocked the world and himself.

Theo forced a smile in response. "The Empire of Death. So you've said."

"Three times at least, Charron," Paul Noret sneered from the seat on her other side. "Before, during, and after your nightly tryst with the green fairy."

Slouched in his chair, Paul looked too much at home in this underground kingdom, like a strange insect god, half man and half praying mantis. His body was long and bony, his face cadaverous. Shadows carved crescents into his lean cheeks and scooped out circles under his eyes, which bulged slightly, and glistened. His hair was prematurely grey, the color of ashes, and aged him a decade or more. Paul was thirty-four—thirteen years older than she was, and ten years older than Averill.

"You should sip the green ambrosia, Noret, and cavort with her yourself," Averill said.

Paul scowled. "Absinthe rots the brain."

"Ahh...but your poetry will soar."

"Not if your twig-bound twitters are any example."

There was a heartbeat of silence. A stinging retort sprang to Theo's lips, but she bit it back when she felt Averill's light pressure on her arm. He leaned across her to taunt Paul in turn. "Twitters? When people hear twitters, they pause. They smile. They listen. If they hear barking, they shut their ears—or throw shoes."

Paul examined his scuffed boots. "These were acquired just so. They cost but a single barking couplet."

Theo relaxed, glad the jab had been too wide of the mark to cut Averill. They were all used to Paul's forays but always *en garde*. They ignored him at their peril. What seemed to be a feint might suddenly pierce the heart. They'd look down to discover their idea, their verse— or their art—mercilessly skewered. But that same deadly skill made Paul chief critic to the group of poets and musicians who had invited Theo into their midst. Since the success of *Le Revenant*, Paul seemed to have doubled his criticism. Was it jealousy? Paul's harsher poems had won praise too, but not as much as Averill's. Perhaps Paul was forestalling vanity from the proclamations of Averill as the new Rimbaud, the new Verlaine.

Absinthe had destroyed Verlaine.

Averill gestured dramatically at the skulls crowning the wide pillar of tibias and fibulas. "We have set ourselves in the Empire's heart, in the sanctity of the Crypte de la Passion."

"It is so perfectly decadent," Theo murmured. The word was a magic key that opened many intriguing doors in Paris. Yet when Averill nodded yes, another part of Theo's mind whispered rebelliously, *So perfectly horrible… So horribly sad….*

"Yes." Averill gave her another conspiratorial smile as if he heard and agreed with each silent pronouncement.

The undercurrent of longing pulled Theo forward. She started to reach out to him then curled her hand tight against her heart. Averill's friendship was precious. She could not bear to shatter what they now had on a futile quest for a foolish amour. She made herself sit back.

"If you think this crypt was named for Christ's Passion, you are wrong, Charron," Paul reproved, his nasal voice smug. "The true meaning is more prosaic—and more profane. Whenever the gendarmes hunted the streetwalkers too aggressively, the women brought their customers down here. Whores have no hearts, and neither does this sepulchral maze."

Averill shook his head. "You are the one with no heart, Noret."

"Who needs such a soggy rag?" Paul rolled his eyes disdainfully.

"A poet, certainly," Theo countered.

"*Exactement.*" Averill ruffled the boutonnière he had pinned over his heart. It was a curious concoction he had created from white paper cutouts. Today, yesterday now, was All Fools' Day. For some obscure reason Theo had not discovered, the French nicknamed it *Poisson d'Avril*—April Fish Day. Their favorite prank was decorating the backs of unsuspecting passersby with paper fish. Averill collected these zealously, declaring the day *Poisson d'Averill*, and the paper fish a personal tribute. He wore the tattered little bouquet pinned to his jacket. Theo frowned. If she included that boutonniere in her portrait, should she attempt to show it was actually a paper fish, and not a white carnation? Unbidden, a tall glass of absinthe inhabited the bottom corner of her imagined canvas, glowing a malevolent chartreuse.

Would Averill be angry if she painted the absinthe? Theo felt a war begin—her not wanting to put the glass there and the glass insisting. *I am truth,* said the glass. *And I am so deliciously, evilly green.*

"I find a brain far more useful than a bleeding heart." Paul arranged his lanky frame in the chair as best he could, crossed his arms and closed his eyes. His lips began to move silently. No doubt, he was composing a poem to prove his point—something perfectly cynical and as gloomy as their setting.

Averill sat up and looked intently about the candlelit crypt. Curious, Theo asked, "Searching for more Revenants?"

He gave her an oblique glance. "Just an acquaintance I thought might appear."

"Someone from medical school?"

"Not from there." His gaze scanned the crowd once more, but whoever the unnamed person was, Averill did not find him...or her. Turning back, he offered an enigmatic smile. "It's not important, *ma cousine.*"

Theo was too startled to pursue the question of the mysterious someone. Her illegitimacy was an open secret, but propriety demanded she be presented as her father's ward. Averill never called her cousin in public. He shrugged as if to say, "Everyone knows."

Someone behind them commented on the performance and Averill turned, inviting himself into the conversation. Paul scribbled a note by candlelight. With her companions distracted, Theo watched the musicians. Their host, Casimir, gave her a brief salute with his violin bow. She smiled in answer. The baron looked both raffish and elegant. Artfully pomaded, his tawny hair curled slightly, glistening in the candlelight. His wide-set eyes were flecked with gold and alight with the same sly charm as his smile. Theo was glad she'd accepted his invitation to this curious event, but grateful only one piece remained to be played.

She saw Casimir quickly search for any other friends in the audience, but it seemed only the three of them had come. Not every poet felt bound to visit the catacombs at midnight. No, she was wrong. In one obscure corner stood the most shadowy Revenant, a young man named Jules Loisel. He seldom spoke and was so shy he had not pushed through the crowd to join them. Theo might not have noticed him at all, except that he looked more incongruous than anyone else—a shabby brown church mouse with pointed chin and darting brown eyes. She felt a twinge of sympathy. Jules subsisted on stray jobs Paul procured from the publishing company he worked for, drearily editing textbooks. Crumbs of crumbs.

Theo shifted restlessly. Despite the eager hum of the crowd and the blazing candlelight, she felt the murky shadows and musty odors of the crypt encroaching. She yearned to escape. Tomorrow she would ride again. Closing her eyes, Theo saw the fragrant green woods and pink cherry blossoms of the Bois de Boulogne. For an instant, she imagined the vital strength of the little mare surging beneath her, the cool wind a sweet current flowing around them. When she opened her eyes again, the shadows had retreated.

Theo lifted her chin and smoothed back the tendrils escaping her braid, adjusting the opal-studded comb that held it in place. Tonight she sported her recent flea market coups. She knew her antique frock coat of sapphire velvet deepened the light blue of her eyes. Beneath it, a fine linen shirt and jabot foaming with Chantilly lace topped trousers and leather boots. Theo wanted her clothes to be festive, but she had not wanted to fret about silk skirts and dainty shoes while picking her way through dank, claustrophobic tunnels.

Officially, the catacombs had been closed to the public decades ago. Visiting them was condemned. Unofficially, there was a thriving business in satisfying perverse curiosity. Averill had insisted on the full tour before the concert. Theo had been startled when their guide met them with his ten-year-old son, but the boy took even more delight in the ghoulish maze than his father did, lifting his lantern to illuminate the carved mottos along the pathway. When Averill intoned their warnings of mortality, Dondre laughed and intoned along with him. "They were what we are. Dust. Toys of the wind...."

With his curling hair and expressive brown eyes, Dondre reminded her of Denis, the laundress' son who had vanished weeks ago. Theo's heart gave a sudden twist. Other boys must be missing, else why was the detective in the alley still investigating such a hopeless case? That memory was far more depressing than the catacombs. She pushed it away and turned back to her companions.

Despite his scoffing, Paul knew the entire history of the place better than their guide. He had told her the quarries were first dug in Roman times. "For centuries, the tunnels burrowed ever deeper, creating this vast labyrinth far beneath the streets of the city."

"Overhead the graveyards filled to bursting," Averill elaborated. "The walls of charnel houses cracked open, and coffins pushed their way out of the earth to create breeding grounds of pestilence."

Paul thrust forward, a verbal duel. "Louis the Sixteenth ordered the quarries consecrated and the bones of Paris began their journey. Napoléon and others continued the venture for decades."

"Decades?" It should not surprise her. The heaps of bones seemed endless, and miles more were hidden beyond sight.

"Ah yes," Averill answered, "for they had to dispossess the dead without disturbing the living. Working only at night, laborers excavated the cemeteries and carried cartloads of bones to their new abode—the mortal remains of six million souls."

Paul stood, his long, thin arms akimbo. "Looking around, I cannot believe a single soul escaped—or that they ever existed."

Theo believed in the soul, but Paul had captured the most depressing thing about the catacombs and their endless corridors of the dead. The heaps of silent bones not only decreed mortality, but seemed to deny immortality as well. Their silence echoed in her own bones.

Lantern aloft, the guide and his son led them ever deeper. When they reached the next large room, Paul turned around with a grim smile. "Victims of the Reign of Terror found their final resting place here."

"Danton and Robespierre lie entangled with Madame de Pompadour and Marie Antoinette," Averill added. His hands entwined in a fluid gesture.

"In this room?" Theo gazed in horror at the mass grave of riot and revolution. All that fury and passion, that vicious violence and lofty hope, reduced to these bleak remains?

"Somewhere," Paul said with relish. "No doubt missing their heads."

Sadness permeated Theo, one with the cold air that sank through skin to muscle, through bone to marrow. The longer they walked, the heavier the bleakness weighed. They crossed wet patches where mineral-laden water dripped continuously from the ceiling, forming small stalactites. The shiny fluid trickled over the heaped skeletons, embalming them in a foul resinous varnish. Damp gravel crunched underfoot like crushed bones. They entered a stretch of dry chambers, and Theo realized she could not hear their footsteps any more. The cold silence was unnerving. No one spoke. Even breath seemed to vanish.

Here the guide stopped them, holding a finger before his lips. "The chalk walls muffle sound." Stepping back, the man raised the lantern high then shuttered the light.

They vanished into darkness absolute. No sight, no sound but the pounding of her heart in an eternity of utter smothering nothingness.

Fingers brushed hers, linked. A hand closed around hers, warm and firm.

"Averill," Theo whispered. Emptiness swallowed the word, but warmth rushed through her, breath returning, blood returning. Life returning. *Not alone in the dark.* Her fingers tightened in answer.

Love filled her, pure and glowing, lighting her from within.

In the surrounding blackness, Dondre gave an eerie laugh, too theatrical to scare them as he obviously hoped to do. It made Theo want to giggle with relief. She heard a rasping of metal, and Averill released her hand just as the guide opened the lantern again. It glowed dimly, a fragile blessing lighting them on their way.

The memory of the tour sent icy rivulets coursing through Theo. She pressed her hand to her lips. After that blinding darkness, the watching skulls and bright candles in the Crypte de la Passion seemed positively cheerful, the murmur of human voices sweeter than music.

The master of ceremonies rose. "Fellow mortals, we offer the ultimate piece to complete our uncanny concert, from the brilliant composer Saint-Saëns—*La Danse Macabre*."

"Your brilliant composer was inspired by a grotesquerie in verse by Cazalis," Paul declared. Annoyed, the man seated behind him tapped Paul's chair with his gloves. The leather fingers gleamed white as new bone in the gloom. Paul turned and glared balefully. "They even call the work a symphonic poem," he added, then assumed an offended silence.

"The poet was inspired by a peasants' legend." Averill bent to her, his whisper barely audible as the musicians lifted their instruments. "Each year, on All Hallows Eve, the Grim Reaper appears at the stroke of midnight." Twelve strokes of the harp strings sounded, quieting the rustle of skirts, the shuffle of boots. "Death flicks his bony hand and calls forth the dead from their graves. He sets his violin to his chin and tunes it…" Averill paused as strange, dissonant chords were plucked on the violinists' strings.

> *Zig and zig and zag.*
> *Death beats a cadence*
> *Stamping a tomb with his heel*
> *Just at midnight, Death strikes a dance tune*
> *Zig and zig and zag on his violin….*

Averill wove words into sound. Theo's gaze darted to Casimir as the music built, his face intent, his bow flashing as the strident commands of the violin strings merged with the percussive clang of the xylophone, evoking the dry bones clattering in a frantic dance as Death compelled the dead to dance for him. Zig and zig and zag.

> *The winter wind blows in the blackest night,*
> *Wailing shivers through the linden trees.*
> *White skeletons dart through dark shadows,*
> *Running, leaping under billowing shrouds.*

Averill's voice whispered like a winter wind rustling leaves, relentless and oddly insinuating. Shrouds fell away. Naked skeletons abandoned themselves to lust, hungering to taste the long-lost sweetness of the flesh. Dispossessed kings cavorted with peasants. Queens coupled with cartwrights. Dismay and delight spun inside Theo as the music quickened. The words licked at her. She trembled at the caress of Averill's breath in the hollow of her ear, at the touch of his lips on the tender lobe. All around her, yellow candle flames leaped and quivered. Then the fervor stilled. The violins sighed, and the notes of an oboe rose—a cock crowing at dawn. Abruptly, Paul leaned forward, his voice joining Averill's to finish the poem.

> *But hush. Suddenly they quit the dance.*
> *They push all in a panic. They flee—for the cock has*
> *crowed.*
> *Oh! The dark beauty of the night blesses the poor world.*
> *Long live death! Long live equality!*

Theo shivered, feeling strangely feverish as a final quiver of sound mingled with the teasing, almost taunting whispers.

Then silence fell.

Chapter Five

Do I reject all authority? No, not all!
When it comes to boots, I acknowledge the
authority of the bootmaker.
                                    Mikhail Bakunin

Pausing at the narrow cross street, Michel glanced cautiously up the rue Lepic. He signaled the gendarmes following him to wait. Lit by the street lamps, a prostitute and her drunken customer tottered along the rising curve of the street. The woman's chartreuse feather boa slithered along the pavement behind her like a molting snake. Someone was always awake in Montmartre, but at this hour they were mostly drinking inside the cabarets. The night breeze carried odors of tobacco smoke and beer drifting out with the music, mingling with the stink of urine and semen that saturated the narrow lane. But Montmartre was still a village topping the modern city of Paris, scattered with midnight lights below, and Michel caught a rustic whiff of cow dung and the bittersweet nostalgia of cherry blossoms.

"It's been three years since the last bombing." The mutter behind him came from Brigadier Sorrell of the *Police Judiciaire*.

Michel ignored him. Sorrell and his three gendarmes were all fuming at having their authority usurped. No crime had been committed yet and prevention was the provenance of the *Police Judiciaire*, not the Sûreté. But the tip was Michel's and Sorrell knew he was one of Cochefert's special agents.

Michel waited for the meandering couple to pass out of sight. He didn't want them raising an alarm. Montmartre had long been home to the city's rebels, both political and artistic. The Montmartrois favored anarchists over *flics* any night of the year. Michel felt Sorrell's boots nudging his heels impatiently. He stepped sideways rather than forward onto the rue Lepic and turned to face him. Sorrell again moved closer, trying to use his huge height to intimidate. Michel was an inch short of six feet, but the other man had four inches on him. Sorrell frowned with heavy brows that were perhaps intended to achieve the same end. When Michel refused to back up further, Sorrell asked, "You're sure your source is good?"

"Impeccable." And secret. If Blaise Dancier wanted his name touted, he'd arrange a parade on the Champs Élysées. Michel nodded in the direction of the basilica crowning the butte Montmartre, the highest point in Paris. "The man upstairs bragged that he would plant a bomb at the Sacré Coeur."

"Bragging is probably all he does," Sorrell snorted. "A lot of drunks are members of the dynamite club." The detectives snickered nervously. They were well aware of their leader's overbearing stupidity, but they would have to go on working with him long after Michel left.

"He bought mercury," Michel explained yet again. With mercury one could make mercury fulminate, an essential of dynamite. "Work continues at the Sacré Coeur. It's an easy and desirable target." This anarchist was no benevolent dreamer. The violence and terror of a bombing followed the criminal Ravachol's footsteps, or Bakunin's school of revolutionary socialism. Such men saw the perfidy of the rich clearly but seemed blind to the same human flaws in the poor.

The street was clear now. Michel guided the men around the corner and up the block. Midway, he stopped at a door and drew his revolver. The others followed suit. Looking down, Sorrell grunted, "It's propped open. You've gotten help from the concierge."

"Yes." It was the worried concierge who had tipped off Dancier. Quietly but swiftly, they entered the apartment house and started up the seven flights of stairs to the top. So late, they had hoped for quiet, but noise filtered down the stairwell. A party to celebrate April Fools' Day. Michel paused on the first landing and looked up, but no one was visible yet. Deep in his gut, anticipation knotted with old anger and older fear. He ignored them all, fixing his attention on taking this anarchist—alive, if possible.

They reached the penultimate floor undetected. Just ahead, the door to the party stood open. Someone was singing and the smell of cheap wine and cigarettes saturated the air. Cautiously, Michel moved to the doorjamb and glanced inside. A dozen someones were celebrating, playing music and waltzing squashed together. He passed the door without being spotted. The commotion inside was good cover for their raid, but Sorrell paused at the door and gestured officiously for silence.

Instead of quieting, the party poured into the hall. They penned Michel and his companions into the far corner of the hallway, bellowing, "*Flics!* Hey *flics,* what's up?" Others squawked out, "*Poulets!*" or "*Vaches!*"—depending on their preference for chicken cops or cow cops.

A floor above, the door they wanted opened and a burly, bearded man peered out. Michel saw an uncanny resemblance to Bakunin, but except for that bearish quality, it was not a face he knew from either the present or the past. Relief loosened the knot in his belly.

The face vanished. The door slammed.

Brigadier Sorrell broke through the crowd and stormed the last flight of stairs. Michel felt a new knot tighten hard inside him. He shouted a warning as the gendarmes rushed to the top floor. Yanking the last man back to the landing, he yelled again for Sorrell to stop. The Brigadier ignored him and kicked in the door. It was rigged from the inside. The explosion sent the splintered door flying outward. The impact sent Sorrell and the nearest gendarme over the railing into the open stairwell. The gendarme screamed shrilly all the way down. Missing half his head, Sorrell fell silently, dead before he hit bottom. A shattered piece of the door hit the third gendarme in the arm, slicing the artery. Blood and brains splattered the hallway.

Michel felt a blast of fury in his gut, like a furnace door swinging open. Instantly he closed it inside a wall of ice.

"Can you do a tourniquet?" he asked the uninjured gendarme, who choked out an affirmative. He let the man tend to his fellow officer. Some of the partygoers, hit by the debris, were screaming and cursing. Useless chaos. "Someone get a doctor."

"*Oui. Oui. Immédiatement!*" Now the *flics* were their friends. One of the more sober women ran down the stairs.

Sidestepping the debris, Michel went through the doorway, watching for traps. The window was open. There were no tripwires. Muffled sounds came from the roof. Running, or waiting with a weapon? He ducked his head out, pulled back, waited a heartbeat. No shots from the bomber. Michel climbed out the window, pulled himself up to the window arch, then onto the roof.

Below, the few streetlamps and windows of the Montmartre nightclubs cast light on the street. Above and ahead, the rooftops caught little but starlight. Michel moved forward cautiously, taking cover at a chimney as his night vision returned. He heard a heavy thud as the bomber jumped to the next roof. There was only one other building before the alley, but its roof line fell away in flat, staggered sections, like a giant's staircase. The bomber had a long head start, but his running and jumping sounded clumsy.

As swiftly as the murky light allowed, Michel moved to the edge of the building and dropped to the next roof. If the bomber had a gun, he'd have taken a shot by now. Ahead, Michel heard an ungodly clatter as the bomber hurled junk at the foot of the next wall. There was the crack of breaking crockery, the soft thump of earth, and the rustle and snap of plants as the bomber pillaged a rooftop garden. Crossing to the edge, Michel slid down the wall close to the far end but still landed in the rubble. He kicked aside an overturned bench, then clambered over spilled earth, smashed pots, and broken branches to the next edge. Below him, he glimpsed the bomber's silhouette above the roof line. The man paused long enough to look back, his face no more than a pale blotch. Then he leaped the three meters down across the alley to the next building.

Michel holstered his gun then jumped down to the next level. Running hard, he made the leap across the alley but tripped forward, skidding on the slippery lead roofing before he slid to a stop and regained his footing. The bomber was clearer now, thundering across the last roof. At the far end, dimly illuminated by window lights, an ash tree grew up from an enclosed garden, its top branches in reach. In a moment, the bomber would be down it, over the garden wall, and vanished into the alleys of Montmartre. Michel raced forward. Still long meters away, the bomber dove and disappeared from sight.

Reaching the edge of the building, Michel looked down into the slender, swaying branches. Farther below, barely visible, the dark shape of the bomber shimmied down a central branch toward the trunk. Michel launched himself after, reveling in the brief, intoxicating flight before his hands closed on a sturdy branch two meters below. He locked his grip as it dipped under his weight, scraping his hands against sharp twigs. It swayed again as the bomber plunged downward with a grunt, shaking the entire tree. Michel quickly gauged his position. The building was four tall stories, too high to jump to the ground. His quarry was halfway down, with stronger holds as he descended. Swinging down to the next limb, Michel followed him through a maze of branches that slapped at his eyes and blocked his vision. Through a sudden gap, he saw the bomber dangle from a thick limb close to the bottom.

Fire burned through the ice inside him. He would not let this killer escape.

As the bomber dropped to the ground, Michel leapt into the narrow space between two limbs. Branches snapped, raking his face and arms, and then he was clear. Plummeting fast, he landed on the bomber's back, broad and hard as a sack of grain under thick, rough wool. The sudden impact sent them sprawling in opposite directions. Stunned by the fall, Michel struggled for breath. He glimpsed movement, saw the bomber kneeling. Michel heard the metal snick of a blade as the man snatched a knife from a sheath at his ankle.

He rolled as the bomber sprang. The blade sliced open his jacket, scoring his upper arm with a hot line of pain. Not his right arm. Michel jumped to a crouch, retreating backward over the uncertain ground. The bomber pursued, the knife slashing viciously. Two feints, then a thrust. Again. Seeing the pattern, Michel stepped in quickly between the feints and seized the bomber's knife hand between his own. He held on grimly as the man gripped Michel's slashed arm with his other hand, grinding his palm into the knife wound. Michel shut off the pain, looking directly into his adversary's eyes. Startled, the bomber stared back, jaw agape. His grip slackened. Michel twisted the man's wrist sharply. The knife fell. A hard *chasse-bas* kick to the bomber's thigh broke his balance. As he pitched back, Michel's whipping *fouetté* knocked him onto his back. In an instant Michel had him flipped and pinned. Another instant had the *ligote* around his prisoner's wrist—one twist tightened the metal strands and stopped any struggle. Michel jerked him to his feet. The man stank of sausage, sweat, and gunpowder.

"You are under arrest."

"*Salaud—je vais te niquer la gueule! Fils de pute! Espèce de con.*" The man bared his teeth, snarling an unending stream of guttural curses. Bastard, I'm going to fuck up your face. Son of a whore. Cunt brain. "*Mes couilles sur ton nez!*" My balls on your nose? That was a new one. Michel dragged the bomber to the doorway of the house and knocked, pounded, until the owner came to let him through the house. Outside again, Michel pushed his cursing prisoner up the now crowded street.

"*À bas les flics! À bas les vaches!*" The crowd began chanting down with cops as soon as they appeared.

"*Espèce de merde! Va te faire foutre!*" The bomber spewed curses. Piece of shit. Go fuck yourself. His accent was Russian, Michel thought, or perhaps from some Balkan state. He walked his prisoner steadily, keeping a sharp hold on the *ligote*.

"*Vache réactionnaire—va encule les mouches!*" The jeering crowd urged him to butt fuck some flies—in cow form. Despite his tension, Michel's lips twitched a little. It was an insult usually extended to useless politicians. The crowd waved their fists over their heads, pinkie fingers sticking out and wiggling.

"*Bouffe ta merde!*"

"*Nique ta mère.*"

"*Brûle en enfer!*"

Michel guessed that "burn in hell" was meant for the anarchist. Otherwise, the deluge of obscenities was all for him. They both took a share of angry buffeting, but Michel got the bomber back to the apartment house without major incident. He locked his prisoner in the concierge's broom closet, verified what had happened in his absence, and then arranged for transport. No marching through the streets for this man.

Michel wanted him safe inside a Black Maria. The wounded officer was doing all right, pale but stoic as he waited for the ambulance. The corpses had been decently covered.

He found the unharmed gendarme outside in the street. The shock of survival had pumped his self-importance. In a fit of inspiration, the fool had lied to the crowd, saying the destruction was caused by a gas explosion. Even if it had been the truth, the Montmartrois would rather believe it was a bomber. There was no point in arguing with the growing crowd of merchants, minstrels, artisans, prostitutes, pimps, and poets who were already exaggerating the damage and proclaiming their own theories of the event. A frenetic gaiety born of fear was overcoming the shock. In a few more minutes, the musicians would have them singing '*La Marseillaise.*' Or, worse than the anthem, they'd begin '*La Ravachole*', the song created to honor that famous bomber. Either would be more provocative than the curses.

Coming up the street, Michel saw Saul Balsam, a reporter who managed to present the facts with less florid embellishment than most. Balsam was often refused interviews because he was Jewish. Michel went forward to greet him. Brown eyes blinked at him from behind wire-rimmed spectacles. They perched on a crooked nose broken two years ago during one of the Dreyfus scandal riots. That case had split Paris like an axe. The minority cried that Captain Dreyfus was innocent, nothing but a convenient scapegoat. The majority opinion was that all Jews were traitors at heart, and therefore Dreyfus must be guilty. The majority had prevailed.

"A fractured gas line, Inspecteur Devaux?" Balsam asked, pencil poised. His lips quirked in a wry smile.

"No. A bomb." Michel gave him a quick and accurate account of the raid. "One officer was severely wounded. Two more are dead because of this man."

"Two heroes gave their lives to capture the bomber who planned to destroy the Sacré Coeur." Saul scribbled madly, adjusted his glasses with his pencil, then looked up. "A great success—despite grievous losses."

"Yes. It must be counted a success."

"After a breathless rooftop chase, Inspecteur Michel Devaux, son of the heroic Brigadier Guillaume Devaux, captured the bomber after...."

"The police captured—" Michel suggested. The memory of his father's death turned his guts to lead, though he had long since schooled his face to show no reaction.

"If you prefer." Balsam shrugged, jotted a note, paused again. "I will include a reprise of recent anarchist activity. Ravachol was executed for murder five years ago?"

"Yes," Michel answered.

"He sang on his way to the guillotine. It was all that was needed to make him a folk hero—not that I can print that without going to jail myself."

Michel ignored that.

"Emile Henry was executed in '94 for bombing the Terminus," Saul went on. "Just after that, President Carnot was assassinated. Stabbed by that Italian anarchist in revenge."

"The same year as the bombing of the Café Foyot and the Trial of the Thirty," Michel affirmed.

"Ah yes, the flowerpot bomb." Balsam smiled grimly. "No one died, but people remember it more than the Café Terminus, where twenty were sent to an early grave."

"They remember the Foyot because of the trial. The perpetrators ran circles around the lawyers and made a fool of the judge." Michel heard the rancor in his voice.

"Can I quote that?" Balsam asked with false innocence.

"No."

Balsam's smile grew broader. "'94 was a good year for journalists, if no one else. No incidents since then?"

"Nothing successful. Tonight proves we must always be vigilant."

"Always vigilant. Excellent finish." Balsam nodded his thanks.

The police van had yet to arrive. "Any news on the Dreyfus case?" Michel was truly curious. He knew Balsam was still investigating. After his conviction, Dreyfus had been humiliated, stripped of rank and honors, his sword broken. His sentence was solitary confinement on Devil's Island.

"His brother has hired almost a dozen handwriting experts. All agree that the treasonous note was not in Dreyfus' handwriting. Clemenceau now thinks Dreyfus innocent, and Zola is intrigued."

The van came up the street, and as Michel had feared, the crowd spontaneously took up 'La Ravachole'—protesting on principle.

There are corrupt politicians,
There are flabby financiers,
And always there are cops—
But for all these villains,
There is dynamite!
Hurrah the blast!
Hurrah the blast!
There is dynamite!
Hurrah the blast
Of the explosion!

The singing grew louder as the van drew up to the bombed building, the horses snorting and stomping. If Michel didn't leave now, the crowd could escalate into a mob. He bade Balsam good night, then fetched his prisoner.

"Mort aux vaches!" Michel tensed as the death threat went up, but he got the bomber locked inside the cage with nothing worse than a few kicks. He climbed in beside the driver. The man instantly cracked the whip to clear a pathway then took the steep but quick descent down the rue Lepic. Michel looked down the Boulevard de Clichy to the Moulin Rouge. Beneath the red windmill the slumming rich mingled with the working classes, all oblivious to the craziness a few streets beyond. Class warfare was put aside in the pursuit of pleasure. Pimps rubbed shoulders with politicians. Diamond necklaces and luxurious *peau de soie* gleamed beside cheap paste and tattered cotton lace. Society ladies did their best to dress like courtesans and courtesans like society ladies.

"*Aristo-rats!*" The bomber howled as if he could see the crowd. The renewed noise and the glimpse of bright lights would identify their location. The man's violent hatred pointed up the foolishness of Michel's musings.

He loved the fierce hearts of the French but hated the chaos they wrought in their wars for power over each other. Chaos was not liberty, whatever pretty theories the anarchists dreamed up. Class hatred was a virulent plague in France. The Commune's attempt to create a people's state had been brutally crushed by government troops, and now, in the Third Republic, the high bourgeoisie ruled by wealth, reviling but envying the haughty aristocrats. Both feared the angry working class while continuing to exploit them mercilessly.

The van clattered on through quieter neighborhoods to the sumptuous area surrounding L'Opéra Garnier where late night *cafés* were filled with chattering clientele in evening dress. A few more minutes and they reached the Seine, its dark water shimmering under the arc lamps. The Black Maria crossed the bridge to the Palais de Justice and rattled under the archway to the courtyard of the Dépôt. Most prisoners were kept here just two or three days before being formally charged and transferred to a holding prison. Particularly dangerous or politically conspicuous prisoners might remain in the Dépôt's cells indefinitely. Michel presumed this anarchist bomber would be one of them. He climbed down from the seat and unlocked the door to take his furious prisoner out of the cage.

"*Vive la révolution!*" the bomber trumpeted as his feet hit the cobble-stones.

Those were Ravachol's last words—cried out, the legend went, by his decapitated head.

Chapter Six

The star on the skyline, the lighthouse on the pier
The cup of fine crystal
Which over my shoulder I tossed nonchalantly
All brimming with wine....

Jean Moréas

Silence lingered like an indrawn breath, then applause rose in the Crypt de la Passion.

Still feeling dazed by the whispered song, Theo joined in the clapping. When the sound faded, Paul gave her a ghoulish grin and settled back in his chair—bored again or needing to appear so. Averill smiled, amused at their impromptu duet. It was well after midnight and Theo bit the inside of her lip to stifle a yawn. She hated looking gauche.

The musicians quickly put away their instruments and came to join their guests. Casimir entrusted his instrument to another violinist, then strolled toward them. Theo offered her hand and he clasped her fingers, lifting them to his lips. The aristocratic flair of his gestures never failed to delight and amuse her. Releasing her hand, the baron nodded to Paul then gave Averill the charming, lop-sided smile that made him look closer to twenty than thirty. She seldom had an impulse to paint Casimir. He was almost too polished to be interesting—the gleaming curl of his hair, the impeccable suits, the ironic arch of an eyebrow. A complete work of art in himself. But sometimes she wanted to capture his golden smile, radiant as sunshine. Theo knew the boyish appeal could be intentionally disarming. The baron had a dangerous side. He had fought duels. Not the usual theatrical Parisian duels of smoke and gesture, but ones in which he'd wounded, even crippled, his opponent.

"Most of the musicians were from the Opéra, but they permitted a few ardent amateurs like myself." A graceful movement mimed the stroke of a bow over violin strings. Though Casimir sometimes wrote poetry, his true interest was music. He had composed a few delicately sinister pieces to accompany Averill's poems. "Were you amused?"

"Absolutely," Averill said.

"Intermittently," Paul conceded.

Casimir laughed. "From you, Noret, that is high praise."

"*La Danse Macabre* was especially poetic," Theo offered.

"Especially challenging, too," Casimir replied. "And what of your challenge, Theodora? Did you submit the pretty portrait to the Salon de Champs de Mars?"

"No. It was not good enough." Theo lifted her chin proudly. She knew the Revenants would approve, for they'd damned the portrait with faint praise—all but Paul. First he'd said that it was bourgeois. Since Paul called Monet and every other great Impressionist bourgeois, that had seemed a back-handed compliment. Almost. Then he'd said, "Imitation Cassatt." That truth was the death knell.

"Bravo!" Paul exclaimed now.

"That took courage, Theo." Averill's eyes searched hers.

She looked away. "Yes, it did."

"It was a charming work," Casimir allowed. "The Salon would have accepted it."

"They'd have awarded it an Honorable Mention," Paul chortled. "The Salon would dote on such a *féminine* presentation."

Theo wanted to smack him, needling her about it now, heedlessly jabbing both her art and her femininity. Theo knew she was far from the petite, curvaceous, submissive ideal of French womanhood. Averill's horrific father criticized her endlessly and made her feel defiant. Her own father offered soft-spoken advice and made her feel uncouth. Theo bit her lip. Paul was not the problem. Theo was still torn within herself. She looked back to Averill, seeing the concern in his eyes. He knew she was thinking of her father.

Anger, resentment, gratitude spun like juggler's balls inside of Theo. As always, gratitude outweighed the rest. For twenty years Phillipe Charron had not known she existed. He could have continued to pretend she did not. Instead, he'd rescued her from her defiant poverty and brought her to Paris. Having lived on crumbs, she knew all too well the value of his support. He would be disappointed, even angry, that she had not submitted the portrait he'd praised. He'd won his success painting elegant society portraits and classical themes. The great Salons were the center of his artistic world. It didn't matter to him that their power and prestige had been waning ever since the Impressionists turned the art world upside down.

Offering distraction, Averill turned back to the Revenants. "Tell us, Paul, what selection of music did you object to least?"

As they discussed the performance, Theo forced the Salon from her thoughts. One adventure in the creepy catacombs was enough, so she needed to impress the images on her mind. There were endless possibilities, but none moved her yet. She scanned again the mortal explorers of the Empire of the Dead. The flames of the tapers showed the rounded softness of a rosy cheek one moment then scooped the eye socket of the same young woman, showing her kinship with the blind stare of the skulls. Theo shivered.

Looking down at her own hands, she found it all too easy to see, to feel, the armature of bone moving beneath the skin. She stared, hypnotized, and felt an image move within her mind. There was a drawing, a painting, hidden there, like the skeleton beneath her skin. She would have to be her own model in this illustration and face the darkness she wanted to flee.

A blaze of red caught her eye. In the far corner of the room, someone was talking to Averill. Intent on memorizing the crypt, Theo had not seen him leave. Averill's back was to her, blocking her view of his companion, but the man gestured dramatically, showing an expanse of crimson lining his velvet cape. Then they bent their heads together, talking intently. Was this the person he'd had been searching for earlier?

Just then, Averill turned and walked back toward her. He looked pleased with himself. Unable to resist, she asked, "Who is the man wearing the cape?"

"Vipèrine," Averill said, tasting the syllables. He nodded over his shoulder. "Apt, no?"

"Oh yes, sinuous as a snake," she agreed, looking back across the room. This man would make an absolutely perfect villain for one of the poems. He was dressed predominately in black, some long robe that suggested a priest's cassock. Draped over it was the rich cape, its lining vivid as fresh spilled blood. Arcane symbols circled the hem, embroidered in heavy gold thread and studded with faux jewels. Most amazing of all, his beard was dyed brilliant cobalt. Theo's lips quivered at the splendid ridiculousness of it all. But she didn't laugh. Vipèrine stood like an actor commanding center stage—or a king holding court.

"He thinks he's the incarnation of Gilles de Rais, with his blue beard," Paul muttered.

"Hubris?" Casimir's nostrils flared with disdain.

"Far worse than hubris—he fancies himself a poet?" Paul snorted with disgust.

"Worse than fancying himself Gilles de Rais?" Averill asked.

"Far worse. You didn't have to read his submissions to *Le Revenant*." Paul gave a theatrical shiver. "Hideous. I rejected them all."

Casimir's hands arced, suggesting a banner or title. "Beware Bluebeard's revenge."

Paul sniggered.

"I have a poem about Bluebeard," Averill said to them. Theo had not read any such. When she gave a questioning glance, he gestured vaguely. "A work in progress."

"Who was Gilles de Rais?" Theo asked bluntly. She hated not knowing already. Vipèrine was an incarnation, Paul had said, so someone long since dead. An actor from the days of Molière? A troubadour perhaps? A magician? Clearly a man fond of extravagant dress in the manner of Oscar Wilde, whom she had not been permitted to mention in polite conversation in Mill Valley, or in her new uncle's parlor, for that matter.

"He was Jeanne d'Arc's first lieutenant, when she fought her holy war to unite France," Casimir said.

"With a blue beard?" It seemed too ludicrous—popinjays preening and strutting on the battlefield, leading a holy crusade with Jeanne d'Arc. Then Theo remembered some of the fantastical armor she had seen in museums, the helmets crowned with plumes, a boar's head or a raven's wings. Medieval aristocrats dressed richly for war, as they dressed richly for everything else. Show seemed even more important than skill—but they skewered their enemies nonetheless. Still, a blue beard did not conjure wealth or daring but eccentricity.

"The color of the beard may be totally apocryphal," Paul replied. "After they burned Jeanne at the stake, Gilles de Rais became the most notorious murderer in French history."

"He was particularly fond of disemboweling," Averill murmured, as if sharing a secret.

"Like Jack the Ripper?" Theo suppressed a shudder at the thought of the killer who had terrorized London a decade ago. "Gilles de Rais murdered women?"

Averill looked at her askance, suddenly uneasy. "No. Children."

"Innocent children!" Heads turned at her outburst, but for once Theo didn't mind being the brash American.

Casimir gave a Gallic shrug, apologetic, bemused. "Only true innocence would satisfy."

"And he's famous?" Anger and horror ruled, despite her best effort to regain a blasé façade.

Casimir offered a placating smile. "Infamous."

"We French know of him, of course, from history," Paul explained in his most professorial voice. "However, the power of his legend was renewed some years ago when J. K. Huysmans published *Là Bas*."

"Most scandalous." Averill fluttered his paper boutonnière. It rustled like a ghostly whisper.

"Huysmans enjoys being scandalous," Paul said dismissively. To Theo he added, "It is a convoluted book. A novel about a novelist writing about Gilles de Rais' ancient crimes. The narrator begins investigating medieval heresies and ends discovering an unbroken tradition of Satanism in France."

"*Là Bas*," Theo repeated. *Down There*. "All the way down to hell, from the sound of it."

"Ah…but don't forget the heavenly section on bell ringing," Casimir entreated. "It made you yearn for the days when church bells sang out the hours of prayer and told the fortunes of their towns—birth, marriage, and death."

"You perhaps, baron." Paul always managed to deride Casimir's title. "They would give me a headache, I fear."

"Breathing gives you a headache." Averill's sharpness no longer sounded playful. Theo feared the vicious depression that sometimes claimed him. The absinthe only made it worse.

Perhaps he saw the worry in her eyes, for he managed a teasing smile. "Shall I loan you another wicked book?"

"Immediately." Despite—or because of—her extreme reaction against their favorite murderer, Theo determined to read the novel at once. It was like a dare.

"I gave you your copy," Casimir said to Averill. "Let me present one to Theo as well."

Averill smiled and shrugged consent. "As you wish."

"Huysmans is here tonight." Paul nodded to a subdued man currently standing beside the flamboyant Vipèrine. The author was small, frail even, with intense eyes under flared brows, and a neat, pointed grey beard.

"Curious. I thought he had found salvation in the bosom of the Church," Casimir remarked.

Averill shook his head, watching the two men with fascination. "Huysmans seeks salvation in one obsession after another. If Satan did not satisfy, will not God be found wanting, too?"

"When he wrote *Là Bas*, Huysmans consulted a corrupt priest who was excommunicated for practicing the Black Mass," Paul told her. "He is choosing no better now, prattling with that gaudy Bluebeard who was once his acolyte."

"You said yourself, the name is apocryphal." Casimir's voice had an undercurrent of distaste. "Bluebeard was a far later appellation for Gilles de Rais. A fairy tale created to frighten little children and nubile maidens."

"If what you say is true, they had good reason to be frightened," Theo said to him.

Casimir smiled. "True enough, *ma chère Amazone*."

Looking across the crypt, Averill murmured, "Vipèrine has promised to help me. I have an ambition to witness a Black Mass. He has chosen an abandoned chapel."

Theo feared he was serious. Averill declared himself apostate but remained fascinated by Catholicism's most tortured visions.

"Charron, you are utterly mad," Casimir retorted.

"I try to achieve madness—but I fear it eludes me." The bitterness was back.

"Achieve your first ambition and the second may no longer elude you," Casimir warned. "Such sights have cast others into the pit."

"Where Satan would devour my soul?"

"A gibbering tidbit, fit only for an hors d'oeuvre." Paul scoffed.

"A lovely line, Noret," Averill said. "Gibbering tidbit. May I steal it for a poem?"

"As long as I critique the phrasing first," Paul replied. "I fear for your rhyme schemes more than for your soul."

"When I attend my Black Mass, I can sell my soul for the perfect rhyme scheme—something truly fiendish which will enthrall all of Paris." Averill's tone was light but his shrug was like a wince.

Theo turned on Paul, tired of his incessant attacks. "Why do you pick on Averill more than the other Revenants? His poems are exquisite."

"But that is why I criticize him more than the others. Charron cannot restrain himself from making everything torturously exquisite."

"An artist must transform pain and suffering," Casimir countered softly. "Why else does he exist?"

Theo kept her focus on Paul. "It is better than making everything unbearably ugly."

"Ah," Paul countered, "you mean I can't restrain myself from telling the truth."

Theo drew herself up straighter, embarrassed to have made such a personal attack. Praising Averill made her feel naked, but still she said, "Averill's poems need that beauty to bring light to their darkness."

"Like a feeble little lantern, snuffed with one breath?"

For a second, Theo was back in the narrow passages of the catacombs. The dim lantern went out. The encompassing blackness choked every sense, as if air turned to earth. She was utterly alone, her soul swallowed up. Alive inside of Death. Then Averill's fingers slid through hers, his palm pressed close, warm and firm. His touch was far beyond simple comfort. She said quietly to Paul, "In darkness like that, a little lantern light can save a soul."

"Some souls prefer to drink the darkness," Paul responded, his voice still sharp. Then, almost apologetically, he added, "Of our poets, Charron has the most talent. He can do better."

"Huysmans likes to drink the darkness—but in quibbling little sips." Casimir smoothly led them back to their other discussion. "But there is no doubt the Black Mass in *Là Bas* was written from experience."

"An invaluable experience," Averill agreed.

"One which you would gulp down without a thought for consequence," Paul snorted. "But if you are so determined, there are certain priests more likely to have covert knowledge of the black arts. Loisel might even be able to help you."

"Jules was a priest?" How odd. Or, how ironic. A true church mouse. Theo imagined him kneeling in a pew, sensitive hands pressed together, praying obsessively. She looked around. Why hadn't he joined them?

Paul shrugged. "Almost a priest."

"A crisis of faith?" Casimir asked

"Sins of the flesh?" Averill suggested.

The almost-priest had two poems in the first issue of *Le Revenant*. In one, Eve appeared as a succubus, probably to Jules himself, and tormented him with a snake. In the other, Mary Magdalene tended the body of Christ with obscene care.

"I prefer to believe Loisel forsook the seminary for the religious ecstasy of poetry—but who knows what arcane wisdom he still possesses?" Paul replied. "Perhaps angels and demons babble in his ears."

"Are his new poems just as...biblical?" she asked.

"They are just as deliriously tormented, but more polished. Convincing him to show them is another matter."

Theo eased back, assuming a nonchalant air as they discussed admittance to satanic rites in Paris. Sometimes the Revenants made her feel like a country bumpkin who would never attain their sophistication. Other times, they seemed like children entranced by outlandish games with secret rules.

Her gaze was drawn back to the man in velvet robes and dyed beard. However theatrical, something about him menaced. She hated the thought of Averill seeking favors from him. Was he truly a Satanist? Men often strove to appear more lethal than they were, as women feigned greater innocence than they possessed. Or greater experience, she thought, mocking herself. Certainly, Averill tried to appear more wicked than he could possibly be.

Vipèrine lifted his head. His gaze met hers across the room. Since he obviously wanted to be looked at, Theo stared back boldly. He was the epitome of what the French called *joli-laid*, beauty and ugliness mingled in a way more compelling than mere handsomeness. It was the face of a corrupt priest, the ascetic twisted with the crudely sensual. Black hair winged back from a high, domed forehead. The long vertical jut of the nose was reversed in the sunken hollows of the cheeks and countered in the long horizontal of thin, beautifully carved lips that suggested a ferocious craving. Under the heavy brows, deep-set eyes glowed black. There was a predatory cruelty in his face.

It gave her a frisson of fear—but the fear only increased her defiance. She refused to look away.

Finally, he gave her a lewd smile and turned to his companions. Huysmans had moved on, but a group of acolytes vied for the favor of the serpent's word. Just then, shy Jules emerged from the shadows, almost as if he had stepped out from the wall of bones. He looked as worshipful as the rest of them. More so. The intense expression transformed his usually pinched features to an angelic purity.

"Monsieur, come with me! I can guide you to the exit." Turning, Theo saw young Dondre approach Casimir, who looked the wealthiest. He tugged on the baron's sleeve and pointed toward a tunnel. "I know the shortest route, monsieur."

Casimir laughed. "From here, my boy, everyone knows the quickest way to escape."

Dondre looked offended. Theo guessed he hoped for a handsome tip. She gave Averill's arm a squeeze, encouraging him to accept the offer. Dondre missed nothing. "Mademoiselle, I am the best guide of all."

"I believe you," she assured him with a smile.

Averill leaned close, his hand lingering lightly on her arm. "I gather we are to follow this Dondre, *ma cousine?*"

Cousine, again. Was he reminding himself that he shouldn't ever be more than a cousin? "Yes, let Dondre light the way."

"Very well, play at Hermes," Casimir said. "Lead us back to the world of the living."

Dondre gave them a broad grin. Theo had to fight the impulse to take his hand. He would certainly be offended by such foolish protectiveness—or maybe take advantage and pick her pockets. He guided them around the crowd and down a shorter section of tunnels. In just a few moments, they came to the ancient spiral staircase leading to the surface. Theo gave him a tip and urged her friends to add to it. She looked eagerly to the staircase while Paul scrounged in his pockets for change and handed it to him.

Dondre closed his fingers tight around the money and grinned. "Messieurs, mademoiselle, I know all the hidden places. You should come back soon."

"Not too soon, Dondre. Mademoiselle can't wait to escape," Averill said, watching her prowl about the exit.

"*Tant pis.*" The boy shrugged elaborately, indicating it was their loss. He stuffed the coins in his pocket and ran back into the catacombs.

"Do you want to lead the charge, Theo?" Averill nodded toward the stairs.

"Like Jeanne d'Arc leading the siege of Paris?"

"Jeanne failed to reclaim the city," Casimir reminded her.

"Perhaps, but she was a fabulous heroine, even to a California girl."

Casimir smiled at that. "Paris was one of her few failures."

"Well, I shall succeed. Up!" Theo forged ahead. Their ascent seemed endless. They followed the tight coil of stone steps round and round and round, until they at last emerged onto the streets. She gazed up the night sky, at the pure and icy glitter of a billion stars. Eternity was that soul-stirring vastness, not the crumbling necropolis lying below. Theo breathed deeply, drinking in freedom with the sparkling air.

"I want a drink," Paul announced.

"Champagne is best after midnight," Casimir said.

Luscious, giddy champagne suited Theo's mood, but Averill countered with, "Absinthe is best anytime."

"Either, both—and beer as well," Paul said. "But where?"

They were on the southern edge of Paris, in sprawling Montparnasse. Like her own neighborhood, it mingled peaceful, bucolic patches with sinful pleasures. But it was Montmartre where Theo wanted to be, her haven. "Home."

"*Le Chat Noir est mort. Vive Le Rat Mort!*" Paul exclaimed.

The Black Cat, Montmartre's most famous cabaret, had closed with its owner's death. But the even more disreputable Dead Rat remained. Theo shook her head. "Not there. Somewhere bright." She craved light and life after all this grimness

"The Moulin de la Galette?" Averill suggested.

"Yes. I want to dance!" New energy rushed through her. Released from the oppression of the catacombs, she felt deliciously wicked again. She would stay out all night dancing with her poets. Dancing with Averill—

Their fiacre was one of many waiting at the exit, the horses shifting restlessly as the midnight revelers emerged from the catacombs and jostled around them. "La Galette," Casimir called up to the driver as Averill helped her into the carriage.

They rolled into the night, the horses' iron-clad hooves clattering loudly on the pavement. Theo laughed with midnight giddiness as they hurried through the streets of Paris, leaning out the window of the coach to feel the night breeze ruffle her hair. She searched for a glimpse of the distant Eiffel tower, glinting like steel lace in the starlight. Almost as much a newcomer to Paris as she was, the tower was not yet ten years old—but already symbolic of Paris herself. The dark buildings grew denser as they drew closer to the center of the city, but lights glowed ever brighter as they rolled through the Latin Quarter, bustling even so late at night. Looking in the *café* windows, Theo saw students drinking, laughing, kissing, and even a few studying earnestly amid the cheerful chaos.

They crossed the Seine, the towers and spires of Notre Dame framed against pale clouds. On the Right Bank, they trotted beside the formal Jardins des Tuileries, quiet in the starlight, and on to the Avenue de l'Opéra, with its elegant *cafés,* and through quieter streets, until at the foot of Montmartre the night came alive again. Lights still blazed at the Moulin Rouge and surrounding *cafés*, and would till the sun rose. The carriage passed the boisterous cabaret, then took the gentler slope up the rue Caulaincourt. They crossed the bridge over the Montmartre cemetery and took the first turn toward the rue Lepic. Except the carriage halted. Looking out, Theo saw some sort of commotion ahead. Gendarmes swarmed everywhere.

The Revenants climbed out of the fiacre and mingled with the people in the street, a peculiar mix of gaudy riffraff, insomniac artists, and sleepy bourgeois in nightclothes. There was an air of hectic gaiety. Some were singing, some shouting, some growling threats. There was a chant that sounded suspiciously filthy, something involving cows.

"What's happening?" Paul asked the nearest chanter.

"Anarchist," the fellow told them. "Blew up a building."

"Destruction is a passion—a creative passion," Paul declared. "Bakunin."

"It was just a gas explosion," a gendarme said, followed by much groaning and argument in the crowd.

"All the buildings are standing," Theo pointed out, hoping it was no more than a faulty stove. She felt a surge of protectiveness. This was her street, these were her neighbors. She didn't want bombs blowing them out of their cozy beds at midnight.

"Not a whole building—just the top floor. Up the street." A woman gestured beyond the curve of the rue Lepic. "The police took away the bomber."

Theo started up the hill, her friends following. They were halted by a gendarme. Undeterred, she wove her way back through the throngs to the rue Tholozé, which was not guarded and ended across from the Moulin de la Galette. The crowd here was obviously from the cabaret. They had rushed into the street at the sound of the blast and most were returning, now that the bomber had been hauled off to jail.

"He was going to bomb the Sacré Coeur!" one fellow told them.

"Too good to be true," Paul said.

"Killed six *flics*," another man announced. "A hero of the people!"

"Murder is not heroic," Theo challenged.

"Disagree with the mob and lose your head," Casimir warned.

"*Aristos* like you don't use their heads," Paul said in his nastiest tone. "They have no brains to put in them."

"Let's use our feet for dancing!" Theo broke in. She did not want her friends arguing.

"I'll ask the band to play the Dynamite Polka," Paul said. Theo presumed that was not a joke.

"I doubt you'll even need to request it tonight," Casimir muttered.

Wanting only to escape thoughts of death, Theo dashed across the street to the Moulin de la Galette. Lit by lights in the garden, the old windmill glowed in the moonless night. She plunged forward, determined to forget both the trouble outside and the grim world of the catacombs. La Galette was the perfect escape. Theo loved the rustic nightclub, with its hodgepodge interior. Decades ago, grain was ground here. Now chandeliers glittered above the polished wood floor and green latticework decorated the walls. She paused on the threshold and closed her eyes, letting the music begin to work its magic and sweep away the sourness of the street. When she opened them, Averill was by her side, a question in his eyes.

"Dancing," she said again, knowing only movement would break her free of the clinging shadows. Averill smiled and offered his arm. Paul and Casimir appeared behind him. Theo and her poets joined the swirling throng, dancing and drinking till the doors closed at dawn.

The sky was paling as they left. Paul led them to a nearby *boulangerie* on the rue Tholozé, promising perfect croissants. He knew the owner, the rotund and apple-cheeked Monsieur Pommier, and coaxed him to open the door to them. The baker's voluptuous wife and elfin daughter were just pulling their bread and morning pastries from the ovens. The shop was filled with the heavy aromas of warm yeast, baked wheat and rye, brandied raisins, marzipan, and melted chocolate. Theo laughed, dizzy and ravenous from the deluge of scents. She bought golden brown almond croissants. Unable to wait, she bit into the one of the pastries. "This is amazing. So crusty!"

"I have my secret pleasures." Paul chose a savory pastry with ham and cheese.

Averill smiled at her. "You are sweetly decorated." Her breath caught when he reached out and brushed the flakes of puff pastry from the edges of her mouth. An innocent touch? Or an innocent excuse for a touch?

"We must have *café au lait* for our picnic," Casimir declared.

"But the cups..." Ninette, the lovely young daughter, looked flustered. Tendrils of black hair framed the perfect oval of her face. Her eyes were chocolate brown and delicately tilted.

"I will buy them," Casimir said.

"Don't be absurd," Paul said. "I will bring them back to her."

"Wouldn't you prefer absurdity, Noret?" Casimir retorted.

Paul rolled his eyes. Since he was a regular, the baker agreed Paul could return the cups later. Theo watched as Ninette poured foaming milk into the fresh black coffee and served them with a charming blush. That splash of pink would be lovely in a portrait that framed her in the golden tones of the pastry, and the crusty loaves of bread on their wooden shelves would make a strong background pattern. The foreground would have coffee in the pure white cups—not the pale, breakfast *café au lait*, but a deep, rich brown. Theo felt a tingling of delicious excitement. The challenge of drawing the catacombs lingered, a murky cloud in her mind, black as the ink she'd use. Painting this beautiful girl in the cozy bakery would be a golden counterpoint. Theo determined to come back soon and see if Ninette would pose. She could work on the portrait on rainy days.

Carrying their breakfast feast, they climbed to the pinnacle of the hill. From there it was a short walk to Sacré Cœur with its wide steps overlooking the city. Theo sat down, savoring the view of Paris and the meal to come. She wished the tree-topped shoulder of the hill didn't obscure the view of the Eiffel Tower. It was strange to have it absent in the vast panorama. Averill and Casimir settled on either side of her, but Paul hovered behind them. Together they sipped their *café au lait*, sharing the quiet morning with the masons arriving to work on the still unfinished basilica. Although it was incomplete and unconsecrated, services were being held inside. Whenever the doors opened, the sound of organ music flowed over them.

Still standing, Paul gave the church a look of loathing. "It is an atrocity."

"It looks like a petrified wedding cake," Theo agreed, though she loved the domed shape seen from a distance, the travertine stone glowing pure white on the peak of Montmartre.

"An atrocity and a monument to atrocity," Paul insisted.

It was not aesthetics but politics that made his voice so hard and implacable. Theo sat up straighter, tension tugging like reins at her shoulders and arms, at her throat.

"It was meant to heal the wounds of war," Casimir said sharply, "and to expiate our sins."

"To expiate the supposed crimes of the Communards—and to celebrate their slaughter," Paul snarled. "The Army of Versailles lined them up and shot them. They entombed hundreds in the gypsum mines below—sealed them in with explosives. Our bomber should have blown the Sacré Coeur to smithereens."

"He is not my bomber." Casimir's voice crackled like ice. "During the Revolution, men such as he slaughtered the innocent monks of La Veillée sur Oise and destroyed their hermitage. What little remained of our town the Communards decimated."

Was that when his chateau burned? Theo wondered. He would have been a child then.

Paul gathered breath to argue, but Averill interrupted, his voice mild. "The basilica was built on the site of the martyrdom of St. Denis."

"Ah yes…they chopped off his head but he picked it up and carried it two miles, plopping it down where he wanted his abbey built." Paul sneered.

"Jeanne d'Arc made a pilgrimage here…" Casimir began.

Paul leaned forward, suddenly earnest. "A true heroine, Jeanne. A valiant warrior and a patriot, she did not desert the people of France. Then she was betrayed by the ruling class—"

"It is too early for argument," Theo broke in. "We don't need to blow ourselves to smithereens." As a peace offering, she gave Paul a bite of her croissant, oozing marzipan and crusted with toasted almonds. Hunger triumphed over zeal. Paul turned his back on the cathedral, sat on the step behind them, and proceeded to devour his *petit dejéuner*. The others relaxed and together they watched a soft pink light bathe the rooftops and spires of Paris.

Averill's gaze was dreamy. "*L'insidieuse nuit m'a grisé trop longtemps….*"

Treacherous night, you have intoxicated me far too long. A new poem? Theo leaned closer, but he spoke so quietly she could barely hear him at first. Ever elusive. Then he raised his head and spoke clearly.

> *O jour, ô frais rayons, immobilisez-vous,*
> *Mirés dans mes yeux sombres,*
> *Maintenant que mon cœur à chacun de ses coups*
> *Se rapproche des ombres.*

O day, O cool radiance, abide, mirrored in my darkening eyes, as now, with each beat, my heart draws nearer to the shadows…. "That's beautiful, Averill," Theo said. "Yours?"

"He wishes," Paul said. "Jean Moréas."

"I have no poems about the dawn," Averill said, looking out over the sun-washed city. "Only the night."

Chapter Seven

Their smiling lips seemed to murmur something
—They dream, they lean upon their small, round arms,
Sweet gesture of awakening, faces uplifted,
Unsettled gazes all around...And think
Themselves asleep in some pink paradise.

Arthur Rimbaud

"*Doux geste du réveil, ils avancent le front, et leur vague regard tout autour d'eux se pose,*" Gilles coaxed the drowsing child to wake, to look around.

Tonight, he would let the poem set the mood.

No frenzy this time. His soul was starved and must be filled, but craving must be bridled by artistry. He crouched over Dondre, curbing his impatience. Ribbons of blood crept from the back of the boy's neck and across the stone floor. They made a beautiful crimson frame for the curling hair, the paling skin. His naked body had a pearlescent glow.

To conjure his lost castle of Tiffauges, Gilles was burning incense. The perfumed smoke rose like soft, black prayers. Prayers to Satan. Candle flames wavered beside the stone walls. They made a fluttering sound, like tiny tongues licking. The shimmer of a scream lingered in the air. When Gilles made the cut, Dondre had shrieked then fainted. The boy was groggy now, barely aware of the pain. It was a rapture Gilles loved, the languishing glory when they bled out slowly beneath him. Sometimes they did not even understand they were dying. So piquant....

"Beautiful, isn't he?" The other was silent, but Gilles did not need an answer.

He always tried to select for beauty, though his sacrifices must fulfill other criteria first. If they were not beautiful enough to please him, the heads could be removed before he took his pleasure. And if they were as beautiful as this boy, the head might be worth preserving. Denis had been irresistible, of course. The martyred saint had been decapitated, and so the saintly boy had been as well. Sometimes Gilles would choose one of the loveliest heads—hold it up and kiss it while he satisfied himself. With the boys, if their pink members were especially pretty, he would cut those off and add them to the display. Dondre was very pink there, genitals plump and rosy against his white thighs. Already Gilles had a priceless collection. His own private museum.

There was a moan. Soft, musical. Barely breathing, Gilles waited until Dondre opened his eyes and peered around him. The boy saw, but did not understand, did not recognize him. He was slipping away. At first Gilles was disappointed. Then charmed. Each death was unique.

He must be quick...but not too quick. Opening his clothes, Gilles stretched out upon his prize, his erect member stroking slowly over the tender skin of the belly. Exquisite, delicate friction. Another soft cry.

"*Mon cheri,*" Gilles whispered, sweet endearments flowing from his tongue. He moved slowly, slowly, drawing out the sensation. "*Mon ange. Mon petit chou-fleur.*"

Dondre trembled beneath him, muscle and nerve guttering like the candle flames. Gilles began to croon a lullaby as life ebbed. The soft cries, his own sighs, the gasping breath were his music. He rocked Dondre gently, soothing him as he stroked. He watched the slow drift down into darkness. He looked deep into his eyes until their gaze fixed upon him. It was a sweet oblivion, sinking into the black well of the fixed pupil as his seed spilled out in the little death.

Gilles shuddered with pleasure. Sighed deeply.

This was his most romantic encounter.

Chapter Eight

Lechery is the wet nurse of Demonism.
J. K. Huysmans

Michel had barely slept. Dreams of bombs and blood haunted him.
New dreams and old knotting together in his brain, his belly.
Walking to work, he paused at the center of the bridge linking the Île
Saint Louis to the Île de la Cité, letting the cool morning light clear the
gloom from his mind. From here, the twenty *arrondissements* curved out
in a clockwise spiral like the shell of a snail, each housing its own diverse
worlds. Alone for the moment in the heart of Paris, Michel allowed himself
to savor the view of Notre Dame. One of the Impressionists should paint
the cathedral at dawn—a grey dawn like today, the muted light flashing
with sudden iridescence like the throats of the pigeons strutting at his feet.
Shreds of clouds floated like pale banners about the spire of the Gothic
cathedral, and washes of sunlight gilded the arches of the flying
buttresses. Just across the bridge, the great willow trailed its withes over
the embankment, green leaves cascading against the ancient stone. Faint
traces of mist still hovered near the quais, but the Seine gleamed silver,
flecks of vivid color rippling in the wake of passing boats.

Michel turned at the sound of footsteps. It was the grocer's wife on
her way to early mass. He nodded to her then crossed over to the larger
island. The morning was relatively quiet. The *café* conversation of a few
early risers mingled with the daily calls and clatter of workmen making
deliveries. He chose a *café* at random for his *petit déjeuner*. He patronized
most of the *cafés* along his route, wanting them all to know him, to feel
free to call on him in need. The coffee was fresh, hot and bitter, the ham
and eggs too greasy. He ate a little, paid, and wrapped up the remnants
of the food in a bit of newspaper.

It was only a block to the Palais de Justice. Skirting the entrance, he
went round to the far end of the building where the feral cats had their
domain. There was an allotment in the budget for the feeding of stray
cats. In turn, the cats helped control the rat population. It was said to be
cheaper than paying for an exterminator. Even with their steady diet of

rats and their official allotment, Michel considered them too thin. He brought them his leftovers almost every day. They came when he called. The tamer ones placed their paws on his knee to demand their shred of ham. The wilder ones watched avidly. Michel tossed a bit toward the white queen with soft grey ears. He had his favorites but did his best to make sure they all got a taste.

When the food was gone, Michel returned to the detective offices of the Palais de Justice. Inside, he went to the washroom and cleaned the grease from his hands. When he emerged, another detective was conferring with the desk officer. His prisoner, a fragile little blonde, sat on a bench, awaiting processing at the Dépôt. She looked like a trampled flower. He had seen her sometimes, this past year, walking the streets by the river.

"Is he alive?" She stared about her, obviously in shock.

Michel saw that her hand was badly burned. Acid, he thought, not fire. "Another *vitrioleuse*?" he asked quietly.

"She splashed her pimp. The press will be pissing themselves with joy."

Michel nodded, frowning. There seemed to be a fashion for certain methods of murder, intensified by lurid stories in the press. Like the man he'd recently captured, many men favored hacking their victims to death with an axe. Journalists especially loved to glorify the vengeful woman with her beaker of prussic acid.

"Is he alive?" the girl asked again. She began to cry.

"Dead, you stupid *pouffiasse!*" the man snapped. She flinched at the insult. To Michel he added, "Acid ate up his eyes—he went head first down the stairs and—." He jerked his head sideways and gave a guttural cracking sound.

The girl curled up in a ball, weeping silently now. Michel felt a swell of pity. The pimp had most likely corrupted her. Juries were sometimes sympathetic to a *vitrioleuse*, if her tale was pathetic enough. Lately they'd been convicting. When women were sentenced to death, it was usually commuted to life at hard labor. This girl was frail and Michel doubted she would survive *travaux forcés* for very long. But there was nothing to be done about it. Michel was about to ask after his own prisoner, but another officer gestured him down the hall toward the chief's door. Michel made his way to Armand Cochefert's office and knocked.

"Enter."

As expected, Michel found the chief of the Sûreté seated behind his desk. Cochefert had been head of criminal investigations for three years now. He didn't leave his office—or his chair—if at all possible. He was a heavy man, almost lethargic. At first, Michel had thought his mind lazy, too. But occasionally the case was important enough, or frustrating enough, that Cochefert would venture into the investigation personally. Once the chief took a case, he was fervent in searching for the culprit. Slowly, Michel had revised his judgment. Cochefert leavened practical intelligence with a sly sense of humor. He knew his men's strengths and weaknesses. If he enjoyed the comfortable world of his office too much, he also knew how to delegate wisely. Michel also approved the chief's liberal leanings, though sometimes he found them too naïve.

"Devaux," Cochefert said, by way of greeting. He looked glum but began with praise. "Good work last night. The juge d'instruction has a confession from your anarchist."

"Already?"

"The villain bragged about it." Cochefert's face tightened with anger. He expelled a sharp breath. "I regret the deaths, but killing our men will get him the guillotine."

Michel nodded. "I had good information."

"Who tipped you?" The chief took a hard-boiled egg from his pocket and peeled it. As usual, his pockets bulged with them.

"Blaise Dancier."

"Odd." Cochefert pursed his lips, pausing between bites of his egg. "Usually he'd take care of someone like that himself."

"Usually," Michel agreed. "He had a favor."

"Ahh...." Cochefert paused. "Just what does he want in return?"

"He is concerned about some missing children. Two of his flock are missing."

"Children?" Cochefert's fleshy face sank into a morose expression. He had a very soft heart where the young were concerned.

"Two boys. But when he asked around, he found several other children who had vanished, both boys and girls."

"If he went to so much bother, we must take him seriously."

"Dancier wants us to be on guard." He paused. "I've begun investigating but with no success."

Cochefert pondered for a moment. "Nothing relevant comes to mind, but assign someone to check the files. I will also contact the Police Municipale to keep a closer eye on the streets. You can take a week—see if you can find evidence to link even two cases."

"And if not?"

"If not, I know damned well you'll go on working it on the side." Cochefert twisted one corner of his luxurious walrus mustache. "But I'll have a special assignment for you soon."

"Of course." Officially, Michel investigated homicides rather than gathering intelligence. Unofficially, as a member of Cochefert's *batallion sacré,* he did what was necessary.

Cochefert tapped a finger against his lips. "Leo Taxil has scheduled a lecture at the Geographical Society."

"There may be rioting," Michel acknowledged. Taxil had been writing an exposé of the Masonic Order, claiming that they were all Satanists. He had promised to produce a repentant high priestess of the order, who claimed to have conducted diabolical rites, participated in orgies, and watched a child sacrifice.

Cochefert nodded. "Taxil has requested police protection. I've ordered a few men stationed in the auditorium to forestall trouble. He's chosen Easter Monday to make his revelations. The bigger the splash the better. We could all end up in the Seine." The chief adjusted his spectacles and poked about his desk, finally pulling a ticket from beneath a file and pushing it across the desk to Michel. "From you, I simply want intelligence."

Michel regarded it dubiously, then picked it up and put it in his coat pocket. "Taxil may have an agent provocateur."

"Quite possibly. The hall will be filled with dupes, tricksters, and troublemakers. I want your eyes, Devaux. I want your assessment." Cochefert gestured vaguely, stewing in malaise. "Anything that reeks of devil worship, I want to know who comes sniffing. Sooner or later, they will be trouble."

"Sooner, most likely."

"The other night there was a concert in the catacombs, and we heard nothing of it till it was over," Cochefert complained. "I don't intend to be caught unawares again. Scrutinize the audience at Taxil's speech. See who is there that we know. Discover any suspicious newcomers, especially these dabblers in the occult."

"Taxil accused the leaders of the Rose-Cross of practicing Satanism. I doubt they will give him any credence by appearing. Not Papus, not even Sar Péladan, though he loves a show. Perhaps Vipèrine will come— he has nothing to lose. Claiming to be a student of the Abbé Boullan was enough to get him thrown out of the Rose-Cross."

Cochefert nodded. "Stanislaus de Gauita's sinking ever deeper into opium dreams. There may be a power struggle to claim leadership of his occult movement. Vipèrine may try an insinuate-and-seize maneuver."

"De Gauita has dangerous enemies—and dangerous friends."

"We must be vigilant. I don't want another 'Magical War.'"

"One was enough," Michel agreed. The magical war between rival Rosicrucians had occurred four years ago. The novelist Huysmans, who worked in the Ministry of the Interior, had been involved. "The station was a wasps' nest of gossip."

The memory seemed to captivate Cochefert. "You must admit, it was a most curious war."

"If you can believe the accounts," Michel countered. Huysmans had denounced the Rose-Cross movement, accusing the leaders of murdering the Abbé Boullan with black magic. Challenged to a duel, he recanted, but the journalist who had published the article did not. There the story became bizarre. Three times the journalist's arrival at the dueling ground was delayed because the horses froze in terror. Each time they stood sweating and trembling for minutes on end, before stumbling on their way. Or so the story went. "Tales of the journeys were more dramatic than the actual confrontation," Michel said. "Both duels passed without serious injury."

"It was claimed that the bullet remained in the chamber of the journalist's gun," Cochefert reminded him. "Such stories, true or not, create their own spells. During the 'Magical War', the city went crazy with rumors. Parisians saw demons lurking everywhere. You could feel shivers of hysteria rippling through the streets."

The trouble began when Huysmans was researching his book on the medieval murderer, Gilles de Rais. It was then that Huysmans made friends with the Abbé Boullan, a defrocked priest. Boullan's Society for the Reparation of Souls specialized in freeing those possessed by succubi and incubi. From all reports save Huysmans', the Abbé was doing his best to have sexual congress with succubi and incubi himself. He was an adherent of Satanism who was known to have debauched nuns and officiated at Black Masses. "Let's hope Dancier's missing children aren't victims of some cult."

"Probably they were beaten to death by their parents and stuffed in a sewage pipe," Cochefert said glumly. Then he brightened. "Have you read Taxil's saga—*The Devil in the Nineteenth Century*?"

"Bits and pieces." Anyone so incendiary was worth checking on. But the stories Taxil spun were beyond belief.

"I read them for amusement," Cochefert confided. "I loved Moloch, the crocodile demon."

Michel tilted his head, admitting curiosity.

"Some mad Parisian tries to summon the devil into his parlor. He sits at a table—candles burning, incense wafting—all the usual paraphernalia. Suddenly the table rattles, bounces and flies up to the ceiling. The whole house shakes. Terror and awe abound. The table crashes back to the floor and a malevolent figure plummets from the ceiling, landing all in a heap. It rises. Behold, it is the demon Moloch, in the shape of a gigantic winged crocodile." Cochefert gestured broadly, miming a display of vast wings. "This Moloch is a demon of talent, a demon of vanity, and a demon of lascivious temperament. He dusts himself off, then proceeds to the piano. He sits down and plays a ditty with the host's wife, ogling her all the while. He sets himself to seduce her."

"Does he succeed?"

"Unfortunately, that was never clear. Perhaps the husband intervened." Cochefert patted his heavy belly, as if he'd dined well on absurdity.

Michel allowed a small smile. "The crocodile is...impressive."

Cochefert smiled more broadly. "It's difficult to completely despise Taxil, not when he can so amuse."

Michel found it easy to completely despise him. The absurdity had an acrid tinge. Michel's father—the man he had learned to call father—had been a brigadier of the Sûreté and a Mason. Michel had little patience with the Church's view that Masons were devil's spawn. He had less still with men like Leo Taxil who exploited such views to gain money and notoriety.

"Why not crocodile demons?" Cochefert supposed, savoring his own amusement. "Electrical current...ectoplasm.... If one exists, why not the other? Miracles happen daily."

"Men are demonic enough," Michel said.

Chapter Nine

*Keep the gem delirious. Laughing ruby. The
flower's most secret heart.*

Paul Verlaine

With practiced quietness, Michel entered the gate and crossed the dimly lit courtyard. Two glossy-leafed camellia trees obscured the recessed doorway. He tapped the brass knocker and waited for Lilias to open the door to the exquisite jewel box of a house she kept for her private encounters. The maid would be there but summoned only if needed. A courtesan's maid needed as much discretion as the courtesan herself. Taking a detective for a lover required even more caution than capturing a politician's favor. Lilias was as daring as she was discreet.

She opened the door and he stepped inside. He was struck again by her delicacy. Lilias was small, with the fragile, brittle beauty of fine porcelain. She had the bearing and self-possession of an aristocrat. He could picture her at the court of the *Ancien Régime*, softly powdered, bewigged, clothed in continents of silk and glittering with jewels. But something raw and ferocious lay hidden below the surface. He could just as easily imagine her carrying the flag through the streets in the Revolution, her feet bathed in blood. Either way, she would be plotting intrigues.

It was said that the most successful Parisian courtesans came from the provinces—it took longer to tarnish their innocence. The ones born in the city had an ironic edge that cut into a man's lust. Perversely, Lilias had triumphed and endured because of that sharpness. Her precision was strangely erotic. Her bitter intelligence and cynicism contrasted with her abandon in the heat of passion. Michel supposed some of her patrons wanted to subjugate that. None had. Though perhaps Lilias offered them the illusion. He would not know. She stirred his desire just as she was.

Her dark brown eyes regarded him levelly. She did not kiss him but offered her hand to be kissed. Black lace gloves made an intricate pattern against her pale skin. He felt the texture against his lips, delicate yet abrasive. The last time he had visited her, she had stroked his naked body wearing the same gloves. The memory sent a jolt through him, hardening his cock. Heat radiated outward. Even his skin came alive, tingling underneath his clothes.

Lilias smiled at him with certain knowledge of her effect. She arched a delicate eyebrow. "Talk first?"

He had meant to—but now he shook his head. She kept hold of his hand, turning and leading him along the narrow foyer. In the dim light, the gesture felt sweetly conspiratorial. They had been lovers for months now, but she made each time feel like their first assignation. Her house was subtly rich, the furnishings refined *Directoire*. Smiling, Lilias led him up the curving stairs to her bedroom. Hothouse roses spilled from a vase, glowing crimson in the lamplight. They were the same roses she chose for her perfume, a fragrance heady with spices and amber—a wanton note of musk subverting the refined elegance.

"I like for you to undress me. Your hands are deft and gentle." Her eyes glittered. "I want them gentle—for now."

First, Michel took off the gloves. Lilias always wore something erotically provocative, as she would for a protector who expected such skillful provocation. He slowly undid the buttons of the gown next, a creation of twilight blue silk overlaid with copper lace that echoed the auburn of her hair. Michel laid the expensive dress on a chair and unlaced her corset, fingertips caressing as he did. He removed the slithering soft undergarments of peach silk and cream lace to reveal still creamier skin dusted with freckles. He reached around to cup her small, perfect breasts. The large nipples hardened, thrusting into his palms. He turned her round to face him. Courtesans were given nicknames, in mockery or in praise. She was sometimes called *La Renarde*. Revealed, her mons gleamed red as a fox's fur.

"Leave your clothes on…for now," she murmured, unbuttoning his fly and taking the hard heat of him into her hand. "Just give me this." She lay back on the bed and guided him into her. The jolt of desire coursed through him, still startling in its intensity. His mind appreciated her. His body craved her. He grew harder even as he began to melt in her fire.

"Not gentle," she whispered. "Not now."

After, she had the maid bring tiny cups of hot chocolate, madeleines, and cognac finer than Blaise Dancier's. Their aromas blended with the spiced rose perfume of her skin, the musk of their sex, the smoke of apple wood burning in the fireplace.

"Talk now?" she asked.

He told her first of his invitation to Dancier's house and his impression of it, and she rewarded him with a wicked little laugh. Then he gave her the details of Dancier's request and his own fruitless investigation of his missing boys and the others Cochefert had since added to his list. "I've interviewed families, friends and neighbors, shopkeepers, gendarmes, carriage drivers and beggars." He shook his head. "The children all vanished without a trace. No one saw anything suspicious."

"Or will say so if they did." Her voice was musical, precise and slightly husky. "You do not think the children ran away? You think the same person took them?"

Michel frowned. "In one case I am having the parents investigated—they've killed the child by accident or design. One of Dancier's orphans was working for a ragman, but I think he ran off with a passing circus troop. And one of the older girls had a crush on a sailor from Marseilles."

"With luck they are married, if not…."

"She's on the streets." He kissed her shoulder softly. Lilias did not like reminders of her early days.

She stroked a fingertip down his nose. "Those cases aside?"

"Instinct says some other disappearances are linked, but instinct is not proof." Michel lay back, staring at the ceiling, his sense of futility growing. "Often I don't even know where they were seized. One boy went on an errand to collect some laundry work, and his mother knew his favorite route to Montmartre."

"You followed it," Lilias said, detached but intent. Her presence was excellent for focusing his mind, as if she was always asking him to look deeper.

"His favorite side street." He summoned the memory—just the usual filthy alley, the usual refuse. Torn posters. Broken glass. Obscenities splashed in paint on the walls, crude images that had embarrassed Mlle. Faraday. He remembered a huge red phallus, giant breasts, and copulating dogs mingled with the usual religious images. A smudged cross scribbled in charcoal. All meaningless. "His mother was making some cake he loved. He never came home."

"How many children?"

"I've set aside a dozen files." Michel took another sip of brandy, letting the liquid fire warm the chill this case gave him. "Recently another boy disappeared. He worked with his father in the catacombs, and the father suspected he sneaked back on his own, hoping to make extra money leading a sightseer through the ancient mazes."

"Many have gotten lost and died in the tunnels."

"Of course, but that is good cover for murder."

"Who else?"

"A *bouquiniste's* boy on the Left Bank seems the earliest. A chimney sweeper in the Marais, a seamstress' daughter in Montparnasse."

"You think he takes both boys and girls?"

"I could be wrong about the girls."

"What other boys?"

"A bootblack's son near the Sorbonne, and Dancier's boy in training as pickpocket around the Opéra and the boulevards. Such various locations…." His hand tightened into a fist. How could he grasp this illusive killer?

"Where then does he take them, and how?" Lilias prompted.

"If he is a laborer, or disguised as one, he could knock them unconscious and carry them off in a cart or even a sack. If they are drugged, he might carry them in his arms, as if they were his own. He would be less visible in a carriage, but would risk being remembered."

"Some men can be hired for any errand." She nibbled a madeleine.

"Yes, or he might have an accomplice who helps him for love of blood or money."

"Then your kidnapper opens himself to blackmail or the chance of being turned in for a reward." Lilias paused. "And the other opens himself to a blade in the night."

"Then the other loves blood more than money—the blood of children." Michel frowned. "If there even is an accomplice."

"Where does he take them?"

Michel caught her gaze and smiled briefly. He wanted her to know he appreciated this indulgence. The case was becoming an obsession. "If he has money, he can rent a room in the neighborhood he plans to hunt, but again he risks exposure or blackmail. I think he has someplace more secure. Perhaps a barge on the Seine, so he can take them away easily."

"We have been talking as if he is a stranger to these children. Someone they know could lure them more easily."

"It's possible, but not with all of them. Dancier's pickpocket would be sharper than that."

"Unless the lure was money. They were all poor."

"He may use a different approach depending on the child, or he may follow some ritual. It's all conjecture."

When he said nothing more, Lilias lifted her delicate eyebrows. "So, you wondered if I had heard gossip about anyone with a predilection for children. Someone with a taste for violence?"

"Yes."

"No, I have not. But I will ask, discreetly." She sipped her brandy.

Michel knew that a wise courtesan kept aware of the professional houses. A possible protector could be recommended there, or she might be warned off someone cruel or stingy. Occasionally a protector asked his mistress to accompany him to the houses. It was well to know what each of them provided. What was allowed and what not. Which might be worth investment, if one were smart with money. Lilias was no fool.

More reluctantly, he added, "I've also considered some sort of satanic cult."

"Ah, there I have intelligence." That surprised him enough that she laughed aloud. She shook her head. "No, I have not been playing in such evil corners, but I have heard rumors that a Black Mass is to be held."

"A Black Mass?" Cochefert would turn cartwheels. "Where? When?"

"Where is a deserted chapel, but I don't know when. I do know the slithering snake who will perform the rites."

He guessed her reference. "Vipèrine?"

"Just so." She laid a finger softly to his lips. "That is all I know now. But I will take pleasure in playing the spy."

When she released the gentle pressure, he said only, "Thank you."

She rose and brought the brandy decanter, refilling their glasses. Michel sipped the rich liquid, grateful for everything she gave him. Lilias was an invaluable ally. She had first provided information on a young man who'd murdered a rich uncle for his inheritance. He'd also been known for the violent streak he indulged with prostitutes. Michel had asked her why she chose to help and accepted the small smile that was her only answer. Lilias was not implicated in any way, so he presumed the nephew had injured her, or someone she cared for. It might be no more complicated than that. Perhaps.

Michel arrested the nephew, and that success was their beginning. A night of champagne and celebration became an affair of six months. Desire had not diminished. Lilias must entertain others, but he did not ask. He could not afford jealousy. Currently, she had no established patron, but she might at any time decide to secure one. Such a man would want sole rights to her bed and pay a small fortune for the privilege. She was already wealthy, but a woman on her own might never feel wealthy enough, secure enough.

If she did decide she wanted a new patron, their trysts would end, but not, he hoped, their alliance. He told himself to enjoy the pleasure, to expect nothing beyond the night. But pleasure could be as addictive as absinthe.

Michel knew she desired him. He could give her few gifts other than pleasure and lack of pretense. He took care never to leave her unsatisfied. It would not have satisfied him. As a gesture, he sometimes brought her small presents. Last time, a bouquet of early violets, dewy and sweet. A bag of roasted chestnuts in winter. Once, truly extravagant, he went to Debauve and Gallias, chocolatier to Louis XVI and Napoléon, and bought four chocolates in a miniscule box. The price was absurd. The tiny size made the confection seem all the more precious. Lilias had laughed with delight, but no more than she had for the violets.

Perhaps next time he would bring his guitar and play for her.

Lilias kissed him lightly, her lips tingling with brandy. She pulled him down to the rug in front of the fire and leaned over him. Her skin was fragrant with the lingering aura of amber and musk. Michel concentrated on the glide of her fingertips along his collarbone, the delicate tickle of her hair framing their faces as they kissed. He began the same sort of touch in return, elusive, almost taunting, across the arched fan of her ribs. He never knew if she would desire roughness or tenderness. It made her all the more alluring. All the more challenging. Her kiss drifted across his cheekbone. A soft exhalation teased the hollow of his ear. Then she bit his earlobe, sharply. He shivered as he felt his flesh reawakening.

"No more talk," she whispered.

Chapter Ten

Each one of my days like a flower that floats
On the water, then sinks:
What place could they find in my fate,
This hope, this regret?

Jean Moréas

Vivid yellow, streaks of sunlight glanced off the blades of the windmill. Their brightness gleamed sharply against the bruised purple clouds lowering in the sky. Deep violet shadows flowed along the dusty streets, the pools of color seductive yet strangely sinister.

Theo lowered her brush, backed up, and contemplated the canvas. The cluster of houses funneling to the windmill lacked detail. The brush twitched restlessly in her hand, but she resisted the urge to elaborate. The clouded sky, jutting blades, the sloping planes of the roofs, would lose impact if she refined the buildings that curved down the hill. She liked the yellow door she saw far up the street. Her painting needed that sort of contrast on the right side, and it would echo the flashes of sun. Choosing a smaller brush, she added a rectangle of chrome yellow to the highest house. Too bright. She muted it so that it didn't pull the eye away from the windmill. A few quick splashes of vermillion suggested geraniums valiantly blooming in the gathering darkness. The newly added yellow and orange gave the shadows a deeper glow.

Stop, Theo thought. *Stop.* She put the brush aside.

What would the Revenants think if she left the painting as it was? Only Paul would approve. Casimir would consider it raw and unfinished. Crude. She feared Averill would frown at it too. He most admired the delicate, decadent voluptuousness of Gustave Moreau. Theo had illustrated her cousin's poems in exquisite, painstakingly rendered detail. But Paris was changing her work, changing her. She would still illustrate Averill's poems in the style he loved, but her painting would go where it would.

The church bells tolled four. There was still an hour before Matthieu came to help her carry back her easel and paints. She would read a chapter of her book then look to see if the painting really needed more detail. Theo turned the canvas around so she would not steal glances at it.

She wiped her hands on a rag, then sat cross-legged in the shade of a chestnut tree. Taking an apple out of her satchel, she bit into the crisp flesh, juicy and tartly sweet. The bright fragrance distracted her from the odors of oil and turpentine that called her back to the windmill. Instead, a still life with apples floated through her mind. Patches of red, yellow, and pale green gleamed as she slowly ate the fruit down to the core.

Finished, Theo searched deeper in her satchel for the book Casimir had recently given her. Drawing it out, she stared at the cover for a minute, reluctant to open it. *Là Bas* fascinated and distressed her. The novel was filled with weird obsessions and unsatisfied quests, overwrought one moment then strangely austere. But it was learning more about the horrific Gilles de Rais that made Theo steel herself before opening her bookmarked page.

'*Association with Jeanne d'Arc certainly stimulated his desires for the divine. Now from lofty mysticism to base Satanism there is but one step. In the Beyond all things touch… She roused an impetuous soul, as ready for orgies of saintliness as for ecstasies of crime…*'

Theo doubted Jeanne d'Arc would be pleased with what she roused. She read on, descending into a darkness as grim as the catacombs.

'*Then as to being a 'ripper' of children…Gilles did not violate and trucidate little boys until after he became convinced of the vanity of alchemy.*'

"Is that an excuse?" Theo muttered under her breath. Apparently so, for the narrator thought that Gilles was no crueler than the other barons of the age.

'*He exceeds them in the magnitude of his debauches, in the opulence of his murders, that is all.*'

A shadow fell across the book. Startled, she looked up to find Averill standing above her. He bent close, lips to her ear, and his whisper sent a spark of excitement coursing along Theo's spine. "*I was born under so fierce a star….*"

Stepping into view, Casimir finished Gilles' most famous quote "… *that I have done what no one in the world has done or could ever do.*" He sounded almost smug. A cat with cream on its whiskers—or a mouse under its paw.

"You're wicked, both of you. All three of you," she chided, seeing Jules lurking behind them.

They had crept up on her deliberately. Theo shielded her eyes as she gazed up at them, standing together, backlit by the late afternoon sun. She was still not fully emerged from the nightmare world of Gilles de Rais. Their words, *his* words, overlaid an image of star-spattered blackness in her mind. The teasing touch of fear mingled uneasily with the teasing softness of Averill's whisper. Her heart was racing, and tiny shivers threaded from the hollow of her ear and down her neck.

"What is happening?" Averill asked, nodding down to the book.

Theo seized the offered refuge. She did not want to talk about the opulence of Gilles' murders, so she turned to the opulence of his possessions. "I was amazed—he was even richer than the king."

"The richest man in France and the most profligate," Averill said.

"He bankrupted himself buying gem-encrusted books and extravagant robes embroidered in gold." Casimir's gestures clothed his own body in a flow of silks and velvets. "Every object in his possession was luxurious perfection. He devised flamboyant pageants where even the least of the pages was garbed like a king and built fabulous chapels for his angelic choirboys."

"He spent even more on alchemists who promised to make gold from lead," a little smile twisted Averill's lips, "and sorcerers who promised to summon Satan for him."

Jules closed his eyes as if praying, murmuring something inaudible.

"What did you say, Jules?" Theo asked, wondering why he tried so hard to vanish. Sometimes it made him all the more obvious.

Startled, he opened his eyes. His lips trembled, but he said, "He lost his soul to black magic. But he was forgiven."

"Forgiven?" Theo hoped not.

"Yes…" Jules hesitated, "…at the end."

"Oh, he was executed," Casimir assured her. "Far too mercifully throttled, then burned."

"But he knelt in church and begged them all for forgiveness." Jules sighed and Theo thought she saw tears glistening in his eyes. "It was granted."

Jules had once wanted to be a priest. Averill was raised Catholic, and Casimir. Was that the reason they understood the excesses of Gilles de Rais better than she could? Like him, they had worshipped in vast cathedrals gleaming with golden artifacts. Like him, they breathed air perfumed with bouquets of lilies and drifting clouds of incense. Priests garbed in embroidered robes chanted rites in Latin, transforming the simple words of Jesus to an impenetrable mystery. Impenetrable to her, but not to them. Did the wafers and wine transform on their tongues to body and blood? Rather than the empty cross of the resurrection that she had gazed on, they lifted their eyes to Christ crucified. It was a world of confession and absolution. Of abasement and glory.

A world of utter damnation—yet one where even the worst sins could be forgiven.

"It's obscene, his love of excess." Theo frowned, still haunted by the images the book had painted in her mind. She stood up, dusted off her breeches. "His crimes were just as excessive."

"Beauty and evil in equal measure," Averill mused.

"Equal!" Theo exclaimed. She could not be blasé about the slaughter of innocents. "How can any amount of beauty equal the horror of those ravished pages and gutted choirboys?"

Her vehemence made Averill glance away. Her heart plummeted at the small rejection. "Averill…" She stopped, hating the uncertainty in her voice.

He met her eyes, apologetic, defiant. "Excess was a drug, a drunkenness. It was both a quest and an escape."

"It was a necessity," Casimir declared. "Think of the void Gilles de Rais had to fill. How could anything compare in glory after Jeanne? The Maid touched his soul, bringing the incandescent light of God into his life."

"Then came the fire of her death—and darkness after," Averill said. "It was God's greatest betrayal."

Jules crossed himself, lips moving silently.

"And Jeanne's," Casimir said. "Greater even than betrayal by a lover."

Theo remembered the anger and abandonment she felt when her California family died. She had raged at Death—but at them as well.

"Her trial was a travesty," Averill added, "and her death without mercy. The Inquisition built the platform high above the pyre, so that fire would torment her longer."

"Horrible. To burn a living saint." Jules' voice was a hoarse whisper, as if he could feel the smoke in his own lungs.

Theo shuddered. "Horrible and heartbreaking."

Did Jeanne truly accept her martyrdom? Did her sense of betrayal rise with the flames? Did she, like Christ, feel forsaken by God? Theo had thought it solely Jeanne's tragedy, but now she envisioned the fire, the pain, the scalding fury, the inner terror all radiating outward, consuming the hearts of those who had believed in her.

"She is a saint," Jules insisted. "She should be canonized."

"She is a heroine to me, too." Spurred by curiosity, Theo asked, "You seem to get on easily with Paul despite his being an atheist."

"He who is furthest is also he who is closest." Jules' voice was low but filled with intensity. "I believe Paul will return to the Church."

"Return?" Theo frowned. She doubted Jules would be concerned about Paul returning to Protestantism. "Was Paul Catholic?"

"Oh yes," Jules answered. Averill and Casimir looked as flummoxed as Theo felt. It was impossible to think of Paul as other than his critical, iconoclastic self. But why had she presumed it was the Protestant church he had disavowed?

"The Prussians burned his village during the war. Paul prayed for the Emperor's troops to save it, but they ran."

"And so was born our atheist anarchist?" Averill mused.

Jules nodded sadly. "It was a test of faith he was not strong enough to endure."

"He was not even ten years old," Casimir said. "Young for a test of faith."

Averill said, "The Jesuits ask only for the first six years—then give the world the rest."

Theo shivered. "That's so cold-blooded."

"Indeed. I can almost picture Paul as a Jesuit." Casimir gave a short laugh. "Better he bring his fervor to literature than burn heretics at the stake."

"He is a lost soul." Jules was whispering again.

"We are all lost souls," Averill replied.

Casimir smiled. "But some of us are more lost than others."

"Like Gilles de Rais." Jules reached out tentatively, almost reverently, his fingers hovering over her book.

Theo wanted to escape from the despair of Gilles de Rais' world, and from bitter memories of her own. She put the novel back in her satchel, ending the discussion. There was a moment of shifting silence then Averill gestured to her canvas, leaning against the tree. "So, Theo, you must show us your new painting?"

With some reluctance, Theo turned the canvas around. There was another space of silence as they all studied it. Surreptitiously, she rubbed her palms against her trousers.

"Raw—but vivid," Casimir commented at last, grudgingly.

Jules moved closer to the painting then retreated. He muttered something inaudible,

"It's compelling," Averill said. "The windmill blades pull you in like a corkscrew."

Theo's heart lifted. He did like it, even if the baron did not. "Yes, that's what I wanted."

"You've found something hidden behind the sunshine. The flowers look like spattered blood." Averill looked from the painting to the Moulin de la Galette, the windmill looking innocent and frisky in the afternoon sun. "It is ominous but enthralling—the ordinary imbued with mystery. Not quite a nightmare, but a dark enchantment. A sorcerer lives in the old *moulin* and his spells spill out over the streets and into the sky." He met her gaze. "A powerful sorcerer."

Her cheeks flushed with pleasure. Always, if Averill liked her art, it was for the same reasons she did. It was a magical resonance of mind and heart.

"Next year's submission to the Salon?" Casimir asked.

It was way too soon to predict, but she played along. "Would they take it?"

Casimir grinned. "Probably not."

"And if they did, it would be skied." Averill gestured toward the clouds overhead. "Almost to the ceiling."

Theo imagined her bold windmill hung so high it would be nothing but dark squiggles. Would refusal be worse, or having it all but invisible? "At least this is not *properly féminine*," Theo muttered.

"But you—" Jules began, then glanced at her breeches and stopped abruptly.

Frustrated, Theo waited for him to finish his sentence. Was he so uncomfortable when alone with the men? When Jules said nothing more about her feminine approach, either proper or improper, she turned back to her painting.

"You scorn the allure of feminine charm?" Casimir asked her, arching his eyebrows. "No doubt you would prefer a *succès de scandale*?"

"But of course!" Theo exclaimed. "What artist wouldn't?"

"I don't think the windmill is scandalous enough." Casimir feigned solemnity. "You would have to add a nude."

"Several daring nudes in the manner of Manet, but stretched out along the street," Averill suggested. "*Le Sacrifice sous le Moulin.*" He glanced at Casimir and they laughed again.

"I don't think I can squeeze in a nude," Theo responded lightly, despite a pang of jealousy. They had known each other for years. Even when she knew their references, she could not hope to match their rapport. Casimir was always amiable but always subtly mocking. Except for his music and his friendship with Averill, she had no idea what was truly important to him—or to Jules, who had been studying his feet since nudes were mentioned, though they populated his poems. Did a woman's presence embarrass him so much? Did he not like them? Did he like them too much? Either way, he could not remain such a prude around Paul and the others and survive.

She wished Paul were here to comment on her windmill. The extreme difference of their views often gave her fresh eyes. "Paul is not with you today?"

With a breath of relief, Jules replied, "He was with us. I will bring him." He turned and walked quickly down the street, moving from sun to shadow.

"Paul took a side trip to the bakery where we bought the almond croissants," Averill said.

Casimir smirked. "Noret is flirting with the baker's daughter."

"Ninette?" Theo felt suddenly uneasy. The girl was lovely but far too young for Paul to romance. "She's barely fifteen."

"Perhaps she writes poetry," Averill said.

"I doubt it. She must be his Beatrice—his inspiration." Casimir laughed. "Paul is so convoluted, such simplicity must be utterly irresistible."

Ninette was not stupid but not quick either. The image of them together was all the more disconcerting because Paul looked older than he was, and delicate Ninette younger. Could the girl's parents permit such a courtship? Theo fought her queasiness. For all she knew, Paul was only ordering a cake, not beginning a seduction.

Then Paul came round the corner, Matthieu beside him and Jules trailing behind. They waved and started up the hill. Paul and Matthieu were eating *éclairs* and talking back and forth between bites. Odd. Paul was the last person Theo would imagine being comfortable with children. Maybe Casimir was right and their open simplicity appealed to Paul because his own brain was usually tied in knots.

"Time to go, mademoiselle," Matthieu said as he approached. "Maman needs me to buy sausage at the *charcuterie*."

"In a moment," Theo said, for Paul had walked to stand squarely in front of her canvas. She waited for his judgment. He stared at the windmill for a full minute. "Theo, this is superb. Startling, yet assured. Not a stroke too many."

She had not expected that! Delight and pride surged through her. "Thank you."

Then Paul shrugged. "Of course, the Salon will not hang it."

Theo gave an exasperated laugh. "I have a year to create a painting to please us both." Was it even worth the effort to please them? Mélanie, one of her good friends from the Académie Julian, had won a pitiful honorable mention for one of the most brilliant paintings at the Salon. But Theo knew her father would be overjoyed if she won even the smallest award.

"It is not Impressionist," Paul said. "Certainly not Pointillist. More in the mode of a Synthetist…."

Theo didn't understand the utter passion of the French to categorize everything. She didn't care what school Paul picked for it, only that it moved him. Superb. Startling. She especially liked startling.

Matthieu was shifting nervously from foot to foot, so she quickly packed her paints and handed him the box. Working together, Casimir and Averill folded the easel. They divided the burdens then made a parade

up and down the twisting streets, past the vineyard, and back up the rue
Lepic. Suddenly inspired, Theo kept walking past her door to the alley.
She'd warned Matthieu to be careful when out alone. He'd assured her
he would be—in the swaggering tone of young boys who weren't afraid
of anything. "I met a detective here not long ago," she told her Revenants.
Let Matthieu listen in and be reminded without her having to sound like a
mother hen.

"A detective?" Jules was horrified.

Paul frowned. "Asking about the bombing?"

"No, he was trying to find a clue to the disappearance of little Denis."
She glanced quickly at Matthieu.

Averill understood instantly. He looked only at her, so Matthieu's
boyish pride would not be injured. "Yes, Theo, you cannot be too careful
in Paris. Especially at dusk. All sorts of dangerous people emerge from
their lairs and stalk the streets."

"You are right, but almost always I have someone to protect me."

"It should be always," Paul said gravely. "Beautiful women are at
risk as much as careless boys."

Casimir rolled his eyes at the *petit* drama she had staged. "Why
did you did not tell us of your adventure before, Theo? Questioned by
the police, no less."

"I told him all I knew, but that was little enough," she said sadly.
Then memory jolted her. "He hasn't talked to you?"

"To me!" Casimir exclaimed in faux horror.

"Yes, you took me to tea the evening Denis disappeared."

"Tea? Ah yes…how corrupt of me," Casimir murmured.

"Mademoiselle, I must get the sausage," Matthieu reminded her.

"But of course. Thank you, Matthieu." Theo took her paint box from
him and he ran off down the street. She wondered if she'd made any
impression at all. The others followed Theo back to her apartment and
deposited her things inside. Theo thanked them and asked when they
would meet again.

"We are all attending Leo Taxil's lecture, are we not? I have procured
tickets enough."

"Yes, I'm going." Theo had been amused when Averill read aloud the
bizarre tales in the *cafés*.

Paul's eyes gleamed with anticipation. "Even the Hyphens will attend
such an extraordinary event."

"Good." Theo hadn't seen them since the last meeting about the
magazine, over two months ago. *Les trois Traits*—the three Hyphens—as
Paul had dubbed them, were three slim, dark-haired poets named Jean-
Jacques, Louis-Patrice, and Pierre-Henri. Professor, student, and fledgling

lawyer, they were a bit more traditional than the other Revenants and sought out each other's company in the Left Bank *cafés*.

"Taxil promises revelations of crazed satanic rites," Casimir said, as if offering a sweetmeat.

Paul rubbed his hands together with theatrical relish. "A deliciously degenerate Masonic priestess who once consorted with demons will be there in person."

Jules licked his lips nervously. "The High Priestess was redeemed when she spoke of admiring Jeanne d'Arc. The demons could not endure even the name and fled, leaving the High Priestess free."

"It should be as entertaining as the Comédie-Française," Averill said.

"You don't believe Taxil's tales of demons?" Casimir asked. "You who want to go to a Black Mass?"

"They're far too amusing to be true," Averill answered.

"No?" Paul challenged. "Surely demons amuse themselves—and with far less hypocrisy than humans."

Chapter Eleven

The invasion of the sharks was just a
harmless bit of vengeance....
Leo Taxil

Behind his podium, Leo Taxil chucked maliciously. "The most distin-guished theologians didn't bat an eyelid when our priapic crocodile demon played the piano."

From his vantage point in the back of the lecture hall, Michel crossed his arms and witnessed the spectacle of Leo Taxil unveiling his gargantuan hoax. Confidence man, cheap tabloid journalist, author of such porno-graphic masterpieces as *Extraordinary Correspondence of the Ecclesiastical F**kers,* and *The Pope's Testicles,* Taxil had seized the Catholic Church by the balls and held tight for a decade. Tonight he had released them, but not without a final twist.

"Nor did the wise theologians blink in disbelief when Miss Diana Vaughan claimed to have cavorted on multitudinous planets. Most amazing."

Taxil's gleeful sarcasm brought cheers of "Bravo!" from the free-thinkers and yet more cries of outrage from the betrayed clergy. An abbot rose from his seat with a cry. "You are a scoundrel, monsieur! A scoundrel!" He was completely overwrought. Several priests drew him back down into his chair and made an effort to calm him.

On stage, Leo Taxil smirked, delighted the abbot had taken the bait. Michel expected him to wag an admonishing finger. How had educated churchmen ever brought themselves to believe the charade of this tawdry sinner's conversion? But he knew the answer. In an age of dying faith, the Devil was more necessary than ever to prove the existence of God. The Church had embraced Leo Taxil, their prodigal son, and spoon-fed him the fatted calf.

They had just not expected him to spit it back in their faces.

The hisses, boos, and applause subsided and Taxil plunged on. "Those naïve abbots and monks who admired Miss Diana Vaughan because she was a converted Masonic Luciferian Sister are victims of their own ignorance." Taxil paused significantly. "In Rome, it's another story. In Rome they know full well that no female Masons exist…."

"No!" a distraught priest cried out. "The Freemasons were your accomplices!"

Michel groaned silently. Taxil had promised them revelations. He had given them revelations. His scandalous exposé, *The Devil in the Nineteenth Century,* was not fact but fiction. There would be no meeting with the heroine, Miss Diana Vaughan, high priestess of Palladism, betrothed of the Demon Asmodeus, who had renounced the evil, erotic devil-worshipping rites and returned to the bosom of the Church. Palladism was Taxil's invention. The High Priestess was only a typist with a perverse sense of humor. But Michel was impressed with Taxil's pecuniary foresight. Before he made his disclosures, Taxil had auctioned off her typewriter to the highest bidder. Michel wished now he'd tried to win it for Cochefert.

He continued his surveillance of the crowd, mentally noting clusters where tension had risen and making sure the gendarmes were aware of them too. Although Michel had seen no obvious plants, he'd marked the likely troublemakers—the most fervent priests, an incendiary journalist or two, and one self-proclaimed Satanist.

"Some months later, my Canon sent me an enormous Gruyère cheese. On its crust, he had carved pious inscriptions and hieroglyphs of frenzied mysticism," Taxil confided. "It was an almost miraculous cheese, for it never seemed to come to an end. I consumed each bit with the utmost reverence."

"Delicious!" Three rows down, a monk burst out laughing and began to applaud. The surrounding priests stared at him in dismay. Taxil did have at least one plant in the audience.

Ignoring both Taxil and his faux monk, Michel turned his attention to Vipèrine, who had chosen a seat very near the podium. Since there were no leads other than Lilias' rumor of the Black Mass, Cochefert had taken Michel off the case of the vanished children. Officially. When Michel last went to savate practice, he'd told Dancier he was continuing to investigate on his time off. The diabolist was at least a plausible suspect— quite capable of provoking some drama to put himself center stage—but was he capable of true villainy? There was little information to be had on him before his appearance in Paris five years ago, not even his real name.

"I presented my public with the consummate she-devil, wallowing in sacrilege!" Taxil proclaimed. "A true Satanist—such as one meets in Huysmans' books."

Huysmans' *Là Bas.* The literary reference made Michel turn to Paul Noret. He was seated with a coterie of poets and artists that comprised the Revenants, one of the innumerable literary groups seeking to make a name in Paris. As far as Michel knew, Noret wasn't a Satanist. But he was an anarchist. His poetry was the most radical, a vicious invective twisted with images of nightmarish violence. His poetry might only serve as a kind of exorcism. Michel knew of no incident that linked Noret to any act of the kind the anarchists proclaimed "propaganda by deed." Words only—so far. But Michel had seen him in the company of Félix Fénéon, the famous avant-garde critic and infamous anarchist.

Five years ago Fénéon had been among those arrested for bombing the Foyot Restaurant. There was a violent explosion and the only person harmed was a friend, another young poet with anarchist sympathies. The bomb left him disfigured and half-blind. Police intelligence pointed to Fénéon and his anarchist circle. There was strong circumstantial evidence, but the Trial of the Thirty was a fiasco. Fénéon's eloquence befuddled the attorneys and won their release. He even continued to clerk at the War Ministry. Michel kept Fénéon under his own personal surveillance. Sporadic surveillance, true, but he only needed to scent trouble to increase his efforts. Now he would add Noret.

"She possesses the ability to walk through walls. Her pet snake writes prophecies down her back with the tip of its tail." Taxil snaked scrollwork on the air with a fingertip.

Looking past Noret, Michel recognized someone else who provoked his curiosity. Theodora Faraday was sitting with the Revenants. He had seen the tall blonde roaming about Montmartre even before he interviewed her. Tonight she wore a gown of midnight blue satin. The deep hue set off her fair skin and pale, gleaming hair. She seemed far too dynamic for most of that coterie, literary aesthetes who lived on their nerves. He had read the premiere issue of their magazine, which had created quite a stir. There were several striking illustrations, but Michel did not remember them being by a woman. He must have assumed Theo to be a man. Or perhaps she assumed a different male nom de plume, as he had seen her assume male dress. Quite illegal and quite flattering. She had very long legs.

"Assuming the guise of Miss Vaughan," Taxil exclaimed, "I revealed the existence of secret rooms hidden within the Masonic temple in Charleston, Virginia. In one, a statue of Eve awaits. When a Templar Mistress is especially pleasing to Master Satan, this statue takes on life. Eve becomes the demon Astarte and bestows kisses on the chosen one."

A tidbit in the grand tradition of Leo Taxil, ecclesiastical pornographer, Michel sneered silently. Lesbian demons on parade.

"Despicable charlatan!"

"No priest will take your confession!"

Taxil moved on to the infamous forges buried beneath Gibraltar and fed by hellfire, and the outbursts faded. The opposing side brooded silently, which Michel thought boded ill. He quietly rose from his seat and stood against the back wall, free to move fast if there was trouble. His gaze roved over the gathering as Taxil embarked on a new tale of Vatican conspiracy. "After Jeanne d'Arc was burned at the stake, the executioner discovered that the heart of our heroine had not been consumed. He threw more burning pitch and sulphur upon it, but the heart would not burn! Finally, in desperation, Jeanne's heart was tossed in the Seine." Taxil raised a pudgy finger to punctuate his words. "Be sure that one day a mysterious angel will carry that heart, not to France, but to Italy, and Jeanne d'Arc will be canonized by the Pope. French pilgrims must henceforth go to Rome to view this miraculously retrieved heart."

Odd. One of the Revenants had risen and was urged back to his seat by Theodora Faraday. Did the mockery of the Maid anger him? Many who cared nothing for Luciferian plots or Vatican conspiracy might still take offence at having France's beloved heroine derided.

Enamored of his own voice, Taxil rumbled on, "Alas, the final success of my hoax was endangered by a Mason who declared these bizarre claims must be a Jesuit plot. Unfortunate Jesuits! I had sent them a fragment of Moloch's tail as evidence of Palladism!"

In spite of himself, Michel's curiosity was stirred. What had Taxil actually sent—mummified crocodile? Cochefert would be captivated with this morsel. Personally, Michel preferred Taxil's story of his first malicious prank—false tales of ravenous sharks hiding in sea caves off Marseilles.

"Fearing my magnificent creation would be suffocated by the evil oubliettes of the Vatican, I have chosen to confess." With a grand gesture, Taxil proclaimed, "I have committed infanticide. Palladism, the child of my mind, is utterly dead. Its father has murdered it." Taxil finished with a bow. Silence hovered for a moment, then cacophony reigned. Applause, laughter, jeers, hoots, and accusations rose in the air like myriad squawking birds. The abbot stood on his chair, gesturing for all the faithful to gather round, but the noise drowned out whatever he was saying.

Vipèrine rose, his height emphasized by his theatrical robes. The gleam of their gold embroidery caught the light and drew the attention of the audience. He lifted his chin truculently, his blue beard pointing at Taxil. "There is only one hoax—and that hoax is that Satan has no worshippers."

Weaving through the stream of the infuriated leaving the auditorium, Michel moved swiftly as Taxil called out his answer, "Ah, monsieur, I acknowledge that he has his worshippers. But that does not mean he exists."

Vipèrine swirled his cape, then flung up his hands. Fire burst from his fingertips. A flaming object winged like a bat sailed to the stage and exploded with spurts of flame and noxious spirals of black and yellow smoke. Screams of panic filled the hall—cries of "Bomb!" and "Fire!" Taxil ducked behind the podium. Gendarmes rushed to guard him. Still twenty feet away, Michel saw that no fire had actually ignited, though the smoke rose in sulphurous plumes.

Chaos reigned as the remaining audience rushed for the doors. Vipèrine raised his arms again, flames flashing from his fingers, and Michel guessed the next smoke cloud would cover his escape. Stepping into range, he aimed a hard lateral kick, driving his heel into Vipèrine's thigh. Vipèrine reeled back with a snarl of surprise and pain. The chemical ball he held bounced across the floor, hissing loudly and leaking darkness.

"Police," Michel said. "Surrender yourself."

No novice to street fighting, Vipèrine aimed a savage kick at his ribs. Michel blocked it and countered with a low undercut to his opponent's shin. Vipèrine lurched forward, grabbed a chair for balance, then swung it sideways at Michel's head. Michel knocked it to the floor, but Vipèrine's back leg sweep tumbled him. Michel rolled as he hit the floor and came up into a crouch. Vipèrine aimed another kick at his head. Michel dodged sideways, but Vipèrine's foot grazed his face. A blaze of pain erupted on his cheek. The iron tang of blood filled his nostrils. Vipèrine had razors set in his shoes. With cold fury, Michel rose and spun into a reverse kick that sent Vipèrine staggering. Another slammed him hard against the wall. Moving in, Michel twisted Vipèrine's arm behind his back, pinning him in place as he pulled out his *ligote* and pulled it tight around Vipèrine's wrist.

"You are under arrest for inciting a riot and assaulting an officer." Blood spilled down from his cheek and onto his neck.

"Let me go now," Vipèrine snarled, "and perhaps I will let you live."

Disgusted with the melodrama, Michel dragged him up the aisle and into the lobby.

Chapter Twelve

Just living life conjures dreams of revenge.
Paul Gauguin

Michel did not summon a Black Maria for Vipèrine. After the panic abated in the auditorium and a semblance of order had been restored, he and the other officers marched his prisoner through the streets. At first, Vipèrine tried to carry the public humiliation off with flair, but their discipline outlasted his theatrics. He was livid with rage and snarling curses by the time they reached the archways leading off the Quai de l'Horloge. To the right lay the detectives' offices. Michel took Vipèrine through the left arch, into the courtyard of the Dépôt, then on to the anteroom. He gave the registrar the charges and waited while the man took down the basic information from his prisoner. The name Vipèrine earned a snicker. Age, twenty-nine. Michel took note of the residence, which was in Montparnasse. Vipèrine hesitated before giving Marseilles as his birthplace. A lie. He'd worked at a Parisian accent, but what lay beneath was something north, Dijon, perhaps, or Rouen. Profession he gave as "Sorcerer." The registrar rolled his eyes, but duly wrote it down. Even standing several feet away, Michel could still smell Vipèrine. His clothing, his skin, reeked of cheap cologne mingling sharply with sweat. Michel could differentiate heavy odors of patchouli, frankincense, and the musk of civet. What woman would find this excess erotic?

Once the information was transcribed, they continued on past the infirmary to the lodge of the Dépôt itself. A commissary waited behind a glass window, and wardens stood by, ready to usher the prisoner on to the cells after the search. The commissary pointed Vipèrine to an embrasure where one of the wardens searched his clothes and body. Another warden took a brief set of preliminary measurements and a description that presaged the formal procedure tomorrow.

When Vipèrine emerged, the commissary looked him up and down, taking in the fancy cape and ruffled linen. "*Salle des Habits Noirs?*" he suggested to Michel. Although the cells were always crowded, "the black coats," gentlemen with more money for amenities, were incarcerated in a separate hall and had their own exercise yard as well.

"*Salle des Blouses*," Michel said. But he felt petty as Vipèrine was led off to the lower cells.

In the end, it hardly mattered where you were put. The whole underground jail was a pit of stench and gloom.

Early the next morning, Michel came to the Palais de Justice to observe the *anthropométric* measuring. He had some small hope that Vipèrine might match a file on record. Michel knew of him only as an upstart magician in Paris, but Vipèrine had a pimp's sort of sleazy arrogance. He might have a more vicious history elsewhere.

Michel followed the stone staircase to the Department of Judicial Identity, the domain of its creator, Alphonse Bertillon. He was now so famous that the cabaret canaries sang songs about *le bertillonnage*. In the prisoners' waiting room Vipèrine sat on one of the narrow benches, stripped to shirt and trousers. His shoes sat beneath the bench, and his fancy cloak hung on a peg. Seeing Michel, his lips drew back in a snarl and skin tautened over the bone, turning his face into a mask of hatred. Michel nodded to the guards and went on into the processing room. Luckily, Bertillon was absent for the moment. When Michel requested to process his prisoner next, the clerk obliged.

The gathering of information began. Vipèrine refused to give any other name, so the registrar wrote that alias on the official index card. Next, he was photographed with a complex technique for synchronized full front and profile pictures. He preened for the camera. Then the registrar gestured him forward for the first step in the *anthropométric* ritual, Bertillon's system of measuring hard bone in adult criminals. Vipèrine stood against the wall while the assistants measured his height against the template. "They say tomorrow will be warmer," the older registrar remarked between notations. Michel murmured agreement. They were forbidden to speak of the case to the prisoner while measuring.

"Spread your arms," Michel commanded. When Vipèrine complied, they assessed the length of his outstretched arms.

"Three-inch vertical scar on the inner forearm," the young assistant said, pleased to add an identifying mark. Birthmarks and prominent moles would also be recorded. A special implement was brought forward to measure the length from the left elbow to middle finger, and another device to take the exact length of the middle finger.

Next they measured the length of his torso. One flaw of the system was the unavoidable variation in the way measurements were taken, despite Bertillon's precise instruments. Yet however cumbersome, *anthropométrie* had made it possible to impose stiffer sentences on repeat offenders. Years, even months, could alter a man's appearance. He might lose or gain weight. He might dye his hair, grow a beard or shave his skull. His visage could be scarred or simply hardened by despair or cruelty. None of these things changed mature bones. That was the evidence they were recording. The system had been adopted by police throughout the world.

"Sit." Michel indicated the free-standing stool. Vipèrine sneered, but did as he was told. Bertillon believed that being seated, and treated with a severe courtesy, helped defuse the prisoner's anger. Michel saw no sign of it in Vipèrine. He followed their commands but answered their questions in monosyllables. All the while he fixed his malignant regard on Michel. When his view was blocked, he stared straight through the bodies of the men measuring his head. The assistant placed the calipers to take the dimensions of his right ear.

"Instrument steady!" Alphonse Bertillon barked as he entered the room. He paused, tall and perfectly erect, his beard trimmed to a thick spade. His gaze darted about his domain, possessive and critical.

"Monsieur Bertillon." Michel greeted him formally, masking his annoyance. It was one thing to be meticulous, another to presume that no one else could perform a procedure.

Bertillon frowned, pointed a finger. It quivered with impatience like an insect's wing. "Do the ear again. Note the contours."

As the assistant repeated the ear measurements with scrupulous care, Michel eased out of his superior's line of sight. He would no more squabble over territory than he would play eye-fencing games with Vipèrine.

"There is a mole by the left corner of his mouth," Bertillon snapped, as if Michel had overlooked this important mark. Such disruptions had increased after Michel inquired if they were investigating the innovative science of fingerprinting. Clearly, Bertillon would not willingly adopt a program created—or even suggested—by someone else.

Another incident might account for Bertillon's antagonism. Bertillon also studied handwriting. His testimony had helped send Dreyfus to rot on Devil's Island. According to Bertillon, Dreyfus had forged a letter to barely resemble his own handwriting so he could claim it a forgery. Bertillon had bragged of his brilliant deductions. Michel had not disguised his skepticism.

"Stand on the stool. Raise your left foot," Bertillon ordered Vipèrine, who posed with mocking grace. The registrar glanced nervously at Bertillon, then bent to take this last measurement. Ignoring Bertillon and the entire process, Vipèrine continued his ferocious scrutiny of Michel and that fixed gaze annoyed Bertillon. If he must glare, then surely he should glare at Bertillon, obviously the most important man in the room.

"Now the eyes," Bertillon decreed.

Vipèrine managed to keep his focus locked on Michel as the registrar tilted his face to the light to ascertain the pigmentation of his eyes and the patterning of color. He possessed far more resolve than Michel had expected. He decided to forego his own questioning until the juge d'in-struction had gone a round with Vipèrine and deflected some of his antagonism.

"No discernible difference in the inner and outer circles, dark opaque brown," the assistant said.

"Tilt his head higher," Bertillon demanded, and examined the eye color himself. "The aureole is actually medium maroon brown in a small circle surrounding the iris, the ground of the periphery is a deeper version of the same shade. Note it."

"Yes sir," the assistant mumbled.

"Such subtleties can determine identification." Bertillon held out his hand for the finished card. Noting the alias at the top, he smirked. "Vipèrine?"

The prisoner refused to acknowledge him. Bertillon gave a snort of derision then stalked from the room, handing the index card to Michel in passing. He returned it to the registrar, who would file it by the measure-ments. Men with heads longer than average were placed in one set of files, average in a second, less than average in a third. Each file was then divided in three according to the length of the middle finger, and so on for the six primary measurements. There were five million cards now, and every new entry was cross-checked for the six signal quantities. An exact match meant that the criminal had been arrested before, no matter what name he gave.

Vipèrine was permitted to put on his shirt and shoes. Once dressed, he faced Michel and smiled. "You will waste away." The stage whisper carried to every corner of the room. "When you look in the mirror, Death will smile from your skull."

Vipèrine turned his back on Michel, refusing to glance over his shoulder as he was led back to his cell.

"If I die tomorrow, I'll be sure to inform you," Michel said to the recorders. They sniggered.

Chapter Thirteen

The sky was grey, there wept a breeze
Like a bassoon.
Far off, a tom-cat, stealthy, discreet,
Miaowed, oh, strangely out of tune.
Paul Verlaine

Lilias smiled lazily and stretched. Her hair tumbled loose about her shoulders, charmingly disheveled. The night was unusually warm, and she'd laid a satin quilt beside the softly splashing fountain in her miniature back garden. The full moon was just waning, and she used the pearly luminescence to advantage. Her pale skin gleamed in its light. She wore a simple batiste nightgown, demure with no decoration but an edge of lace and a few rosebuds of pink ribbon. Of course, Lilias knew how to make demure wickedly seductive. Sated, Michel kissed the hollow of her throat, each nipple, then laid his head in her lap and pretended they were young and innocent.

A fantasy quickly dispelled when she said, "The rumors of the Black Mass grow ever wilder. A virgin sacrifice is to be offered. Assuming they can find a virgin…."

"When?"

"Perhaps a month? They will want to build anticipation." She gave him a mocking kiss.

"In Paris?"

"Yes. The most demented whisper they will bribe the priests at Notre Dame." The corners of her lips curled with mirth. "Most simply repeat what I first heard, that it will happen in a private chapel. Where that chapel is will be the last thing I learn."

"Vipèrine is to play the priest?"

"Yes, the same nasty snake that slithered free of the cage you put him in." She drew a fingertip across the healing razor slash on his cheek.

Vipèrine had been released before Michel ever questioned him. The charges were not that serious, but Michel felt a cold ire that some influential idiot had gotten them dismissed. "You're sure? A Satanic ritual?"

"Yes. And I believe that the man who arranged his freedom is the same to whom he's promised the virgin sacrifice." When he started to ask who, she laid her fingertips across his lips. "I know he is a cabinet minister, but his identity is better hidden than your elusive kidnapper's."

"No one with the power to open Vipèrine's cell door would want his name associated with such scum," Michel said scornfully.

"There is a scent of evil about Vipèrine," Lilias said. "Some find that intoxicating."

"It is only cheap cologne." Then he paused. "He and the kidnapper could be one and the same."

"Do not build your hopes," Lilias said. "There is little chance this tawdry orgy is connected to your missing children. The fake virgin will squeal with fake pain and fake pleasure while everyone rolls about in crumbled hosts and sacramental wine."

"I am grateful nonetheless." While Michel could imagine any number of fools yearning to mix sex and sacrilege, he doubted many could stomach a child sacrifice. "Such rites are still illegal. I can arrest Vipèrine."

"And the minister?" She smiled tauntingly.

"Oh yes, I will arrest him, but I imagine he will escape even more easily than Vipèrine."

"A pity," she said.

Even if there were plans to rape or murder some young girl, the minister could plead ignorance. Unless there was direct proof, Cochefert would buckle to pressure. "The press might hear about it," Michel suggested. "Saul Balsam could do wonders with the story."

"Ah…scandal." She smiled dreamily, guiding his hand between her thighs. "The very thought of the high and mighty taking such a tumble makes me wet."

Michel left Lilias sleeping and walked home at dawn, pleasantly weary. The wind scuttled newspapers and debris about the streets and dissipated the cool grey mist as he went. Belatedly, he remembered his plan to bring his guitar. Another time. He did not have the peace of mind to play well for an audience, even of one. The missing children haunted him.

He welcomed the distraction of the vibrant sunrise as he approached the Pont Louis Philippe. Rose, crimson, and vermillion framed the silhouettes of the buildings and blossomed in the rippling waters of the Seine. He crossed the bridge to the Île St. Louis. Walking past his building, Michel went to the far point of the Quai de Bourbon, relishing the glory of the light. The sparkle of red in the water evoked not blood but petals tossed out in a parade. When the colors finally paled, he walked back and climbed the stairs to his apartment.

Michel unlocked the door and stopped on the threshold. Someone had been here. He wasn't sure how he knew at first, but his next breath picked up a residue of scent. Breathing deeper, he identified a cologne reeking of patchouli, civet, and the acrid smoke of incense.

Vipèrine—the snake with important enough connections to be released without trial.

A scent of evil, Lilias had said. Perhaps, after all, that was what polluted his home. But that fading scent would prove nothing to anyone else. Would there be evidence? He saw no marks on the lock. Had Vipèrine climbed down the air shaft to the open bedroom window? And what exactly had he done? A bomb was Michel's first thought, but as he began to explore the hallway for trip wires or loose boards, memory exhumed Vipèrine's sibilant hiss.

"You will waste away."

Poison, most likely. Yet he could not discount explosives. Michel moved slowly from the hall into the salon, then the bedroom, and study, searching for hidden wires, a book misplaced, a package planted beneath the couch or between the slats of the bed. He opened his guitar case gingerly, examined the instrument, but nothing had been disturbed. Nothing. Michel went last to the tiny kitchen, and found the odor strongest. Furious, exasperated, he washed everything with which he cooked, everything from which he ate or drank. He checked what foods might have been opened, injected, tampered with in any way and threw away anything the least suspicious. Wine. Cheese. Flour. Sugar. Salt. He paused. Should he have them tested? Extravagant and pointless. Patchouli was not proof. But he would tell Cochefert.

He had imagined Vipèrine nothing but a demonic peacock, flaunting his colors and shrieking loudly. He had been wrong.

Chapter Fourteen

Mysteries abound….
Charles Baudelaire

Rising on her toes, Theo looked down the long central passageway to the entrance to the Bazar de la Charité. The double doors were the only way in, so Mélanie and Carmine should be easy to spot—if only the crowd didn't keep blocking her view. Her height gave her little advantage over the top hats of the boulevardiers and the plumes and gargantuan bows ascending from the hats of the ladies. Ordinary Parisians mingled with the fashion-plate extravaganzas, thrilled to see members of Tout Paris that they had only read about in the society pages. Even sweeter, the elite were playing at being saleswomen and waitresses in the booths of their favorite charities.

Theo had arrived early to secure a place in line for the cinema demonstration—a line already long in front of her and getting longer and longer behind. Just then, she saw Mélanie making her way through the throng. Her friend looked exquisite in a dotted Swiss dress foaming with ruffles. Tiny flounces cascaded down the skirt, growing ever larger and ending in a huge flounce. What a challenge that would be to paint! Would it be too trite? '*Woman in a White Dress*' was a genre unto itself. Would it be possible to paint a portrait of Mélanie that wasn't too pretty? Maybe Theo should try that for next year's Salon, completely dazzling, completely sincere prettiness! But could she capture the ambition and anxiety lurking behind the huge doe eyes?

"How wonderful!" Mélanie squeezed in beside her, magically unrumpled by the crowd, black hair serenely coiled in a perfect chignon. She wore some unusual scent, white flowers blooming beside a shady forest pool. At her throat, a Wedgewood cameo of the virgin huntress Diana seemed the perfect image for the fragrance. "Look—there is even a Gothic cathedral!"

Together they admired the faux medieval interior of this year's Bazar de la Charité. Not long ago this was an empty lot near the Champs Élysées. The promoters had erected a huge wooden structure and created a quaint village inside it. High overhead, the painted canvas ceiling suggested a cloudy sky. Gauzy streamers drifted down from above and festoons of paper lilacs and roses bloomed in a lush imitation spring.

"I can tell you want to paint it, Theo!"

"Perhaps I only want to imagine painting it." Theo laughed. She shifted, trying to imagine different vantage points. She did love the fanciful mix of historical village and strolling men and women in modern dress, but she had never tried such an ambitious interior. "I meant to bring my sketchbook, but I was afraid of being late and ran off without it."

"You can come back tomorrow," Mélanie said. "But where would you draw without getting jostled?"

"Maybe near the entrance—with you on one side and Carmine on the other?" Theo suggested. "We could trade places and protect each other's drawing arm."

"It's a good idea, yes, if you like modern scenes."

"But you wish to evoke the purity of the Ideal." Theo pressed her hand to her heart.

"Oh, you make me sound so silly." Mélanie laughed then said very seriously, "I do want images that inspire, that resonate with history."

"You did *le grand art* perfectly for the Salon and they all but slapped you." Theo felt renewed anger for her friend.

"Honorable mention is hardly a slap," Mélanie replied, but her voice was subdued. "If it didn't receive a medal, something must have been lacking."

Mélanie had painted Cassandra. The canvas was of modest size, but great intensity. In the foreground, the scorned prophetess wept alone on the battlements of Troy. Her grief, her despair, were palpable, not theatrically staged gestures. The sunset sky glowed in muted hues of gold and bronze, streaked with forbidding clouds of charcoal grey. Shadow draped the prophetess like a shroud. A dying glory, the sun sank beneath the horizon in streaks of blood red and royal purple. Far below, the dark horde of the Greek army pretended to depart for their ships. Isolated, the tiny Trojan horse waited on the plain. The strong diagonals of the composition created an unsettling effect, mysteriously predicting the reversal of fortune. Tomorrow, the miniscule figures, no bigger than ants, would rule Cassandra's world.

"Don't let them make you doubt yourself," Theo said with quiet fury. "Yours was better than the grand prize winner."

Shrieks of panic rose behind the curtain hiding the cinema presentation. Mélanie looked at Theo in alarm. Then came a burst of relieved laughter. Everyone in line relaxed. Soon, a group of dazed looking people emerged from behind the curtain and went through the turnstile, and another group was admitted.

"Where is Carmine?" Mélanie tried to peer through the crowd. "She is always late just because she thinks punctuality is bourgeois."

"She's never late to class—just everything else," Theo laughed. "Oh! I see a hat that must be hers."

"*Bonjour!*" Carmine Dougnac hailed them as she made her way through the throng.

"Oh my!" Mélanie exclaimed when the parting crowd gave a better view of Carmine's chartreuse plaid dress and latest hat, an elaborate creation of emerald green straw, lime green plumes, black netting, and purple roses.

Theo laughed. They were an odd assortment, the three best women in Theo's first class at the Académie Julian. Carmine was already a professional. She painted delightfully bizarre animals—horses riding bicycles, monkeys at the roulette table, a daring young cat on a flying trapeze. She preferred to amuse and provoke, but she also made oodles of money with her sentimental pet portraits. Her printmaker father had paid for her classes at the Académie Julian to improve her skill—even though women were charged double for the same lessons.

"*Mes petits choux-fleurs!*"

Theo wondered yet again why "little cauliflower" was a French endearment as her friend kissed them on each cheek with a cheerful smack. Carmine could make Theo feel positively polished sometimes. She was so earthy, so brash. Small and sturdy, like the roan pony Theo had loved in childhood, she was just as feisty. Her olive skin and brown hair had a rosy cast, like her name. Even her eyes were a ruddy chestnut brown.

Carmine adjusted her tip-tilted *chapeau.* "I wore a wide brim today, the better to slice through the crowd."

"I love this one!" Theo said. "The purple roses are so decadent."

"And I love your new painting!"

"What is it? I must see it," Mélanie said eagerly.

"Le Moulin de la Galette," Theo told her, "but transformed by storm clouds."

Carmine spun her fingers like pinwheels. "Bold."

"Not too bold, I hope?" Mélanie teased.

Carmine rolled her eyes. Theo laughed. "So bold no one will buy it!"

"Don't you care?" Mélanie asked plaintively.

"I don't need to," Theo said. "I just finished a portrait for which I've been paid a fortune—in croissants."

"Better than gold." Carmine grinned at her.

"Now remember, this is a charity event." Mélanie became all earnestness again. "We must each be sure to give something."

"There are a hundred and fifty charities to choose between. I'm sure I'll find at least one worth a franc." Carmine grinned. "Though the boutiques will beckon to my purse."

"Any purchase goes to charity. There is a school for the blind with many orphaned students. I have ten francs for that. They teach those with musical talent to play the organ," Mélanie said primly. Then her face brightened. "Monsieur Braille taught there. Do you know he adapted his system from a secret spy code that soldiers used to read in the dark of night?"

"What a marvelous bit of history." Theo smiled. "They shall have a donation from me. When we have finished, let's have a cozy tea at Ladurée." She loved the salon's gilded interior.

"Or, supper if the line does not move faster," Mélanie said plaintively.

"This is the most modern exhibit. Everyone must see it." Carmine gave her wicked smile. "All two thousand of them."

The line crept forward as another set of people went through the turnstile. As they drew closer the deep blue of the curtains made the hidden interior all the more alluring.

"Theo, did you read the *Petit Journal* yesterday—the editorial on suffrage?" Carmine lifted her brows in provocative challenge.

"Did I read about the superior wisdom of France compared to the United States?" Theo retorted. "Did I discover that French women live under a rule of benign order, unlike the profound disorder in the state of Colorado where women serve on juries and are free to vote?"

"What of your state?" Carmine asked. "Are they so enlightened?"

Anger tightened Theo's back and sharpened her voice. "The amendment failed in California last year."

"Did you march in the street to protest?" Carmine asked her.

"It failed after I left, but yes, I marched to promote it."

"Then you are truly French!" Carmine laughed then became vehement. "The women of France fought in the Revolution—we led the march on Versailles! Again, in the Commune, we joined the struggle for liberty. Are we not worthy of equal rights and privileges?"

"You cannot want the vote." Mélanie looked truly appalled. "Politics is the man's world, as home is the woman's. If she enters into masculine troubles, how can she create a haven for sheltering those she loves?"

"If she has no choice, then she's just a servant in her supposed domain," Theo protested. "Controlling your money, owning property, having a vote, it's all necessary to being a person, not just some decorative attachment, a pretty bauble."

Mélanie shook her head. "I wouldn't want the vote. Let men deal with sordid politics."

"I want a say in just which stupid, sordid idiot runs my world," Carmine declared.

"If you feel that women belong in the home, why did you apply to the École des Beaux-Arts?" Theo challenged. Mélanie's impeccable technique had just earned her a place within those sacred walls. She and two other women were the first ever admitted. It was the fulfillment of a dream for Mélanie, who lived a quiet and all too proper life with her widowed mother.

"Artistic skill befits a woman as well as a man. Women cannot expect to outdo men at the pinnacle of their skill, but they can still strive for excellence," Mélanie said stiffly.

"They promised to admit women almost a year ago," Carmine said, "then danced around in circles—with us still on the outside. They have opened their doors at last, but do not fool yourself. You will not be given classes equal to the men's, no matter what they say."

"We share the oral lecture classes," Mélanie said defensively. "Of course anatomy is segregated. But we will have the same models—we will simply study them independently. They have promised."

"Have they kept their promise?" Carmine asked pointedly.

"...Not yet. No male nudes have been permitted. But classes have barely begun."

Carmine huffed, but Theo forestalled further arguing. "It's a beginning, at least."

Finally, they passed through the turnstile into the dimly lit room behind the curtains. Their host briefly explained the system while his assistants readied the machine. "Monsieur Joly has improved upon the kinetograph of Edison and the innovations of the brothers Lumière, giving our machine greater smoothness. No longer is just one person at a time able to view the magic world of cinema. This entire audience will experience the wonder of our films," he proclaimed proudly. "The *Cinématographe Joly* is a most marvelous creation—a camera, a printer, and a projector all in one!"

The mechanism operated something like a sewing machine, shuttling the slotted film through the teeth of the projector. "Up and down, in and out, move and pause," their host chanted, his hands moving as if pushing fabric under a needle. Theo almost laughed, but the man was so serious she didn't want to hurt his feelings. When she tried for a closer look at the intriguing machine, the projectionist and his assistant blocked her.

Their host pointed at the screen. "Attention! Three magical films for your viewing pleasure—each almost a minute!"

The lamps were dimmed and they were in darkness. The air filled with quivering light and the screen with flickering images that cast a spell over the audience. Theo gasped and sighed with them, tingling with excitement at the visions unfolding before her. First there was a wonderfully sweet and silly moment of a woman feeding her baby daughter porridge. The baby was chubby cheeked and got the gooey stuff all over herself and her mother, who threw up her hands in dismay. Murmurs of awe wove with bursts of laughter. "It's a miracle, a modern miracle!" was whispered all around. After the baby came a glorious scene of boys having a snowball fight, running, falling, and rising to send their missiles flying through the air. Theo wanted to be with them, to gather the white snow in her hands and hurl it with the same laughing abandon. Weaving through her enchantment were elusive distractions. The machine made a soft clattering as it ran the film, and a swish as the spools unwound and fell into a box beneath the projector. The booth had a curious smell, a dizzying hint of the ether used to lubricate the mechanism.

The last film was the most startling. Iron struts of a bridge framed train tracks that curved away out of sight. Suddenly, a train turned the bend. Like a black beast, it rushed toward them, spewing a cloud of white smoke. Theo was transfixed. There was no sound, but her mind filled with the grinding sound of steel wheels and piercing whistles. Her heart raced as the engine with its jutting grill charged forward. The next instant there was nothing but smoke and black iron as the train seemed to hurtle off the screen into the room. Frozen in place, Theo gasped in delighted terror. She gasped again when Mélanie clutched her arm as blackness swallowed them.

Almost instantly the lights came on. Everyone laughed with relief to find themselves still alive and filled with wonder at this joyful present the modern world had given them. They smiled at each other as their host hurried them out as quickly as the turnstile would let them pass. Outside the booth, the air buzzed with anticipation. Some of the waiting crowd tried to catch a glimpse inside while others studied their faces to see if it would be worth the long wait. Exhilarated, Theo grinned at them all. She wanted to see the films again—but the line was very long. At the end, she saw Paul and Jules patiently waiting their turn. She would have gone to speak to them, but Carmine declared herself famished. Theo waved and they bowed in return.

Theo felt hungry, too. She followed her friend to the buffet by the entrance. There she purchased and devoured a *croque monsieur* with such dry ham and greasy cheese she needed a second glass of cool fizzy cider.

Carmine had a slice of berry *clafoutis* and Mélanie chose a *petite quiche*. When they were done, they all sat back with sighs of contentment.

"What next?" Theo asked. "A stroll among the boutiques?"

"Did you bring your Tarot cards, Carmine?" Mélanie asked. "You promised to tell my fortune."

"You didn't tell me you read Tarot cards." Theo was bemused. Irreverent Carmine was interested in the occult?

"I didn't tell Mélanie, either. The sneaky minx caught me working on a design."

"We can't let any of the organizers catch us," Mélanie whispered. "The good Catholics would probably throw us all out as devil worshippers."

The gleam in Carmine's eyes suggested this was an exciting prospect, but she shook her head. "This place is too noisy for a full reading," she began, but at Mélanie's stricken look, she relented. "I will do a simple three card spread for you."

"Thank you." Mélanie leaned forward eagerly.

"First clean the table and your hands, both of you." Carmine frowned at Theo's greasy fingers. The task was quickly accomplished with their handkerchiefs, then Carmine took an oblong bundle from her purse and unwrapped it. "I always keep the cards in silk for protection." They were large and stiff, but she handled them with practiced ease. Theo watched the flow of colors and tantalizing glimpses of painted images. Carmine drew out a few and laid them face up on the table. There was a man in a belled cap with a little dog, a woman holding open a lion's jaws, and a dashing knight on a white horse. "Here are the Fool, Fortitude, and the Knight of Swords."

Theo was entranced. "You designed these yourself? They are beautiful, Carmine."

"I am pleased with many of them, especially the ones with animals! But they are still too much like the usual decks. I want to use the traditional symbols, but in a more modern fashion. My father says he will print them if I do all the designs."

"How exciting for you," Mélanie said, restraining her impatience.

"I can design a deck now, when I'm young and inventive, and another when I'm a crone filled with wisdom." Carmine laughed. "I expect it will take me a year or more to think it out and execute it."

"So long?"

"Yes, I have a new teacher, Moina Mathers. Her name is pronounced Mina, but she spells it with an O. She says the old Celtic form has greater power." Carmine smiled fondly. "She has already given me new insights.

But the images themselves will be the challenge. I don't want pictures just on the Major Arcana, but on the minor cards as well."

"The Major Arcana?" Theo knew almost nothing about the Tarot.

"The ones you see here with the pictures, like The Fool on the edge of the cliff. There are twenty-two of them. They bring depth and power to a reading. Most of the Minor Arcana you know from a deck of playing cards. Only their court cards have pictures, like the Knight."

"Can I look through them?" Theo held out her hand expectantly.

Carmine frowned. "I'd rather you touch them only if you are shuffling them to have your fortune told. I will show you the pictures, but each deck needs to preserve the connection with its owner."

Theo wanted to see the images close up and feel the texture of the cards in her hands. "Well, I must have a reading too—but not in this madhouse!"

"I don't care!" Mélanie insisted. "I've been wanting one ever since I saw your sketch!"

Carmine gathered the cards and handed them to Mélanie. "Then you shall have one."

"What should I do?" Mélanie looked perplexed now that she actually held the Tarot in her hands.

"Frame a question in your mind and shuffle them. Don't tell it to me until after I read them. Or never, if you prefer." Mélanie began to shuffle very awkwardly and gazed at Carmine in dismay. "Do it slowly, until they feel right to you. Closing your eyes may help."

Mélanie closed her eyes and shuffled the cards several times. At last she opened them. "And now?"

"Cut three times, from left to right," Carmine instructed. Her demeanor was quieter and more serious than Theo had ever seen before. Art, politics, people, all were up for a tongue lashing, but Tarot cards were not to be mocked. When Mélanie cut the cards, Carmine chose one group and restacked the pack with it on top. Then she placed three cards face down in front of Mélanie. "This reading is a time progression. Sometimes it is past, present, and future. Sometimes it is the present moving into the future."

Carmine turned over the first card and Theo drew in her breath sharply. Upside down, the image showed a stone tower struck by lightning, its jagged streak vivid against the black night sky. People fell from the ramparts, and huge stones plunged to earth as the high walls crumbled. Fire spouted from the cracked top and sent orange tongues licking around the windows.

"The Tower—reversed." Carmine frowned fiercely. Mélanie said nothing.

"What is it?" Theo asked, not all that eager to know but hating the silence.

"Let me see the rest." Carmine turned over the center card. "Next is the Ten of Staves."

After the spectacle of The Tower, the simple staves looked both innocent and meaningless. "How would you paint this?" Theo asked.

Carmine thought for a moment, then answered, "The background, a wall of fire. Against it, a wall of interwoven staves."

Mélanie looked pale. "Still—that is not as bad as the first card, is it?"

Carmine shook her head, but in a way that might mean "yes" as easily as "no." Having begun, they had to finish, so Theo asked, "What is the last card?"

Carmine turned it over and Mélanie gave a small cry.

The card was Death—a dancing skeleton wielding his scythe. Heads lay scattered on the field in front of him...the head of a king stared blindly at the head of a peasant. Theo felt she was back in the catacombs.

"The Death card rarely means physical death," Carmine said quickly. She looked at each of them and added, rather defiantly, "There is no card, however dark it looks, that cannot lead to brighter things."

"You have to tell us what they mean," Theo insisted. They could hardly pretend the cards were not there. Mélanie nodded mutely.

"First, there is something I must tell you..." Carmine stared at the Tower.

"What is it?" Theo asked, trying to restrain her impatience. Carmine loved to dramatize, but she seemed truly upset. She was as pale as Mélanie, her olive skin sickly.

Finally she looked up at them. "Every morning I draw out a card to contemplate. This morning I drew the Tower—reversed."

"This morning?" For a second, Theo wondered if Carmine was making it up. But however much her friend might prod and provoke, she would not deceive any more than she would cover what she meant with pink sugar frosting.

Now Carmine said, "Drawing that card twice cannot be coincidence. Maybe the message is not for you. Maybe the cards are still trying to speak to me."

"Do you think so?" Mélanie looked relieved then horrified at herself.

"I don't know. But they are not happy cards, so I decided to tell you that before I do the reading. Let it be a buffer for you."

Mélanie nodded. "But they may truly be for me. I understand."

Carmine laid her hand down beside the first card. "The Tower signifies a great disruption. Suddenly, the world you know will be blasted as if by lightning. Where you expected safety and security, you will find nothing but upheaval and chaos. Sometimes the card means some literal catastrophe, a disaster that spares no one. Sometimes its meaning is personal, internal, and you will find it is your vision of the world that will tumble into ruin."

"And what brighter thing awaits?" Theo couldn't keep the anger from her voice. The Tarot was supposed to be a harmless diversion to please romantic Mélanie.

"After the Tower falls, you may find unexpected freedom."

"What does it mean that the card is upside down?" Mélanie asked.

Carmine's lips tightened, but she continued, "The fall of the Tower should be a blessing in disguise. It can mean the toppling of a despotic regime—or being broken loose from confining ways of thinking. But since it is reversed, you may find yourself imprisoned."

"But you are warned now, Mélanie. You can cope with it better," Theo knew she should hold her tongue, but the images throbbed before her. The longer she looked, the more alive they seemed.

Carmine didn't chastise her but touched the middle card. "Next is the Ten of Staves. The element of Staves is fire. They are cards of action and creative energy, but here, under the weight of the ten and trapped between two grim and powerful Major Arcana, their energy becomes a terrible oppression, a blind cruelty. There are destructive influences at work that you cannot control. There is no escape. You must face whatever comes with all your courage until the energy has consumed itself."

That left the last card, with its skeleton overlord. Carmine grazed it with a fingertip. "As I said, this card rarely means physical death."

"But it can?" Mélanie asked, her voice wavering.

"Death finds everyone. But most often the card means the dying of an old way of life. A rebirth into light after the darkness of the scythe has cut the old bonds. The other cards cloud this, but Death also promises release."

Carmine took up the Tower, and gave a bitter smile. "Until today, I've loved this card. For me it signified the forces of Revolution."

"But I'm not..." Mélanie began, then stopped abruptly.

"Everyone is a revolutionary if the stakes are high enough," Carmine said.

"Or a reactionary," Theo began, feeling argumentative, but then she noticed Mélanie's chastened expression. "Does it have a meaning for you?"

"Yes. I'm afraid I do know what it means," Mélanie admitted. "When we began, I asked what my future would be." She looked at each of them in turn. "I've been worried that everything will go wrong at the École des Beaux-Arts. The first day of classes…some of the male students spoke rudely to me…pushed me."

"Pushed you?" Carmine exclaimed. Mélanie had said nothing about this before today. Theo had thought the men of the École would be protective of someone so very feminine. She had expected them to patronize Mélanie, not shove her about.

"I didn't want to tell anyone," Mélanie admitted. "They tripped me then pretended it was an accident. They laughed at me all tangled in my petticoats. It was humiliating!"

"Beasts," Theo hissed. She wrestled with her temper, knowing the hot flare of her anger for a reaction to the fearful Tarot cards as much as to Mélanie's nasty encounter.

"Now they are threatening to protest," she told them.

"Yes, it would make sense if the reading were about the Beaux-Arts," Carmine said with obvious relief. "With the admission of women, their old ways are being overthrown. But they are so reactionary they will cling to the falling stones. Instead of the revelatory experience you hope for, Mélanie, it will oppress your spirit. You may become trapped by their rule, by your own fears and crushed dreams."

Mélanie didn't seem any happier, but Theo preferred this to destruction and death. "Let old notions die and you can be reborn to a new and better creativity."

"Exactly." Suddenly, Carmine gathered the cards and shuffled, paused, shuffled again. At last she stopped and laid the top card face up in the center. Half hidden behind a veil, a mysterious woman held open an ancient scroll. "The Priestess."

"She's like Cassandra, whose warnings went unheeded," Mélanie whispered. "We should believe you. You got the Tower so you would be forewarned."

"Perhaps. I don't think the Priestess is me," Carmine said.

"It must be you," Mélanie said. Theo agreed completely.

"I think it is Moina—she is far more the Priestess than I am." Carmine gathered up the cards with shaky hands and thrust them inside the silk bag. She stood up. "I must go and tell her about this. I will ask for a reading. When I see you again, Mélanie, I can tell you if these cards are truly yours or meant for me."

Stunned, Theo and Mélanie watched as Carmine abandoned them, pushing her way through the crowded bazaar.

Chapter Fifteen

In that day the sun shall become black like
sackcloth of hair….

Oscar Wilde

Smiling hesitantly, Mélanie turned to Theo. "This is all a little crazy, no?"

"Yes. Crazy." Theo felt icy jitters skittering along her nerves and wished for the hot burn of anger again. "Let's go. We're too upset to enjoy the bazaar anymore."

Mélanie looked distressed, but she shook her head. "You go if you want, Theo. I promised my mother to give money to her favorite charity, and talk with the sisters. She wants to be remembered in their prayers."

"I'll walk you to the booth." Theo wanted to leave, but now that Carmine was gone and the cards with her, fear seemed foolish. "Then we can meet by the *café* in half an hour? We'll take a carriage to Ladurée?"

"Yes! We'll have tea and *macarons*. They are famous for their pretty *macarons*. All different colors and flavors…." Mélanie pressed a gloved hand to trembling lips.

Theo's anger came to the fore and she welcomed it. She was angry at Carmine for frightening Mélanie. She was angry at herself for wanting to flee. Theo did not believe in Tarot cards or crystal balls. Fuming inwardly, she walked with Mélanie as far as her charity's booth. Within the little church the decorator had created sat the blind orphans with a nun protecting them. How strange it must be for them to sit so dutifully in this alien environment they could not see, looking charmingly pathetic to the passersby. But it was a worthy charity, and she added her promised francs to Mélanie's. "By the *café*," she repeated.

Theo remembered a booth with lace near the cinema display and made her way back. She paused there, admiring the exquisite creations of black silk and pure white laces. What infinite patience went into their creation! There was a simple muslin blouse trimmed with the less fashionable blonde Alençon lace, but even that was beyond her budget. She reminded herself she needed paint more than a replacement for her wardrobe. She must go to Sennelier's for new tubes of viridian green, alizarin crimson, and lamp black.

Beside her someone whispered that the Duchess of Alençon herself was there, sister of the Empress of Austria. Glancing up, Theo saw her, sitting proudly in her chair, not selling, but nodding to those who had come to gawk. Her shoulders were draped in the finest shawl her city's lace makers could offer. Her highly coiffed hair gleamed in the light.

Refusing to be a gawker, Theo left the tempting lace behind and began a slow stroll back toward the *café*. She hated the sense of dismay that was creeping back over her. When would Mélanie be ready to leave?

Huge sound erupted in the bazaar. A violent explosion silenced the chatter of voices, the clatter of coins. Within that thundering silence, a concussion of air shoved Theo forward. She fell, but caught herself by clutching the edge of the booth. The front of paper mache caved under her grip, and she scrambled for another hold. Regaining her footing, she glimpsed light and spun around. Sheets of orange flame were racing up the velvet curtains of the projection booth. Dark smoke coiled. Even as she watched, the fire sent blazing tendrils along the streamers of crepe paper and silk banners that fluttered above the booth of laces and leapt to the canvas ceiling.

"Fire!" a voice cried out a warning.

"Fire! Fire! Fire!" Screams rose all around her. She felt the surge of terror like another explosion. It stunned her with its power. Hordes of people raced down the aisle toward the entrance. Theo watched, mesmerized, as the flames glided along the ceiling toward them. She dragged her gaze away. Time was moving slow as cold molasses but she knew there was none to spare. The booths were nothing but luscious tinder for the conflagration to devour. What had happened? Pressed against the side wall of this booth, she could no longer see the room that held the projector. That whole corner of the building was aflame. She remembered the slow turnstile that reluctantly released one person at a time.

Screams. Shouts. Curses. Fear and rage rose like flames from the crowd thundering past. A woman supporting her elderly mother was knocked aside by a man. They fell to the floor in front of him and he trampled over them. The crowd followed, oblivious in their panic. Theo moved to help them, but already they were invisible. The crazed rush pushed her toward the door, where the crowd jammed together in a seething mass

Hot, sharp pain slashed her back. Theo cried out in terror. Glancing back she saw it was not the fire but a man with a cane. Snarling with rage, he hit her again, cutting her cheek. Then someone rammed him from behind and his fall shoved her forward. Theo dove even as she fell and landed sliding on a table of pamphlets. The man who had struck her lay screaming on the floor as the mob stampeded over him. Shaking, Theo pulled her feet under her, stood atop the table and looked around. Geysers of flame rose from the tops of the booths and poured through their flimsy walls. Overhead, patches of fire spread along the ceiling. Like huge birds of prey they opened scarlet wings, then plummeted to seize their prey in burning talons.

She saw a woman with a bright red boa, not of feathers but living flames that wrapped around her neck. Theo wanted to scream, but she swallowed back her cry. Somehow the screams rising around quieted her—as if they all were screaming for her. She did not need to scream.

She needed to escape.

Calm wrapped her, strangely cool in the dreadful heat. She watched the men beating their ways to the forefront of the crowd. Their canes rose and fell as they struck each other and any woman who dared cross their path. If she had a cane, she'd beat the cowards herself. Anyone who fell was crushed underfoot. The pile of bodies was growing, and the men were climbing over a heap of women and children to get through the narrow admission door.

Fear and fury both urged her forward but Theo did not move. She'd be burned alive before she could fight her way through that stampede. She scanned the burning walls. There must be another exit, but she could not find it. She felt the screams inside her beating like trapped birds against the thin wall of her control. Some of the crowd knelt and prayed, hope already incinerated. Her gaze was riveted by the Duchess sitting rigid in her burning booth. A man bowed before her, beseeching. Was she too terrified to move? No, Theo saw the knowledge of death in her face, and a grim determination. She said something to the man. He flung up his hands in despair, then whirled and vanished into crowd.

"Theo! Theo!" At first it was a scream like all the other screams. Then it was her name. It was Mélanie, carrying a little girl along the edge of the crowd.

"Mélanie," Theo called as her friend maneuvered through a collapsing booth.

Reaching the table, Mélanie thrust the girl into Theo's arms. "Save her!"

Theo wrapped her arms tightly around the child's back. The little girl locked her legs around Theo's waist and her arms around her neck. Mélanie saw her safe in Theo's grasp then turned back into the sea of chaos and fire. Theo did scream then. "Come back!"

"They are blind! They are trapped!" Mélanie let the press of the crowd carry her back toward the charity booth. Theo glimpsed a woman inside, crouched on the floor, her arms spread over a dozen little children. Then flames from a burning booth between them leapt up to block her view.

The terrified crowd crashed against the table. Holding onto the little girl, Theo struggled to keep her balance. She steadied herself against the edge of the wall but didn't trust it to hold her. She heard a sob against her shoulder. "I'm Theo." She pitched her voice low, hoping the sound would carry under the screams of the crowd and the insane crackle of the flames. "What's your name?"

"Alicia." The girl trembled against her but did not panic. She gripped Theo tighter and gave another sob. Was her blindness a blessing or a terrifying curse amid the screams and crackling flames?

Theo searched frantically for an escape route but found only horror. The ceiling was a river of fire. Heat scorched her lungs with every breath. Choking smoke clogged the air. Dark shadows fell—chunks of the tarred canvas ceiling that clung to whomever they touched. A black smoldering cloak covered a man completely. He staggered into a burning booth and fell thrashing to the ground. Fire danced up the dangling ribbons of a woman's straw hat. She snatched at her hatpins with white gloved hands, then lifted them burning from the great wheel of fire swirling around her head.

Theo heard a loud crack. Another booth disintegrating? No. At the far end of the aisle, she saw an axe split an opening high on the wall. Hope surged through her, more desperate than fear. She clambered off the table, clutching Alicia close. "Hold tight!"

Grabbing a chair, Theo knocked through the crumbling walls of two burning booths. The next would not give way. There was no way left but the aisle. Theo plunged into the seething crowd, shoving fiercely against their forward press. For an instant the black smoke parted and she could see the hole. The crack of the axe came again, the split widened. A cry went up, and the tide of the crowd swerved for the breach. Theo ran with them, choking and coughing with every breath, fighting to keep her balance against the violent shoves from behind. Flames burned up all around them, consuming the last wreckage of the booths.

Theo held Alicia tight, struggling not to fall with rescue within sight. They had almost reached the back wall. A man in a bloodstained apron climbed through, helping the women and children up to the window level where the wall had been cracked open. Other rescuers reached down to take hold of the beseeching hands. A woman and her boy went through. One of the crowd moved to help the man in the apron lift a heavy woman up to the window. It was Paul Noret. Theo almost burst into tears. Her friend had not beaten his way to the front with the cowards. Four more women were lifted up to the window. Shrieks rose behind Theo as a vast section of the ceiling fell behind them. Chunks of blazing wood flew through the air and struck the waiting crowd. She handed Alicia to Paul to lift through, and let others go next. There was still time. There must be.

"Theo!" It was a hoarse scream. She turned and saw Mélanie struggling through the crowd, through the smoke and flames, carrying another child—its hair was on fire! No, the hair was red, with a pink bow. Another little girl. The crowd parted on either side of her. Then she saw that the flames at Mélanie's feet were not burning debris. The hem of her skirt was a deep ruffle of fire. Mélanie reached the child out toward her. Stumbled. Fell.

The man in the apron seized Theo and lifted her up to the breach. Paul gave her feet a shove. "No!" Theo cried, struggling to get back to Mélanie, to the child. Hands grasped her from above. She was pulled through the opening, hauled back through the arms of a line of men in a flame-infested space between the buildings then pulled through a shattered window. The man holding her released her. Then she was inside a huge kitchen. It must be the Hôtel du Palais. Someone stood by with a bucket to douse any flames. She was not on fire. Another quickly checked to see if she was burned. He wiped her face with a wet napkin. She saw soot and blood.

"Cane?" Her voice grated, hoarse from the smoke. She felt an echo of the cowardly blow as he cleaned the wound.

"Oh mademoiselle," he said, shaking his head sadly. But when he knew she was hurt no more than that, he turned to help the next arrival.

Theo looked for Alicia but didn't see her. Many victims were being shepherded outside. She swallowed a sob of relief when the flame-haired child Mélanie had held was carried past her. Then a man clambered through, his whole face raw with burns. After him came a woman who had ripped off her burning skirts and petticoats. But it was not Mélanie.

Theo did not know she had run back. She was yanked to a stop close by the breach. A man gripped her arm. She tried to pull away, but his fingers were a vise. Spinning round, she saw a grim, soot-streaked face. She jerked savagely against his grip. He tightened more and pulled her hard against him, holding both her arms. She stared past him to the fire. "Mélanie!"

"No?" It was all he said.

A wild anger ran through Theo. She struggled violently, but he held her fast. "Let me go!"

"No." His voice was low but its very quiet commanded. Her gaze met his, and something in his intent eyes brought her to her senses. "You cannot go back."

The breach in the wall drew her again. A wall of fire blazed beyond it now. The next woman they lifted through had flaming canvas clinging to her back. The man with the bucket threw water on her. She screamed in pain, laughed in hysterical relief. For a few moments Theo had only heard this man's voice. The screaming had been part of the conflagration. Suddenly it became separate. Everyone who came through the wall now was on fire.

"I cannot go back." If she did, she would die.

"Good," he said, seeing her aware. "Tell me your name."

Her throat was raw, but she got the words out. "Theo. My name is Theodora Faraday."

"Michel Devaux."

"Inspecteur Devaux." She remembered him now. She swallowed, moistening her throat as best she could. "You can let me go now, monsieur."

He released her, waited an instant to make sure that her control held, then turned back to the line. The fire raged, and every second could be a life. She did not get in his way again, but she pleaded, "I must help. Let me join the line. I'm strong."

He glanced back, impatient, but understanding. "They have found their rhythm. They are a team. Go outside. Help the injured."

Paul came through the window. His sleeve was on fire, but the rescuers quickly beat it out. Seeing the question in her eyes, he shook his head.

Together they went outside.

Almost at once, Theo saw Alicia in a group of waiting children. She looked completely unharmed, her striped pinafore barely rumpled. Theo went over and hugged her, and was given a wonderful hug in return, tight and damp with tears. She told the woman attending this sad little band what little she knew of Alicia. The woman nodded as if she knew it all already, so Theo kissed Alicia's cheek and turned back to where Paul stood waiting silently.

"I want to find Jules. We were separated." Paul did not say how, but Theo had a vision of slashing canes. Hesitantly, he added, "Jules thought he saw Averill and went to say hello. It was right before the explosion."

The words plunged her into a freezing well. Cold shudders racked her, but she managed to gasp, "Let's look near the entrance."

Neither of them wanted to show their panic. They walked hurriedly around the corner to the rue Jean Goujon. The sound and smell of the fire that had followed them outside now grew stronger with every step. Theo shivered again, the ripples of cold running along her spine all the more bizarre in the radiating heat. A cloud of smoke billowed overhead, black against the innocent blue sky. Crimson geysers shot above the rooftops. The fire roared louder and louder. Screams and howls were all but drowned in its fury, but still the watching crowd winced with the cries. The bazaar was a piece of hell on earth. The entire building was burning ferociously, but panicked victims still clambered over the crush of bodies and ran screaming into the street, flames streaming from them like scarlet wings. Coats were thrown around some to smother the fire. Others were doused in a nearby watering trough.

Searching through the crowd, they found Averill's mother. Aunt Marguerite stared at Theo without recognition, her beautiful, heavy-lidded eyes hazy and unfocused. Shock had unnerved her, Theo thought, perhaps drugs as well. Her aunt fervently sought their false joys and false comfort. Her daughter Francine stood beside her, arm cradled in an improvised sling, smooth cheeks grimy and tear-streaked. "Theo!" She made it sound like an accusation. "Have you seen Averill?"

Paul moved closer, gripping her arm.

"We had only just entered when the explosion came. Even so I was trampled—they broke my arm!" With her free hand, Francine pushed angrily at people pressing toward the fire, fearful of being jostled.

Her aunt looked at Theo, finally seeing her. "Averill went back!" She began weeping.

Like the screaming all around her in the fire, Theo let her aunt weep for her, fear for her. "I will find him."

She turned and her Uncle Urbain was there, solid as a wall, blocking her way. He glared at her, his cold eyes glittering. "You're injured, Theodora," he said, in the soft, insinuating voice she hated. "You're bleeding."

Her hand flew to her cheek. "Someone hit me with a cane."

He licked his lips, and Theo felt naked under his scrutiny. She wanted to strike him. His eyes met hers and he smiled. He pulled out his pocket handkerchief and handed it to her. "That is too insignificant an injury for me to tend."

"How fortunate." Theo dodged him and maneuvered through the crowd.

She saw Averill approaching. She ran to him and embraced him more fiercely than she had ever dared. He was alive, strong and slender in her arms. She felt his heart pounding. Or was it her own? Averill held her tightly, but only for a moment. He whispered her name, kissed her just above her cut cheek, then stepped away. Paul was still with her aunt and cousin when they returned, but her uncle was no longer to be seen. Averill's mother clutched his lapels and wept soundlessly. He murmured comfort then looked over her shoulder to Theo. "Please, can you accompany them home?"

"Father can take us, Averill," Francine said.

"Yes. Find your father, Averill," her Aunt Marguerite pleaded. "We must all leave here!"

"He must help with the injured. So must I." He looked at Paul. "I don't have treatment for that burn yet, but I will soon."

"It can wait. I need to find Jules."

"And Casimir, if you can. He wasn't waiting for us inside—I don't think he'd arrived yet," Averill added, though he was pale and tense with worry.

Paul gave him a brief salute then moved into the crowd.

Her uncle returned, his eyes gleaming with an elation that made Theo nauseous. "Take the family home, Averill," he ordered. "I will gather supplies from my laboratory and return. You should come back as well."

"Yes, Father," Averill replied, his voice subdued.

Her uncle was much thicker set than her elegant father, with a longer face and heavier features. His eyes were as blue as Averill's, but small and chill, always measuring the extent of his control over those in his domain. "Theodora, you will go with them."

"No. I will await the end."

"Nonsense," her uncle said. "Why would you stay?"

But Averill understood at once. "Who is inside?"

"Mélanie, my friend from the academy. She handed me a little blind girl then tried to save another child."

"She was very brave," he acknowledged. "Maybe…."

Theo shook her head. When she closed her eyes, she saw the Tarot spread. The Tower falling, the wall of flames with its imprisoning staves. Death.

"I'm sorry," he said softly.

When she opened her eyes, her uncle's irate face loomed behind Averill's shoulder. "I am not leaving," she snarled, all her patience burned away.

"Suit yourself," he snapped back. No doubt he would complain to her father about her lack of discipline and uncouth manners. "I will be back swiftly, Averill. Be ready."

"Yes, father," Averill repeated. Theo hated how dead his voice sounded.

Staying beside Averill, Theo looked through the crowd and caught a glimpse of Paul talking to Jules. In the chaos, desperation and grief clashed these few bright moments. She saw a husband and wife reunited, weeping with joy. It made Theo want to weep too, but the tears were a hard knot in her throat. A woman sobbed because her husband had gone back for their child and not returned. Theo thought again of Alicia. At least she and Mélanie had saved one life. Suddenly, she realized that she would have to tell Mélanie's mother what had happened. She might already have heard there was a fire. The news must be speeding through Paris. Guilt and misery wrapped her like a cloud of grey smoke.

Averill said something, but she was so upset she didn't understand him. "What?"

"There is Casimir." Averill walked swiftly, and Theo hurried after him despite Francine's protest. Casimir stood alone, gazing transfixed at the inferno. Theo was shocked to see tears running slowly down his face.

Averill laid a tentative hand on his arm and he turned to them, staring blankly. His eyes caught the reflections of the blaze. "Is someone you know trapped inside?" Theo asked quietly.

When he spoke, his voice was a hoarse whisper. "It is a terrible way to die. In the flames."

"Yes," Averill echoed. "Our country home burned a year ago. One of the servants was trapped. The screams were the same."

"I remember." Casimir nodded. "I know what it's like to lose a home."

"Your family's chateau," Theo said. The Revenants had been there once on a picnic. Theo had sketched the fire-scarred ruins. At the time it felt a bit too grim to be picturesque. In comparison to this, that day now seemed idyllic. And Paul's village had been burned in the war. Fire haunted them all.

"You are hurt." Casimir said, looking at the cut on her face. "But not burned?"

"No, not burned." She told him her story, and Paul's.

Looking at the blaze, Theo had little hope of more rescues. The screaming inside had abated. The crowd stood quietly, the roar of the fire louder, a wind-beaten sound like vast wings. Timbers crashed inward as the building collapsed. There was a strange sound—like a rifle shot.

"What?" Someone cried out.

"Skull exploding," a low voice said. Bile rushed into Theo's throat, and she fought not to be sick. Turning, she saw Michel Devaux. His soot-streaked face was bleak with exhaustion. How had he known what the horrible noise meant?

All who could be saved had been, but still the crowd was growing. Ghoulish sightseers came to view the disaster. Her heart a tight knot in her chest, Theo waited until the fire burned out. Less than an hour had passed since the explosion, and there was nothing standing but a few charred posts, black sentinels marking the smoking graveyard of the Bazar de la Charité.

Chapter Sixteen

Blood flowed at Bluebeard's—in the shambles—
at the mummers, where the windows blanched
under God's seal. Blood and milk poured forth.
                                    Arthur Rimbaud

Gilles hesitated. That was unusual. But sometimes the shell that encased his spirit did not yield to his desires—as if this creature whose flesh he wore did not know the lust to murder. Hypocrite.

"Go on," the Raven urged. "You asked for her. You actually asked for a girl."

"Yes." Gilles had to have this girl. But now he faltered. Perhaps it was the suddenness of her acquisition? Gilles always planned, to ensure his safety. He anticipated to increase his pleasure. And he waited—to let the darkness grow and overtake him, so he would not hesitate.

"Well?"

He wished the Raven would cease his cawing, just for the moment.

"Alicia." Gilles tasted the delicate licks of the syllables on his tongue.

"Please." Her soft-voiced plea tinted the darkness with a feeble glow. Usually their fear, their despair, their pain was part of the emotional feast he craved. Yet now he felt a rare sympathy, an ache deep in his belly.

The Raven bumped him, pushing him forward. Gilles almost turned and struck him. Exercising restraint, he drew a deep breath then moved forward.

"About time." Another raucous caw.

Gilles walked around Alicia, studying her fragile form as she cowered on the tiles, trying to cover herself with fluttering hands—soft and white as baby doves. Her blind face followed the sound of his movements. The Raven had already taken all her clothes. It was cold here, colder than Gilles' own dungeon, and her pale skin was pocked with gooseflesh. She whimpered, the tiny sound raising prickles of anticipation all over his body, as if her cold and fear imprinted its pattern there. He paused, savoring the subtle thrill.

The Raven misunderstood. "We are safe here. The walls are thick. There wasn't time to take her to the country."

Gilles supposed he should be glad the Raven had waited for him—sometimes he was too greedy. The Raven had introduced him to many wicked delights and imagined himself master. In his first life, Gilles had sent his aides out to gather the sacrifices. Sillé, de Bricqueville, Henriet, his beloved Poitou, they all understood his sovereignty. They brought the children to his castles at Tiffauges, at Machecoul... Gilles stopped and looked about, silently lamenting his lost kingdoms. At least the ruins he did possess were evocative.

The Raven jabbered on. "I waited until another child was being reunited with its mother. The supposed guardian barely glanced at me when I called the girl's name. As soon as I lifted her up, my face was hidden."

"Risky."

"Where's your gratitude for my risk? Look how pretty she is."

"Lovely. Luminous." Gilles watched Alicia weeping silently. She flinched when he touched her face. He lifted a tear on a fingertip, sipped it. One of his favorite rituals. Her tears were sweeter than he expected. She looked up with her blind eyes. Her lips trembled, dripping soft little pleas like rosary beads, small and round and almost silent. Gilles felt another pang, like an egg cracking open inside him. Sorrow fluttered about inside him like a dove. He watched Alicia's hand, the fingers quivering, helpless. It was as if she reached inside him. Gilles shivered.

"She hugged me," the Raven gloated. "Then she was uncertain. She didn't know my voice. Too late!"

"Too late," Gilles echoed. The darkness beckoned—but still he wanted to retreat.

"I liked watching her as we came here. Staring. Seeing nothing. Twitching at every sound." He laughed.

Gilles laughed in answer. Why did it sound like a sob? "Still hoping for escape."

"I like them to watch, but having her just feel..." The Raven's voice thickened with lust.

Gilles felt the dove beat frantically. Death throes?

Going to the table, the Raven lit another candle. Lifting it high, he smiled. "She thought she escaped."

"Inspired," Gilles whispered, almost choking on the word. Images pierced him with horror, cold then burning. Excitement stirred like a snake. It rose up, devouring the bird.

"A...li...ci...a," the Raven singsonged the syllables. She lifted her head, turning toward the sound of her name. "Remember this, Alicia?"

Holding his breath, Gilles watched the Raven glide the candle flame beside her face. She gave a sob of terror and tried to crawl away. The other man strolled beside her, dripping hot wax along her spine. Her sobs tangled in Gilles' breath, his heartbeat. What a fool he had been to hesitate! His dread, his sorrow, his sympathy were offerings to the waiting dark. They were the human skin he would strip off to let his naked soul revel in Evil.

The Raven turned to him. "Turn her. I want to watch her face."

Gilles loathed being ordered but he complied, kneeling and embracing Alicia. She struggled, but it was futile. The other dropped a low necklace of wax drops along her throat and down her budding breasts. Her keening was sweeter than choir song. When the wax hardened, Gilles peeled off a few rounds. "Moonstones and pink sapphires."

"You and your poetry." The Raven sniggered.

Fool. "It is a light in the darkness, like your candle."

"My candle has better uses." The Raven laughed again.

"Show me," Gilles murmured.

Chapter Seventeen

The spell of stifling night and heavy dreams....
Paul Verlaine

Panting, coughing, Michel took cover in the bombed ruin of a bakery. He had to get back to his sister. His father was dead—shot by the soldiers. They would have killed him if he hadn't run—they killed children too. He had to have sense. That was what his father said. How much sense did his father have, getting shot?

Hot tears ran down his face. Michel scrubbed at them ferociously. Only babies cried. Tears helped nobody. He lifted his head, searching for a safe way back. There was none. His world was on fire. Everywhere he looked, flames climbed into the sky. Black smoke climbed above them. The vast dark cloud filled the sky like a soldier's helmet—or an executioner's hood. It looked like the shadow of the devil looming over Paris.

"The soldiers were supposed to join the workers," Michel whispered. "Join them—not kill them."

The sharp crack of a carbine merged with the crackle of burning wood. A bullet shattered plaster at his shoulder. Michel dodged and ran.

His eyes, his throat, burned from the smoke. Grey ash drifted down like filthy snow. It covered the ground and coated the piles of rubble in the streets—barricades erected by the people against the government army invading from Versailles. The workers were retaliating against Paris herself. The monument in the Place Vendôme had been pulled down, a hollow thing filled with rats' nests. The Tuileries were ashes. Now the Palais Royale was burning—the rue de Rivoli was a boulevard of flame. He knew people were trapped in the burning buildings. Some were still screaming. He could smell their charred flesh. Sometimes he heard their skulls exploding.

The Communards were running past him toward the Palais de Justice. An old woman scuttled through the wreckage, swinging a can. *Une pétroleuse.* They threatened to burn Notre Dame and La Sainte Chapelle, to pour gasoline over the rooftops and ignite it.

His mother had loved La Sainte Chapelle. She would not want it to burn.

Then he was inside the church. His mother's corpse lay on an altar, emaciated from starvation. Her open eyes stared upward. Michel looked above him, where the tall windows of stained glass glowed. But now all their colors were the hues of fire. They throbbed. Crimson. Orange. Gold. Yellow. Blood red. Then the glass broke and the fire rained down, cutting him to pieces....

Michel woke gasping. He trembled in the aftermath of the nightmare, trembled with fear, then with fury, to be so overcome by the corrosive images that ate into his soul.

It was not the Charity Bazaar fire burning in his brain. It was the Bloody Week—the Paris Commune of 1871—the great insurrection of the Paris working class after the ignoble defeat of France in the Franco-Prussian War. That brief reign of the proletariat had ended in carnage. More people died in that urban civil war than had been executed in the Revolution. Thirty thousand men, women, children, or more. Most shot without trial.

He had been six years old. Had helped his father and his cousin Luc load guns when the government troops attacked and the Commune and recaptured Paris.

Michel got up, splashed water on his face, scrubbed his body. But he couldn't scrub the memories from his mind. It had been May then, too. *Le Temps des cerises.* At Père Lachaise cemetery, in the last days, Communard heroines tucked the ripening cherries behind the ears of their lovers. Then they went to the slaughter. The poignant love song had taken on a deeper pain after that.

> *But cherry season's all too brief a time*
> *when, dreaming, one goes out to pluck*
> *two pendants for the ears*
> *cherries of love in skins like*
> *blood drops dripping down beneath the leaves....*

Sometimes he forgot that he hadn't always been Michel Devaux, son of Guillame Devaux, brigadier of the Sûreté. Before his rescuer took him home, covered in soot and blood, he was Michel Calais, son of the Communard Marcel Calais, executed by the firing squad, and Agnès Calais, starved to death during the Prussian bombardment. Brother of Marie Calais, raped and bayoneted by Versailles soldiers. A fate he barely escaped.

I'll always cherish cherry season
a time I keep within my heart,
an open wound….

With a sigh, Michel put on fresh clothes. The others would have to be cleaned.

A smoky pall clung to them. And to him as well….

The victims of the Commune were long dead. The victims of the charity bazaar fire awaited his attention. It was time for Michel Devaux to take his place in the world.

It was a hideous day. Grief and despair covered them all like a heavy shroud, slowing movement, thought, breath. More than 125 bodies had been removed from the wreckage and carried to the Palais de l'Industrie. Identifying them was another matter. All were carbonized—black, twisted forms burned beyond recognition. Michel, like many of the Sûreté, helped with the aftermath. He met with Cochefert, but the officer in charge of the investigation was the Prefect of Police, Monsieur Lépine. The National Guard was given the chore of sifting the ashes for what belongings might be salvaged.

"Not long ago, these walls were covered with the paintings of the Salon." Cochefert stared around the bleak interior. With a huge sigh he returned to the list he held and marked off more names of those who had been identified. Michel was grateful that Cochefert was bearing the news to the families. Michel had done so as well, but for now he was helping to examine the corpses, making note of possible ways to identify them.

Cochefert was especially good with the grieving relatives. His compassion was huge, as sincere as a stranger could offer. Michel appreciated it all the more because it wasn't a quality he possessed. He tensed and seemed cold while simply trying to retain his composure. He did not find it difficult to be calm in the midst of violence. It was dealing with emotional wreckage that ate holes in his belly. Here especially, where a terrible hysteria of bewilderment and rage churned beneath the mournful surface.

Noise jarred the constrained conversations around them. Another body had been claimed and was being nailed into a pine coffin. Or mahogany, perhaps. The undertaker had hurriedly returned with more expensive housing for the wealthy cadavers. The stink of the scorched corpses, which Michel had forced himself to ignore, invaded him again. He caught himself trying to hold his breath. Foolish. He inhaled deeply. The odor was nauseating, overwhelming, clotting every sense. Then, then after a moment, it faded. Michel returned to the task at hand, searching for some scrap of identification on the pathetic corpse of a young girl. He found a comb with jeweled butterflies annealed to her skull. Sensing someone watching, he looked around. Saul Balsam waited quietly, head cocked, pencil in hand in hope of an interview. *Bonjour* seemed ludicrous on such a gruesome morning, so Michel simply said, "Monsieur Balsam."

"Inspecteur Devaux," Saul greeted him then took out his notepad. "I have been interviewing Monsieur Gomery, the butcher who broke the window of the Hôtel du Palais to reach the bazaar. He told me you helped with the rescue effort?"

"Yes, but not in an official capacity."

"Why were you at the bazaar?"

"Like everyone else, I wanted to see the cinema presentation. I decided to have some wine first, to fortify myself before squeezing through the crowds. When the fire broke out, I thought there might be a way through the walls and went in search of it."

"So you organized the men?"

"No, the rescue was already underway. I helped, that is all. I would rather you do not mention my name."

"It never hurts to have a police hero."

"Perhaps, but I would prefer the working men get full credit." Saul nodded. Michel knew he would take him at his word, not presume it was false modesty. He'd made a couple of quick suggestions, no more. A curious pride linked him to these workers. They had been caught up together in a resoluteness that transcended the fear and horror. For once he had felt part of a whole that had nothing to do with his chosen profession.

"You and your compatriots must have saved a hundred people."

"Close to two hundred," Michel told him.

Saul looked around at the terrible display. Michel saw his jaw tighten. "How many of these bodies were men?"

"Only five." Michel was being generous, one was an adolescent groom.

"It is a great scandal. The men—if you can call those rich brats men—beat their way to safety over the women and children." Saul sneered. "It was the simple workers who risked their lives to save strangers."

"The duchesse d'Alençon acted with the courage her class claims. One of her servants begged to carry her out. She told him her rank gave her the privilege of entering first, and so she would leave last."

"Yes. She was valiant," Saul admitted, then added, "The duc escaped unscathed."

"Baron de Mackau returned to the fire seven times and saved seven women. There was a doctor—curator of the wax museum of the Hôpital Saint-Lazare—who ran back into the building to try and save his daughter," Michel said.

"Tried?" Saul asked.

"Both died, but he had already saved his wife." He gave Saul the man's name, and one or two others he'd learned. "Many of the bourgeoisie joined in the rescue attempt." When Saul frowned, Michel conceded, "But the butcher, the plumber, the street sweeper were heroic. You have your story in them."

Saul glanced at his notes. "Many were saved by being doused in a water trough?"

"You can add a cabdriver to your heroes. He grabbed General Munier as he ran down the street with his clothes ablaze, and flung him into the watering trough of the Rothschild stables. The Rothschilds opened their doors when other families shut them against the burning victims." Michel watched Balsam scribble the information.

"Did you hear the explosion?"

From down the aisle came a wrenching cry. "No! No, monsieur! Stop!"

Michel turned to see one of the white sheets covering a body swept into the air, swirled, dropped—like a magician flourishing a cape during a magic trick.

It was Vipèrine.

Surprise and anger stung Michel like vicious slaps. He had not seen Vipèrine since his release. Today he was not dressed in an outlandish occult costume, but in mourning so elaborate it might as well be one. He had uncovered half a dozen bodies, displaying them for his quavering band of followers. No one searching for family or a friend would do that. Another gendarme, angrier than the first, muttered, "*Bougre de canaille*." Michel could only agree. Buggering dog. The insult was audible to Vipèrine. He smiled.

Michel's nostrils flared with disgust, as if the avowed Satanist emitted a sulphurous stink worse than the stench of burnt flesh. Vipèrine probably wanted to steal fragments of the dead for some ludicrous spell. As Michel moved forward, Cochefert was there, blocking him. He lifted an eyebrow, looking like a mournful walrus. Michel realized that he had let his anger rise to the surface. Instantly he swallowed it back. Tempers must be controlled or there would be violence. Cochefert nodded and stepped aside.

Vipèrine departed, trailing acolytes. Michel recognized one of the Revenants, the shabbiest one, and made a mental note that they were connected in some fashion.

"We've had too much of this nonsense," Cochefert said. "Sightseers visiting the catastrophe."

"Ghouls," Michel muttered.

"In Vipèrine's case, perhaps literally," Cochefert muttered back. "We must expect the curiosity seekers. He wasn't the first, and he won't be the last. We had another case earlier. The count de Montesquiou."

"Ah…the hero of *À Rebours*," Michel said. The aristocratic dandy was much satirized in the press, and Huysmans had filched many of the count's eccentricities for his decadent novel. Michel had read about parties where liqueurs were matched to wafted perfumes. There had been an unfortunate tortoise which had jewels glued to its back to provide amusement for the guests. It didn't survive the embellishment. "The horror tantalized him?"

"Yes. He minced along the line, lifting the sheets with the tip of his cane, with much the same result as Vipèrine. Someone nodded at his cane and asked if he had been at the bazaar."

"If he had, we would have heard. Montesquiou is always conspicuous."

"True, but many of his ilk are alive today by virtue of just such a cane applied to women and children. Sensing he might find his own used to thrash him, the count scuttled off like a crab." Cochefert's satisfaction made Michel smile, his first since the fire. It was another gift his boss possessed, to leaven with humor without making light of what was important.

Michel went to the line of exposed corpses to help replace the sheets. Bending down to cover a body, he stared into a blackened face locked in a scream of agony. Inside the gaping mouth, the stub of tongue looked like a shriveled mushroom. And deeper, a hint of gold glinted. He crouched beside the body, staring intently.

"Cover the body, Devaux," Cochefert urged. Then, sensing his intensity, "What is it?"

Michel turned to him. "We must find their dentists."

The chief gazed at him numbly for a moment, then understanding sparked in his eyes. "It's never been done, but yes, yes! We will find out the dentists of those still listed as missing. Their records can be compared to the teeth of the victims. I will go speak to the Prefect."

Michel watched Cochefert depart then looked around for his next task. Across the expanse of bodies, he saw the American artist who had behaved bravely in the crisis, Theodora Faraday. *Thee-o*, she called herself. She was with an older woman in mourning whose face looked blank, as if grief were a blunt instrument that had struck her full force and crushed all other emotion. For a moment, Michel had been able to distract his mind with the fascination of the forensic questions, but watching Theo support this emotionally wounded woman brought the misery of the situation back.

He made his way through the unhappy throng and offered his help. Theo thanked him and introduced him to Madame Besset. "She knows of her daughter's bravery in saving two of the children. I've told her that Mélanie did not escape."

He remembered Theo crying out "Mélanie" when she tried to go back through the wall.

"We must try to find her here," Theo said with grim determination.

"She would have come home if she escaped." Madame Besset's voice was flat despite the pathos of her words. She looked at the lines of victims, her eyes blank. "She always came home to me."

Michel knew there would be an empty room in her heart from now until her own death. "I will help you search."

"How could this happen?" the mother demanded suddenly. "How could they have a display that was so dangerous?"

"They have arrested at least one of the organizers of the event," Michel replied. There must be someone to blame, and the precautions had been ludicrous. Men had been instructed not to smoke inside the bazaar, nothing more. Workmen left piles of rubbish under the pine floors. He had given this speech in various forms already, trying to adjust the details to suit the person standing before him. They all wanted a reason, but most were too shocked to digest the information. Some only wanted someone to punish.

Theo asked, "Was the *cinématographe* the cause of the explosion?"

Madame Besset was stunned with grief, but Theodora Faraday was quite aware and deserved the full explanation. "Not the projector. A lamp was ignited by a spark," he said, omitting the stupidity of an assistant who lit a match. "Both the ether used to lubricate the mechanism and the nitrate film were extremely combustible. The bazaar itself was only a temporary structure, and too easily consumed by the fire. It was a terrible accident."

"She always came home to me," Madame Besset repeated, her voice hollow as an echo.

"Come with me." He led them first to the bodies that had been identified as female. "Madame Besset, I must warn you that the victims are burned almost beyond recognition. Pieces of jewelry more than anything, have enabled us to identify bodies."

"Mélanie was wearing a lovely white dress," her mother said. "Her best afternoon dress, dotted Swiss, with touches of lace and a huge ruffle at the bottom."

What little color there was in Theo's face seemed to drain, but she lifted her chin and added, "Mélanie had a cameo at her throat, Diana the huntress, white on Wedgewood blue."

Michel met her eyes and nodded. She knew the white dress would be ashes. One stricken man had identified his wife from the remains of her red corset. Grandparents recognized the brace on the leg of a child. One corpse had a collar of pearls embedded in her neck. The most unnerving discovery had been a wedding ring, found not on the woman's hand but pressed into her heart. Michel took them farther down the line, checking the notes he had made. He remembered two bodies with some sort of round brooch adhered to the throat. When he uncovered the first blackened body, the mother gave a keening cry and turned aside.

Theo moved closer, looked carefully. "No. That is not the brooch. It is too large."

She turned to him, her eyes brimming with tears—tears she did not permit to spill. She had the valor of a Communarde. Michel moved down the aisle, and Theo guided Madame Besset after him. For the next body, he found a damp cloth and wiped some of the ash from the cracked oval. It was blue and white. A woman with a bow, and beside her a deer.

Theo pressed a hand to her own throat, swallowed hard. "That is Mélanie."

"No!" Madame Besset cried out.

There was no doubt, but Theo said nothing more. Madame Besset drew back and glared at her in accusation. Michel knew that look. How dare Theo be alive when her daughter was dead? What right did she have to be whole and unharmed, and not some blackened remnant? Anger was easier than grief. It did not matter whom she hurt, if it kept grief away.

"Madame Besset, as Mélanie's mother, you must make the formal identification." It was the truth, and he guided her gently towards the clerk. Theo meant to follow them but stopped when he shook his head. Once he had settled the poor woman in the chair and made certain she was calm enough to fill out the brief form, he returned to Theo. "I may ask one of the men to escort her home. I think it wiser."

"Whatever she wants," Theo answered quietly. Michel knew she had asked the same questions of herself, and that there was no real answer. She had been brave and resourceful to have escaped. And lucky. She would stay with Madame Besset unless Mélanie's mother could no longer bear to look at her.

Theodora asked him how many had died and how many had been saved through the break in the wall. After he answered, she said, "If I do not have a chance to speak to the other rescuers today, please tell them how grateful I am."

"I will," he promised.

"And what of Alicia?" she asked.

"Alicia?" He did not know the name.

"The little girl I carried to the wall. The child Mélanie gave me."

"Ah. All the children were taken home by relatives."

"But she was an orphan."

"Then someone from her orphanage came," he assured her. "No child was unclaimed."

"I am glad she is safe," Theo said.

A wail rose up. They both turned to see Madame Besset weeping. Shock and anger had given way. Now there was only pain. Theo hurried to her side. Gently, she helped the distraught woman to stand then guided her from the charnel house of the Palais de l'Industrie.

Michel turned back to find himself confronted by another family searching for answers to their tragedy. In reply to their furious questions, he began the litany again. "Ether was used to lubricate...."

Chapter Eighteen

But, yes, I've wept too much! The dawns are dismal.
Every moon is pitiless, every sun bitter.
                                    Arthur Rimbaud

Michel had spent the entire night helping with the identification of the fire victims. Many of the bodies were claimed, if only by process of elimination. The Consul of Paraguay had the same idea that Michel had suggested, and dentists had been summoned to examine the cadavers' teeth. He was almost asleep on his feet when an equally exhausted Cochefert appeared and handed him a hot *café au lait*.

"Drink it, Devaux," Cochefert said. "Then take a carriage to the Montmartre cemetery. There is a murder to investigate. A child."

"Yes, sir." Michel drank the scalding liquid gratefully, handed the cup back, and left.

He drowsed fitfully in the carriage but forced himself to sit up when they turned onto the Boulevard de Clichy. Soon they turned up the short street to the entrance of the Cimetière Montmartre at the western base of the butte. Less than a century old, this was the second largest cemetery remaining inside Paris.

The carriage pulled into the circular driveway. Michel stepped out onto the gravel and drew a deep breath. The smell of living things was an infinite relief—new grass, spring flowers, tree bark, even dark earth. The dawn light was cool and grey, the green of the leaves lush even in the dimness. The grass gleamed, wet with dew. His senses were parched, and he breathed deeply, taking in the scents like water for thirst.

Turning, he saw a gendarme come over the crest of a low rise shored up by a grey stone wall. Behind it on his left, slabs and mausoleums were set along wide branching pathways. On the right, another section was tucked under the bridge that led up the hill to Montmartre. Michel climbed the steps to greet the gendarme. He wasn't unseasoned but he looked greenish. An odor of vomit clung to him. This was going to be bad. Weaving among the trees and tombstones, Michel saw three more officers and a young man standing beneath a tree nearby and went to meet them.

They were not looking at the body—another warning of the ugliness awaiting him.

Then he saw the corpse.

Michel had thought that anything would bring temporary relief from the ghastliness of the burned cadavers, but he had been wrong.

A young girl, perhaps ten or eleven, was propped against a granite tombstone. The skin of her abdomen had been sliced round and laid between her wide spread legs. Her intestines decorated her like a thick, glistening necklace, framing her tiny maimed breasts and open belly. Her nipples had been removed and lay in her open palms. They had been burned. Other red burn marks glowed, intimate and lurid against her white skin. Her eyes had been cut out. Michel didn't see them. The killer might have committed some obscenity with them, or kept them as a memento.

Michel closed his eyes. He took a deep breath. Another. Exhaustion made it difficult to fight the heave in his guts. For a moment, he literally could not make his feet obey him and move forward. The horror of it stripped his defenses. She was a child—a child barely than his sister had been when she was raped and murdered by Versailles soldiers. Fury and revulsion knotted inside his belly as the old images superimposed their agony on the present. Vengeance, the urge to murder, he understood too well—but not the lust to destroy innocence.

Look past the grotesquerie. Look past the twisting pain of memory. Catch her killer.

Michel opened his eyes. He made himself approach. He found, if not the calm he wanted, a cold anger that awakened him. The little girl had not been killed here, or the ground would have been drenched with her blood. She was posed carefully, as an artist might. That did not mean the murderer was an artist, but Michel did think he considered his murder art. The killer wanted to shock, to horrify. But he also wanted to mesmerize. It might not be enough to have admired her after he first arranged her. He might need to see her again or to see the shock of those who discovered her. Michel told three of the officers to explore different sections of the cemetery. It was probably useless, as it would be easy to slip away between tombs in the dim morning, but it must be done. A bridge nearby arched over two sections of the cemetery. Michel thought he saw a figure move out of sight, but it might be only a swaying branch. He gestured a young officer he knew, Inspecteur Hugh Rambert, to go have a look.

He nodded toward the young man standing beneath the tree. "He found the body?"

"Yes," an officer answered. "His name is Averill Charron."

A Revenant. He knew the young man's poetry. Morbid poetry did not make a murderer, or there would be a thousand in Paris alone. But a morbid sensibility in a man who had supposedly discovered a corpse needed to be questioned

Perhaps she was his latest poem.

Michel told one of his remaining men to allow only police to enter the cemetery, the other he set to guard the corpse. Then he went to Averill Charron. The poet looked to be in his early twenties. Only slightly shorter than Michel, he was trim and fit, if not in a blatant way. His defensive posture straightened as Michel stopped before him. His fair skin looked pasty from shock.

"Monsieur Charron," he said. "I am Inspecteur Devaux."

"Inspecteur," Charron replied tersely.

He was tense, sullen, frightened. Natural enough. His eyes were curious, the irises tinted a crystalline blue with only the thinnest dark rim to set them off from the whites. They were even lighter than those of the beautiful blonde, Theodora, who frequented the group. Charron was beautiful too, beautiful enough for it to have caused him problems. Perhaps he wanted the problems? Perhaps not. It was probably irrelevant, but Michel laid the thoughts out in his mind like pieces of a jigsaw, to be shifted until they formed a pattern. He chose a relevant question. "Do you recognize this girl, monsieur?"

Charron looked over at the corpse, looked away. He hesitated a little too long before answering. "I've never seen her before."

"You *have* seen her," Michel insisted.

Charron frowned, shook his head. The confusion seemed genuine, yet he spoke a little too carefully, not looking at Michel. "She seems familiar, that's all."

"Familiar?" Michel put all his skepticism into his voice.

Now Charron looked at Michel defiantly. "This is not some scene from Zola."

Surprised, Michel paused. It was exactly what he had been thinking earlier. In Zola's novel *Thérèse Raquin* the murderer went to the morgue to look for the body of his victim. Michel waited a heartbeat before inquiring, "So, I have not found my Laurent?"

Surprised in turn, Charron flushed. "No."

"I am glad to hear it." The scoffing tone earned him another angry glare. Michel remembered reading the novel as a youth and asking his adoptive father if such things happened. Guillame Devaux had said they did indeed. Killers came to the morgue. They returned to the scene of the crime. When Michel first started as a detective, he looked closely at the too helpful young man who said he had discovered a murdered prostitute and proved him her killer. However illogical, the guilty sometimes reported their crimes. Some killers were horrified by what they had done, trapped in a coil of terror and guilt. Others thought themselves too clever to be caught. Charron might be either. There was no blood on his clothes, but he could have changed them. Michel asked, "Did you touch her?"

"No!" Charron's teeth chattered a little. He clenched his jaw to stop them. "I thought of taking her pulse, but it was obviously pointless."

"Taking her pulse," Michel repeated.

"I am a medical student."

Interesting. The cuts on the body didn't look surgical, but they could be deliberately crude. Michel scribbled a note, to unnerve Charron if nothing else. There was some bit of information eluding his brain. It would come. "Why were you here so early, Monsieur Charron? Were you visiting a grave?"

"No." He took a moment to gather himself before answering. "I go to the cemeteries sometimes to write poetry. The quiet... The mood...."

The explanation he gave was entirely plausible for who he was. That did not mean it was the truth. Michel continued to probe. "How often?"

"Some weeks, several times," he said defensively. "Sometimes not for several months."

"To the Montmartre cemetery in particular?" Michel asked.

"Montmartre. Montparnasse. Père Lachaise."

"Père Lachaise," Michel repeated, memory tugging him.

"Yes." Charron's tone sharpened. "I went to visit the memorial of the Commune."

Michel knew the reference was meant to antagonize him. Charron would assume that a policeman would despise the Communards. Michel felt a pang in his chest, thinking of the plain stone monument in the cemetery. Keeping his expression impassive, he quoted, "*Aux Morts de la Commune*."

"Yes," Charron replied. For a moment he seemed perplexed, then took up his litany. "I go to the Batignolles to pay my respects to Verlaine. I go to Montparnasse to visit Baudelaire."

"And today?"

"*J'ai voulu communier avec Hugo*." Charron's acerbic reply called on his earlier reference to the Commune, on Victor Hugo's liberal sentiments, and on his own desire to commune with the dead. The poet playing word games.

"You got up before dawn because you desired communion with Victor Hugo?" Michel asked flatly.

Charron sighed heavily. "No, I couldn't sleep. Tuesday I was at the fire. It was horrible—my sister's arm was broken in the panic. I helped attend to the burn injuries. Finally, I went home but I couldn't sleep. It was no better last night. I didn't want to stare at the ceiling again. I've been walking in Montmartre most of the night—"

The rambling stopped abruptly. "Can anyone verify that?" Michel asked.

Charron bit his lip. After a moment he said, "I went to the Cabaret du Néant for an hour perhaps. Otherwise, I avoided people."

The Cabaret of Nothingness, where the patrons sat at coffin tables and watched an optical illusion in which a man dissolved into a skeleton. Would someone who had just murdered a young girl dally with such nonsense? Or did he go there before, for inspiration? As a secret joke? In any case, he might have an alibi for an hour at least. "What time?"

Charron shrugged. "Two?"

Michel could smell the absinthe on his breath. However, the scent was faint, and he didn't seem to be drunk or even hung over. He might have been shocked sober. "Tell me, Monsieur Charron, do you believe that a poet must arrive at the unknown through a relentless disordering of his senses?"

Charron stared at him. "You read Rimbaud's poetry, Inspecteur?"

"In Paris, even chimneysweeps read Rimbaud."

"You are probably right." Charron gave a short, harsh laugh. "Yes, I believe a poet must seek the unknown. He must break the bonds of convention by any means possible." He paused and looked at Michel intently. "Every class has conventions which imprison the mind, the soul, as tightly as a coffin."

"And must he become monstrous?" Michel prodded him once again with Rimbaud.

"He must become a seer."

The missing bit of information flashed in Michel's mind. "Dr. Urbain Charron is your father?"

"Yes." Hearing the name, the younger Charron's nostrils quivered as if they scented rottenness.

So, there was trouble at home. Michel had heard of something unpleasant about the father. Work with the criminally insane? Or with prostitutes? Vivisection? He would have to look into that. "You are following in his footsteps?"

The Revenant's face became a mask. "I am not at all sure it is the right field for me."

"No?"

"No," Charron responded icily. "I'm not fond of blood."

It was an effort not to murmur *touché*. Michel doubted it was true but it was an excellent retort. Instead, he told Charron he was free to leave. There was no reason to charge him, but he would be investigated, discreetly.

The officers returned from searching the cemetery and bridge with nothing to report. Bertillon's men were arriving with equipment to photograph the body *in situ*. It was another of his innovations, one that Michel considered more useful than the complex system of measurements. He gestured for the men to wait, glad that Bertillon was not with them. He wanted to survey the scene without any distractions.

First he examined the girl head on, the way the killer had presented her. Even disfigured as she was, it was apparent she had been pretty. Had she been raised within the *demimonde* and sold accidentally or deliberately to a sadist? Snatched from the street? Michel could not help but think of his vanished children, but not one of their bodies had been found and this girl was blatantly displayed. Curious, he began to circle around the grave, wondering if the killer had only posed her from the front, or if, like a sculptor, he had considered her body from other angles. He could not tell. Two trees and some low bushes framed the gravestone against which she was placed, and ivy crawled everywhere. She would be partially visible from the back, but that might not be a deliberate act. Then he stopped. Pushing aside the bushes, he moved closer to the back of the gravestone.

In the center was a cross marked in thick black charcoal. Rising off to one side were strange smears like wings.

Chapter Nineteen

Darkness, woe, come flooding back....
Paul Verlaine

bruptly, even while weeping with distress, he precipitates himself into new debauches and, raving with delirium, hurls himself upon the child brought to him, gouges out the eyes, runs his finger around the bloody, milky socket....'

Theo shut *Là Bas*, feeling queasy.

Violence against children was unforgivable.

It was not just a novel. It was history. This vile man had lost himself in orgiastic brutality, maiming and murdering innocents. The author even seemed to feel sorry for him.

Theo glowered at the book, then slid it back into her knapsack. She would finish it—eventually. The present had its own violence. Averill had come late yesterday to tell her of his gruesome discovery in the cemetery, but she suspected that what he told her only hinted at the hideousness. Theo wanted to comfort him, but she felt so hollow herself she could not to find the right words. There were no right words, only platitudes that quivered like rickety bridges over the blackest suffering.

Theo rose from her bench in the garden behind Notre Dame and walked to the willow overhanging the stone embankment. Parting around the island, the Seine flowed past. Impatiently, she looked toward the Left Bank, the world of the Sorbonne, of students, printers and poets and artists, as bohemian in its way as Montmartre.

Where was Carmine? Mélanie's voice echoed in her mind. *"She is always late just because she thinks punctuality is bourgeois."*

Theo had seen Carmine only once since the fire, after taking Madam Besset home. They were both subdued, almost silent. Neither of them had been able to cry. Theo almost wept when she identified Mélanie, but could not indulge in tears when Madame Besset's loss was so much greater. She wondered where Mélanie would be buried. She should have a beautiful sculpture over her grave, a Greek maiden like the ones she painted.

Clouds drifted overhead. The spring breeze, moist and cool, caressed her skin. It carried a subtle scent of bright green grass, a bolder one of golden marigolds, even a hint of primrose. Theo let the natural perfumes comfort her. The memorial service for the victims of the fire had failed to do so, and the grisly *Là Bas* only aggravated her anger.

Two years ago, Theo had stood over new graves in California, devastated. A year ago January, when she was newly arrived in Paris, Averill had invited her to Verlaine's funeral. "Our literary world will be there." The flamboyant church was dedicated to St. Genevieve, the patron saint of Paris, the service solemn but marvelous. She'd met Casimir for the first time, and remembered how enthralled he was by the organ music. He was just coming out of mourning, too, for his grandfather. Feeling they shared a bond of grief, Theo asked if Casimir missed him much. "A man most ancient and utterly corrupt?" He'd smiled lightly. "I mourn Verlaine far more."

After the service, the three of them joined the most famous writers in France on the long walk to the cemetery. As the chill drizzle gave way to clouded sunlight, the memorial transformed into a celebration. Everyone shared stories of Verlaine in all his glory and pathos. His poems were quoted around the grave like benedictions. Even the absurdity of his tawdry mistress trying to reclaim the sheet that covered him merged instantly into the myth of the poet. The tragicomedy continued when they turned to leave. Their umbrella and a dozen others had been stolen from under the tree where they rested. An Irish poet named William Butler Yeats pointed out the fleeing thief and recognized him—Louis XI—a poor, crazy, homeless man that Verlaine had taken under his wing and renamed because of his likeness to the medieval king. At last, the clouds parted and azure sky graced their return home.

That day, Theo had felt herself on the brink of something momentous. For her it was a death that signified a rebirth, a winter that promised a bright spring. This spring, too, was bright and glowing. But Death stalked her, stepping out from Mélanie's Tarot card, twirling his scythe.

Hearing the crunch of gravel, Theo turned to see Carmine approaching. She also wore mourning. Nodding toward the cathedral, she said, "You look anything but consoled, Theo."

"The sermon wasn't the tribute I hoped for. The priest informed us that the fire was God's judgment on us. We were wicked for indulging in the irreligious scientific and social ideas that abound in these sinful modern times. But if we repented, we would not be punished. Otherwise we should expect to be burnt to cinders. It was hateful."

"Pompous, flatulent fool," Carmine muttered. "I warned you."

"Yes, you did." Theo paused, feeling sad for the thousands who had come to the church in a futile quest for comfort.

"I have a better tribute to Mélanie. There are rumors of a protest at the École des Beaux Arts. Many of the men grudge sharing their privileges with women students. If it happens, I will protest their protest," Carmine said. "And you?"

"I will go with you!" After the men's treatment of Mélanie, Theo felt bound to support the other women.

They sat watching a butterfly, grateful for its beauty. Carmine asked, "Remember when I drew the Priestess from the Tarot deck?"

"Of course."

"You were probably angry that I left so suddenly."

Theo swallowed. "A little angry. Shocked."

Carmine nodded. "It was as if the Priestess spoke to me. Summoned me. That's why I knew the card wasn't me. I felt I had to leave."

The memory disturbed Theo but she was fascinated, too. "Leaving saved your life."

"Yes. That morning I'd drawn the Tower, just as Mélanie did. I would have been trapped, too."

To call it coincidence seemed cowardice. "I don't know what I believe."

"To me, the mystical is all around us. Not to see it is a kind of color blindness."

Theo winced. "That hurt."

"It was meant to pinch at little," Carmine admitted. "But it was unfair."

"It is so far beyond my control, it frightens me," Theo confessed. "But I've always prided myself on facing my fear."

"Moina Mathers wants to meet you today."

"Your Priestess?"

"Yes. I've decided to study with her." Carmine paused. "We think it's important that we read the Tarot for you."

Theo felt her stomach plummet, but Carmine looked at her so earnestly she didn't refuse. Because of Mélanie, Theo knew she must confront the cards again.

As they started to walk, Carmine looked up to the cathedral. "Did you know they were going to tear down Notre Dame?"

"Tear it down!" Theo was stunned. She loved the elegant façade and glowing rose windows. Most of all, she loved the crazy collection of gargoyles perched on the ramparts. They were named for their gurgling and gargling as they poured rainwater from their snouts.

Carmine nodded. "Then Victor Hugo wrote *The Hunchback of Notre Dame* and everyone fell in love with it again. Sometimes we artists have power."

"Sometimes." It was an interesting conversation Carmine was offering, but Theo found concentration difficult. The Tarot cards had resumed their taunting dance in her brain. On the Right Bank they bought a ticket for a horse-drawn omnibus. When it arrived they climbed to the open-air seats on top. Theo was restless. She turned to Carmine. "Tell me about your priestess.

"Her family is quite a *cassoulet*—her father is Polish, her mother English. Moina was born in Switzerland but has lived most of her life in Paris and London. Her brother, Henri Bergson, is making quite a stir in philosophy."

The Revenants had talked about Bergson.

"She married an Englishman named MacGregor Mathers. He is a bit mad, in the way the British can be. The last time I was there he wore a kilt and performed a sword dance."

Theo tried to smile. "That sounds quite dramatic."

"He was actually rather good, though I could have done without the lecture on tartan plaids." Carmine rolled her eyes.

"But you are impressed."

"I find Moina compelling. McGregor is intense, but perhaps too much the autocrat. They are both serious about their occult studies. Between them they must know a dozen languages and MacGregor translates ancient texts. The one he's about to publish is called *The Book of the Sacred Magic of Abra-melin the Mage*." Carmine intoned the title. "They are discreet about it, but I'm sure they are exploring magic."

"Exploring magic," Theo repeated. She knew Carmine didn't mean parlor tricks. A week ago this would have been enticing. Now she felt uneasy.

"Moina designed the cover for MacGregor's book." Carmine frowned. "Most of her painting is for his projects."

"Isn't she unhappy, sacrificing her own art?"

"No. Utterly devoted." Carmine paused. "Theo, have you been able to paint?"

"Paint?" It was difficult to even say the word. Theo felt as if a giant hand was squeezing her lungs. A cloud of sooty darkness hovered behind her eyes. "No...I've only drawn a little."

Nightmares flung her sweating out of sleep—into the waking nightmares of memory. First had been the torment of not being able to paint at all, then of being compelled by the hideous images that haunted her night and day. Flames burned inside her brain until she thought her skull would explode. For the first time in her life, she was afraid of color. Afraid of hot scarlet, and orange, and yellow that burned white. Afraid of the vivid licks of azure that tipped the ends of flames. Perversely, she was scrawling compulsively in charcoal, her fingers black, the smell half nauseating, even the gritty sound repulsive, but she could not stop. Clouds of smoke obliterated the white pages. Black flames burned to the edges of the paper. Rage and fear and grief drove her fingers into scrawling patterns....

"Theo, are you all right?"

She took a deep breath. "I will be."

"I've been drawing Mélanie over and over again. Trying to keep her alive."

Mélanie came to Theo too, but she could not bear to draw her. She swallowed hard, refusing to cry on the omnibus.

They were silent again until they reached the suburbs. The flats in the sixteenth arrondissment were attractive, but less expensive than the ones closer to the center of Paris. Theo nudged Carmine, pointing out a new building in the sinuous lines of Art Nouveau. "Look, it seems to have grown out of the street."

"It's beautiful. Unique." Carmine gestured toward the rest of the block. "I really hate Haussman's renovations. I wish Paris were still medieval, full of nooks and crannies and quirks. Sometimes I go to the old churches just to slide back a few centuries."

"I love the broad sweeping avenues," Theo countered.

"Ploughed through the homes of the poor." Carmine huffed.

Theo didn't try to defend that. "I find Paris very beautiful. Perfectly elegant."

"We call Haussman the Alsatian Attila. When he rebuilt the city for Napoléon III, he demanded uniformity. All new houses must be six stories high and stand square with their neighbors. The roofs must cant at the same angle. There must be a pretty little balcony running the length of the second floor and another pretty little balcony on the fifth," Carmine complained.

"I love the balconies," Theo protested.

"It's so regimented!"

"But Carmine, the modern buildings blend with the older ones. Most are built of the same limestone—all those pale shades of cream and buff."

Limestone from the quarries that housed the catacombs. The thought silenced Theo.

They got off the omnibus on the rue Mozart. The tree-lined street was pleasant, even if a prime example of the Alsatian Attila. Carmine led her to the Mathers' buuilding, and together they walked up several flights of stairs. A young maid opened the door. Despite the serving girl, Theo could tell that the Mathers did not have much money. But everywhere talent and imagination enlivened their home. The apartment was furnished with low divans and other touches of the exotic. The air had a scent of incense and roses, of cinnamon and clove. Piles of sketches lay about, men in kilts and fairy goddesses. Others evoked ancient Egypt, a temple with lotus columns, pagan gods with the heads of beasts, a figure that looked like a priestess.

Moina Mathers came to greet them. Her voice had a beautiful resonance, and Theo relaxed in her presence immediately. She had a warmth, a glow that both brightened and soothed. Willful brown hair framed her face. Her eyes were vivid cobalt, her skin a warm olive. Moss green, her flowing dress was in the Arts and Crafts style fashionable a while ago. On her it seemed timeless. Since Carmine used Moina's given name, Theo suggested the same. She preferred informal manners.

Gesturing to the sketches, she asked, "Are these for a play? They are evocative."

Moina tilted her head and smiled. "We plan to give performances of ancient Egyptian dances—as we envision them."

Theo wondered just what *envision* meant.

"Carmine said that you wanted her to read the Tarot for you." Moina held up a hand. "I know. That was before the fire. All the more reason to carry through. Questioning will open paths for you. Trust will come in time."

"I don't know if I could ever trust the Tarot." Since Mélanie's reading had come so devastatingly true, Theo was wary. Could such a sinister coincidence be mere chance?

"The Tarot did not cause the fire," Moina said, as if she could read Theo's mind.

"No, of course not," Theo answered, but realized that was part of her fear, however irrational. She thought of Mélanie's Cassandra, doomed to see the future and not prevent it. She thought of Mélanie's charred corpse, wearing the Wedgewood cameo that Inspecteur Devaux had cleaned. Yet, Carmine survived because of the cards. Mélanie might have too, had she not misunderstood the falling Tower for the École des Beaux-Arts. The cards were not a trap, but they could mislead as easily as reveal.

"You can say no, Theo." Carmine looked at her directly.

"No, I can't." She could not walk away. She needed to prove to herself that the foretelling of the fire was only a terrifying fluke. "Let's begin."

"Usually I consult the Tarot only for our students," Moina told her. "But what happened at the charity bazaar was quite extraordinary. My husband agrees with me that it is appropriate to read for you."

With a prickling along her spine, the conversation with Carmine and Mélanie returned. She disliked Moina's dependence on her husband's approval.

Moina smiled serenely. "MacGregor is my husband, my friend, and my teacher."

Once again, Theo had the disconcerting feeling that Moina could read her mind. Though more likely, her thoughts were plain on her face.

Moina tilted her head. "Carmine thought it would be better if I read the cards, Theodora. But if you prefer, Carmine could do it."

"Moina could watch and comment," Carmine added.

Theo was curious about Moina, but she had to admit to herself the offer relieved her.

They went into a pleasant little alcove where afternoon sun filtered hazily through embroidered curtains of red gauze. The rosy light edged the black-on-black design of Carmine's cut velvet jacket, an array of poppies. Theo could imagine Carmine dressed in perfect Gypsy regalia, a silk scarf bright with scarlet flowers wrapped around her hair, kohl painted around her eyes, and a multitude of gold chains draped about her neck. Theo felt another surge of gratitude. It was the first image she'd had in days that did not conjure the fire.

Carmine unfolded the silk protecting her Tarot deck. Despite her uneasiness, Theo wanted to see the images close up and feel the textures of the cards in her hands. "Three cards?"

"Too few," Carmine said. "I only did a brief reading for Mélanie because it was so crowded and noisy in the bazaar. My grandmother first taught me the Tarot. I will use her special six card layout."

Theo nodded. She could hardly refuse Carmine's almost mythical grandmother.

Carmine handed her the deck. "Remember to pose a question in your mind as you shuffle them."

"Can't they just tell me whatever I need to know?"

"If you prefer."

Theo began shuffling the cards. They felt large and awkward, difficult to manipulate. Part of her still insisted the whole thing was silly. Yet over and over she saw the images of the flaming Tower and of Death. Theo pushed those images away and tried to look into the future without asking anything specific. She painted a lazy question mark in her mind as she shuffled, a stroke of mental calligraphy. The cards felt cool and smooth in her hands, yet warm and alive, too. She had not expected that. Then they seemed to fall into place smoothly, and she felt a quiet descend. How strange.

"I think that must be right." She set them down, remembering to cut three times.

Carmine's hand hovered over the piles. She chose the center one and placed it atop the others, a different order than she had chosen for Mélanie. She put one face down on the table. "My grandmother always laid them out one at a time, so I will too."

Theo was holding her breath. She let it out in a shaky sigh. "Show me the first."

"This represents the past," Carmine said at last, and turned over the first card. "The Seven of Staves."

It looked like an ordinary playing card to Theo. She felt nothing. "Before you tell me what this card means, Carmine, tell me the image you will paint for it."

Carmine looked up at Theo. "I see a wounded Amazon. She holds a long stave to support herself. Behind her the other staves stand like a fragile fence. Beyond them, fire and smoke on a hillside with an army approaching." The image came alive in Theo's mind, and she nodded for Carmine to continue. "You are in the midst of a monumental battle, Theo, a battle that will call for all your strength."

"A battle?"

"You have achieved a victory, but it is not the end. The respite may even be an illusion. Another ordeal lies ahead."

Memory pierced Theo. Her courage had been tested in the fire. She'd won a great victory, but at a terrible cost. "Mélanie had a card with Staves. She was trapped in the fire."

"Fire is the element of that suit, but Mélanie's card wasn't the seven. Your card says you can win the battle, but you must keep fighting no matter what the odds."

"I don't give up." She nodded for Carmine to go on.

"The present—the heart of the matter." Carmine turned over a new card and drew a sharp breath. "The Devil."

"The Devil," Theo repeated, frowning at the ugly, looming goatish figure and the chained minions at its feet…its hooves. The figure of the Devil had horns. The male and female figures below did too, and tails, but otherwise were human, even attractive. Incubus and succubus? "At least it's not Death."

Carmine looked at Moina but neither of them spoke. The silence was palpable. "What?" Theo demanded. "It's bad enough when you talk, saying nothing is worse."

"There is a malign force at work—a power both seductive and repugnant." Carmine met her hostile look. "You may be chained by your own passions."

Theo felt perplexed, then relieved. The cards must be wrong. But even as she shook her head, Moina added, "You may be ensnared in a maze of evil instigated by another. Theodora, is there anyone in your life that you see as destructive—perhaps even evil?"

"Evil?" The idea of a devil running around was ridiculous, but not all evil decked itself out in horns and pitchforks. People committed evil acts. Robbery. Murder. Children were abducted and tortured. She heard less certainty in her voice. "I don't know anyone evil."

Carmine was watching her sharply. "Not even a forbidden temptation that threatens to take hold?"

Theo began a denial, then bit her lip. Falling in love with your cousin was forbidden by the Catholic Church. It also wasn't wise. Her heart might be broken. But a big looming Devil with scaly skin and hairy goat legs? Averill with cloven hooves peeking out below his elegant but often rumpled suit? She swallowed a laugh. "Not really."

"The Devil can be a figure of anarchy," Carmine suggested, rather reluctantly.

"Anarchy?" *Paul?* Theo's thoughts jumbled together. Paul's violence was all talk, an idea he played with to vent his frustrations. Wasn't it?

Moina leaned closer. "Sometimes this card means addiction to a substance, or bondage to a person." She touched the man and woman on the card. "See how the chains only drape them? They enslave themselves, from lust, or from fear."

Hot tears pricked Theo's eyes. What if Averill could not escape the clutches of absinthe? He did not heed her warnings, or Casimir's. As for his parents—"Oh."

"Oh, what?" Carmine asked immediately.

"I do know someone who might be as terrible as that Devil." How could she have forgotten for an instant? "My evil unc…" Theo bit back the word.

Carmine gave her a knowing look. Her friend had certainly untangled the polite sham knitted over Theo's parentage. "Urbain Charron is my guardian's brother. He's a horrible, domineering man. I even think of him as evil Urbain."

"What does he do that is so evil?" Moina asked.

"He's a doctor. He treats women, though I can't understand how any woman could trust him. Fine ladies consult him at his office, but he also performs surgeries at the asylum. He cuts out their wombs to make them more docile. And he does hideous experiments on animals. Vivisection." Theo's stomach lurched at the thought of their torment.

"That is truly evil," Moina agreed. "Yet it took long for you to think of him. He does not have you in thrall."

"No." But he did seem to have Averill in thrall.

"Might it be anyone else?" Carmine asked. "Even someone you do not know well but have glimpsed?"

Vipèrine came into Theo's mind like a fairy tale villain, evil eyes glittering above his fantastical blue beard. That reminded her of Gilles de Rais, of Averill and Casimir whispering his words as if it were a game. Gilles de Rais—there was true evil. But he was long dead. She shrugged. "Let me see the next card."

"Your future." Carmine placed another card opposite the first, making a V with the Devil at the bottom. She turned it over and frowned. "The Moon."

Theo glared at the new image, disliking it on sight. High in its center, the profile face of a quarter moon was drawn within a full round. Its pearly whiteness was the only brightness and was hypnotic. The thickly clouded sky and the barren grey land below were glum and dismal. Two forbidding stone towers glowered in the background. In the center of the landscape, a wolf and a dog howled up at the hovering moon. They crouched on either side of a murky pool, where a black scorpion crawled out of the polluted water.

"Truth is hidden within illusion and deception," Carmine told her. "I think this weaves together with The Devil. The Moon can be the card of the inspired genius, but it can also be the card of the lunatic, the drug addict—the tortured soul."

"Beware when crossing the landscape of The Moon," Moina warned. "You may feel trapped within a nightmare. Yet night's darkness promises a new dawn."

Carmine laid two more above the others. "These are your choices—paths you might follow. They may be what you hope for or what you fear, but each is linked to the cards beneath. When Theo nodded, she turned one over. "The Page of Cups, reversed."

Theo saw a charming and elegant young man in a medieval tunic. Rich, vibrant, the colors evoked the glow of satin, the lushness of velvet. One hand was at his hip, a rose dangling from his fingers. The other held a jeweled goblet.

Carmine began, "The Page is a romantic soul. Imaginative, poetic, even visionary...."

Averill. Hope and fear wove together inside Theo, pulled taut.

Carmine hesitated, perhaps reading Theo's face. Moina spoke softly. "This card is ill-aspected. Water follows fire, an element hostile to it. This person is beset by turbulence and troubles, perhaps even violence."

Carmine nodded. "His visions disturb his peace of mind. His imagination lures him to unwise, even destructive actions."

It may not be Averill, Theo thought. It could be Jules, or even Casimir. It did not remind her of Paul, but he also was a poet. "Well, at least the Page is not the Devil."

"You cannot be sure of that," Carmine chastised. "The Page, however charming, may be consumed by some inner blackness. He is entwined with you and, one way or another, you are both entwined with The Devil."

Theo thought of Averill drinking his absinthe in search of oblivion, wandering at dawn in the cemetery and finding not solace but murder. He said the police suspected him because he found the body—a devilish sort of mess. She felt like snarling. "Show me the other choice."

Carmine turned over a knight in black armor charging on a white horse, his sword upraised. Storm clouds roiled, blown by winds that whipped back his cape and the plume of his helmet, and bent the distant trees. Theo remembered seeing that card before, when Carmine first displayed the deck. It had not been in Mélanie's layout, but because she'd seen it before, it seemed unusually resonant.

"The Knight of Swords." Carmine sounded intrigued. "Your temperament, and possibly your beliefs, will clash with his. He possesses strong intuitions but suppresses them to serve his will. He will not share his thoughts easily, his emotions even less so."

"Ally or enemy, he acts with total conviction—and he can be ruthless," Moina said.

"That sounds like Paul. He's always sure he's right. But ruthless?" Theo frowned. Paul did wield his ideas like a sword, but Theo thought much of it was to shield his emotional uncertainty.

"Perhaps he is linked somehow to The Devil," Carmine suggested.

"Perhaps?" Theo snapped. "Everything is perhaps."

Carmine gave a little apologetic shrug, but her lips curved in a catlike smile. Touching the card she continued, "Or perhaps you will become allies and go into battle together."

Unbidden, Theo remembered Inspecteur Devaux—easy enough to imagine him a knight pursuing evil, sword at the ready. But he had no real place in her life. She watched as Carmine placed the sixth card face down at the top, forming a rough circle. "This is the outcome."

The card she turned over was Death.

There was a terrible silence, but Theo's heart thundered furiously. "*Of course, the Death card need not mean physical death.*"

Carmine's face went sickly pale to hear her old reassurance thrown back at her, but Moina's calm voice was firm. "That is the truth."

Theo was shaking with rage. "Maybe I'll be luckier than Mélanie."

"Oh, Theo!" Carmine said, and started crying. Theo could not cry. Anger was the only thing holding off terror.

"Theo, you are facing a great battle, against a great enemy," Moina said quietly. "You will meet Death, on the physical plane or the spiritual. You must prepare yourself."

Theo was too furious to speak.

"Do you want another card, Theo?" Moina urged. "To clarify what is here?"

Theo did want that. She wanted almost every single card clarified. She wanted them nailed to the people they were supposed to be, to identify them. But she was afraid that more cards would only bring more layers of mystery, more terror. She did not want to see the Tower shattering. She did not want to see more Staves that were fire or Swords that threatened to cut her to bits and pieces.

In the hallway, the front door opened and closed. For an instant, they all froze. "My husband's errand should have taken much longer. I am sorry." Moina rose at once and went to meet him. Their voices were hushed. Theo expected the husband would be polite and leave them to themselves. Instead he came and stood in the doorway to their alcove, almost posing. He was a slender man with military bearing. His eyes glittered in a gaunt face and his whole being radiated intense energy. He looked at Theo and Carmine in turn, demanding their attention with his very silence. When he had it, he crossed to the table and stared at the cards.

Theo tensed with anger. It felt an invasion to have this stranger studying her Tarot, guessing at her secrets. Fighting the impulse to turn them face down, she curled her hands into fists.

Seeing the movement, MacGregor Mathers gazed into her eyes. "From what I can see, you will need every ally you can muster."

Theo gave him a thin smile. "For that, I will have to know my friends from my enemies."

"Yes." He nodded toward the cards. "That will certainly be a problem."

The intimacy was shattered. Moina asked if Theo had any other questions, but her focus was on her husband. Theo shook her head. Carmine gathered the Tarot cards back into their protective silk. After the obligatory courtesies, they departed. Theo begged off any further discussion and made her way home alone.

Chapter Twenty

Cold nothingness now clasps my flesh....
Paul Verlaine

Yes, fired." Cochefert glared at the morgue attendants. His cold voice increased the chill of the modern, refrigerated autopsy room. "If anyone sells so much as a scrap of this body, you'll be tossed on the dung heap."

Michel noted the attendant who looked away uneasily and knew Cochefert did too.

The chief waited for the man to meet his gaze again, then laid his hand tenderly on the unknown girl's shoulder. "This child's body has been violated enough. Remember what I've said—all of you," he added, looking around once more. "Now, get back to work."

The attendants glanced at Cochefert uneasily. No doubt some had work to attend to here, but none wanted to remain under his critical eye. After they filed out, Michel turned to him. "It's been a decade since anyone's been caught," he said, though the morbid trafficking was probably just more secretive.

"It is usually the killers whose bits and pieces people beg for, but victims' remains are popular, too," Cochefert muttered. "I'll have no ghouls like Godinet working here."

Michel nodded. Godinet had been the best-known body thief because of the Pranzini scandal, but he had just carried on the morgue tradition. Many unclaimed corpses were used for medical experiments. Godinet had been assigned to strip skin for study. Tattoos he'd saved for his own collection, but he had made a tidy profit selling off what he stole from the autopsies. Medical students had begged him for breasts to be made into tobacco pouches. Cops and journalists alike had hunted macabre memorabilia—an ear, a finger, enough skin to cover a book. Women came too, lusting after the most intimate parts of a killer.

Pranzini was guillotined after a gory triple murder with a machete. He'd chopped through the necks of a courtesan, her maid, and her little girl. After the execution, Godinet had many requests for pieces of the notorious killer and gave a detective a section of Pranzini's very white skin. The man took his prize to a leather worker and ordered it made into three chic card cases, each lined with blue satin. Two were given as presents to high-ranking police officers. They had not been pleased to receive the grotesque gifts but did nothing. The scandal broke because the detective stupidly told the oblivious leather worker that his material was not, after all, a peculiar sort of pigskin. The leather worker went to the press, and soon several heads were ready to roll. The press, the public, the church were in an uproar over the sacrilege. Godinet claimed there was nothing holy about refuse lying around on the morgue floor. His defenders said the church shouldn't kick up a stink unless it was ready to give up its saintly bits of bone. That caused even more outcry. Finally it was decided not to punish the very men who had captured the killer. Only the morgue assistant was dismissed. Godinet died soon after. No one seemed to know just how.

"Our evidence is scant, but I've shown it to our juge d'instruction," Cochefert said. "He is appalled. I believe he will be most helpful."

That meant he would keep his nose out of the investigation, at least until they made an arrest, and that he would promptly provide any warrants needed to ensure it. "I will keep him apprised of any crisis," Michel assured his boss.

"Once we have an *inculpé*, he may order a *mise au secret* for this case."

Michel nodded. If so, they could hold the accused indefinitely while the juge d'instruction examined the evidence and independently questioned the prisoner and witnesses. It would give the police more time to build their case. Lately there had been talk of judicial reform due to abuses—beatings, bribery, even starvation. Once again the liberal faction had suggested that the accused should have a lawyer present during inter-rogation by the juge d'instruction, not just at trial. Disgusted as Michel was at the mistreatment that sometimes occurred, he doubted the reforms would much affect police interrogation. Looking at the little girl on the granite slab, Michel knew this case could easily tempt him to abuse her murderer. To Cochefert, he said, "First we must capture our killer."

"I've informed the newspapers that we will display her, starting tomorrow." Cochefert contemplated their victim mournfully. "It's been almost a week and no one has claimed her."

Michel ignored the disgust curdling in his gut. The morgue offered free street theatre for the masses. The bourgeoisie could titillate themselves with death while pretending shock at the degenerate behavior of the poor. Michel detested the policy of showing unidentified bodies, but it had proven effective in the past. "We will need extra guards to control the crowds."

The chief looked more glum than usual. "Hoards of women will descend to weep over a pretty child like this."

"And men, for more perverse indulgences than tears."

Cochefert's shoulders heaved in a bearish shudder. "It will be a circus."

"If possible, we should put a watch on the body for the duration. I'm convinced whoever killed her will want to see her again." Michel paused, his certainty increasing. "He posed her in the cemetery like an obscene sculpture. People will be flocking to view his work. He will want to see their reactions."

Cochefert nodded. "You've kept men at the cemetery?"

"Charron came twice. Most of the other Revenants have been at one time or another." Michel was glad Theodora Faraday had kept away.

"Charron returned?"

"Suspicious," Michel acknowledged. "We also have a witness to his presence that morning."

"What witness?

"We asked the gendarmes on patrol to question the local carriage drivers in case they saw something suspicious. Since a child was involved, they've been more cooperative than usual. Three came forward with sightings. One turned out to be a father recapturing a runaway girl, the second a parent taking a sick boy to the doctor."

"And the third?"

"A fiacre driver passing the cemetery around dawn on the morning of the murder saw a young man of Charron's description lurking about." The driver, a cocky fellow, had obviously enjoyed having a part in the unfolding drama of the crime. "But that does not place our suspect there earlier than he said, or in bloodstained garments."

Cochefert twisted his moustache and frowned. "Wasn't there an earlier verification?"

"Yes. A waiter saw Charron at the Cabaret du Néant."

"Why did he remember him?"

Michel repressed a sigh. "The waiter has read his poems and is smitten."

Cochefert rolled his eyes. "Not as questionable as his mother swearing he was tucked between the sheets…."

"It is not an alibi, only a verification of his story."

Cochefert nodded morosely. "Whoever our killer is, he must feel invulnerable."

Michel agreed. "We have one advantage. He does not suspect we know the murders are linked."

"Anyone might draw a black cross." Cochefert played devil's advocate, though Michel was certain he agreed.

"Religious symbols are common graffiti, but the cross was freshly done. And there are the wing-like smudges. I've gone back to where Denis was abducted. The cross I found there has the same wings, so my men are reinvestigating the neighborhoods of the other kidnappings."

"And?"

"And we've found another. Only one so far, but we will broaden the area. To keep this clue secret, we have not asked if anyone saw such a mark."

Cochefert toyed with his mustache, musing. "The first cross was at the site of the kidnapping. Here it is where the body was found. The only body that was found."

"I know. Yet I am sure they are part of the same puzzle."

"Do you think he is now displaying the bodies because he feels safe?"

"Perhaps he grows bolder. It does seem odd when he has taken so many." He lifted a hand when Cochefert readied himself to argue again. "I'm certain some of the others are his."

"Then he is mocking us."

Michel frowned, an idea stirring. "We've considered another possibility. There might be two killers."

"A shared madness? It would not be the first time."

"Perhaps one wants secrecy…."

Cochefert picked up the thread instantly. "…and the other wants to shock."

"If they are at odds, there will be trouble," Michel finished. Was Vipèrine sacrificing children to the devil in hopes of gaining some unholy power? Did two Revenants share a lust for blood, cloaked behind aesthetic mysticism? Was Averill Charron controlled by his vivisectionist father? A doctor who tortured animals for what passed as scientific curiosity might want to escalate to more challenging prey.

Cochefert smiled. "With a little luck, they will slit each other's throats."

Chapter Twenty~One

When I came hither I slipped in blood,
which is an evil omen; and I heard,
I am sure I heard in the air a beating of
wings, a beating of giant wings.
Oscar Wilde

*B*rooding, Theo watched Averill pour absinthe into the bottom of the wine glass, a layer of liquid peridot. Next he balanced the flat, perforated silver spoon across the top of the glass. He set a sugar cube atop the spoon, then took the carafe of chilled water and drizzled it over the sugar. Slowly, the chartreuse liqueur underwent its metamorphosis into a pale, opalescent green.

Theo wanted to sweep away the paraphernalia cluttering the table and pour the evil green liquor on the pavement. But that would be pointless. She did not even know if absinthe was the Devil she should fear. Or if Averill was the Page of Cups....

Averill lifted the spoon, lowered it into the glass, stirring until the rest of the sugar dissolved. He did it all far more carefully than usual, Theo noticed, giving each gesture his total concentration, presumably so no random thoughts of murder and mayhem might distract him. For days he'd talked compulsively of the charity bazaar fire and the murder in the cemetery. They haunted him, Theo knew, but still she wondered if they were a distraction from the deeper pain of his sister's death a year ago.

Theo was haunted too. Tomorrow she was to meet Carmine at the École des Beaux Arts protest—but that was not a distraction. It would be for Mélanie's sake and would keep the pain of her loss close and sharp. But that was tomorrow.

Today, Paul had summoned them to the Café des Capucines to talk about the next issue of *Le Revenant*. But their chief critic had yet to arrive. Besides Averill and herself, there were Casimir, Jules, and the Revenant they'd dubbed the student Hyphen. The others were all sipping their first absinthe. Averill was already on his second. Theo indulged in a *blanc-*

cassis, the crème de cassis tinting the bubbling champagne a fuchsia that was a satisfying clash with the milky chartreuse of the absinthe.

"*C'est l'heure verte*," Averill lifted his glass in a toast.

The green hour. Creating absinthe was an act of alchemy, a ritual performed each afternoon. The interior of the *café* was perfumed with its scent, licorice sweet with a sharp herbal undercurrent. At first, Theo had loved the bittersweet perfume and found the elixir a quintessential part of the magic of Paris. It had become a darker sorcery since Averill could not or would not stop his indulgence. Did he now love absinthe even more than he loved his art?

"To Oscar Wilde," Casimir added his own toast. He had told Theo that the extravagant *café* was Wilde's favorite. The decadent oasis of plush garnet velvet and glowing stained glass ceilings was just across the street from where he had lived while writing *Salomé*.

"Salomé," Theo murmured, conjuring the memory. Not long after they attended Verlaine's funeral, Casimir had invited them to see the play, which Wilde had written in French. An actress he was courting had a small part in the avant-garde production. It was Theo's second outing into Averill's Paris and her discovery of its living, beating, poetic heart. She had been dazzled as the penniless theatre company performed its own alchemy with only the magic of words and shifting light. A full moon hung above the stage, its pure pale color corrupted as the play unfolded its tale of obsession, seduction, and death. Pearl slowly clouded and turned to tarnished silver. Silver was slowly stained scarlet. By the end of the play, crimson light drenched the set and actors like flowing blood. Theo had been transfixed by the beauty and exquisite terror of the night.

"Wilde is still in prison, isn't he?" The student peered from beneath the fringe of brown hair that all but covered his eyes.

"He'll be released at the end of this month," Casimir answered. "When he comes to France, I have vowed to visit him."

"You believe he will return here?" Jules asked.

"Where else would he go?" Casimir asked in turn. "In London he'd be snubbed, in America he'd be shot. Wouldn't he, Theo?"

"Snubbed and shot," Theo admitted, though she might have secretly pointed him to the right bar. That last rough-and-tumble year working at The Louvre bar in Mill Valley, she had learned many things that nice society girls weren't supposed to know. What mysteries remained, Averill had been willing to illuminate. From the beginning, he'd treated her as an equal. There were no forbidden topics. He'd told her it was common for schoolboys to experiment with each other. Most came to prefer women, some never did, and some desired both. He'd been amused to hear that some of the girls at finishing school were far more intrigued by each other than the muscular riding instructor she'd thought so alluring.

"What is Wilde like?" the student Hyphen asked.

"Oscar revels in his fame," Casimir said. "He has to be the center of attention. He loves to delight and he loves to shock—if not to the extreme his trial brought about."

"The judge called it the crime of the century," Averill sneered. "You have to wonder what he thought of Jack the Ripper."

Averill had said little, Theo realized. Neither for pleasure or from compulsion.

"The judge probably thought the Ripper performed a public service," Casimir replied. "Wilde's trial was a circus. He thought he could whip them with his wit, but they sledgehammered him with their morals. Two years at hard labor."

"Two years does not seem so terrible," Theo said.

"It was supposed to be a death sentence," Averill replied, animated now. "Most prisoners die of exhaustion. Their health gives out. Or their sanity. He must be amazingly strong to have survived."

"What happened to Wilde's lover?" Theo asked, earning a shocked glance from Jules.

"Nothing happened to Lord Queensbury's son." Casimir's voice dripped disdain. "Such creatures usually escape. Bosie is a rancid piglet. Vanity without talent. Utterly self-centered."

"Did you ever see *Salomé*?" Theo asked the student, trying to draw him out again.

"No, I joined the Revenants after it had closed."

"The words dripped color and glittered like jewels. It was like watching a painting by Gustav Moreau come to life." Theo hoped the mention of Averill's favorite painter might stir a response from him. He only swirled his absinthe, watching the color glow in the afternoon light.

"Truly magnificent—but it was almost a catastrophe," Casimir added. "The only theatre they could afford was condemned, all but falling apart around them. There was a fire backstage the night of the first performance. The actors were beating out the blaze on costumes."

Theo shut her eyes against the image of flaming clothes. No one had died during *Salomé*, except on stage.

"Topping that, they broke the wax head of John the Baptist they had borrowed from the Museé Grévin," Averill added.

"So much for any profits—despite being sold out." Casimir opened his fingers as if coins were falling through them.

The student Hyphen sighed regretfully. "I wish I had been there."

"Casimir, Averill, and I met Paul and the others in *café* afterward, by accident. We pulled our tables together so we could all talk about the play." Theo still had the program, designed by Toulouse-Lautrec, as a keepsake. "It was our inspiration."

"We talked of how Salomé's ghost would dance through Herod's dreams. And how John the Baptist would have haunted Salomé." Casimir smiled at Theo, urging her to continue.

"Casimir proclaimed that Salomé would only want a ghost with a body. Averill said that would be a revenant, a ghost you could touch."

"Like a succubus," Jules whispered. "A spirit that lusts."

"We decided to do a magazine with poems touching on the theme and publish it for *La Toussaint*. So *Le Revenant* was born," Casimir said, then looked up as Paul appeared with the missing Hyphens and settled at their table.

"The theme is our focus," Paul said as if they were arguing with him. "*Le Revenant* does not proselytize a new movement in poetry. We welcome all superior work, be it from the Symbolists, the Decadents, the Parnassians, even from the naïve Romantics. We are artistic anarchists." He looked around at them all and nodded with satisfaction.

"*Garçon,*" Averill summoned a passing waiter and ordered another absinthe.

"Averill…" she started to ask some question to engage him, but he looked at her blankly, lost in some inner turmoil.

"For once we're all here." Dispensing with pleasantries, Paul pulled out a notebook and turned to Averill. "How many poems do you plan for the next issue?"

When Averill only stared bleakly at the street, Paul poked him with his pencil. "*Tu as le cafard?*"

Theo wondered how having a cockroach ever came to be equated with depression.

"Poems?" Paul repeated with another prod.

Averill frowned. "I have only two that seem right. Another two I am unhappy with but know will improve. Bits and pieces of others."

"What two are finished?"

"Another Salomé poem. Cupid and Psyche."

"Bluebeard?" Paul asked. "You did promise me Gilles de Rais."

Averill shook his head. "Something about Bluebeard is incomplete, imperfect."

Bluebeard again. Theo frowned. Sometimes Gilles de Rais seemed like a revenant walking through Paris. Present but never quite in sight.

"I want Bluebeard," Paul insisted. "I want that ultimate darkness."

Averill gestured in frustration. "First I must finish the poem of my little Venus."

"Venus? Greek myth?" Paul asked. "Erotic?"

"No. It's about the girl I found in the cemetery," he whispered, no louder than Jules.

Shaken, Theo wondered how Averill could bear to write about her. And yet, for the past week, she had been obsessed with the fire, with destruction, with death. Her scrawled sketches of the burning building, the charred wreckage, had not exorcized the most terrible image from her mind. Over and over, Mélanie came toward her in a white skirt circled with flame. It was too horrible. Theo had resisted making a drawing. Now she felt she would not be free until she did.

"Not fairy tale or myth, but your little Venus appears to be a revenant," Casimir said.

Paul scribbled in his notebook. "Yes, that might work."

"There is another Venus poem I began earlier. A pantoum."

"Excellent." Turning to Theo, Paul explained, "The second and third lines of the preceding stanza repeat in the next, repetition creating rhythm."

"I want to make them a duet of sorts. *Grand et petit...*" Averill trailed off, staring into his absinthe. Theo didn't know what was wrong. Suddenly, he lifted his head, looking round at them. "The poem is frozen!" he blurted out. "I must see her again, or I won't be able to finish it."

Paul's eyebrows ascended. "I do not want to dig up a grave to raise your revenant."

"No! The papers say she has not been identified. They have put her on display. I must go to the morgue." Averill sounded desperate. He turned to Casimir. "Come with me."

Casimir hesitated, but conceded. "Of course, if you wish it."

Theo was appalled. How much death did Averill need to see? Did he only feel alive when it was close? The fire at the bazaar, the body in the cemetery, were cruel strokes of fate. But Verlaine's funeral, the catacombs had been events he sought out. Of course it was Casimir who had invited them all to the catacombs, but Averill had been the most eager to attend.

A hollow ache filled her stomach. Theo had to admit that she did understand Averill. She understood what it was to be haunted, to be possessed. Mélanie was her revenant, begging to exist if only as a painted image.

"I will go with you too," Theo said quietly, though she hated the thought of the morgue. She had discovered it by mistake after exploring Notre Dame. It stood at the eastern tip of the Île de la Cité, where bodies found in the Seine could easily be brought by boat. Theo had approached cheerfully, mistaking the colorful crowd for something festive. Rich and poor, young and old were gathered outside. There was even a puppet show. All sorts of pastries and drinks were being hawked. Then she heard one of the many vendors promoting his curative ointment, his *"pâté de morgue."* Realizing where she was, Theo watched, stunned, as parents hustled their children inside, a family outing to view the corpses on display. Ever since, Theo had avoided the somber building. Until today.

"I too would like to see this little Venus of yours," Paul said. "The Revenants should all go, especially those who avoided the catacombs or did not witness the fire."

Theo wanted to clobber Paul. "Must everything be an aesthetic show? Misery, grief, horror?"

Paul sat back and surveyed her. "Anger is much improved with aesthetics."

Before she could respond to that back-handed compliment, Casimir whispered in her ear. "Paul is clever, *chère Amazone.* Our Averill must go. Will not a little human padding protect him?"

"Perhaps," Theo said reluctantly.

"An artist must have courage," Paul asserted. "No one escapes their fears, but the artist must face them, conquer them."

"The artist must gaze deep into the abyss," Jules agreed fervently. "You must search out your demons—even stir them."

"Maybe demons should be treated with more respect," Theo ventured, feeling a coward as she did. She had completely believed what they said—until she had a Devil to beware.

"Demons make better muses than angels," Paul replied. "They spend more time communing with mortals. They infest reality."

"I've had more than enough reality," Theo said. *More than enough hellfire.*

"You are more real than the rest of us," Averill murmured to his absinthe. "You are sunlight. We are shadow."

For a moment, no one spoke. Theo heard nothing but her own clamoring heartbeat. Averill had never given her such an extravagant compliment. But it wasn't just his words, it was the catch in his voice as he said them. It was almost as if he'd said he loved her. Almost.

"You underestimate us, Averill," Casimir said. "We are more substantial than shadow. We are dense as night."

"Shadow. Night. Wolves baying at a blood red moon," Jules intoned.

Theo felt like she was staring into the depths of the Tarot card, seeing the Moon's reflected light quivering in the oily waters of the fetid pool. She felt a sudden chill.

"To the theatre of the people?" Paul gave a feral grin. "To the morgue!"

"The theatre of the people?" Theo looked at the long line gathered to enter the morgue. Despite her doubting tone, she knew Paul was right. Parisians considered the whole of their city a stage to enact the drama of their daily lives. Yet why would anyone choose to play out a scene here, unless they had to? At least the catacombs possessed a morbid glamour.

"The show is free and changes frequently," Paul said, glancing down the line waiting outside the sober building. "Of course, you must provide your own dialogue."

"The only problem is when the actors are absent." Casimir gestured to the crowd. "When there are no corpses to provide entertainment, the people riot."

Theo looked about, fighting uneasiness. The carnival atmosphere she had witnessed before was gone. Parents kept their children close and shushed them if they became loud. The line was dominated by women with fervid eyes and tear-streaked faces. They sighed vastly to draw attention, then squeezed out another tear so they could dab at their eyes and display the expensive lace on their handkerchiefs. Some obviously imagined themselves the next Sarah Bernhardt, but a few wrenched Theo's heart. They looked so haunted, so fearful of discovering the child within was their own.

Paul pointed to one. "*Le Fausset* comes often."

The faucet. Theo winced. "All that grief is just for show?"

"If it's not for amusement, then she's crazed." As usual, Paul adopted a scornful pose. A little ahead of her, Averill looked agitated and Casimir concerned. Jules appeared oddly peaceful. His lips moved as if whispering a prayer. The Hyphens clearly wished they were elsewhere but had not dared refuse Paul's challenge.

Theo struggled to maintain her poise as they approached the door. The feverish atmosphere infected her. She felt like ants were crawling all over her skin. Only a week ago, she had stood in just such a snail-paced line with Mélanie and Carmine to see the cinema. Closing her eyes against that memory, Theo saw instead the black train rushing off the screen, drowning them in darkness.

"Soon now," Casimir whispered. Theo opened her eyes. He was speaking softly to Averill, who stared fixedly at the door ahead.

Finally, they entered the public viewing room in the center of the building. It was cold inside. Ahead of them stretched an enormous window with green curtains. Inside *la salle d'exposition*, framed like a department store display, were a dozen black marble slabs in two rows. Today three bodies were laid out in the front, naked except for a cloth draped across their hips. Their clothes were hung nearby to help with identification. They were adults, a man and two women. No children. Then Theo glimpsed a small figure at the far end, almost out of sight, seated on a cloth-draped chair. Did they do that to make the children seem more alive? It seemed even creepier. Some sort of fabric draped the body, but no clothes hung beside her. Averill must have found the little girl naked. The small body posed on the chair was pathetic and disturbing. There was no way the morgue could create any feel of normal life. Theo felt even queasier than before.

The crowd thickened around the last window, blocking the little girl from sight. The bodies before her were given only cursory attention as everyone waited for their vision of pathos.

Suddenly, Jules laughed loud enough to be hushed. He twitched nervously then looked abashed. "Forgive me."

The line moved until they stood directly in front of the window. A muscular old man lay on the first black marble slab. He had a jutting nose, a strong jaw, and a mane of grey hair almost to his shoulders. He reminded Theo enough of the uncle who raised her to sadden her. Her eyes stung with tears but she blinked them back. The present was sad enough. Pushing old grief aside, she looked at the man again. The clothes hanging beside him looked like a farmhand's Sunday best. Theo guessed he had come into Paris seeking adventure. Had he been robbed? There was a mark on his head. Was it a killing blow, or had he only fallen? She moved on past two women lying on the next slabs. One looked bloated by the river, her clothes little more than rags. The other had slashed her wrists. Beside her was a garish dress and clashing feather boa.

Averill had already moved on, his gaze fixed on the little girl's body in the chair. Theo stopped, looking down, letting him have his moment with her. She glanced behind her. Casimir was hanging back as well. All the Revenants were ready to offer succor but only if Averill needed it. Theo heard the crowd muttering, urging them to move forward. A flash of anger warmed the cold gloom that had settled on her. Averill looked wretched yet utterly rapt. Deciding he'd spent long enough alone, Theo came to stand beside him. She tried not to look into the window, studying her feet instead. The old man, the sad women, had been awful enough. Then her own cowardice angered her. An artist must look at grief, at ugliness, as well as joy and beauty.

And so Theo looked, really looked, at the little girl sitting on the chair.

A cold hand squeezed her heart, her throat. For a moment she could not breathe and choked on her own silence. The name came out a whisper. "Alicia."

Averill turned to her. "Theo?"

"I know her!" Everyone in the morgue turned to look at her. Most looked puzzled. Theo realized that she had spoken in English. Her voice still catching, she whispered in French, "Averill, I know her."

He stared at her, his eyes wide. "Who is she?"

"She was at the fire," Theo gasped. "I saved her from the fire."

"Are you sure?" Casimir asked, moving closer.

"Yes. Yes! I saved her but she's here. She's dead."

Suddenly it was all back. Alicia clung to her as screams and fire rose up around them. Mélanie staggered toward her, dressed in flames. She held out another child as Theo was lifted away to safety. She was saved. Alicia was saved—

Alicia was dead.

Theo sank to her knees. Shaking. Sobbing. Coldness poured over her. She was drenched in grief, drowning in death. Averill knelt beside her, put his arms around her, held her. She loved him then and hated him. He had brought her here, to see death. To see that everything was pointless. She drew back, struck him hard with her fists.

"Alicia! The name of your poem is Alicia," she cried.

He gripped her wrists, his hands hard. His voice was soft, urgent. "Theo! Theo…don't."

"Theodora, control yourself," Paul said coldly.

Averill did not try to make her behave. He pulled her against him. Held her tighter.

"Let her cry, Noret. Don't be a beast," Casimir hissed angrily.

"This is why they have the display," Paul said. "It is not just a bread-and-circus spectacle. You can identify her, Theo. That is more useful than your tears."

"Yes, Theo. Paul is right." Averill kissed her forehead. His lips were soft. Theo shuddered. She pulled back and looked at him. His eyes were filled with concern.

"Theodora," Paul repeated sharply.

She looked beyond him. Everyone in the morgue was staring at her. Now she was part of their drama. She wanted to scream at them. Hit them. She wanted to vanish. Theo choked back her sobs. "I know her first name, that's all."

"The police do not know her first name. They do not know that she was at the fire." Paul beckoned the guard, who was already watching them closely.

"Please, Theo, stand up." Averill slid an arm under her elbow, helped her to rise. But the black sea of meaninglessness pulled her down again. Her knees buckled. Casimir moved swiftly to her other side, helping Averill lift her. She stood between them, her legs like jelly. They waited until she steadied. Lips close to her ear, Averill whispered, "Can you walk?"

"Yes." Theo pulled away from them both. Slowly, she began to walk toward the door the guard indicated. Averill had found Alicia. Tortured. Alicia had trusted her, and Theo had abandoned her to a death more hideous than the fire.

She stumbled and Averill was there, gripping her arm. "Theo, let me help you."

Theo could not fight him again and leaned closer. She could not ward off the memory of Alicia's tight, fragile embrace. Unable to stop herself, Theo looked back.

Vipèrine stood in front of the window where Alicia was displayed.

He was smiling.

Chapter Twenty~Two

It begins as it ends, with the laughter of children.
But poison now insinuates into our veins, even after
the trumpets resound, summoning back the ancient
discords.

Arthur Rimbaud

Michel was instructing two detectives to follow Vipèrine when a guard hurried up to him. A woman had recognized the girl on display. Following him back to the hallway, Michel was stunned to discover Theo Faraday sitting on a bench with four Revenants clustered around her. She lifted a tear-streaked face. Seeing him, she looked startled—then angry. Why angry?

"Mlle. Faraday." He nodded formally. "Monsieur Charron."

"Inspecteur Devaux." Charron's eyes flared defiance.

Had Michel found his Laurent after all? But if Charron had any culpability, he was now *en garde*. As were they all, he thought, introducing himself to the others. Noret he was informed about, the baron was a known dandy and vicious duelist. The self-effacing one, Jules Loisel, he had seen with Vipèrine. "First I would like to speak to Mlle. Faraday, then each of you separately. Please do not discuss what has happened with each other."

Charron said, "Mlle. Faraday should have an escort."

"Mademoiselle?"

"I will be fine," she replied steadily enough, but she sounded hoarse.

"This is ludicrous," the baron said. "Mlle. Faraday can tell you the name of the little girl. Other than that, we have no information of value to you."

"Monsieur Charron has already provided important testimony in this case. You may have information you do not know you possess." To mollify them, he added, "I realize that this is an unpleasant task."

The men glowered but did not protest. Michel opened the door to the office and gestured Theo to the chair in front of his desk. He regretted he had not been observing the parade of spectators when she came through. As he watched, her hands clenched and unclenched the black gabardine of her skirts. She continued to wear mourning for her friend. Her jaw was set, and her eyes flashed. Was her anger a defense against the shock?

"Can I bring you water. A sip of brandy?"

She shook her head. "No—thank you."

"You recognized the victim we have on view in the morgue?"

"Victim!" She lowered her face, so he only glimpsed her fury. She clenched her fists tighter. Finally, she choked out, "It's Alicia."

"Alicia?" For a second the name meant nothing. Then he remembered. Something dark and chill settled over him. "The girl you saved from the fire?"

She nodded. Her lower lip trembled and she bit it.

"You are certain?" He did not doubt it. He only wanted her to keep talking.

"Mélanie died!" she burst out furiously. "She died saving the children—and all for nothing. Alicia is dead! Murdered!"

Michel waited, giving her time to regain control.

Theo drew a long harsh breath, glaring at him. "The other little girl—the red-haired little baby girl—is she safe? Are any of them safe?"

"I cannot be certain now," Michel admitted, "but I presume so."

"You presume?" Theo was visibly shaking now.

"I was not in charge of the children, Mlle. Faraday. I was not even present in an official capacity," he reminded her quietly. It was true, but guilt carved into his gut. "Many people were simply trying to help the injured. The woman who organized the children was the wife of one of the hotel workers."

"Anyone could take them! A killer did!"

"She would have felt only relief to have a child claimed," he said. "But even with the chaos surrounding the destruction of the bazaar, it was a huge risk to kidnap even one child."

"Not if the killer said the orphanage sent him. Alicia was blind!"

Blind. Michel felt his professional composure falter, remembering the terrible suffering the child had endured. He looked away then made himself meet Theo's accusing glare. "We will talk to the school, and interview the woman again."

Theo shook her head, choked with anger. For a moment she studied her hands, twisting in her lap. At last she said, "I know it is not your fault, or hers."

"The only fault is her killer's, mademoiselle."

But he felt ashamed of his failure and knew the hotel worker's wife would as well. Michel had spoken to her only once, to thank her. One or two children remained at that time. Could Alicia have been taken when the woman's back was turned? Surely the girl would have struggled, cried out. Did she believe her killer was sent to claim her? The chill he felt deepened. The killer could have known her name. He could have overheard it. Or he could have been told it—by Theodora Faraday. She was quick, but he didn't think it had occurred to her. Yet.

"You have great physical courage, Mlle. Faraday," he said. "You must find another kind of courage now. You saved Alicia from the fire, but not from her final fate. Now you can help us find her killer."

She lifted her head and met his gaze. "I will do anything I can."

He believed her. "Alicia did not tell you her last name?"

"We gave each other our first names." She flinched. Michel knew she was remembering the moment when he held her—prevented her from rushing back to try and save her friend.

"Was that the last time you saw Alicia?"

"I saw her outside, the one time. I hugged her." She swallowed hard. "I meant to go back but realized that I had to speak to Madame Bessett."

"Why did you come today?" he asked. "You did not recognize her photograph in the paper, or seeing her here would not have been such a shock."

"I couldn't look at it. I'd seen so much death." She could barely hold back her tears.

"Please, mademoiselle. Tell me why you came to the morgue."

"Averill—Monsieur Charron—wanted to see her again." Suddenly she was stiff. "You know he found her body in the cemetery? He was concerned that she had not been identified."

"So, you thought you might recognize her?" Perhaps she would tell him more if she kept correcting him.

"No." She regarded him warily now. "I...we...only wanted to help Averill...Monsieur Charron."

"All of you came to support him?"

She hesitated. "Some came as a challenge. Facing death."

"Yes, that is a common reason," he said. "A common excuse as well."

"It is a common need." Anger flared in her eyes.

He thought she was not defending herself but her friend. He prodded her. "Was that Monsieur Charron's reason?"

Theo squared her shoulders but did not meet his gaze. "Finding Alicia's body upset him. He began a poem about her. He needed to see her again to finish the poem."

"To finish his poem," Michel repeated without inflection.

Now she glowered at him. "Yes. It was a way to confront the terrible things he felt, to face them and move on."

"Or to embrace them," Michel said. He probably should not goad her. She was visibly shutting herself off from him. Charron was a friend. A lover? A relative? Except for hair color they looked oddly alike.

"I have been drawing the fire," she challenged. "Not to embrace it, but because it burns in my brain. Is that so hard to understand?"

"No. I understand." But Michel did not think Theodora had the same perverse sensibility as her poet friends. She wanted to be wild, perhaps even wicked in a small way. She did not know that small ways were like small tears in the soul that let evil drip in. That could be ripped wider to let it pour in. "How did you become acquainted with the Revenants?"

"My…guardian…is Monsieur Charron's uncle. I was invited to stay with his family when I arrived in Paris. Averill liked my drawings and introduced me to his friends. It was an incredible opportunity." Suddenly she stood, vibrating with anger. "I have told you everything I know."

"Very well." He knew where she lived, after all, if he needed to speak with her again.

At the door she turned back to him, still furious. "That horrible man was here today—Vipèrine. He likes to imagine himself as Gilles de Rais, who murdered more children than they know how to count. Why don't you question him?"

"I have, mademoiselle." It was a half-truth, or half-lie, and he felt cheapened by it. So he added, "And I will again."

Vipèrine had appeared at the morgue early this morning then returned this afternoon. Each time he brought some fawning acolyte, first a young man—the Revenant Michel had recognized—then a pretty girl. He hoped Vipèrine would not manage to elude his detectives. He wanted to know where the man had his current lair. If he needed any more proof that Vipèrine had broken into his apartment, it was the surprise on the serpent's face. He had expected Michel to be dead by now.

Michel escorted Theo to the corridor, then summoned Averill Charron. He had dark circles under his eyes but managed to make fatigue look poetic.

"You have not been sleeping well, Monsieur Charron."

Taking the offered seat, Charron regarded him with cold disdain. "Finding mutilated bodies gives me nightmares."

"The Revenants is the chosen name of your group, is it not? So the idea of embracing revived corpses is not repugnant?"

Charron glared. "Of course it's repugnant—except as symbol."

"Does Alicia haunt you? You've been writing a poem about her?"

"You can draw the darkness out of yourself…put it on paper," Charron replied. "You cannot escape what is terrible, but you can transform its ugliness into beauty."

"You would not be someone then, who seeks out the darkness, creates the darkness, in order to have a subject for your art?"

"No," Charron answered sharply. But when faced with Michel's silence, he added, "Yes, but no more than any other poet. Darkness and light. Beauty and terror. "

"You told me you were not Laurent. Yet you are here to view the corpse that you found during a morning stroll in the cemetery."

"You make it sound, make it feel, like something other than it is. I told you—if I am depressed, the trees, the graves, can be soothing. Cemeteries are preternaturally quiet."

"Does it bother you that Death has the ultimate power? Do you wish to take the power for yourself?" Had Charron wanted to make certain that Theo saw his handiwork? To show her the futility of her rescue?

"Stop making me out to be a murderer."

"Is that what I am doing?" Michel asked.

"Yes. That is exactly what you are doing." Charron scowled at him. "I can't decide which is more offensive, when you pretend to be more stupid than you are, or more clever."

"Perhaps you created the murder in order to create the poem. The pose you chose for the girl was most picturesque." Michel opened the folder beside him and dealt out the crime scene photographs.

"Stop it!" Charron stood up. Pale blue irises blazed against the bloodshot whites of his eyes. But he gazed at the photos with horrified fascination. Did he feel horror after the fact? Feign it? Or was he what he said, an artist obsessed with a fearful creation?

"Will you be able to finish your poem now, Monsieur Charron?"

Charron regarded him with loathing. "With your help, it is guaranteed."

He had spirit—even rage—not far below the surface.

Michel laid the photograph of the winged cross on the top. Charron looked perplexed, "What is the significance of this?"

If he was an actor, he was a good one. "I am searching for someone who can tell me just that."

Abruptly, Charron reached out and turned over the photos. "Not I—I did not kill this girl." He paused. "Alicia...I did not kill Alicia."

Either Charron was innocent, or he had barricaded himself effectively. "One last question. Were all the poets with you today also at the Bazar de la Charité?"

"Yes—everyone waiting in the hall." He smiled coldly. "So we are all suspect."

Michel returned the smile. "It would seem so."

"Is that all?"

"For now." Michel followed him to the door. Outside, he saw Theo seated. He didn't like her pallor. "Mlle. Faraday has had a shock. I do not think she should be alone. Perhaps you should take her to your parents, or one of her friends?"

Charron scowled but then went swiftly to Theo's side. He took her hand, fingers pressed to her wrist above her glove, and tested her pulse. Leaning close, he talked softly to her. Theo shook her head vehemently. Charron spoke more forcefully and helped her to her feet. For a moment, she looked unsteady. Then she drew a long breath. With a quick nod, Michel directed a guard to escort them out the back entrance. There was no need for them to deal with the circus inside the *salle publique* of the morgue.

Casimir Estarlian walked with them as far as the door but made no effort to leave. Etiquette said a member of the *noblesse ancienne* should not be kept waiting, but Michel decided to question the others first. They'd all had the opportunity to see Alicia. They'd all visited the cemetery. But Estarlian had been with Theo in Montmartre the day Denis was taken. The baron looked at Michel expectantly. Michel turned to the other two. Jules was sitting by himself, telling a rosary. Noret regarded him distrustfully. Michel would have preferred not to be a recognizable face to the anarchist, but there was no help for it. "Monsieur Noret?"

"Inspecteur?" Noret examined him as he might a cockroach.

Michel gestured him to the chair and ran through his questions. Noret's information didn't differ. He spent most of the interview sneering monosyllables. Finally, he asked, "Do you really think I am the sort of man who slices little children into bits?"

Michel studied him silently for a moment. "I think they would have to be aristocrats' brats, or progeny of high bourgeoisie, for you to deem them worthy of slaughter."

Noret's eyes narrowed to slits. "Why would my politics be of concern to you?"

"I've read *Le Revenant*. It was pertinent to my investigation."

"I assure you, I do not believe children bear the sins of the fathers. And Charron would much prefer crimson ink to bloody wounds."

"Whoever did this would prefer to give that impression."

"Could you have caught him if he danced blood-stained through the streets?"

"It would have made our job simpler."

Noret gave a snort of laughter.

"You went to the cemetery," Michel reminded him.

"I believe we all went to the cemetery. It is not every day a friend trips over a corpse," Noret said. "You should not make too much of it, Inspecteur. Poets are impudent—they exploit experience."

"Nietzsche," Michel responded. Noret looked startled and Michel thrust deeper. "Do you consider yourself beyond good and evil, Monsieur Noret?"

"I consider art beyond good and evil."

"And would you consider this art? Michel placed a photo of Alicia in front of him.

Noret started at it stonily, though he looked greenish and his nostrils quivered as if at a noxious odor. "That pushes the boundaries of art past my limit."

Michel covered the photograph of the corpse with one of the winged cross. Noret stared at it blankly, then retorted, "Art? I should say not. Should it mean something to me?"

"Preferably."

Noret eyed him distrustfully then looked at the photograph again. "A clumsy cross. Is this murderer some sort of religious maniac?"

"Perhaps." Michel didn't think he would discover much more. He asked a few questions about the fire. Noret had spent much, but not all, of that day with Jules Loisel. They had all, briefly, helped Charron tend the victims, and so all had time to snatch Alicia.

He dismissed Noret and summoned the younger man. Loisel was flustered, yet there was something sly and secretive about him that Michel distrusted. Nor did he like the company he kept, dividing his time between anarchists and Satanists. His accent wasn't Parisian. Michel discovered he was from a small village in Normandy. The local priest had taken an interest in him, and Loisel had entered the seminary to train for the priesthood. It was a common enough story. He was one of those poor young men for whom service to the Catholic Church was more a practical salvation than a spiritual one. But now he was a poet, not a priest, living like a beggar in Paris.

"Why did you leave the seminary?"

"I questioned the teachings. I was unhappy. There was a woman. A crisis of faith…" Loisel bit his lip and relapsed into silence.

"And what can you tell me of this visit to morgue?"

Loisel repeated the same explanation but with a peculiar fervor. He tended to speak either too softly or too loudly. "This was all for the sake of Monsieur Charron."

"Did you visit the cemetery for Charron's sake?"

Loisel looked guilty and frightened. It was almost impossible to understand his next whispers. "Curiosity…macabre…perverse. Ashamed."

"Did you recognize Alicia today?"

Loisel looked at him wild-eyed. "No!"

"But you saw her the day of the fire."

"No!"

"Wasn't she pointed out to you?"

"I don't know. I don't remember!" Loisel looked ready to bolt, so Michel tried a different approach, asking how he had joined the Revenants. Relieved, Loisel spoke quickly, "I take odd jobs. Once I made a delivery to Monsieur Noret's office. I knew his writing. I showed him poems I thought worthy. He told me he would publish them. He befriended me."

"The poems in *Le Revenant*?" Loisel had a long and strangely salacious epic about Mary Magdalene and the dead body of Christ. In another, a nightmarish Eve performed tricks with a snake that a brothel keeper would envy. Perhaps Loisel should go to work for Leo Taxil.

"Yes." He sat up straighter, pride and defiance glittering in his eyes. "There were just two in the first issue, but I will have my own section in the second."

"May I see them?" Michel asked.

Loisel gaped. A policeman was probably one step above a demon in his hierarchy. But he closed his mouth, swallowed, and refused politely. "I have shown them only to Monsieur Noret. He has made invaluable suggestions. I am still reworking them. They must be perfect."

"Perfection is difficult to achieve," Michel said.

Loisel's jaw set stubbornly. "What else is worth the struggle, the torment?"

"Can you tell me the themes?"

"Death. God. The Devil. Lust. Love. Time. Beauty. What every poet writes about."

Michel nodded, though Noret's list would have differed. He had reread the first issue of *Le Revenant*, and poems by these poets in other literary magazines. Noret's were often violent, especially the ones in the more political publications. Loisel had talent but little restraint. The baron's were polished and elegant, revealing little emotion but hinting at hidden depths. Charron's were brilliant but too carefully controlled, as if he feared to unleash his emotions. Most were morbid. Loisel, Charron, and Estarlian all presented death seductively. Charron and Estarlian both had poems about Salomé, full of blood imagery. Yet, Paris was hardly lacking in poets who explored the dark realms of the psyche.

But Michel had seen this failed priest in other company. "Monsieur Loisel, you know a man who calls himself Vipèrine."

Loisel went very pale. "That...that...can have no relevance," he stammered.

"You came with him to view the bodies after the fire, and this is your second visit to the morgue. You were here with him this morning."

The poet shook his head mutely, then licked his lips. "Death is one of the great themes. The death of a child is the ultimate tragedy."

"And the murder of a child is an even greater one?" Loisel was speechless again, so Michel asked, "This Vipèrine is a diabolist, is he not?"

"Do you believe such things?" Loisel whispered.

"Don't you? Or did belief die with your crisis of faith?"

"I cannot say." He shook his head. Michel maintained a dubious silence until Loisel swallowed hard and said, somewhat louder, "If one believes in God, one must learn the snares of the Devil."

Michel thought that most snares were quite obvious. He laid the photograph of the cross with the wings down in front of Jules. The poet looked frightened, but asked, "What is it?"

"This version of the cross has no significance for you?" Michel pushed it closer.

Loisel shoved back the chair and stood. "Truly, I know nothing. I have seen nothing."

Michel was tempted to badger him, but it was only frustration. Better to leave some questions to pursue later. "You can go."

Watching Loisel sidle out of the room, Michel reminded himself to remain detached. He must not want Vipèrine to be guilty, or Charron—any of them. Unless he studied the evidence dispassionately, he might overlook something. There was no guarantee that the killer had returned to the cemetery or the morgue. The Revenants had. Charron's father had. But so had a multitude of bartenders, cab drivers, milliners, tourists, and prostitutes—with and without their customers.

Michel invited Estarlian in. The baron answered his questions with icy politeness. The Revenants had heard of Alicia from Theo or from each other. They were all at the fire—with two thousand other people. Estarlian said Noret had encouraged them to come to the morgue, but it was to support Charron. "Instead, it was Theo who needed us, so it was a wise decision. Don't you agree, Inspecteur?"

"You did not only come to the morgue, Monsieur le Baron. You went, alone, to the cemetery and visited the tombstone."

"Why should I not? My closest friend had a horrifying experience. I went to see where it happened. To comprehend and to commiserate." Beneath the cold politesse, Estarlian simmered with anger. If he was lying, he did it superbly.

"What did you feel when he told you what he had discovered?"

"What would you expect me to feel? Shock. Horror. Disgust!" He paused for a moment, visibly seething, then stood. "Really, Inspecteur, this is ridiculous. I do not know what you expect to learn from us. We are not the sort of people who create obscene public spectacles."

"No? Poets are exempt?"

"The Revenants are exempt. I cannot speak for other groups. We have no Ubu Roi chanting obscenities like a crazed nutcracker." He gave a slight laugh. "Well, perhaps Noret, on occasion."

Ubu Roi was a play which had created a scandal earlier in the year. The first word that the bizarre Ubu spoke was '*merde.*'That single bit of scatology set off a riot in the theatre. With the taboo broken, Michel presumed it would soon become a commonplace vulgarity.

"Please sit down again," Michel said quietly. "There is another case about which I must ask you—unrelated to this."

Estarlian paused, frowning. "Another case?"

"The disappearance of Denis Armand. The son of a laundress who lived near Mlle. Faraday in Montmartre."

"Ah…yes. She mentioned it. So, I am her alibi?" He lifted a mocking eyebrow. "And, of course, she is mine. I don't remember the exact day, but I did take her to tea around that time."

"Do you often do so?" Michel asked.

Estarlian lifted an eyebrow. "Does that have some relevance to the disappearance of the little boy?"

None, except that she had said that the baron was not her lover. "Sometimes I discover what is relevant by asking questions which do not seem to be. I imagine that writing poetry may proceed in the same fashion."

Estarlian actually smiled at that. "Very well, Inspecteur. I do not see Mlle. Faraday often. I try to make her welcome to Paris because she is Averill Charron's friend. Perhaps every other month I escort her to her favorite tea shop, to the opera, to the ballet. We have ridden in the Bois de Boulogne. She is always an interesting companion—unique."

"Do you remember anything about that afternoon?"

"It was the last time we went to Ladurée. It was chilly and threatening to rain. She had a new dress, lavender and grey—not muted but stormy, like the sky."

"What time did you escort her home?"

"Perhaps five. It was dusk."

"And afterwards?"

The baron hesitated, obviously reluctant. But he could not know what the others might have said already. He offered a disarming smile. "I have a small apartment in Montmartre. It is mine but Averill shares some of the rent. We both find it...convenient. For amours, of course, but Montmartre inspires us both. We sometimes go there to work. I went to see if he was there."

"And was he?"

"Yes, but I did not speak to him. We have an agreed signal. I knew he did not wish to be disturbed. I returned home."

"Did you see him that weekend?

"I had business out of town, I believe. Yes. I was gone that weekend."

Michel nodded. He would question Charron again to confirm what he had just learned.

"Is that all? I am sorry not to be of more help. This is truly a despicable case." Estarlian's lips thinned with anger. "A poor young girl murdered and put on display for the masses to gawk at. The very idea is repellent."

"Yet we have discovered her identity."

Estarlian looked perplexed. "Ah...yes. Not this display at the morgue—I understand the necessity, however unpleasant. I was thinking of how my friend found her. Appalling."

Michel reached for the folder of photographs taken at the crime scene. He had no intention of revealing that Denis' murder was linked to Alicia's, but he would show the baron the new mark. The Revenants would, of course, discuss what had happened today. He hoped Theo would not remember the cross in her alley. It was just one scribble among more eye-catching offenses, but she was observant.

Estarlian lifted his hands in protest. "Please. I do not want to see your photos. The corpse in the window was pathetic enough."

"Yet you came to the morgue and visited the grave."

"For my friend's sake."

Friend. Did he mean it in the intimate sense? Could the baron be Charron's partner in this? Michel opened the folder. "I will not show you anything repellant."

The baron inclined his head. "Thank you."

"When you went to the cemetery, did you notice this?" Michel laid out the photo of the back of the gravestone. Estarlian went very still, staring down at the photo. Michel felt electric excitement crackle along his nerves. He kept his voice calm. "You recognize it."

"I did not see this at the cemetery."

"But you have seen it." Michel had no doubt. "Where?"

Estarlian responded with another question, "This has something to do with the murdered girl?"

"Perhaps. Perhaps not," Michel said. "So you must tell me where you saw it."

"It is some meaningless scribble," Estarlian said, his jaw tensing. "Graffiti is everywhere in Paris—even graveyards."

"This mark is not everywhere. Tell me where you saw it."

Estarlian was reluctant, smoothing his gloves over his fingers. Michel did not push, for now the baron was implicated by his own silence. Still studying his gloves Estarlian said, "I have seen something similar by the Seine—but it was months ago."

Months? Frustration warred with eagerness. "Where exactly?"

"Near the Pont Neuf. There was a dog groomer…" Estarlian glanced up briefly, almost defiantly, then looked down again. "She was supposed to pick up the wretched poodle that belonged to Averill's grandmother and take it for a bath. She did not come. Averill and I were going to the *bouquinistes* that morning, so we were given the errand of finding the woman."

Michel forced himself to silence, waited.

"We found her where she usually washed the dogs—but she was quite mad with grief, poor woman. Her little boy had vanished."

"Why did you notice the mark?"

"She was kneeling in front of it, praying—it was, after all, a cross of sorts." Estarlian shrugged. "Probably it is meaningless. Everyone said the child must have fallen in the Seine."

"When was this?" Michel asked.

"It was barely warm enough to be washing dogs outside. Last October?"

"Can you show me where you found the mark?"

"It will have been rained away by now." The baron frowned. "But of course I can show you where it was."

Estarlian was right. All that remained was a blurred stroke and a faint line that might have been the upper sweep of a wing. Michel would never have noticed it. Asking others on the bank, he learned that the grieving mother was no longer here. She believed her child had drowned and left Paris not long after he disappeared. She had not been on his list.

Now he had three victims marked with a winged cross. Had the little boy been snatched here? Killed here? Standing in the shadow of the bridge, Michel stared across the Seine. This site was too close to the Palais de Justice. He felt as if the killer was laughing at him.

Whoever the killer might be.

Chapter Twenty~Three

My peers are fired even as I am…
ardent and breathless before life's
intensity, its bright fires of knowledge.
Emile Verhaeren

"Down with women! Down with women!"

The shouts of the male students clanged in Theo's head, as she watched them march inside the huge iron gates of the École des Beaux Arts. She had woken groggy and wretched after crying late into the night, but determined to meet Carmine here, for Mélanie's sake.

"They are yapping dogs." Carmine didn't yap, she snarled.

"Puppies with power," Theo agreed unhappily. Her headache grew worse with each angry shout. She probably should have gone back with Averill yesterday, but she'd needed to be alone after seeing Alicia in the morgue.

"Out with the women! Out! Out! Out!"

"No!" "Stop!" "Cowards!" Cries rose from the crowd as a new pack of male students drove the two distraught women students across the vast courtyard, through the gate, and into the street. The protesters outside quickly drew them into the center of a protective circle. Theo had seen the same arrogance and brutality when she marched for the vote in San Francisco. Why had she expected Frenchmen to be any better, especially when they granted their women even less power than American men did? Her friends were the exception, and even they preferred the image of the perfect muse—a seductive, destructive Salomé who would rend their souls the better to inspire their poems.

"Go back to your embroidery!" a whey-faced student taunted.

"Go back to your diapers!" Another student surged to the front of the pack. He looked like a scruffy fox—a rabid fox. "You can use baby *caca* for your paints!"

"They are the ones full of *caca*," Carmine fumed. "Only men can create *le grand art*! You remember Mélanie's Cassandra."

"It was beautiful!" Theo affirmed as insults pelted them like rocks. "It was everything they say art should be and it had soul. It had passion."

"That's why they didn't give it an award. Too much life. Not posed pain—real pain. They need their art to be dead, like a rabbit strung up for a still life."

The futility of Mélanie's sacrifice tormented Theo, but Carmine brought back Mélanie's hope for her art, her courage in fighting for what she believed. The demonstrating women shared that hope and that courage.

"Your brains are stuffed full of ruffles!" the whey-faced one sang out, winning hoots of laughter from his friends.

Theo thrust off the smothering misery of the morgue and stalked to the gates, looking into the paved quadrangle where the irate students marched and shouted. Men she presumed to be professors and administrators hovered anxiously in the background, but some of the male students and teachers squeezed through the gates to join the growing crowd supporting the women. Turning to look across the street, Theo saw a man who must be a journalist scribbling madly in a notebook. Behind him, half-hidden in the arch of a corner doorway, a young woman watched the protesters. Theo caught her eye and beckoned her to join them. She smiled a little but shook her head, looking anxiously from side to side.

"You're ruining everything!" a petulant voice called out. "All sorts of stupid new rules and restrictions came trailing on your petticoats."

"We don't need new rules!" Theo shouted back, adding her voice to the other women. "We don't want special treatment! We want the same treatment, the same classes, the same models!"

"And the same medals!" Carmine yelled. "That's why you're really afraid! You'll have to compete with women for the prizes you've been keeping to yourselves."

"Why should I be afraid of that!" another student taunted. "No woman is better than I am!"

Remembering Mélanie, Theo seethed with scorn. "These women got higher scores than you did."

That brought a deluge of cries. "Liar!" "Bribery!" "You don't belong here!" "You belong on your backs!"

The whey-faced student yelled out above the others. "Go find yourself a husband!"

The scruffy fox lifted his cane above his head, waving it furiously. "Yes! A husband will teach you to paint with your tongue!"

The men laughed and wagged their tongues at them. The crass insults gave Theo a surge of furious energy. "Did you swing the same cane at the Charity bazaar?" she yelled at the fox. "Did you beat your way through those women too?"

"I was never there!" he yelled back, though the whey-face one suddenly turned even paler and backed out of sight. The fox looked stunned, then shrugged off the defection.

Theo put a hand to her head, remembering the painful cut that some man had inflicted. Hot anger flowed through her. "You are just as much of a coward!" she accused the fox. "More of a coward. Your life's not at risk—just your vanity!"

Suddenly, the woman she had seen half-hiding in the doorway darted from her haven and ran down the street. Perhaps because of their silent communication, she came straight to Theo and Carmine. She was quite petite, barely five feet. She had a gentle, shy countenance, lit by eyes full of steely determination. The young woman pointed back down the cross street. "The police are coming," she warned. "I saw them at the end of the block."

"Let's hope they arrest these men!" Carmine said. "But with our luck, they'll punish us for daring to protest."

"Go now," one of the women students said to the protesters. "But thank you for joining us."

"We should leave," Theo said to Carmine as the women began to disperse.

"I will walk with you to the corner and circle back around. I don't want to be arrested!" the young woman said.

Quickly they walked down the rue Bonaparte toward the quai. "You're American, aren't you?" Theo asked their companion.

She nodded. "Yes, and you?"

"From Mill Valley, California. That's near San Francisco. My name is Theodora Faraday."

"And I am Julia Morgan. We were neighbors. I am from Oakland. I came to Paris last year because the École promised women would soon be admitted."

"You see they will use any excuse to refuse you," Carmine muttered, squaring her shoulders. She set her hat at a jauntier angle and plucked at her sleeves to puff them out.

"I want to study architecture," Julia said firmly. "This is the most prestigious school in the world. There is no equivalent."

"What are you doing meanwhile?" Carmine asked.

"I am working in the architecture atelier of Marcel de Monclos and submitting my designs to international competitions."

"Have you won any?" Carmine asked.

"Indeed I have. I am gaining a reputation. Surely the École will admit me."

"Surely they will," Theo affirmed.

"Perhaps," Carmine said gloomily.

Julia stopped when they turned the corner that brought the Seine into view. "I must go back to work."

"*Bonne chance*," Theo wished her good luck. Tiny and soft-spoken as she was, Julia obviously had the tenacity to triumph over the forces allied against her sex. "I can cross the bridge and walk to the Charrons' from here," Theo told Carmine. She could not think of it as Averill's home. He felt as much a prisoner there as she had.

"I will walk with you—I need to burn off some of this energy, or I will go home and pick a fight with my father!" Carmine laughed at herself, then eyed Theo more seriously. "Let's stop for a cup of chocolate and you can tell me what has been bothering you."

With so much happening, Theo had hoped Carmine did not notice how glum she was. "I did not sleep well," she equivocated, then was furious with herself.

"You did not sleep well because?" Carmine asked pointedly.

"Let's sit." Theo pointed to a small *café* near the next corner. They went inside and Theo chose a little booth in the back, far from the other customers. The croissant she ordered was stale but the food calmed the wooziness she felt. The quiet interior and the warming hot chocolate subdued her headache as well.

"Tell me," Carmine insisted.

"It is as terrible as Mélanie's death," Theo warned. "Worse."

"Worse?" Carmine laid a hand over hers. She wore coquettish little black lace gloves. Theo stared at them in fascination, her mind trying to find some escape. But there was none. "The little girl that I helped Mélanie rescue from the fire is dead. She has been murdered."

For once, Carmine was speechless. Theo told her of Averill's discovery of the body and of yesterday morning at the *café*—how her cousin had begun a poem about the murdered girl that he could not finish and needed to see her at the morgue.

"Artists are ruthless. If they are not, then they are not artists," Carmine said. "Seers must not lie about what they see."

Theo smiled faintly. "Paul says the same."

"You don't believe it?"

"It was something I thought I believed. Perhaps I still do, but with my head, not my heart. My heart just wants to mourn."

"I think perhaps your head is judging the impulse of your heart.

You want to find a way to exorcise the horror, but your head says it is selfish or unseemly. Your heart is more honest."

"Perhaps you are right, but it is hard not to feel guilty."

"No emotion is more useless than guilt. Your art is as worthy a tribute as any tears."

Theo continued about the visit to the morgue. "It's a horrible place— a ghoulish picnic."

"Death makes people feel alive. Especially the death of strangers." Carmine gave a philosophical shrug.

When Theo at last described seeing Alicia's pale corpse, what detachment she had faltered. She had to fight off crying yet again. Carmine gripped her hands more tightly. Theo managed to finish the rest of the events, ending with her silent trip back to Montmartre with Averill. "I promised to visit him this afternoon. He's worried." Theo felt wretched for her fury at the morgue. Anger and grief had flung her about like the waves of a tempest.

"So you are all suspects, I suppose?" Carmine broke into her thoughts.

"Yes." Theo bristled. "I told the detective to investigate that blue-bearded creature I saw at the catacombs and then at the morgue. He looks like he would enjoy murder."

"This is truly bizarre, Theo." Carmine paused. "But it is less bizarre if it is deliberate."

"Deliberate?" Theo stared at her blankly. Of course murder was deliberate.

"I believe Alicia was not taken at random. She was taken because you rescued her."

Theo stared at her. "No one hates me like that. No one would devise such a convoluted way to torment me—by torturing an innocent child!"

"Hate. Love. How could anyone do such a thing? The Tarot said you are in the middle of a battle between good and evil. What you describe is the epitome of evil."

It was too terrifying to believe. Theo envisioned the images of The Devil and the gleaming Moon spread out before her. She saw Death. The memory was a sinister undertow pulling her toward darkness. "I still don't trust the cards. Mélanie was certain the Tower was about her entry into the École des Beaux-Arts. It made perfect sense to all of us."

"The cards did not mislead us, we misled ourselves," Carmine said earnestly.

Theo still felt deceived and knew Carmine could see it in her face.

"The cards did not cause the fire. The cards could not have caused Alicia's terrible murder."

Theo frowned. "But they didn't help me stop it."

Carmine leaned forward. "Three cards were too few for a clear picture. Let me give you another reading. Take what help you can, Theo."

"Not now." Not ever would be better. The cards had allure when they were a charming myth, something half-believed for the pleasure of it. Not as a premonition of horror. Theo pushed away her chocolate and stood. "I promised Averill I would visit him after the protest."

Carmine stood as well. "I still want to walk with you."

They left the shabby little *café*, crossed the Pont du Carrousel, strolled alongside the Louvre, and continued into the gardens of the Tuileries. The cool green of the ordered park and the rain-like music of the fountains helped soothe Theo's frayed nerves. "Look, the *giroflées* are blooming."

Carmine smiled. They knelt briefly to sniff the fragrant wallflowers. Their bright gold contrasted with the vivid scarlet of the geraniums and charming faces of the purple pansies. As difficult as it had been to relive yesterday, Theo was glad she'd shared her unhappiness with Carmine. Sensing her mood, Carmine linked an arm through hers and they walked in silence through the gardens and along the boulevards, sharing the comfort of each other's presence until they reached the entrance to the Charrons' residence.

Carmine kissed both Theo's cheeks and walked back toward the park. Theo remained outside, still hesitating. She hungered for Averill's comfort, the sound of his voice, his touch—yet the thought of him feverishly writing his poem about Alicia was a physical pain that made her shy away. But she had promised, so she went up the steps to the door and pulled the bell.

Her favorite of the maids, Bettine, greeted her warmly and asked if she was joining Madame Charron's gathering. Theo heard skittish laughter from the parlor. The sound cut across her nerves like a serrated blade. It was Friday, and every Friday her aunt's friends took turns playing hostess at their cocaine parties. The drug was quite the rage with Parisian high society ladies, having taken over from morphine. They considered cocaine quite harmless, but Theo knew it could be utterly destructive. When young Henry Faraday inherited the ranch she had called home, he sold off everything—the house, the land, the horses she loved—and partied for a year. Much of the money entered syringes. Another chunk went for liquor bottles and loose women. The rest to gambling. And for the car, of course, the one he crashed and died in—too drunk to crawl out before the gasoline fumes ignited and burned him alive.

Theo looked askance at the parlor, dreading that sharp, artificial exuberance. "No, Bettine," she began, but just then Aunt Marguerite appeared in the salon doorway. She looked startled to see Theo but beckoned to her. There was no escape.

"Do I look presentable?" Theo whispered to Bettine.

"Yes, miss. Everyone else in tea gowns, of course," the maid warned.

Theo entered the parlor with its traditional *Toile de Jouy* wallpaper of frolicking shepherds and shepherdesses and its plush red velvet sofas. Vases of fragrant pink and white tea roses were set about on the tables with artful casualness. Theo greeted her aunt formally and was introduced to her friends. She was glad she had not worn black for Mélanie today. Her muted lavender shirtwaist was a suitable color for mourning but would not lead to questions she did not want to answer and answers these women did not want to hear. She perched on the nearest chair, hoping she could flee soon. Tea was being served in the best sterling service. On the table in front of the largest sofa, a platter of elaborate petit fours was all but untouched. With their smooth marzipan coating tinted in various pastels, they looked exquisite but hardly real. On a separate table, jeweled hypodermic needles were laid out. The atmosphere was hectic, the women laughing too much, their movements quick and nervous.

"It seems a sprightly party, Madame Charron," Theo lied, smiling too brightly at the ladies gathered in the parlor.

"Sprightly indeed." Her aunt's eyes glittered with excitement. To the others she said, "Theo is quite artistic, you know. She is the ward of my brother-in-law, and he permits her to study painting."

Permits? Theo prickled.

A woman in chartreuse ruffles straightened her already perfect posture and frowned severely. "The world of modern art is degenerating."

Beside her, a lady in puce said fervently, "True, but women can help lead it back onto its true path of virtuous ideals. We have forsaken our spiritual mission."

Theo fought the urge to argue. What miniscule chance she had of changing their minds would shrink to zero with the cocaine buzzing through their veins. Her aunt was unhappy enough without Theo making a scene. Instead she composed a painting in her mind with the wildly clashing colors of the gowns lurid against the red velvet sofa. She put the petit fours in the center, sugary sweet, their pastel tints vapid versions of the bright green and pink dresses.

"You are fortunate that your *guardien* indulges you so," Puce said archly, "but of course he is also a painter." From her tone Theo could not tell if the woman thought he was her father or her lover.

"Yes. He understands the artistic impulse," her aunt answered for her.

"I am very fortunate," Theo affirmed. She knew how lucky she was to have been given this world. She had freedom and money enough to keep that freedom. But if she had to, she would tend bar and paint on her own, as she had in Jagtown on the fringe of Mill Valley.

"Theo is living in Montmartre now," her aunt said, rather slyly, Theo thought. Hoping to stir up some controversy? Theo saw disapproval on most faces, but at least one duplicated the envy she sometimes saw in her aunt's eyes. Then her aunt touched Theo's arm and gestured to the hypodermics. "Two of us bought new accessories. Tell us your opinion."

"Show me your new…accessories," Theo said, feeling utterly hypocritical. But she could endure another few minutes before making her escape.

"I found this at—"

"Don't tell her where you got it," her aunt said sharply. "She may be biased by the maker."

Theo knew that argumentative edge. With great caution she examined the gold syringe set with peridots and emeralds. Beside her, Aunt Marguerite proudly displayed a silver syringe set with moonstones, opals, aquamarines and turquoise. At last Theo said, "The gold is a beautiful, balanced classical design and is perhaps the most technically excellent. But the silver has an innovative beauty that I find more appealing."

That seemed to satisfy them, if not provide a clear victory. Theo begged for tea to distract them from further discussion. She guessed that her aunt's prize came from L'Art Nouveau, Theo's own favorite luxury shop, filled with gorgeous objects in the most modern and inventive styles—glass by Tiffany and dazzling jewelry by Lalique. Her uncle would not see it, or her aunt would have bought something more conservative.

"I knew you would love it," Aunt Marguerite whispered conspiratorially as she handed Theo her cup of tea. Her aunt smiled with delight, and for a moment Theo saw the vivacity that must have once sparkled in her. That vibrant Marguerite should be holding salons for poets and artists, not cocaine parties for bored ladies of the bourgeoisie. The Marguerite that Theo liked was all but crushed by evil Uncle Charron. She was not permitted to hold any opinion that differed from his—unless it was frivolously feminine enough not to threaten his authority. Perhaps Theo could encourage her to live vicariously a bit more. She would invite her aunt to help her choose a new dress from a creative designer in one of the less expensive boutiques.

As if to prove she had a happy marriage, Aunt Marguerite began to brag about her children. She emphasized Francine's docility and spoke fervently of how pleased Averill's father was with his success at medical school. Theo knew how well he did depended on how ardently he was pursuing a poem and how much absinthe he drank. It was his sister Jeanette who'd urged him to quit school, to leave home before their father broke his spirit. Become a poet. He'd listened to Jeanette and left, despite his mother's tearful entreaties to stay. But when Jeanette died, he yielded to Marguerite's tearful entreaties to return.

When the conversation flagged, Theo begged a headache. Her aunt excused her. "You'll stay for dinner, won't you? You won't want to miss a chance to see Eulalie—" she gave Theo another sly sideways glance. "—or Averill. I don't think either of them is home just now."

Did her aunt know she was attracted to Averill? Could she possibly approve? Theo managed a bland smile as she rose. "Thank you, Madame Charron. Your meals are always delicious."

She left them to their gossip—she was probably the main topic now. In the hall, she asked Bettine when Averill was expected home. It did not matter so much now that she was committed to dinner, but she was surprised when Bettine gestured down the hallway. "Monsieur Averill is at home, mademoiselle." Bettine gave a nervous glance down the hall then whispered, "He is in his father's study." No one was supposed to go into Uncle Urbain's study unless invited.

Theo thanked Bettine and made her way to the end of the hallway, bright in the glow of the crystal chandeliers. She hesitated, then knocked lightly at the door of the study. "Averill, it's me," she called, wanting him to know it wasn't his father.

After a long pause, Averill responded, "Come in."

Theo turned the handle of the door and went inside.

Chapter Twenty~Four

I, whom some call poet,
within the muted night
I am the secret staircase;
I am the staircase Darkness.
Within my deathly spiral
the shadow opens its dim eyes.
                              Victor Hugo

Here no lamp shone and heavy burgundy velvet curtains muted the sun. Waiting for her eyes to adjust to the shadowy interior, Theo inhaled the opulent scent of books, their expensive paper, ink, and leather mingling with aromas of pipe tobacco and lemon-polished wood. Ahead of her, the massive carved desk gleamed dully. But no one sat behind it. Papers were scattered across the top, their black-spattered whiteness striking in the gloom.

There was a soft noise off to the side. Theo turned. Averill emerged from the dark corner of the study, his shirt white as the paper.

But something...someone...lay in the room between them.

A woman. Naked. Hideously murdered—her body cut open from throat to sex, the exposed organs glistening horribly like entrails on a butcher's block.

Theo lurched back toward the door, fear and disbelief choking the scream rising in her throat. Only a gasp escaped.

Averill gave a sharp bark of laughter. Hard as a slap. "She's wax."

"Wax," Theo rasped, her mouth so dry she could barely hear herself. She saw now there was no blood. None on what she had imagined was a woman. None on Averill. The edges of the open body were smooth.

He turned on the newly installed electric lamp. Artificial brightness illuminated the thing lying between them. It rested in a display case with sides that lowered, leaving the figure reclining in full view. The cavity showed larynx and lungs, heart and intestines. Inside the womb, a tiny child. The wax skin gleamed softly.

"She looks real," Theo whispered.

"A month ago…a week ago…you would not have thought she was human." His eyes glittered with accusation. "You would not have thought I could murder someone."

"I had no time to think. I was shocked." Anger burned over her shame. "After what we have both seen, do you truly blame me?"

Averill looked ashamed now. He lowered his gaze, shook his head mutely.

She gestured at the figure. "What is it?"

"She is my father's most prized possession—an anatomical Venus from Italy."

"She looks like a Botticelli," Theo said. The red gold hair evoked the Renaissance painter. Even the shape of the body resembled the work she had seen in the Louvre.

"A slaughtered Botticelli—very neatly slaughtered." He gestured to where the front of her torso sat propped on a chair, small perfect breasts, curving rib cage and rounded belly. A lid of molded wax.

Theo stepped closer, horrified and fascinated by the perfect creation, so incredibly detailed. The face showed tiny russet hairs inset for her eyebrows and eyelashes. A rope of pearls was woven through her long hair and another circled her neck demurely. She reclined on a long cushion of pink velvet that matched the pink flush of cheeks and lips… and the soft pink of the lips revealed beneath the auburn curls between her legs. Her face was turned toward Theo, her green glass eyes half-open, her lips parted slightly.

"She would win a prize at the Salon, wouldn't she?" Averill asked. "She's just the sort of erotic image they dote upon. So perfect they can pretend she's the ideal of beauty—even if they go home and…" He stopped himself.

"She's obscene."

"Isn't she, though." He picked up the missing section. "She wears a breastplate, like Jeanne d'Arc, but a breastplate of her own waxen flesh. Lift it off and see the hidden treasure trove. Replace it—" He lowered the section back onto her, "—and you have a wax sculpture beautiful as a Renaissance Venus."

"Thank you," Theo said, relaxing a little once the gaping cavity was covered. Yet once you knew her secret, it was difficult not to think of the butchered version.

"You're welcome." It was almost a sneer. Theo winced at the harshness. This close she could smell the absinthe on his breath. "Tell me, Theo, is this Venus a victim…or a seductress?"

"Averill…" She faltered.

"Father used to keep her in his office." Averill lifted an edge of the figure's ribcage to release a curl trapped in the seam of the body. "He showed her to me to lure me into medicine. He knew a young boy would be fascinated by such a replica. It's a favorite theme in painting too, you know—the dissection room. Doctors gathered around the corpse of a beautiful whore, eager for the pillaging."

Theo fought a surge of queasiness. Averill was angry at her, trying to upset her. "You didn't mention her before."

"Why should I have?" He was sneering again, bitter and impenetrable. She hated when the absinthe dragged him into its shadows. He raised the sides of the case and enclosed the anatomical Venus back inside her glass coffin.

"You told me so much," she whispered, her heart twisting at his coldness.

"Father brought her here after you left." Averill's eyes flashed with sudden anger. "Maybe he knew how much I missed you."

"I did not want to leave *you*," she said.

"I didn't want you to leave—but I helped you." His hand was hard on her wrist, pulling her closer. She forgot how strong he was sometimes. His gaze was still accusing. "From the first, I could talk to you."

"You can talk to me now. I'm here."

"I've been talking with Venus. But she's not as amusing as you. She has no opinions of her own." He smiled grimly. "Probably why Father dotes on her."

Abruptly he released her wrist and walked to the desk. "I began a pantoum for this Venus—I did tell you, didn't I?"

She ignored the sarcasm dripping from his voice. "Yesterday at the *café.*" Was it only yesterday?

Lifting one of the pages, Averill read,

Elle t'invite à sonder la mort,
Pour découvrir de tendres secrets.
Son corps s'ouvre comme une porte,
Où se dénouent des rêves vermeils.

He stopped abruptly, despondent.

The poem uncoiled in Theo's mind. *She invites you to explore death. To discover tender secrets. Her body opens like a door—where unravel crimson dreams.* Then she remembered. "Two poems."

"Yes—unhappy twins. *La grande et la petite Venus.*"

"Twins?" He'd told her the child in the cemetery had been nude. She had been displayed. Tortured. Alicia had been tortured. Cut open like this?

Her vision wavered. Theo thought she would faint. She walked to the desk and gripped the front of it, feeling the wood hard against her hands. She must not show weakness now. She must not swoon. She must not weep. Averill would take pity on her but he would stop talking and shut himself away.

He came to her swiftly. His hands took hold of her arms, tight enough to bruise. Yet his touch was meant for comfort, she was sure. He could not know he was hurting her. She stood up straight and instantly he released her. She faced him. He was so close, his gaze searching hers. Then he closed his eyes and some emotion rippled under his skin. Pain— or was it still anger?

"*La petite Alicia.*" Averill turned away and went to the far side of the desk. Bending down, he rifled through a wastebasket and drew up some scraps of torn paper, sprinkling them on the desk like confetti. "I've ripped up the poem about your little girl—but I can't rip the words out of my brain, any more than I can rip out the images I have of her."

"I know you have to write it." The words were reluctant, almost a whisper. Averill could not help that he was haunted by Alicia, any more than she could help that Mélanie walked through fire in her dreams.

"You will hate me." His gaze was unflinching now, and there was a grim satisfaction in his words.

She responded vehemently. "I will never hate you."

"You hated me yesterday."

"No!" Was that why he was so upset? It must be. Yesterday she had refused his help. Now he was refusing her. "I hated that Alicia was dead. I didn't hate you any more than I hated the whole world."

A smile twisted his lips. "The whole world hasn't made a poem of her murder."

"Perhaps, in a little while, I will want to read the poem."

"Will you? You don't want to read this one." He gestured to the reclining Venus. Then, watching Theo closely, he quoted,

Pour découvrir de tendres secrets,
Tes doigts cherchent dans le doux abîme
Où se dénouent des rêves vermeils,
En éveillant un plaisir impie.

To discover tender secrets, your fingers search in the sweet abyss where unravel crimson dreams, awakening a blasphemous pleasure. The repeated lines made it more nightmarish, more perverse. Theo shuddered as the images pried at her mind, but she refused to look away.

It was Averill who dropped his gaze. "I don't know how else to exorcise the horror. If I don't write the poem, I will become the darkness. But even if I do—" he broke off, despairing.

"What?" she pleaded.

"It's all tangled." He shook his head, still refusing to face her. "All knotted. Impossible."

"I will untangle it—or cut the knot." Theo went to him, gripping him as he had taken hold of her, hard so he would feel the force of her promise.

He pulled away. "At first, I thought that you were like Jeanette, come back to me. A new sister."

"At first?"

He lifted his eyes to hers, defiant now. "Now I don't think of you as a sister, except as Baudelaire meant it—the sister of my soul."

"I feel the same," she whispered.

"I thought I could save you. If only from loneliness." He laughed softly. "Then I thought perhaps you could save me."

"Save you from what?" She knew he was dreadfully unhappy—who would not be miserable in this wretched house? But why did he hate himself so much?

"You are sunshine, so bright you hurt my eyes," he whispered, cupping her face in his hands. "I want to look—then I want to snuff it out."

"You can't snuff out the sun." Her heart was hammering wildly, but she smiled a little. This close, the scent of him filled her. Absinthe mingled with the fresh smell of his linen, washed in lavender water, and the teasing musk of his skin.

"I shouldn't love you," he said. "I destroy what I love."

He loved her. She could see desire in his eyes, burning like blue flame. She could see the pain too, even if she barely understood it. He pulled her against him, his body lean and hard. She was stunned by his force, by the power of his hands. Joy and fear mingled in a crazy cacophony. One moment she was stiff in his arms, unsure, then she melted against him. He kissed her, his lips lush and warm against hers even in their fierceness. Her mouth opened beneath his, taking him deeper. The bittersweet taste of absinthe was suddenly delicious. Intoxicating. Behind her closed eyelids, the blackness flamed scarlet and gold and black. She wanted to plunge into it. She wanted to escape yesterday. Averill was the only one who truly understood that. They needed each other. Needed understanding. Needed oblivion. She pressed the length of her body against him, matching his ferocity.

With a moan, Averill broke away. He looked hungry, as if he could devour her. Then the flame died in his eyes. He was suddenly weary, despondent. She kissed him again, trying to call him back to her. "Averill…"

"It's wrong," he said, tense and trembling in her embrace. "It's impossible."

She thrust away all the arguments she had made herself. "Other cousins—"

"—No!" he broke in. "I'll pull you into my darkness."

"I'm not afraid of your darkness."

"You're lying," he said.

Once it had been true. Now she wasn't sure. She tightened her arms around him. "Why can't you come into the light? Just a little?"

"Because I see myself too clearly." He pushed her away hard.

Theo stumbled against the desk. Shocked, she watched him stalk across the room. "Averill!"

He stopped for one instant, pressing his fists to the door. Then he walked out and left her alone.

Chapter Twenty~Five

*Idealism enslaves thought as
politics enslaves will.*
Mikhail Bakunin

When Michel went to Urbain Charron's luxurious office off the Champs Élysées, he was told that the doctor was lecturing at Salpêtrière Hospital. He thanked the secretary, regretting that he had no excuse to explore further. Though the rich neighborhood was well patrolled by gendarmes, the office would be quiet at night and well equipped for slaughter. He hired a carriage to the Left Bank. Salpêtrière had first been a gunpowder arsenal, then a notorious insane asylum—a fetid dumping ground for diseased prostitutes and beggars, and an equally insalubrious hospice for aged and feeble women. But in the last fifty years the asylum had been reformed and expanded to become one of Europe's most advanced institutions, specializing in neurological disorders.

When Michel asked the guardian at the desk where he could find Urbain Charron, the man mistook him for a doctor and told him the lecture was in progress, he'd best hurry. Michel did not disabuse him but followed his directions along the hallways to an infirmary door. Beyond, he heard a low voice but no clear words. There were also what sounded like small whimpers of pain and an odd mechanical whirring. Michel prayed it was not to be an experiment in vivisection.

When he entered he was shocked to see a naked woman spread-eagled on a table directly in front of him, her knees lifted and held back with leather cuffs and chains. Some sort of rubber gag was wedged between her teeth. She was the centerpiece to a group of a dozen men standing on either side, observing her. Something was suspended from the ceiling on a pulley, and held in the possession of a solid man in a highly expensive suit who stood with his back to Michel. The noise ceased abruptly as the man turned, holding the suspended object—some sort of motor with a gun-shaped implement at the end of a snaking tube.

"You're late, doctor."

"I apologize," Michel said, not wanting to be dismissed from the lecture. This must be Urbain Charron.

The doctor frowned and gestured for him to join the others. "With all due respect to Hippocrates, the modern vibrator is far superior to the classic method of manual vulvular massage. Truly a tedious procedure. While water therapy remains a useful alternate approach in the case of incarcerated hysterics, this new technique is without parallel. Restraints such as we have employed today will keep violent, frenzied, or vituperative patients under control until they achieve hysterical paroxysm." He nodded to the left. "You will be able to test the efficacy of the device yourselves in a few moments."

Glancing to the side, Michel saw two other patients pinioned and gagged while they awaited treatment. He was convinced that Charron had chosen their position to provide shock value to his lecture—and to humiliate the women.

"Such extreme methods are usually unnecessary in private practice, though some women gain a sense of security with the confinement." Charron turned on the vibrator again. The woman on the table jerked at the sound. She stared at Charron with hatred and then at the mechanism with abhorrence mixed with longing. He smiled slightly and turned it off. "This current portable instrument is far superior to previous models. It delivers five thousand pulses per minute and will quickly induce paroxysm. Women suffering from less severe cases of chronic hysteria can have their symptoms quickly alleviated by this suitably professional approach. While some need only come monthly to your office, others will feel compelled to have treatment weekly or even more often."

An eager murmur swept through the men as they considered how many lucrative patients they would be able to alleviate with the vibrator.

Charron turned on the vibrator, pressing it between the woman's labia until she moaned through the gag. He turned off the instrument and parted the woman's labia further. "You can see that her sexual organs are engorged and lubricated. The clitoris is erect. She is close to paroxysm. Like most hysterics she cannot achieve a natural release through union with the male but must have this perverse stimulation."

The woman flushed and her breathing grew more rapid. She looked desperately from one face to the next. Most of the men showed nothing more than scientific curiosity. Others showed disgust. A few were aroused and hiding it as best they could. Urbain Charron's expression was somber, but his eyes gleamed. He turned on the device again, then waited, deliberately, Michel thought. Shame, fear, and lust flashed across the woman's face. With the gag she could not form words, but she began to whimper. Charron pressed the buzzing head of the device against her exposed clitoris. Helpless, the woman thrust up, trying to attain more stimulation. Her eyes widened and a choked scream began building in her throat.

Michel turned and left the room, feeling tainted.

A few minutes later, Urbain Charron emerged. "That was most unprofessional."

"It depends on your profession. I am with the Sûreté."

The doctor stared, eyes filled with wariness. He swallowed hard. "My daughter?"

That was a curious first response. But he had lost one daughter. Did he fear to lose the other? "No."

Charron frowned angrily. "Has my wife been injured?"

"No. I apologize." Michel already detested the man, but there was no point in making him fear for his family's lives. "I've come to ask about your son."

The wariness returned full force. Charron assumed an air of disdain. "What has the Sûreté to do with drunks?"

"Very little, except when they place themselves in the center of a murder investigation."

"What?" Urbain Charron looked stunned, then outraged. This time his response did not appear fake, which disappointed Michel immensely. But he expected his killer to be good at deception.

"Your son didn't tell you he found the corpse of a child in the Montmartre cemetery?"

"No!" Charron snapped. "What was he doing there?"

"Seeking inspiration for his poetry. Or so he says."

"How typical. How degenerate." At first Urbain Charron had been angry, now he became calculating. Modulating his voice to a soft, patient, and subtly threatening tone, he said, "You cannot trust him, Inspecteur. My son is…not well. His perception is distorted."

"His choice of entertainment is peculiar," Michel said, "but he seems lucid."

"Appearances can be deceiving. Many of the patients here can assume the semblance of sanity."

"He is insane?"

Urbain Charron hesitated. "Unstable. The brilliant often are."

Michel wasn't sure why the doctor was stirring up doubt, but he was. Only, the man appeared uncertain how far to go. "Why did you presume I'd come about your daughter?"

The doctor glared at him, his eyes like chips of ice. "I have no intention of discussing these matters with you."

Michel could not demand it at this point, but he allowed himself a final prod. "The murder victim is one of several kidnapped children. I would like you to confirm your whereabouts on the evenings in question."

Urbain Charron swelled with outrage. His large hands closed into brutal fists, and he looked about to strike Michel. That would be grounds for arrest. But Charron guessed his intent and subsided. "You are insulting…" Charron said in a sibilant hiss, "…but the murder of children may justify it. My secretary will be instructed to give you the information you need—as long as you come and go before I arrive in my office. I do not wish to see you ever again."

Michel took his leave. Charron had said *the murder of children*, but he could have inferred more than one death from the kidnappings Michel had mentioned. Early next week he would gather the information Urbain Charron had so generously offered. Either the doctor was smug in his innocence, or he'd arranged alibis to cover the crimes. Michel could confront him again once he possessed more information.

A vile man. A glutton for power.

Taking another fiacre back to the Palais de Justice, Michel pushed this new puzzle piece around in his mind. Urbain Charron revolted him. The malicious torment he inflicted on the helpless women at the asylum had no direct relevance, but that, combined with his vivisection experiments, convinced Michel he was capable of almost anything. The doctor could easily be the evil genius behind these crimes, moving his son about like a pawn. Even if he was not involved with the kidnapped children, having such a father would warp any man. Had Averill Charron suffered ugly abuse at his father's hands and now inflicted it on children as powerless as he once was?

What would it be like to have such a man for a father? Both Michel's fathers had loved and protected him.

The fiacre stopped outside the Dépôt. Michel got out—and staggered. He stood exactly where his adoptive father's body had lain. Feigning calm, he forced himself to walk to the wall of the quai, to stare blindly at the Seine. Almost every day of his life, he walked past this place. He lived in Guillame Devaux's house. Michel had expected the March anniversary of the Commune to trigger guilt. He had been on guard. Now, unexpectedly, gratitude had left him vulnerable, and a single misstep unleashed the flood of pain.

Reality disappeared in the onslaught of memory. He heard the bomb explode outside the Palais de Justice. He saw Guillame Devaux lying dead in the street, his face contorted with agony, his body scattered in pieces. The man who had saved Michel's life had died because of him. He had loved Guillame Devaux as a father, and had come to hate him for not being his true father.

Michel had been eighteen. Old enough to know better, young enough not to care. The Commune cast a long shadow and Michel had found its darkness brighter than the pallid light of everyday life. He'd still felt bound to the past, to the Communards he'd worshipped with a boy's fervor. He'd still felt bound by blood to his cousin Luc, who had been the glowing symbol of that worship. Now Luc, hero of the Commune, had returned. Luc, who was dashing, articulate, brave—and utterly ruthless.

In 1883, Paris was again a shambles, the mammoth stock market crash only a year behind them. Wild speculation and borrowing had spiraled out of control. Banks all around France had collapsed and finally *l'Union Générale* floundered. The Catholic bank blamed its demise on the Jews and Freemasons, as if its own gluttonous greed, its falsified reports, had no bearing. France plummeted headlong into a recession that would last another decade. Guillame Devaux, brigadier of the Sûreté, had helped keep the peace in turbulent Paris. But keeping the peace meant oppressing the people. He'd spoken soberly of the perils of anarchy and warned of worse bloodshed, but the words Michel had once found wise constricted him like a straightjacket.

Defiant, he'd wanted words of passion, of rebellion. At her trial, the Commune's great heroine, Louise Michel, had cried out, "You decree that any heart which beats for freedom has the right to nothing but a lump of lead. I now claim mine. Let me live and I will go on crying for revenge. I shall avenge my fallen brothers. If you have any courage, you will kill me!"

Twenty-five thousand Communards had died or been executed, but they had not given Louise Michel her lump of lead. She had been deported. Now, twelve years after the fall of the Commune, she'd returned to Paris, her fiery spirit unquenched. Continuing her fight against oppression, she'd led a huge demonstration at the Esplanade of Les Invalides. Afterwards, a huge crowd marched across Paris. Loaves of bread were looted from bakers' shops. Louise Michel was charged with instigating the looting. Ever fearless, she'd turned herself in to the police.

Montmartre was in an uproar. Their heroine was arrested because some tag-alongs had stolen bread. Who could blame them? They stole because they were starving! Anger simmered hotly under the cold, heavy lid of fear. Everyone believed the protesters would go to jail—or worse, be gunned down just as during the Commune. The *cafés* were filled with furious arguments and songs of revolution.

Michel had shared their zeal. He remembered sitting in Le Rat Mort on a cold, wet day, drinking red wine and feeling like a man. Surrounding him were tables filled with the glorious riffraff of Montmartre—musicians, artists, poets, radical journalists and even more radical anarchists. Craziness became the ultimate sanity, bourgeois sobriety the death of the spirit. Michel's hair had grown long and shaggy. He tossed it out of his eyes as he quoted Kropotkin's *Anarchist Manifesto*, "We demand bread for all, work for all, freedom and justice for all."

That was when his cousin reappeared, sliding into the chair beside him. "For words such as those," Luc said, "Kropotkin was sentenced to five years' imprisonment."

He looked a little like Michel's true father, with finer bones and a more olive coloring than Michel had inherited. Luc's easy surface charm barely concealed an inner ferocity. Michel responded to both instantly. The past was not dead. It was alive, here, now, with this man. Michel had found his true family again.

Luc filled him brimful of tales of woe and triumph. He told Michel how he'd fought at Père Lachaise cemetery, the final bastion of the Communards. Michel envisioned the thick early morning fog that gave way to drizzling showers. He saw the cherry trees dripping rain like tears. Then the army blew open the gates and rushed upon them. The Communards fought hand to hand with the enemy amid the tombs. Most died in the battle. Those captured were lined up against a wall and shot. Luc claimed he was the fabled last man on the barricade, that he fired the last shot before he walked off into the mist. Paris wasn't safe, so he took a new name and vanished.

"Where did you go?"

"Many places, Algeria, Madagascar, Dahomey. I was dealing guns two years ago in Abyssinia. I had a partner, but he took sick, Arthur Rimbaud."

"The poet?"

Luc smiled. "A poet? Oh, I doubt that. Rimbaud was a cold-blooded, mercenary creature. He read nothing but books on engineering."

Filled with hero worship, Michel believed him. Now he thought his cousin knew what stories would thrill him, as he had when Michel was a child. Of course, Luc told him stories about his parents, things he barely remembered, things he never knew. And, of course, they talked politics. The dream of anarchy—the triumph of the honest poor over the corrupt rich.

"What would be the perfect revolutionary act?" Luc asked him one day.

"For me? To rescue Louise Michel."

Luc smiled. "And how would you achieve that?"

"She goes to trial in June." Michel had fantasies, but he knew they were just that. "She will be heavily guarded."

"In shackles."

That stirred his anger. "We could organize—"

"—and be gunned down in the streets, as always."

"A distraction then. A disruption."

Luc waited.

"A bomb." A spear of ice pierced Michel. He knew that Luc had led him to the idea.

"A bomb in the Palais de Justice." Luc's eyes glittered.

Michel hesitated. "An explosion to cause panic and in the chaos rescue Louise Michel?"

"Yes, of course." Luc leaned closer. "And how would you do it? Do it and escape?"

They argued about various targets within the Palais de Justice and about the structure of the time bomb. Michel could visit his adoptive father at will. He could saunter off and explore various parts of the building. Luc suggested the Café Louis, where the lawyers gathered for lunch. Somehow, he even acquired an advocate's robe. "I will walk unseen among them." He laughed. Michel argued that an empty trial room would be the ideal target. But there were seldom empty rooms. Cases piled up endlessly. Reporters flocked the halls along with the accused and their lawyers.

Luc shrugged. "We can send a warning."

"They would clear the building, but what if they searched for the bomb?"

"Stupidity can be fatal."

Michel had imagined killing. In fantasy, he'd climbed the ramparts, fighting to the death and taking the enemy with him. But even at the height of his rebellion, he was by then enough Guillame Devaux's son not to want to murder anyone. Perhaps Marcel Calais's son had also seen enough horror. He'd watched his mother starve to death. He'd seen bloody, bloated corpses in the street, crawling with maggots. He'd seen his sister raped and bayoneted. The soldiers had threatened him with the same before Guillame Devaux entered the abandoned building and saved him.

He was also enough Guillame Devaux's son to know of the million things that could go wrong when carrying out a crime.

Luc scoffed. "Do you think we'll blow ourselves up? We are not idiots."

The longer they talked, the more Michel resisted. The heroine of the Commune might be freed by a well-executed plan with many participants, but the most likely outcome would be slaughter in the streets. He felt both a coward and a fool when he expressed his doubt, but Luc only said, "I believe you are right. Rescue is impossible. Louise Michel might even refuse us. She is willing to be a martyr to the cause—to take that lump of lead into her heart."

"You thought all along it was a crazy idea," Michel accused.

Luc grinned at him. "I believe in crazy ideas. How else can I be an anarchist?"

Without his glorious plan, however futile, Michel felt bereft.

Leaning forward, Luc lowered his voice. "We cannot rescue Louise Michel, but nothing else needs change."

It had all changed for Michel. For a second he felt only confusion, then a cold weight sank to the pit of his stomach. "The bomb."

Luc's smile was hard. "Propaganda by deed."

Michel argued fiercely, "In *Le Révolté* Kropotkin says a structure based on centuries of history cannot be destroyed with a few kilos of dynamite."

"A few kilos are a beginning. Wave after wave of us will crash down on them. In the end, we will obliterate them."

"Or they us," Michel said.

Finally, Luc just laughed at the idea of no one dying. "What does it matter? I will try to stay alive, but if I die killing them, I will become a martyr for those who follow."

"Many are innocent," Michel protested.

"There are no innocent bourgeois," Luc said scornfully. Then, quoting Robespierre, "Pity is treason."

"Robespierre was a monster." Suddenly Michel was furious. "Pity is human."

"You haven't the belly for a revolutionary," Luc sneered. "Your father would be ashamed of you."

"My father fought to build a new world. All you want is to destroy."

They argued and Michel stalked off in a rage. When he went back to Luc's room the next day it was empty. Luc was gone. There was crumpled paper thrown away, bits and pieces of wire scattered about. There was a grainy substance Michel knew must be gunpowder. Luc planned to bomb the Palais de Justice. But when and where?

His cousin had acquired an advocate's robe. Luc had a sense of drama. He would not be able to resist walking invisible amongst the enemy. Michel knew where his father kept his extra weapons, knew the location of the key. He ran home, unlocked the drawer, and took out the weapon. His adoptive mother stood in the doorway, crying, not understanding what was wrong, only that something was. Then Michel looked up to find Guillame Devaux standing in the doorway. His father did not look perplexed at all, and Michel realized that he knew about Luc Calais. His belly became a black bottomless pit in the knowledge of his own stupidity and the enormity of his betrayal.

"Where has he gone?" his father asked him.

"The Café Louis."

"Stay here," his father said. "Give me your word."

Michel almost refused. He almost lied. Yet to have his word trusted was a terrible gift. "I give you my word," he whispered.

And then Guillame Devaux was gone.

Five minutes later he heard the explosion. From half a mile away, it was no louder than a gunshot. His word made no difference now. He ran to the Palais de Justice. The street outside and the courtyard leading to the *café* were almost impassable. But the police knew him and let him through. His father lay scattered in pieces—a bloody arm, a leg, the agonized head still attached to the cratered torso. He had found the bomb and carried it out of the *café*, hoping to fling it into the Seine.

The police took Michel to the detective's station. Overwhelmed with guilt, he went silently, but he did not think he could endure trial and prison. Dying would be easy, a cage unbearable. He told them he had warned his father. That at least was true. His father's compatriots did not arrest him. They brought him brandy. They offered sympathy. At first, he wondered why they did not suspect his involvement, for he must have been seen among the anarchists. But no one treated him like a leper. Finally he realized that they thought he'd been acting as a spy. His father had covered for him.

Michel thought his culpability would come out when they arrested Luc, but they did not capture his cousin. No one knew his true name. No one had seen him in Paris since the explosion. There were endless places Luc could have gone, but Michel only knew where he'd already been—Abyssinia, Algeria, Madagascar, Dahomey. Running guns, he'd said, but those names suggested a stint in the French Foreign Legion. Their troops had been used against the Communards, but after the slaughter, many desperate rebels had fled there.

So Michel lied his way into the Legion.

Chapter Twenty~Six

*I have kissed thy mouth. There was a bitter
taste on thy lips. Was it the taste of blood?
But perchance it is the taste of love…They
say that love hath a bitter taste….*

Oscar Wilde

Theo stood for a moment, stunned, then ran after Averill. The hall was empty, but she heard the front door slam. She would not chase him into the street. Clenching her fists, she sagged against the wall. She felt scraped bare, inside and out. Emotions raced along her nerves like fever chills, hot and cold ripples of anger, fear, and fierce desire.

Closing her eyes, Theo drew a deep breath. She could not continue to prop herself up in the back hall. The dinner invitation would give her another chance to talk to him.

She went upstairs to the guest room. Exhausted but too agitated to sleep, she paced and fretted, tried to read, paced again. "He loves me too," she whispered fervently.

Whatever problems there were could be dealt with if they faced them together. At last she managed to doze fitfully until Bettine came to tell her it was time to change. After a sponge bath, she put on one of the dresses she kept here, a gift from her aunt. The taffeta skirt and bodice were striped in tints of pink and draped with fine net and white lace. Over them was a little corset of cerise satin embroidered with pink roses. It was a pretty dress and Theo knew she looked pretty in it, if more girlish than she liked. Bettine added some of the fragrant tea roses to her hair.

When she took her seat in the dining room, Averill offered one apologetic glance then avoided her gaze. The first course of tomato aspic looked like jellied blood and quivered unpleasantly. Theo forced herself to eat it. Aunt Marguerite chattered. The cocaine had left her a mass of jitters. She hushed under her husband's cold stare. Francine made an attempt to draw her father out, sulking when rebuffed. He frowned at Theo but refused even to look at Averill. *Grand-mère* looked disapproving of everyone, especially the son-in-law who had banished her new puppy from the dining room. Theo was grateful for the uneasy silence. Her headache had returned full force. The clink and scrape of silver against china grated on her nerves. The candle flames flickered too brightly, distracting as snapping fingers.

Cod with pearl onions in a pale, bland cream sauce came next, valiantly garnished with parsley. Her uncle roused himself and began speaking of such current events as he deemed worthy for ladies' ears. He looked at Theo pointedly, even as he continued to ignore Averill. Had he learned of their trip to the morgue? Or the murder? Getting embroiled in such events was considered crude by society—not mischance but inherent lack of character.

As the fish course was removed and sweetbreads placed before them, Uncle Urbain addressed her directly. It was an accusation, if not the one she expected. "You could not resist joining the furor at the École des Beaux-Arts today, could you, Theodora?"

"Yes, I was there." She prickled with defiance.

Her uncle seized the argument. "You seem quite proud of your selfish indulgence when you should be ashamed. Because of you and your ilk, the École has been closed for a month."

"The male students started the protest. They are the ones who should be ashamed." Theo kept her voice level, but under the table she dug her nails into her palms. "They assaulted the two women students and ran them out of the school."

"You see, only a meager two were even able to pass the test."

Averill spoke up. "The women are held to a higher standard than the men."

Her uncle swiveled, furious that Averill had taken her side. "You—"

Theo interrupted him. "Many women tested higher than the men but were not admitted."

"You cannot know that," her uncle sneered.

Theo drew breath to argue, but Aunt Marguerite chirruped her distress.

"If you say so." Theo attacked the sweetbreads. Arguing with her uncle was always pointless, and for whatever reason he'd taken up the incident as a cause. He was glaring at her and at Averill, probably planning retaliation.

Her aunt struggled to find a topic to distract him. "Francine was asking if we would go to the country this summer?"

He frowned. "Have we not always?"

"Yes, but she hoped we could go to the estate and I believe it still needs repairs."

"Wasn't there a fire?" Theo asked, helping her aunt along.

"Yes, perhaps six months before you came to stay with us. It was quite terrible."

There was a brief pause, and Theo presumed they were each remembering that fire.

Averill gave her a tight smile. "It remains in ruins. Brambles are overgrowing the stone—very picturesque."

"As picturesque as the baron's decrepit estate?" Theo asked.

"Not at all picturesque." He turned his attention to *Grand-mère* then, said something to make her giggle.

"Next year, I will attend to the repairs." Her uncle's voice was sullen.

"But why postpone the work again?" Marguerite asked him, earning a deeper frown. Theo could see her struggle. The cocaine had left her skittish and argumentative, but she had too much experience of her husband's wrath to persevere. Instead she sat, her eyes darting around the table, her hands moving spiderlike from one bit of jewelry to the next then scuttling up to twist her hair.

"I chose to invest in my laboratory instead," Uncle Urbain explained as if to a moron. "I needed to expand the space, modernize the equipment, and improve the soundproofing."

"That was far more important, of course," her aunt murmured.

Far more important to have a place to vivisect his specimens, Theo snarled inwardly. Did he really need soundproofing? Averill said he cut the poor animals' vocal cords. She pushed the sweetbreads around with her fork, unable to take another bite. After a few moments, they were replaced with a sampling of cheeses.

For some reason, her uncle considered the discussion a triumph. He turned to his daughter and said in a cajoling tone, "Perhaps this year we will go to Deauville. You would like that, of course, Francine?"

"Yes, Father."

"And you, my dear?" he asked, turning to his wife. "Deauville would appeal to you this summer, would it not?"

"Of course."

Uncle Urbain did not turn and ask her, but Theo thought she would be invited eventually. If she did not go, she would not see Averill for a month. That would be impossibly painful. Yet it would be misery to watch him subdued under his father's domineering presence, day after day. But they could escape together. Averill could take her to paint the cliffs over the sea and the boardwalk. And Deauville meant the race track. That would be exciting. Or perhaps Averill would beg off. They would have Paris to themselves alone. Theo felt a flush of excitement radiating between her thighs, hot and sweet. Feeling her cheeks heat as well, she glanced at Averill. He was studying his food in a most determined manner.

They had finished the cheeses when Casimir was announced. With no pretense at subtlety, *Grand-mère* indicated the baron should sit beside their nubile Francine. He smiled, kissed her hand, then made small talk to everyone else with polished politeness. Francine sat hunched, casting yearning, resentful glances at him. Dessert was presented, a crumbly crusted tart with tiny wild strawberries and whipped cream. Theo still had little appetite but the fresh brightness of the berries tantalized her into a few bites. Casimir mentioned that he would soon be away for a few days, in Dieppe. This time, Averill exchanged glances with her. They knew Casimir was going to greet Oscar Wilde upon his release from prison.

Oblivious, Aunt Marguerite made pleasantries about the sea air. "It is still too early for the best weather. There will be rain. You should wait a month."

"Perhaps you're right," Casimir replied, as if he was actually considering it.

The baron was amiable as always, but Theo saw tension in his posture. He glanced from Averill to her uncle but avoided Theo's gaze except when offering pleasantries. After dinner, the men went to the library for brandy and cigars. The women sat in the parlor, Theo's tension winding tighter as she waited for a chance to speak to Casimir and Averill. She suspected the unexpected visit had something to do with the morgue. Her aunt asked Francine to continue on in *Les Misérables*. Francine read for about twenty minutes in her soft, inflectionless voice until Aunt Marguerite abruptly suggested they retire. Her eyes had a glazed eagerness. There would be a much-desired sleeping potion waiting by her bedside.

Theo loitered in the parlor, allowing her aunt and cousin to precede her out the door. When she entered the foyer, she heard raised voices behind the library doors. Her uncle exclaimed, "Murder!" But the rest was a blur of sound. She was tempted to eavesdrop, but the servants were still moving about the house. Frustrated, she went upstairs to her room and waited a few minutes for the women to settle into bed, then went to the head of the stairs. At last, she heard the library door open. Catching a glimpse of her uncle, she ducked out of sight until he ascended to his room. Returning to the overlook, she saw Averill and Casimir below. As she descended the staircase, she heard Averill say, low but angry, "Why did you tell my father we were questioned at the morgue? He was already furious about the cemetery."

"Better he is forewarned in case the Inspecteur pays another visit. I was at the morgue with you. As a supposed suitor for his daughter, I must be forgiven—and you with me."

"He will only blame me for implicating you."

"He is mad. One can only do so much." Casimir shrugged. "Forgive me?"

"As always."

Theo did not want to eavesdrop. She wanted to be included in their conversation. Approaching, she called out their names quietly. They turned, startled. "You are talking about the interrogation at the morgue?"

They looked at each other almost guiltily. Then Casimir faced her squarely. "In part. The Inspecteur is troubled because I remembered another winged cross."

"A winged cross?" She was completely perplexed. Casimir realized it at once and looked annoyed that he'd said anything. He glanced at Averill again. Theo was annoyed in turn. "I will not have hysterics again."

"You weren't shown the photo of a winged cross of the back of the grave?" Averill asked.

"No." An image teased the edge of her mind but would not take form. "I wonder why."

"Because the Inspecteur does not think you capable of murder. The rest of us are suspects," Averill said.

"It was a charcoal scrawl." Casimir shrugged again. "Probably meaningless."

"Then why was it important enough for a visit? You said you saw another?"

"By the Seine," Casimir said. "People who scrawl on walls must have a limited repertoire."

"Scrawls mean nothing. This mark does. Tell me."

Casimir told her the sad story of the poodle washer. There did not seem to be a correlation, yet Theo was uneasy. "No one ever found her son?"

"He probably drowned. The Seine was right there." Casimir frowned. "No doubt the detective exaggerates the significance of this scribble—but I was obliged to show it to him."

"Of course," Theo said. "There is a madman killing children."

"If this detective even bothers to hunt for him," Averill added. "He seems perfectly pleased to seize whoever is at hand."

Theo shook her head. "I believe he is more competent than that. He just provokes us to see what will happen."

She lingered, but Averill seemed determined to wait her out and continued to find questions for Casimir. He must not want to be alone with her again after what had happened in the library. Reluctantly, Theo bade them good night and climbed the stairs. Reaching the top, she paused and looked down. Averill and Casimir were still talking at the front door. Casimir stood with his well-tailored back to her, gloves in hand. He did not see her, but Averill glanced up over Casimir's shoulder, briefly meeting her gaze.

Then he took Casimir's face in his hands, leaned forward and kissed him.

Shock seared through Theo like a bolt of white lightning. The pain was a blinding brightness in her brain, flashes of burning heat and burning cold in her body. Averill stepped back from the embrace and smiled at Casimir. He opened the door, slid his arm over Casimir's shoulders and led him out into the night.

Theo fled down the hallway to her room. Once inside, she sank to the floor as demons of pain and anger rent her with searing claws, trying to rip their way out. Heart and belly and lungs and brain all screamed at her. She could not breathe, could not think.

But she must think. She must make sense of what she had seen. Pushing herself back on her feet, she began pacing. That kiss was utterly deliberate. She was sure Averill had kissed Casimir tonight to drive her away. Tonight. But that was not their first kiss. There was nothing hesitant in it. Nothing hesitant in the casual drape of Averill's arm over Casimir's shoulders as he led him out the door. They were lovers. If he had warned her, would her heart have been safer? Did he not trust her? Did he despise himself? Had it not been Averill's secret but Casimir's? That would be a double betrayal.

Bettine knocked, but Theo sent her away. She undressed herself and tried to sleep, but images tormented her unrelentingly, what she had seen—and more that she imagined. She rose and paced again, wanting to smash the mirror, the windows, Casimir's smiling face.

Averill had tried to warn her when they joked about school crushes. When he said most boys experimented, she thought it a subtle way of confiding that he had too. But he also said most men turned to women. She knew he consorted with actresses and other disreputable beauties. So he desired women as well. The kiss he gave her had been savage, passionate. Was it only anger? Only desperation?

Even now, would he tell her the truth?

Exhausted at last, Theo fell asleep. At dawn she dressed and let herself out of the house. The morning was a morose grey, sky and air merged in a faint pervasive rain that was little more than mist. Wetness and misery swathed her like a veil as she searched for and finally found a carriage to take her back to Montmartre. It wasn't until she stopped outside her door that she remembered what happened before that revelatory kiss—the conversation about the missing children and the mark left on the grave. Theo went farther up the street and turned onto the rue de la Mire. The image of Inspecteur Devaux examining the wall superimposed itself on the stairs. This was where Denis had been abducted. Theo descended a few steps and there, amid all the crude and ugly images, was the black cross. A cross with wings.

Even knowing what she would find, Theo was dumbfounded. Images and emotions swarmed, a black cloud in her mind. Back in her apartment, she splashed cold water in her face to try and clear her head, then ground coffee and put water on to boil. Anything to wake up. But she could not wake up to a different reality. Dread was like some horrid yeasty substance swelling inside her. Was it no more than bizarre coincidence? If several children had been killed, was it so very odd that they knew more than one?

Yes, it was very, very odd.

Could one of the Revenants be involved?

No. She knew them.

But last night had proved that the one she knew best, she knew least of all.

"No." She said it aloud. None of her friends could slaughter a child. One of them must have an enemy who wanted to implicate them. But what enemies? Paul would have political enemies, of course, and an endless stream of rejected poets bent on revenge. Theo bit back a laugh that threatened to turn into a sob. What enemy would contrive these horrible murders because his poems had been spurned?

Theo saw the Tarot cards laid out before her, The Devil squatting in their midst.

She saw his nearby companion, the Page of Cups. So charming. So tormented.

"No."

She felt the presence of evil envelop her, like a foul breath tainting the air.

Chapter Twenty~Seven

The film of night flowed round and over us. And
my eyes in the dark did your eyes meet...
                                          Charles Baudelaire

Michel had an assignation with Lilias tonight. For once, he felt more reluctance than anticipation. There was still time to send his regrets, but he had done so the weekend following the fire and the discovery of the linked murders. Lilias would not tolerate being taken for granted. He would be a fool to lose her.

And she might have news for him. He desired that more than he desired the escape of pleasure in her arms.

In a bistro near the Sorbonne he ate an oyster sandwich and sipped a brisk Beaujolais. At two, he went to his appointment at the university where he spoke to a history professor specializing in religion. Shown a photograph of the winged cross, the professor theorized at length about the Cathars and the Albigensian Crusade. When the earnest academic began on the secrets of the Templars, Michel excused himself. He had a fortifying coffee across from Notre Dame, then sought out the priest who had been recommended to him. Unlike the professor, he did not pretend to any knowledge, only stared at the cross in bafflement.

"Could it be a symbol for one of the angels?" the priest asked.

Frustrated to be questioned himself, Michel replied, "It's not one used by the church?"

"No, except the obvious symbol of the cross," the priest said. He looked relieved, no doubt guessing it was involved in a crime. Michel thanked him for his time and left. There was one more expert he meant to consult, but Huysmans had put him off till Monday.

Michel returned to the morgue to gather his officers' reports. There were no new suspects though all of Paris continued to file past the display. He had to warn himself continuously that it might be only strange coincidence at work that connected the Revenants with the children's killings. Like a savage clock, his brain ticked off cases where innocent men had died because of just such absurdities. Instinct told him to follow this trail, but he must guard against forcing the pieces to fit his theory.

If no new suspects had emerged, there was new evidence. Searching in a wider arc than before, Michel had discovered one more cross, and Inspecteur Rambert another. Alicia remained the only victim they had found, so also the only one with the symbol where her body was displayed. A discrepancy. But even in the chaos of the fire, it had been a great risk to snatch the girl. The killer dared not take time to scrawl his mark. With the cross on the grave and the remnant the baron had shown him, they now had five kidnappings marked with a cross. Five murders, Michel was certain. How many more remained a mystery. The discoveries had given Michel a brief surge of satisfaction, followed by a deepening depression at their failure.

Earlier in the week, Inspecteur Rambert had returned in a fury from the orphanage. The assistant who had been sent to identify the charred remains of the blind children had not even bothered to acknowledge that there was one child missing, but had simply told the officers to bury all the pathetic little corpses in a pauper's grave.

"*Sac à merde*," Rambert had fumed.

"He did not murder her," Michel pointed out even though the callousness and incompetence angered him as well.

Rambert stalked off muttering, and Michel had quit for the day as well. Though he had been in the morgue only an hour, the smell overlaid the odors of the Paris streets and the lingering aromas of Notre Dame, incense, candle wax and lilies. Gathering fresh clothes from home, he went to the nearest public bath house and scrubbed himself until he was sure any lingering scent was in his mind, not on his skin. Later this month he would allow himself the indulgence of a lavishly tiled Turkish bath. The steam, a massage, would force him to relax.

Clean and somewhat refreshed, he ate a simple supper of brie and baguette in the waning evening light. After dark, he made his way through the quiet streets to Lilias' home. He still had not brought his guitar. Choosing a song, practicing, would have given him a needed distraction. He tried to put the murder of Alicia out of his mind, but the ugliness preyed on him. A blind child raped, tortured, murdered. What torments had the other children suffered?

And if at the hands of a Revenant, which one? Charron still seemed the most likely, but it might only be happenstance or even some sort of misdirection. Jules Loisel seemed too emotionally weak to commit such havoc, but Michel had met other killers who used the power of death to counter their weakness. The baron was the most athletic, a duelist, someone far more used to violence than he appeared—but violence against men, not children. He had not feigned his surprise at the photograph. He had visibly paled. What of Noret? These were not political crimes. There was a sick passion in them. Had they been rich children, Michel might have constructed some twisted theory. But they were sexual crimes, and all of the children poor and vulnerable. Perhaps Noret's sexuality was as twisted as his cold-blooded anarchist politics, but buried, a sort of self-loathing….

Michel made himself stop. The case was devouring him. He must push it away as best he could. He was grateful that he would not have to hide his concern entirely from Lilias, yet he could not go to her submerged in gloom. He must make an effort.

He should have known himself better. And Lilias. In her presence, all his reservations fell away and desire overwhelmed him, blazing out from his groin. He did not want to talk. If he started to talk, he would never escape the case. He was going to try to read her, to give her what she desired this night. But she read him too well. He supposed courtesans must have that skill even more than *flics*, if they were to triumph in the *demimonde*. She led him upstairs, the grip of her hand hard. In the bedroom, she kissed him. Just for an instant, slow and lingering. But it was not a seduction, more a reminder, for then she bit his neck, his lip. The metallic taste of blood trickled onto his tongue. He lifted her, carried her to the bed, stripped her. Her naked skin glowed on the moonlit sheets, nipples and mons enticing him.

"Now," she said, opening her legs to him, and he entered her fiercely. He felt the warmth and wetness of her sex close around him.

It was ruthless, violent, but not quick. He buried himself in her heat, but every time climax approached he stopped. She helped him there, sometimes with stillness, sometimes with a touch that eased the building pressure in his balls rather than inflamed them. He took her legs over his shoulders for a deeper angle and plunged into her over and over. He used his finger to penetrate her other orifice and felt her hand moving between them, rubbing her clitoris. She came suddenly and violently, her vagina gripping him in rippling spasms. He cried out and lost himself finally, like a bullet flying into darkness.

After, they shared pâté and caviar, and drank a bottle of lush Cabernet Sauvignon. In the soft candlelight, the rich wine looked almost black.

"You have news?" he asked. She arched a delicate brow, and he silently cursed the concern that had swooped from his brain without thought. He should have taken time to offer well-earned praise of her skill. "I'm sorry. This case is consuming me."

She said nothing about his lack of courtesy but answered the question. "Yes, of a sort. I still know nothing about your missing children, but there is news of the Black Mass."

"What news?"

"I now know the time but not yet the place. This mass will be held two weeks from tonight, just after midnight—not Saturday, but Sunday morning to profane the Sabbath."

"Vipèrine will conduct the ceremony?"

She gave a little shrug. "Supposedly he has a defrocked priest to do it."

Michel was dubious. "He'll let someone else take center stage?"

"Much of this is only a step beyond rumor—but it is difficult to imagine him surrendering the spotlight. Perhaps he will play the summoned Devil."

"When will you learn the place?"

She lifted a hand. "I cannot promise to deliver this information. I have pretended to have a client who is interested in such things. But a client who is not yet willing to give his name. Perhaps my refusal to give a name will exclude me."

"I know you do not want to be implicated."

"A little implication will not harm me, but I draw the line at attendance."

"That is understood."

"In case my source decides not to confide in me, you should shadow cabinet minister Williquette."

"Williquette?" Michel scoffed. "He is a mouse."

"Some mice dream of becoming lions. Instead they become rats. The minister is ambitious enough to seek power however he can, including black magic."

"True." Michel frowned. "He is influential enough to have had my previous charges against Vipèrine discarded."

"Gossip says the snake is playing pimp to the minister, who has a penchant for pubescent girls." He sat up at that, but she pushed him back. "He prefers *jeunes filles* older than your victims, thirteen or fourteen."

"Still, it is suspicious."

"Very suspicious." She gave him a feline smile. "I have gleaned a bit more. Before he moved on to grander schemes, your wily serpent used to be a pimp in Rouen. One of the courtesans with whom I spoke remembers him working for a madam she knew in that city, L'Anguille."

"L'Anguille? I wonder what particular eel-like talents she possesses."

"Who knows? But I am told her house catered to clientele with more aberrant tastes."

"Then my instincts were right. He has the soul of a pimp."

"Your instincts are quite excellent—a snake consorting with an eel." Then her smile faded. "Michel, there is talk of a virgin sacrifice at this Black Mass. I doubt they would seek witnesses to murder, but I do fear a true rape rather than a staged one."

"Vipèrine is perfectly capable of the rape." He fought a surge of disgust. "He is a leading suspect in the cemetery murder but I find him too obvious in many ways."

"Being too obvious can be a sort of protective coloration," she said.

"True. And if he did not kill Alicia, he is still capable of murder." Michel told her about Vipèrine's visit to his apartment and his presumption of poison.

"You're sure?"

"Only Vipèrine wears that abominable cologne. He threatened me. He broke into my home but tried to leave no trace. Poison is what makes sense."

"There will be people at this Black Mass that might kill rather than be revealed as Satanists. So take care, *mon ami*. I would prefer you did not die."

"I am always careful. And I am quite alive."

Her fingertips teased down his torso, whisper soft but with the hint of nails here and there. "Ahhh," she said. "Alive, most definitely."

"Long enough to share the little death."

Chapter Twenty~Eight

Swarming city—seething with dark dreams
Here, even in full sunlight
Pale specters stalk each passing stranger.
                                    Charles Baudelaire

Astonished, Michel stared at the woman who burst into his office at the morgue. She wore a scarlet shawl tossed over a nun's habit. Her face was heavily made up, with pink circles of rouge and lips painted maroon. A prostitute with peculiar customers? Then he saw that dark lines bled down the sides of her cheeks where tear streaks of mascara were smudged, and her eyes were red with weeping. She was out of breath, almost gasping, pressing a hand to her side as if her corset pinched her. She must have run here from the detectives' headquarters.

"Inspecteur Devaux?" Her voice quavered.

When he nodded warily, she thrust a note at him. Michel opened it, read it, and crumpled it in his fist. The woman made a small mew of fear. He smoothed his features along with the note and read it again.

Devaux—
Come to the Grand Guignol. Now. Someone tried to grab Lalou
Joliette's daughter.
Blaise Dancier

Only an attempt, he thought, relief tightly woven with concern. The child was safe.

"I'll come." Michel nodded to the woman who took a deep breath and dashed out the door, not waiting for the ride he'd have offered. Not a prostitute, but one of the actresses from the Grand Guignol, he realized, remembering the clash of costume and garish makeup.

Lalou Joliette was Dancier's most recent mistress and a rising star. Probably this was an attempt to get ransom from Dancier. Stupid. But stupidity was rampant. Could this be related to the other abductions? Unlikely but not impossible. The other children were from poorer families.

Was the attempt on her child revenge for Dancier's tip about the children? Almost impossible, though Dancier had been asking questions. Michel needed to leave a man in place at the morgue, so he decided to go alone. First he sent a note to Cochefert, explaining why Dancier needed help and asking for two men to follow to the Grand Guignol. He penned a second note to Huysmans, postponing their meeting until tomorrow, then headed out the door.

When he told the cab driver the Grand Guignol, he got a cheeky grin. "A little early for a show, isn't it?"

Michel ignored him and clambered inside. The man sensed his impatience and set off briskly. le Théâtre du Grand Guignol was on the bottom edge of Montmartre in a seedy neighborhood. Michel knew that Dancier's investment had proved an instantaneous success. There was nothing else quite like it. Three or four short plays alternated horror with bawdy comedy—screams of terror with screams of laughter. But gruesome gore was the irresistible centerpiece. The Grand Guignol bragged that every night someone was carried away in a faint.

The driver let him off at the mouth of rue Chaptal. The theatre, once a derelict convent chapel, stood at the end of the cobbled cul-de-sac. Michel glanced at the alley walls as he walked but saw no winged cross. A man came across the courtyard and opened the iron gate. They had only a passing acquaintance, but he recognized Oscar Méténier, one of the owners, by his fabulous handlebar moustache. Michel received a terse *thank you* for his swift arrival.

"Dancier is with Lalou and her daughter." Méténier admitted him and secured the gate behind them. His dark eyes were filled with concern. "I'm keeping this locked for now."

"Post a guard. I have men coming."

"I'll send out a stagehand."

Oddly enough, Méténier was the son of a police commissioner. Once he decided the theatre was his true calling, he'd made dramas from the seamy side of life he'd seen working for the police force. His daring *Mademoiselle Fifi* had been the first prostitute to saunter across the stage in Paris. She wasn't a courtesan—the romantic Camille and others of her ilk had long been acceptable—but a coarse street walker. But his whore was still a heroine. The audience cheered her murder of a German officer. It was almost thirty years since the war, but Germans had not been forgiven for their bombardment of Paris.

Méténier led him across the courtyard. "We have delivery men in and out all the time, especially Mondays. New props. Fabric for costumes. Materials for the sets and lighting. This creature hid behind a bouquet of flowers in case anyone noticed him, but no one did."

Michel felt a surge of frustration at that. He said nothing, but Méténier glanced at him and nodded. "It's always the way, isn't it?"

"More often than not," he acknowledged.

Méténier paused to unlock the carved oak door of the theatre. The door was under an archway and there, toward the bottom of the stone portal, Michel saw the winged cross drawn in charcoal. His heart stuttered then began to beat more rapidly. Keeping his voice even, he asked, "Have you seen that mark before?"

Méténier glanced down and frowned. "No. I'll send someone to wash it off."

"Don't," Michel said sharply then added, "Wait till it's been photographed."

"If you wish." Méténier studied his face for a moment, then motioned him inside. After seeing the winged cross, Michel felt his senses heightened. The click of the key as Méténier relocked the door seemed sharp as the cock of a pistol.

Michel did not tell him not to mention the mark to Dancier. There would be no surer way to have the information passed on. Money trumped any loyalties left from an abandoned career in police work. Méténier led Michel into the tiny oak-paneled lobby. "This is where he tried to seize her. She plays here when rehearsals are in progress."

The air smelled of dust, paint, sweat, flowers—and chloroform. There was a scattered bouquet cast at the foot of a wrought iron staircase. The rag lay nearby. The kidnapper had not seized an unexpected opportunity, as with Alicia. This time, he had come prepared, with chloroform at the ready, flowers for concealment. Michel went over and examined them. "The bouquet is trampled. Is this where they struggled?"

"Probably. Darline usually sits on the staircase steps with schoolwork or her toys. The kidnapper must have thrown the flowers down when he grabbed her." Méténier rubbed the back of his head, cleared his throat. "I do know Blaise trampled them afterwards."

Dancier was in a frenzy of rage. Michel was not surprised. He looked at the flowers again. White stocks gave out a hint of cool spicy fragrance. Mixed in were some daisies, a pink tulip, baby's breath and ferns. Even trampled he could see that that most of the blossoms were faded. These were flowers from a poor seller who could not afford better blooms. There were dozens, perhaps hundreds of such flower girls the kidnapper might have bought them from. The chloroformed rag was a cheap washcloth, impossible to trace. The flowers were at least possible. "The little girl plays here alone?"

"After school and on holidays, if her grandmother isn't free to watch her."

"Frequently?"

"Often enough for someone to notice."

"How old is she?"

"Ten, I believe."

"But she managed to escape?"

"Yes. I'll let her tell the story, it's worthy of the Grand Guignol—except for the happy ending." A smile flashed across his face.

"Did anyone see the kidnapper?"

"No, our attention was on the rehearsal and then on Darline. Blaise did chase after him—but he had no luck."

Michel decided to talk to Blaise Dancier and the little girl Darline, rather than gather any more secondhand information. He took a moment to embed the layout of the foyer in his mind then walked farther into the theatre. The would-be kidnapper must have paid his francs for a view of the interior of the building. The mood was Gothic, for Méténier had retained the interior of the chapel with its elegant spandrel ceiling. At night, the audiences sat on wooden pews and gawked at angels overhead. Murals depicted the seven deadly sins. The small size of the theatre, the smallest in Paris, would only increase the impact. The Grand Guignol had fewer than three hundred seats, and the stage looked no more than twenty feet square. The players were all but in the audience's lap. Getting splashed with fake blood or struck with a bouncing sheep's eyeball would be a common event.

Turning to Méténier, he asked, "Do you remember if the door opened? I would think he'd check to see how many were inside and how close they were to the foyer."

"My attention was on the stage. I didn't see or hear anyone until Darline ran through the door screaming."

Looking about, Michel saw a few stagehands working quietly and some of the actors sitting in corners talking. Just then, the men Cochefert had sent arrived. There was the photographer from Alicia's case, and also Hugh Rambert, who had done several interviews. Good choices. Michel asked Méténier to wait and took the two men back to the lobby.

"No body?" The photographer looked about, puzzled why the scene was deserving of his efforts.

"Attempted kidnapping. The man is dangerous," Michel said sharply.

"Yes, sir." The photographer looked unconvinced.

"Do not discuss the case with anyone. Refer them to me if need be." He wanted to limit the information going to Dancier. "I want photographs of the flowers and the rag you see here. And I'll want a photograph of the interior of the theatre, just what you can see from the door. But first, inside the archway of the door, there is a chalked cross with wings. Take a photograph of that as well."

Both men paled. They remembered the mark on Alicia's tombstone. The photographer nodded soberly and began to set up his equipment. Michel took Rambert inside the theatre. The young officer possessed a husky build and a placid face, handsome but also slightly silly. His ingenuous gaze proved invaluable in interviews with the bourgeoisie, and criminals underestimated both his competence and his tenacity. "Inspecteur Rambert, please interview all the stage hands and actors you see here. See if they remember anyone suspicious wandering about in the last few days."

"Yes, sir." Rambert went off immediately.

Michel rejoined Méténier, who led him backstage, past painted backdrops, tables of props, and racks of costumes. There was a room for the bit players to change and do their makeup, and three or four doors with names stenciled on them for the stars. Méténier knocked at the one with the name Lalou Joliette.

Inside, Dancier's voice snapped, "Come in."

"I'll be on stage if you need me." Méténier hurriedly departed.

Michel opened the door and paused on the threshold, wondering if the kidnapper had ever made it this far when scouting the theatre. It was another miniscule room, already crowded with Dancier, radiating fury, the softly sobbing Lalou Joliette, and her daughter. The actress sat at her dressing table. When Michel entered, she turned and pressed trembling hands to her bosom. Tears glistened in her eyes, but no mascara was smudged. Her daughter sat on a chair behind her, but seeing a strange man, slid off it to bury her face in her mother's shoulder. The actress wrapped her arms around the girl with equal parts maternal tenderness and theatrical awareness. Michel thought the theatricality looked more like second nature than cold calculation. The mascara had probably been cleaned with the same automatic professionalism.

Behind Lalou were several costumes on hooks and stands. Michel noted a streetwalker's outfit of cheap satin, ripped and torn, and a pink froufrou negligee for a romantic farce or seduction scene. A dressmaker's dummy wore a silvery knit simulating chain mail. There was a small open case filled with what must be doll clothes, for an elegant china doll lay atop them.

Dancier managed the introductions. "This man is going to help us," he told Darline then glared at Michel as if he no longer believed it.

"You must protect us, Inspecteur Devaux." Lalou gave him a beseeching look from velvety brown eyes.

Feeling like an actor in a bad melodrama, Michel replied, "I will do everything I can to solve this crime. First, I would like to ask Mademoiselle Darline a few questions, in your presence, of course."

"You must tell the Inspecteur what you remember, my sweet one." Lalou said to her daughter.

The girl stepped forward, still honestly frightened but now aware of being the center of the drama. Michel knelt beside the child, not too close, but bringing him down to her eye level. He waited until she actually looked at him, then asked, "Did you recognize the man?"

"I don't know!" She burst into tears, huddling against her mother, who stroked and soothed her.

"Don't you think we asked that?" Dancier glared daggers at him. He was furious with himself for not having caught the kidnapper, Michel knew, and his temper was aggravated by the confined space. But it was pointless to suggest he leave and walk off some of the tension.

"I must ask again. Perhaps she remembers more now that she is safe." *I don't know* might mean nothing more than the child was confused. It could mean that she had seen the man but not often enough to say where or to give him a name. It could mean she did recognize him but was afraid to say so.

"Then ask," Dancier snapped. Michel stared him down. Dancier knew better than to undermine his authority. Dancier glanced away, then said to Lalou and her daughter, "Do your best to answer. I've called in the smartest *flic* I know."

Michel accepted the oblique apology and turned his attention back to the child. "Mlle. Darline, you've been frightened but you are here with people who love you." He could not say people who will keep you safe since she would no longer believe that. "I need you to be brave and help me to catch the man who tried to steal you away."

"Did his own little girl die?" she asked plaintively. "Does he need a new one?"

A budding actress, Michel thought, used to hearing her mother recite. Or perhaps the Grand Guignol had a future playwright. "That is possible. Perhaps he is lonely. If we find him, there are lonely orphans who need parents. Then he won't frighten any more little girls." He made himself stop and take a breath. The story was absurd but might reassure the child. "Close your eyes and imagine yourself back in the lobby. Tell me what you were doing."

"Mama was rehearsing. I played with my doll." She went over to the case he'd seen earlier and picked up the doll. "She's beautiful, like mama."

"Yes, very beautiful," he agreed.

"I always play there unless there is going to be a matinee. There are no matinees today."

"I see," Michel said.

"She's very good, very quiet. No one minds," Lalou broke in. "They love her."

"Of course they do," Michel replied, but he kept his attention on Darline. "Was the lobby empty until the man came?"

She shook her head. "Someone brought paint, and a lady brought black netting."

"They are building a new set. People have been in and out all day." It was Dancier this time, needing to say something.

Michel spared him a quick warning glance then turned back to the girl. He wanted to keep the images vivid in her mind. "Some people came. Then it was quiet again. What game were you playing with your doll?"

"I was making her into Salomé. Mama had beautiful costumes made for her…to commemorate her roles." Darline spoke the last carefully, obviously quoting. It seemed vain on the mother's part, but perhaps it was an amusing way for the little girl to share more in her life…or her dreams…for Lalou had not played the lead in *Salomé*. "I was making my doll a new cape. Monsieur Dancier gave me a pretty cravat."

Dancier must be truly smitten if he'd given Lalou's child one of his precious cravats. Michel continued. "Where were you sitting, Darline?"

"On the staircase. I'm not in the way there."

"Did you see the man come through the door?"

"He had flowers."

"Did you see his face?"

She shook her head and repeated, "He had flowers. White ones and pink ones."

Michel squelched his disappointment. He'd held out hope even though Méténier had already said no one had seen the man's face. But the little girl did have an eye for detail. "Did you notice what was he wearing?"

She scrunched her face. "A black coat."

"Shoes, boots? A hat?"

She shook her head.

"Did he have any smell?"

"Just the rag," she wailed again. "The horrid smelly rag."

"Ssshh…" Michel made it a soothing sound. He was pushing too hard. "You are doing very well." He was afraid the mother would interrupt, but Darline calmed down quickly, so he asked, "Did he come right over to you?"

"He went to the door. I thought he was going inside."

Michel nodded. "But he came back."

"I didn't see—he sneaked up! But I smelled the funny smell. I looked up, and he covered my face with the rag."

"How did you get away?" Michel could not imagine her escaping.

"Mama told me that if a man ever grabbed me, I should try to kick him or hit him in the place between his legs."

"Excellent advice." He almost smiled, imagining Dancier sharing the same internal wince he did.

"I was cutting up the pretty cravat to make a cape for my doll. I had scissors. I stabbed him there with the scissors. He yelled."

"They were very sharp scissors," Lalou said, then added defensively, "She sews very well, very neatly."

"Seems she stabs neatly too." This time, Dancier winced visibly.

Michel allowed the smile now. "We are all very impressed with how clever you were."

"And brave," Dancier added.

"I screamed." Darline did not believe him. "I screamed and I ran into the theatre. I tripped and fell."

"Now you know the secret that all brave men know," Michel said. "You can be scared and still be brave. You did just the right things."

"I did?" Darline looked to Dancier for confirmation.

"You were brave. They will call you Darline of the Scissors." Dancier raised his hands and mimed snipping. Darline giggled.

Michel tried a few more questions, but the girl could not remember anything more. The seamstress was summoned to take Darline to another room. Michel sat in the chair across from Lalou. "Mlle. Joliette, have you noticed anyone suspicious hanging about the theatre?"

"There are always strange people, but not strange enough to make me worry."

"Or near your home?"

"Home?" She gasped, but it was only fear, not recognition. Wide-eyed, she turned to Dancier and cried, "Oh, Blaise, we won't be safe at home!"

"I'll put you up in a hotel," Dancier said at once.

"Thank you," Lalou whispered, but Michel thought he caught a hint of disappointment. Her fear was real but she had also tried to play Dancier for more than she got. Her lover's home would be even more secure than a hotel, but as far as Michel knew, Dancier had never had a mistress in residence.

"The Élysées," Dancier offered, as compensation. "Darline will be escorted to and from school, and you'll be escorted to the theatre.

"Will you take me to the Élysées?" Lalou asked.

Dancier frowned and shook his head. "Jacques le Rouge will get you there safely. I've already put aside some important business."

Michel wondered if there really were business that couldn't be put off, or if Dancier wanted to go hunting for the kidnapper. Either or both. Life and crime must go on.

"There are some things I need at home. A change of clothes…." Lalou bit her lip nervously, worried now about seeming too demanding.

"After we finish the interviews, we can conduct Mlle. Joliette to the hotel," Michel offered. "We can stop at her current home for anything she needs to take with her. While she packs, Inspector Rambert and I can ask a few questions of the neighbors."

"That's good," Dancier said. "Jacques will go book a room at the Élysées, and stay with you until I come tonight."

"*Merci, mon cheri.*" Lalou gave him a grateful smile. Michel wondered how the desk clerk would react to Jacques le Rouge sauntering through the lobby of his plush hotel. Whatever his reaction, Dancier's name would get a very nice little suite with no argument.

Michel turned back to Lalou. "Mlle. Joliette, this man might be a stranger who seized an opportunity but he might also be someone you know—" She shook her head vehemently, but Michel went on, "—or someone who is associated with the theatre."

Dancier shifted slightly, becoming more attentive.

Michel continued, "I would like you to make a list of your admirers."

Lalou just looked at him for a moment. He wondered if she might not be able to write, but she drew out some paper and a pen. "I have many admirers," she said, with a proud tilt of the chin. "Most are gentlemen. But there are also women who wish to emulate me. I cannot believe any of them would wish me harm. Or my daughter."

"Jealousy," Dancier suggested. "Your beauty. Your talent…."

It was a sop to her ego, but she smiled at him.

"Perhaps, though no one has been spiteful to me."

"You may not remember everyone right away," Michel said, handing her the pen. "I will copy what you write now. But you will keep the original in case you think of anyone else."

She picked up the pen then bit her lip. Michel knew she didn't want to list her lovers for Dancier to read, and Michel didn't want him to see an intriguing list of suspects. But there was no way to prevent it. If he took the original, Dancier would demand another. "There must be men whose vanity was injured by your refusal," he suggested. "Or it could be someone who works for a past suitor, someone who has seen you with your little girl."

"Yes, of course." She began to write.

"Include the men who have visited since Le Grand Guignol opened, and before that anyone who caused you any difficulty." When she finally paused, he added, "Mention also if any delivery people acted peculiarly."

Dancier made an exasperated sound. "Everyone gawks."

Michel turned to him, "Many would enjoy having a peek inside such a controversial theatre—or seeing a lovely actress. But it must be investigated."

She nibbled a nail and Michel prompted, "Has anyone shown your daughter a little too much attention?"

"Oh no." Lalou shook her head. He sighed inwardly, doubting she would have noticed anything but the most flagrant disregard of her own charms. But then she bent over the paper and scribbled another name at the bottom. She gave Dancier a last nervous glance and handed the list to Michel.

Copying it gave him a chance to look for names he recognized without showing any response. First he went to the last scribble, and saw cabinet minister Williquette. Lilias believed he had engineered Vipèrine's release and wanted to attend the Black Mass. This made him a new suspect in the abductions, one totally separate from the Revenants. But the minister's penchant was for pubescent girls with budding curves. Michel copied Lalou's list in the order of his own interest, then placed it beside her on the dressing table. He singled out a name he knew, a financier with a bad reputation but only for roughing up women. When he pointed to him, Lalou made a moue of distaste. "He came once. I was polite, no more."

He pointed to another name, trying to be casual.

"The baron? He is always gracious," she said. From the warmth in her voice, he gathered she had no complaints about Estarlian. Lalou went on, "We were closer when I played a handmaiden in *Salomé* last year. He wrote a little song for me, but I didn't have the training to play it on the lute. We did use one piece he wrote. He came by perhaps a month ago with lovely roses. It was most kind of him, as I had not seen him or his friend in quite a while."

"His friend?"

"Another poet. He has strange blue eyes and an unusual name."

"Averill Charron?" he asked, and she nodded. Two Revenants then. "Only the one friend?"

She shrugged a little at that, gave a nervous little sideways glance at Dancier. Only one other that she'd slept with, Michel surmised. He asked her about the Revenants, and she shrugged again. "Last year they were working on publishing a literary magazine. *Salomé* inspired them. I had absinthe with them once or twice, but I do not remember all their names. One was quite rude and ill-tempered."

"Paul Noret?"

"Perhaps. Yes." Michel could sense Dancier's attention growing ever more intent. He picked three more names at random and asked some questions. None of them seemed truly suspicious.

"I can't think of anyone else, and my daughter needs me," she said to Michel. "She needs my comfort."

"Of course. Monsieur Dancier and I can talk outside so as not to distress you further."

As expected, she looked upset at being deprived of her protector, but Dancier was ready to burst out of the tiny room and jerked his head toward the door. "Let's go."

"Lead the way." Michel followed as Dancier sped through the theatre and back outside.

In the courtyard, he whirled and confronted Michel. "Is this the same case I tipped you about?" he asked, watching Michel closely.

Michel would not lie, but it would be dangerous to give Dancier much information. He was careful not even to look in the direction of the winged cross. "I believe it is the same case."

"Is someone targeting me? Taking kids I know?"

"I do not think you are the target." Before Dancier could start asking questions Michel said, "Tell me your version of what happened."

Dancier fumed a minute, then replied, "I was watching the rehearsal. There was a muffled yell, then Darline burst through the door screaming. She fell about halfway down the aisle, so I went to help her first." He scowled at Michel.

"Of course you did. That was most important."

"I asked what frightened her, and she said a man grabbed her. So I ran out into the lobby. Empty. And the courtyard. Empty. The alley. Empty." He glowered at Michel again. "I got to the street and there was nothing suspicious—no one running, or trying to look like they weren't. I started grabbing people and asking them who'd just come from the rue Chaptal, but he'd the sense to blend in as soon as he hit the street. Or he was already out of sight."

"Nothing struck you as odd?"

"There was a fiacre standing by the curb. That made me suspicious, that maybe he was going to throw her inside and drive off. Then the driver stumbled out of a bistro and tried to climb up. I grabbed him, but he stank of beer." Dancier shrugged, shook his head. "I went up and down the street for a few more minutes…."

"…but nobody saw anything suspicious," Michel finished for him.

"Anyone ever tell you your job is *merde*?" Dancier inquired.

"Frequently."

There was a pause, then Dancier said, "I like Lalou."

"She is very pretty."

"Those eyes." Dancier rolled his own dramatically. "She's got great legs. The Jeanne d'Arc role really shows them off."

"Jeanne d'Arc?" Michel felt a shadow fall across his memory but could not see its form.

"Yes, she plays the Maid. And damned well too," Dancier said with pride. "It's one of the new plays. Lots of drama. Makes everyone feel patriotic, religious, and gives them thrills to polish it off. The fire is very convincing. Lalou gives one really stupendous scream."

"New, you say. How long have they been performing it?"

"They just started last week."

Michel had not paid any attention to the billboard. "Is there a poster?"

"Yes, of course. It's important?" Dancier asked, but it wasn't really a question.

"I don't know." Michel's shrug was honest. The shadow took on form, of sorts. Theo had said Denis' mother told her son tales about her namesake, Jeanne d'Arc. The baron had seen the dog washer worshiping in front of a scribbled cross—a cross that may have been drawn by her child's murderer. Religious mania had always been a possible motive. What about Alicia, who had almost burned to death in a fire? Had that evoked the death of the Maid of Orléans? "I do know that at least some of the disappearances are linked."

Dancier leaned forward intently. "And what links them?"

Michel shook his head. "There is always a danger in trying to force pieces to fit."

"You have any suspects yet?" Dancier asked. His voice was light but his body vibrated with new tension.

"I have some suspects," Michel admitted, but held up a hand as Dancier moved in on him. "There are more than I questioned Mlle. Joliette about. I have no real evidence against any of them—only curious coincidences."

Dancier's eyes glittered dangerously. "I trust your instincts."

"My instincts told me to examine the coincidences, nothing more."

Dancier moved closer still, chest pressed to Michel's warding hand. It felt scorched by his anger. "You forget I gave this to you."

"No. I don't forget. It's the only reason I've given you any information at all," Michel said coldly. "Neither do I forget that you may be overzealous in your ferreting out of enemies."

"You want me to give you anything more, you'll give me this," Dancier snarled.

"Then I will go without." Michel thought for a minute Dancier would hit him, but he only turned and stalked off.

Michel spent an hour helping Rambert question the various stagehands and players. By the time he was done, Dancier had come back and was listening on the sidelines. He still held himself tensely but had apparently decided to forget the refusal. When Michel approached, he said, "I've got them to change the playbill so Lalou won't have to perform tonight."

A safe topic. "Good. Her daughter needs the security of her presence."

Dancier nodded. "I sent Jacques le Rouge off to wait in the hotel. You be sure and escort Lalou and Darline to their suite."

"Of course."

Mercurial as ever, Dancier relaxed, adjusted his cravat, and gave Michel a wink. "Guess what—Méténier's going to give me a part in one of the shows."

"Playing yourself?" Michel asked.

"Lacenaire," Dancier replied, naming the infamous dandy criminal Baudelaire had called a modern hero. "Bit of a come down—he was never very successful. But he knew how to play to the crowd."

"You can give me a ticket for that performance," Michel allowed.

He laughed. "I'll perform sublime atrocities and you'll have no reason to arrest me."

"It will be a vast relief." Michel smiled, but Dancier's boast brought the killer to mind.

After they parted ways, Michel summoned Rambert. Together they escorted Lalou and her daughter to her apartment, which was closer to l'Opéra than the Grand Guignol but still not in the most fashionable neighborhood. The avenue was busy with pedestrians and street traffic. Michel glimpsed a fiacre at the head of the next block. It looked to be waiting at the curb with no driver. Hardly unusual, but Michel didn't like it. It was the only memorable thing Dancier had mentioned. Michel sent Rambert to check on the driver while he took Lalou and her daughter inside. They waited in the hallway while he searched their apartment, which was expensively furnished if overelaborate—and free of any threat. While the actress packed, he spoke to the neighbors on either side. They were both horrified to have the police asking questions, as was the concierge. By that time, Lalou was finished and anxious to leave. Michel had her wait in the foyer of the building while he checked outside.

The fiacre had left and Rambert was waiting. He said that the carriage had been empty, but the driver had tapped him on the shoulder as he looked inside and asked if he wanted a ride, all the while balancing a cheese crêpe from a street vendor, and a bottle of beer. Dancier's version of the fiacre driver echoed again.

"What color was his coat?" Michel asked.

Rambert frowned. He closed his eyes to recapture the image of the driver. "Black."

What did a black coat mean? There were hundreds of cab drivers with black coats. Nonetheless, alarm bells were clanging. "Description?"

"Youngish, dark brown hair, brown eyes, no obvious scars or marks."

"Ugly? Attractive?"

Another frown. "The attractive side of ordinary. Average height. No one you'd notice."

"I want you to stay and interview the other neighbors in Lalou's building and the nearby shop keepers. Ask about anyone suspicious in the last few days—especially loitering fiacre drivers." Then, gathering his charges, Michel chose a carriage driven by a portly, grey-haired man and escorted Lalou to her hotel via a circuitous route, making sure that no drivers in black coats followed. He supposed the kidnapper could eventually find the hotel if he was set on Darline, but not today. When he handed Lalou over to Le Rouge, he also warned them both not to open the door to anyone unexpected. Lalou looked newly terrified, le Rouge disgusted that Michel had bothered with such a blatant warning.

He returned briefly to the morgue to find out if anyone suspicious had viewed Alicia in his absence. He also spoke to Rambert, who had returned with a single sighting. A flower girl had seen a dark-haired cabdriver waiting near the apartment yesterday and again today. "I asked if he bought flowers, but no."

"Too much to hope," Michel agreed. He gestured Rambert into a chair and reviewed the case with him.

"Beer might mask any lingering smell of chloroform," Rambert noted.

Michel nodded. "A beer in hand would also explain another beer spilled earlier on a black coat."

"Not much." Rambert sighed in frustration.

"You have one piece I don't," Michel said to him.

"The man's face."

"Yes. I think, Inspecteur Rambert, that you should spend some time hunting for our elusive driver."

Rambert gave him a pleasant smile. "There are only a few hundred stables to look through."

Chapter Twenty~Nine

Have you felt the fog of terror encroaching—the awful clutch
of night squeezing your heart into a crumpled paper ball?
                                    Charles Baudelaire

Feeling as if she was wandering in an endless nightmare, Theo
approached the morgue. She had gone first to the detective offices at
the Palais de Justice, only to be told that Inspecteur Devaux was here.
Alicia was on display for a few more days, and he was conferring with
his men. The same crowd of gawkers and vendors still milled around the
front of the building. To avoid them, she went around to the back door
that she had walked through five days ago—five days filled with constant
upheaval and relentless searching.

Saturday, she found Paul playing billiards with the student Hyphen
in Montmartre. Paul gave her the address of Jules' pitiful garret in
Montparnasse, which proved a grim expedition. He wasn't there Saturday,
and the landlord growled that he never was but he paid the rent. She'd
gone back Sunday, and Jules opened the peeling door a crack when she
knocked. He was flabbergasted to see her standing there. When she asked
if she could come in, he'd refused outright. She supposed the police would
find that suspicious, but even in Montparnasse he couldn't be carving up
children in such a ramshackle building without discovery. He was just
ashamed. So she'd taken him out for lunch and learned what she could.
The last two Hyphens had been easier. Monday she found one at his
father's law offices. The last appeared in his university classroom today.
Her quest was important, and bicycling through Paris had kept other
miseries on the fringes of her mind—until she tried to sleep. She lay in
bed, mind and body filled with shards of shattered glass. In each one
Averill was kissing Casimir.

Theo shivered and pushed the memory away again.

Gathering her resolve, she rapped on the door and waited. Some
would feel going to the *flics* was a betrayal. Paul especially would be
angry. But what was his fuming in the face of these murders? And she
was certain the other children had been murdered. Alicia was proof. Theo

would save the detective a little time and perhaps learn something in return. She knocked louder. Finally an attendant opened the door and led the way back to Inspecteur Devaux's makeshift office. He was sitting behind the same desk and greeted her politely, gesturing to the chair across from him. A flicker of curiosity gleamed in his eyes, but otherwise there was only his usual well-schooled calm.

Last time, she'd been angry at his ruthless probing and insinuations. Today his control steadied her. He had dealt fairly with her emotional outburst. She trusted him to think through her discoveries, to investigate rather than presume. "I have some information for you."

"And what is your information?"

"You know there was a strange symbol on the grave where Alicia was found and another on a wall beside the Seine where a little boy vanished. A cross with wings."

He said nothing, but Theo saw him glance at a folder beside him. His fingers moved slightly then stilled. Photographs of the crime scene? She felt a tremor of resistance, of dismay, but held out her hand. "I didn't go to the cemetery, but there is a similar design in the alley by my home. I remembered seeing it the day we first met. I returned to make sure."

"Yes, it is the same mark," he acknowledged reluctantly, but then he did open a folder and hand her one photo. "Here is the one drawn on the gravestone."

Theo looked at the scrawled cross intently. She frowned.

"What?" he asked instantly.

"It is the same design, but much cruder."

"Cruder?" For once the Inspecteur looked perplexed. "Less light to draw by? Less time to make his mark?"

"Perhaps just a heavier stick of charcoal," she replied. "But the drawing in my alley has more graceful movement to the wings than this."

He retrieved the photograph, staring down at it for a minute. Then he put it away and looked up at her again. "Did you tell your friends you'd seen the symbol in your alley?"

"No."

"Good. Please do not tell them."

"I will not promise that," she said flatly. "I have to use my own judgment."

He had the sense not to argue and nodded briefly.

Theo went on, "So, there are three cases—three at least—where children we had met vanished and a mark was left."

"Yes." He waited, watchful. When she waited in turn, he offered more. "The cases are dissimilar, but I must believe they are connected.

The cross drawn on the back of the gravestone was too deliberate to be chance. I do not think the others are random scribbles."

"I believe you are right," Theo said unhappily. "After I heard about the second cross, I talked to all the Revenants. Each of us knew at least one child who has vanished in the last nine months."

He leaned forward, his gaze intent. "Tell me who the children were."

"Everyone at the fire could at least have heard Alicia's name, from me or from Paul. I knew Denis and so did Averill, Casimir, Jules and Paul. Averill often told silly stories about his grandmother's poodle, so we'd all heard of the lady who washed him even if we didn't meet her." She hesitated then. "I didn't ask questions as a policeman would but as a troubled friend. I didn't try to discover how many Revenants knew each child, only if they knew one at all."

"You presume your friends are innocent. I understand." He nodded for her to continue.

"I found that Jules knew a seamstress' child who went missing that no one else has mentioned. Two of the Hyphens…."

He gave her a quizzical look, and she explained about the Hyphens. "Two of them live near each other and knew a bootblack's boy who vanished. The professor also knew the boy of a *bouquiniste*. That is five children."

"Five," Inspecteur Devaux repeated. He bent his head and made a note.

That was absurd. He would remember the number. Theo sensed the note was only to distract her. He was hiding something. "How many more children do you know about?"

He looked up but said nothing, his face a smooth, cold mask…

"Tell me—I can at least tell you if I knew any of the others."

If possible, his expression grew even blanker. He did not want to give away any information.

"Surely you want to know? There is no roundabout way for you to ask me now." She welcomed the simmer of anger rising to the surface, burning away the fear that cold mask evoked. "Tell me their names or what they did."

His lips tightened, but he relented. "Some names may be relevant, others not."

He named two children and Theo felt a surge of relief. "I didn't know them."

Then he said, "There was a boy named Dondre…."

"No!" At her gasp, he stopped speaking. Theo pressed her hand over her mouth, holding back another cry of protest. Tears blurred her vision and she blinked them back. He'd told her she would need courage, but Theo had not realized how much it would take.

The Inspecteur waited a moment, then said quietly, "He disappeared early in April."

Theo had regained her control, but she felt a terrible dark weight settle over her. "We went to the catacombs for a midnight concert."

Recognition ignited in his eyes. "All the Revenants attended?"

"All whom you questioned at the morgue. The Hyphens were not there though they were told about it."

"Were they at the Charity Bazaar?"

"They say no, and none of us saw them there."

"The kidnapping of Alicia was a crime of opportunity."

Theo nodded, also doubting the Hyphens could be involved. "They did come with us to the morgue but fled after I caused a scene."

"You were shocked. It was understandable."

For a moment there was silence, then she whispered, "Six children, at least."

He told her several other names. She did not recognize them. But that did not mean the poets might not know them. When he was silent, she said, "So many?"

"Many children go missing, run away."

"But you think these were kidnapped. Kidnapped and murdered by the same man?"

He hesitated, still obviously reluctant to discuss the case. But she had brought him valuable information and might do so again. "We've only managed to find three more crosses, but we do not know for certain where all the children were taken or where their bodies were discarded. Alicia is the only one whose body was found."

"The only one?"

"Yes. I fear the killer is growing bored with his private amusements and wishes to share them with the world."

"Do you think the cross is symbolic of some sort of religious obsession?"

"I have shown it to a priest, who says it's not the mark of any cult of which he is aware. I know of someone familiar with the world of satanic ritual. I have an appointment to see him this afternoon."

He would want her to leave. "I know you must consider us suspects, but—"

"But you think someone is framing one of you, or some of you?"

"Yes, exactly." She was relieved he'd had the same idea.

"It is far more likely that at least one of you is implicated." His voice was flat and hard.

"I told you—" Theo heard her voice sharpen and subdued it. She'd give him no excuse to dismiss her. "The day I recognized Alicia in the morgue, I also saw Vipèrine. He has a blue beard in imitation of Gilles de Rais who practiced black magic and murdered children."

"A colorful image," he said. Her anger must have showed because he held up his hand and added, "I am investigating him, as well as others."

"What…" she began, but stopped when he shook his head. Of course he would not tell her anything about that. At least she had the assurance that he was not looking only at the Revenants. "I knew some of the children. And I want to help my friends."

His expression grew even sterner. "It would be better if you left the investigation to the police, mademoiselle."

"I've brought you information you didn't have before, haven't I?"

"Yes, but I would have discovered it eventually. I would prefer not to worry about you as well as the children. Do not persist in this."

He made her feel like a child when he put it that way. But she had no intention of stopping. Feeling defensive, she attacked. "Arresting the wrong person, however convenient, will not end the murders."

He regarded her coldly. "Nor will protecting the killer."

"Believe me, Inspecteur, I would not protect anyone at the expense of a child's life."

"I do believe you." He held her gaze for a long moment. "But loyalty or affection may mislead you."

"I am not so easily misled." The image of The Moon rose up in her mind, mocking her.

"Do you know Darline Joliette?" he asked abruptly.

"No," she answered, though the very question made her tense.

"Lalou Joliette?"

She floundered because the name was familiar. "I don't know."

"She is an actress."

Theo remembered. "She had a small part in *Salomé*. The baron wrote some music for the play."

"And for her particularly?"

"Yes. He saw her for a time, I believe."

There was something in his hard look that made her defensive. "He shared her company with Averill Charron."

Theo jerked back as if he'd slapped her. Heat flared out over her skin, but her heart felt small and cold. Trying to keep control, she asked, "Why is she important?"

"Darline is her daughter. Someone attempted to kidnap her yesterday but failed."

"I am glad they failed," Theo whispered, still struggling to stay calm.

"Seven children, at least, that the Revenants knew." He leaned forward. The coldness thawed and his voice was quiet but earnest. "Listen to me. Some monsters cannot hide what they are, but others are quite adept at appearing human. They are like the character in that English novel—the story of Jekyll and Hyde. But it is not some fantastic potion which releases the monster within them. Their own lust provides the chemistry."

Theo shook her head but she knew he was right. As if they were auditioning for a play, her friends appeared in her mind in a Jekyll and Hyde transformation, their faces turning lecherous and cruel. Violent. Demonic—the evil Devil of the Tarot.

"Inspecteur Devaux…" Theo hesitated. He waited. Sometimes his stillness could be so unnerving. "You will think I am crazy."

"I doubt that."

"When I was at the Charity Bazaar with Mélanie, a friend told her fortune with three Tarot cards." He did seem to sneer a little, the slightest quiver of his upper lip, but she forged ahead. "She predicted the fire."

He frowned. "We know it was an accident. She could not have been involved."

"Of course not," Theo said. "I never implied that she was."

"You think she foretold the fire?" His face became a total blank which was better than him laughing in her face. He had enough courtesy or curiosity to ask, "What were the cards?"

"Carmine laid out three. The first was The Tower." That probably meant nothing to him. "The image is a tower struck by lightning, surrounded by flames and people fleeing. It was upside down. Carmine said that meant that Mélanie might be trapped by some catastrophe. The second card also foretold her being trapped. Its element was fire."

When Theo paused, he looked at her expectantly. "And the third?"

She knew it was melodramatic. It was also horribly painful. "The last card was Death."

The Inspecteur frowned. He spoke very reluctantly. "That does not seem like the sort of reading you would give a friend or even a customer."

"A fake would arrange visions of love on the horizon, or wealth, or something else pleasant and amusing. Or if the person was unhappy about something, there would be a promise that all would be better soon. At worst, a fake would give a mysterious warning, not a threat of death."

"Perhaps they were not truly friends?" he suggested.

"Carmine liked Mélanie. She believes in the Tarot."

"And you do as well?"

"I would rather not believe, but now I do."

"What happened to this Carmine during the fire?"

"She left before it began."

He actually looked suspicious again.

"Carmine was frightened. She'd gotten the same card herself that morning."

Michel shook his head. "Has this Carmine laid out the Tarot cards for you as well?"

Theo felt a weird mix of reluctance and amusement. "Yes. I think perhaps it was true as well. The cards said I would be in a battle of good and evil."

Again a look of blank disbelief. "Indeed?"

Theo enjoyed trying to perturb him. "I think that you may have been represented as well—as a knight who would be involved in the same battle but would disagree with me."

A smile flashed briefly across his face. "A knight?"

"The Knight of Swords." She saw the card again, the charging knight in his shining black armor with a windswept plume on his helmet and upraised sword.

"That seems appropriate." He smiled once again. It lasted a second, then vanished utterly. "Did the Tarot reveal the killer?" he asked sardonically.

"The Tarot thinks the killer is in league with The Devil," she answered.

"I think we can all agree on that, if only symbolically. Do you have his name?"

"No." Amusement flipped to annoyance. She most certainly would not mention the poetic Page of Cups. She pursued her other idea. "Carmine has some friends who have studied the occult, the Mathers. If the killer's cross has some deeper meaning, perhaps they will recognize it."

"You should not involve yourself in such a dangerous enterprise." His voice hardened.

"Yet only the other day, you told me I must have courage."

"And now I tell you not to be foolhardy. Searching out black magicians—" he began.

"Not all occultists practice black magic." Theo wished now she had not revealed their names. "Her friends are scholars. Surely not everyone in Paris is suspect?"

"Until they are cleared, yes." There was only the faintest lift of an eyebrow to lighten the statement. Then his voice hardened into a command. "I have my own source for this information, mademoiselle. Do not interfere further."

He could not command her obedience. Angry again, Theo stood. "I will continue to investigate. If I learn anything of interest from my interference, I will let you know."

She made it to the door before he said, "Mlle. Faraday."

She turned, reluctant to argue further, but he only added, "Please—be cautious."

His voice was cool, but there was true concern in his eyes. Her emotions went topsy-turvy again, and she smiled with amusement. "Do not fear, Inspecteur Devaux. I will call for you—if I have need of a knight."

Chapter Thirty

I saw the low sun daubed with mystic horrors
Lit up with long, livid, curdles of light,
Like actors playing out an ancient drama....
                                    Arthur Rimbaud

After Theo left, Michel spent the early afternoon conferring with his men about any last suspicious incidents at the viewing in the morgue. He assigned one to investigate the schedule he'd obtained that morning of Doctor Urbain Charron's whereabouts at the time of the kidnappings. Then he made the initial arrangements for Alicia to be sent to the funeral home that had volunteered its services. There had been a huge outpouring of money and gifts. She would be treated better in death than she ever had been in life. He dreaded the hordes that would come to the funeral, but he must attend. If—when—he captured her killer, he would visit her grave and tell her even though he did not believe she would hear him.

Before he went to his delayed appointment with Huysmans, Michel checked in briefly with Cochefert about Theo's occult scholars, the Mathers. The chief blinked and looked upward, perusing his memory. After a moment, he said, "MacGregor Mathers. Moina Mathers. Promise of ancient Egyptian ceremonies—fancy dress and all that."

Egyptian ceremonies sounded far better than a Black Mass with children sacrificed on the Devil's altar. But who knew what was actually involved? Michel pictured people tottering about with gilded jackal heads and skimpy linen kilts, totally failing to evoke the somber beauty of the authentic art he'd seen in the Louvre.

"British. Bookish." Cochefert smoothed his moustache with care. "Nothing against them so far."

Michel was dubious, if only because these supposed scholars could influence Theo Faraday. But he did not think all such dabblers were necessarily dishonest, only foolish. Was he being foolish to dismiss them? Remembering what Theo had said about the Tarot reading, he felt puzzled and deeply uneasy.

The question about the Mathers had diverted Cochefert. He was telling Michel about one of the prominent Parisian occultists. "Sar Péladan started out as a bank clerk, you know, but managed to transform himself into mystic royalty. Sar is Assyrian for King…."

Michel listened with half his attention. Péladan was all too familiar, with his gaudy satin robes and his luxuriant curling beard. Had Vipèrine taken his costume cue from Péladan? Not necessarily. Such theatrics were quite common. Expected. No one would believe you possessed magical powers if you dressed like a dreary bank clerk. While Cochefert expounded, Michel brooded on Theo's visit. Should he offer to accompany her when she visited these Mathers? Probably she would refuse him. Would she ask Charron to escort her? Michel frowned. He thought not. Theo did think of this as her investigation. She did not want to believe her Revenants guilty, but neither did she want them influencing her impressions.

Occultists would distrust a detective as much as Michel did them. If the Mathers did have information, they would tell Theo more if she came unimpeded by a policeman. And if anything would be likely to make them help, it was murdered children. He might have more information to work with, but Theo would make a far more emotional appeal.

On the other hand, he could gauge if they were lying only by being there.

"Péladan believed the artist should be a knight," the chief was saying.

"A knight?" Michel asked, surprised to have the image presented twice within an hour.

"Yes. The act of artistic creation was to be the quest for a kind of Holy Grail," Cochefert told him. "The enemy was once again those evil stiflers, the bourgeoisie. Artists were to engage in a perpetual war with them—swift strokes of paintbrush and pen against the ponderous bludgeon of convention."

"I have my own quest," Michel said. "I am going to brave Huysmans in his den."

"He breathes not fire, but fumes of acid," Cochefert warned. Michel smiled at the chief and took his leave.

Once outside, he decided to take a fiacre rather than walk as he had planned. Having cancelled once, he could no longer afford to play the *flâneur* and wander through the Jardin des Tuileries, pleasant as it would be. Michel did have the driver take him past the gardens before turning off to the Place Beauvau. The Ministry of the Interior wasn't far from the fashionable Champs Élysées. Would Huysmans be able to help? Michel had condescended to Theo about her occult source, but his own, however famous, was also dubious. Curious stories still circulated from when he wrote *Là Bas*. The Abbé Boullan, the defrocked priest Huysmans had consulted about diabolic rites, once warned him to avoid his office. Huysmans stayed home. That day a great mirror fell across his office desk and shattered. It would have killed him. Uncanny coincidence? An elaborate plot? The incident made a believer of Huysmans.

The Abbé's fatal heart attack only increased Huysmans' fervor and terror. Michel presumed Boullan's sudden death was presaged by decades of debauchery. Huysmans believed he had been murdered magically by his rivals and claimed further vicious attacks on himself. He could no longer sleep at night because he was pummeled by invisible fists. Huysmans had declared his cat suffered from these attacks as well. It was all too perfectly preposterous.

The fiacre brought Michel to the gates of the Ministry. Set around a square courtyard, it was an elegant traditional building of creamy limestone, tall narrow windows, and a steep lead roof. Armed with his briefcase of photos, he entered. Everyone within knew of Huysmans, the famous author who constantly complained of having his true calling interrupted by the demands of his job. At present, he was *chef de division* in the Sûreté Générale, identifying undesirable aliens for deportation. Michel was swiftly directed to his office and knocked on the door.

"Thank you for seeing me, Monsieur Huysmans," Michel said when his knock was answered.

The author was a small, neat man of restive energy, with dark, compelling eyes. In person, he radiated the same bitter discontent that permeated his novels. "I could hardly refuse the detective who captured the Montmartre *anarcho.*"

Michel gave a small nod at the compliment. Huysmans gestured him to a chair and returned to his own seat behind the desk. On the wall above and behind him hung a small mirror—no longer of a size to kill him if it fell. Files belonging to the department were scattered about on the desk and tables, but far more books and papers were obviously dedicated to Huysmans' current project. Michel saw various editions of the Bible and the lives of the saints. A book on Gothic art lay open to drawings of Chartres Cathedral. Huysmans' last book, *En Route*, had described his surrogate character's emersion in the rituals of a Trappist monastery. Evidently, the author was continuing that religious journey. It was a difficult one for a scornful intelligence easily overcome with disgust at all the stupidity and corruption that plagued the Church. Yet those difficulties were the substance of his work, played against the seductive purity of faith and the inspiration of its art. And perhaps, for such a complex intelligence, a longing for simple goodness was a temptation sweeter than any lust.

"Your *anarcho* proved to be Russian, I believe," Huysmans said.

"Originally, yes."

"You saved me the work of deporting him." He gave a cynical smile. "Instead, the guillotine will insure his departure."

"Undoubtedly."

"We have enough radicals of our own. I don't know why we need to import them as well," Huysmans complained. "But what can you expect when the Jews and Freemasons are running rampant in France?" He paused and looked at Michel expectantly.

"Ummm." Michel managed a small, noncommittal sound.

Mistaking it for approval, Huysmans continued, "Once, when I complained of the fortune we spent tracking *anarchos*, the poet Valéry suggested that it would be cheaper simply to give them the money instead."

"Some would instantly become bourgeois and settle into comfort," Michel replied. "But others would stock up on dynamite."

Huysmans nodded glumly. He sat back in his chair to watch Michel. "Your note said that you are investigating a murder."

"More than one. I've come here because of a mark at the crime scenes, perhaps a religious symbol, perhaps something more. One of my suspects calls himself a Satanist though it may be nothing but amateur theatrics."

"I have left off those investigations." Huysmans gazed at Michel with solemn intensity. "I ventured into the blackest darkness. It was not possible to emerge unscathed. I found I must make a definitive choice—either the muzzle of a revolver or the foot of the cross."

To Michel, such portentousness seemed another form of theatrics. He tried to direct Huysmans' ego to the matter at hand. "Still, your memory of occultism may assist me."

Huysmans' mouth turned down in an expression of disgust. "The whole world comes knocking on my door, searching for access to this obscene knowledge. I once refused a countess who came begging to wallow in sin and degradation."

"I have no desire to wallow. I want to stop a killer."

"That is not a request I can refuse." Huysmans regarded him glumly.

Michel opened his briefcase and evaluated the photographs of the winged cross. Alicia's gravestone was the clearest, but Theo thought it crude. He chose the photograph from the Montmartre alleyway and laid it down on the desk. "Does this have any meaning for you?"

Huysmans looked at it for a few seconds, then stared at Michel in blatant disbelief. "Is this some sort of joke?" His lip curled in a sneer. "I will not be made a mockery."

Startled, Michel lifted one hand in a placating gesture. It was odd to feel so much on the defensive. "I assure you, the question is sincere."

"Sincere?" Huysmans bit off the syllables, his lips and nostrils pinched and quivering.

A fierce rush of energy swept away Michel's first surprise. If Huysmans was angry, there was something to be angry about. "What does it mean?" he demanded.

Still glaring, Huysmans was silent long enough that Michel wanted to shake him. At last Huysmans said, "We know the black cross was on his shield. The swan is disputed—but there are many who believe the swan was set on his crest."

"Whose crest?" Michel's throat was tight.

Huysmans' voice dripped disdain. "Gilles de Laval, baron de Rais."

For a moment, Michel felt completely disoriented. "Gilles de Rais was burned at the stake five hundred years ago."

"For crimes of perfidy, sodomy, murder, witchcraft, and heresy." It was a litany.

Michel heard Theo's voice in his mind, accusing Vipèrine at the morgue. "*He likes to imagine himself as Gilles de Rais, who murdered more children than they know how to count.*"

It seemed his killer was even more insane than he'd imagined. To Huysmans, he said, "I am afraid his spirit lives on."

Huysmans blinked, looking as disoriented as Michel had felt a moment ago. Then he asked, "Just the one mark? One murder?"

"Many mysterious disappearances. One discovered murder." He hesitated, then added, "Five marks found so far."

"Five cannot be chance."

"No."

"There was no *fleur de lys*? For his service in the war, the king granted him the right to use the *fleur de lys* as well."

Michel shook his head. "None that we've found."

"Perhaps your killer discounts Gilles the warrior. It is Gilles the aspiring magician he emulates. The swan is the alchemist's symbol for mercury, you know."

Michel didn't know or care unless it led him to his killer. "He slaughtered children. So does this man."

"I visited Tiffauges." Huysmans' voice lowered to a confessional whisper. "I saw the crypt where the children were sacrificed, the chamber where the remains were incinerated. The castle was imbued with a kind of stale horror, an invisible smoke that tainted the nostrils and throat."

The castle was far afield from Michel's concerns, and Huysmans' morbid memories farther still. "What can you tell me about Gilles de Rais?"

"You have not read *Là Bas*?" Huysmans regarded him suspiciously.

"I read it when it was first published," Michel quickly assured him. "But I remember only bits and pieces of it. As a Parisian, the contemporary section had the most impact."

Mollified, Huysmans gave him a brief history. "Gilles' parents died when he was about ten. After that, he was raised by his grandfather, Jean de Craon, an old man even then, and thoroughly corrupt. As a boy, Gilles was allowed to run wild. He was married off young, a marriage that was essentially meaningless. Soon he sought out the court, where his youth and riches let him cut a dashing figure. He had his own army which the dauphin was most pleased to use. Gilles was judged a courageous, even a reckless warrior."

"And he served under Jeanne d'Arc?" Michel's heart clenched tight inside his chest.

"He was there when Jeanne first knelt before the dauphin, recognizing him even though he was in disguise. It was her first miracle, but not as great to Gilles as her triumph in battle. He rode to victory after victory by her side. He reached a glorious pinnacle of faith and fame." Huysmans paused. "Her capture and death were devastating blows from which he never recovered. After her death in the flames, he began his quest for a magical solution."

"Solution to what?"

"Despair, I would say. Gilles de Rais would probably have said he wanted immortality, infinite wealth, and ultimate knowledge." Huysmans paused again. "In his quest, he descended into a bottomless pit of depravity and madness. His few remaining acts of good, all his acts of evil—everything was done in extraordinary excess, at extraordinary expense. The richest man in France was wholly bankrupt when he was arrested for heresy."

"Not murder?" Michel frowned.

"They would not arrest an aristocrat for the murder of meaningless peasant children. In that era, they were little better than livestock." Huysmans made a moue of distaste. "But heresy threatened the power of the Church. Once there was proof of that, the evidence of the murders could be included."

"What else?"

"I see no need to recount information I spent months—years—gathering. Read my book. Read a biography." He continued in a less aggrieved tone, "If you want to show me other evidence, perhaps I will know something directly relevant."

Michel pushed aside his own possessiveness about the case and evaluated the remaining documents and photographs he had brought with him. There was no need to show Huysmans the hideous photos of Alicia's wounds. Michel did remember that Gilles de Rais sometimes eviscerated his victims though that was not his only mode of murder. He indulged in other atrocities, slow strangulation, dismemberment, bludgeoning. Michel picked out the list of missing children. "Do you see any correlation to Gilles' victims? Their work? Their names?"

"Usually the children were anonymous, known to us only as the son or daughter of the grieving parent. Sometimes the age was given," Huysmans said as he took the pages. But when he actually looked through them, he paled. "This is extraordinary. We know a half dozen or so names of the hundreds he may have murdered. But the first known victim is the son of a man named Jean Jeudon. The first victim on your list is also the son of a man named Jeudon. And here too, Jamet—a boy chosen by Gilles de Rais for demonic sacrifice."

Michel wished the *bouquiniste* had a more common name than Jeudon. And Jamet had been the boy Dancier said he was training as a pickpocket.

Huysmans looked over the names again and shook his head. "Nothing else emerges. The other names mean nothing to me."

Jeudon was the first on Michel's list. Was he truly the first victim? Perhaps that name was all the killer needed to begin this orgy of slaughter. Once the modern Gilles had murdered an innocent child, he could follow no other path but madness. "A medieval monster comes to life," he said, more to himself than Huysmans.

"I now understand something about Gilles de Rais which I did not even when I devoted myself to studying him."

"And that is?" Michel asked.

"His faith. No, for I always understood that sin and redemption were interlocked in his soul." Huysmans' eyes shone with his own fervor. "The unsullied soul of Catholicism endures in the unsurpassed beauty of its art, its music, which can transform both sin and suffering. The creation of such beauty and the besmirching of it were both Gilles' light and his darkness."

"What did the children know of this unsurpassed beauty?"

"Let us hope that their very innocence transformed their suffering before God."

"Forgive me, Monsieur Huysmans, but perhaps your own search for faith makes you too generous."

"Not at all. Gilles never stopped worshipping, never stopped abasing himself before the glory of God, even as he questioned it, even as he defied it and defiled it. He was center stage in his own fabulous drama."

"That I can believe," Michel said. Gilles de Rais probably only believed in God and the Devil to give more importance to his own gore-sodden soul.

"Once he lost his saintly Jeanne, he turned to Satanism. It was his revenge on God, yet it was also his path to salvation."

"You believe he was saved?" Michel's tone was flat.

"The forgiveness of God is infinite."

"I hope not." Michel did not believe a killer like Gilles should be saved. It made him hope that the soul existed, so it could be damned.

Leaving, Michel thanked Huysmans and affirmed that he would reread *Là Bas*. He decided to take the long walk back to the Seine and search the stalls of the *bouquinistes* for the biography Huysmans' recommended. There had been nothing about the heraldic symbol in *Là Bas*, or he would have remembered it. The killer must have had other sources to be able to find the symbol and to know the children's names. Any of the Revenants might be able to beg or bribe their way into the archives.

Gilles de Rais had been an aristocrat. Estarlian was of noble birth and a baron. Would that make him more likely to identify with the historic figure? Perhaps, but others might crave that distinction for the creature who lived inside. Paul Noret might have a hidden Hyde who was everything that his Jekyll personality despised. Jules Loisel might desire the elegance, distinction, and power implied in a title. Charron—any of them—might think Gilles de Rais the ultimate decadent artist, carving the flesh of his angelic choirboys after listening to them sing Hallelujah.

And Vipèrine… Lilias had said that Vipèrine was to conduct a Black Mass. He was the only suspect known to be dabbling in the slimy malevolence of Satanism. An icicle streaked Michel's spine, for he remembered that Lilias also said that Vipèrine was from Rouen.

Jeanne d'Arc was burned at the stake in Rouen.

Tonight, Michel would read about his killer's secret mentor, whispering in his ear from beyond the grave.

Chapter Thirty~One

Every hideous vice has a lair—
Paul Verlaine

"*Merde!*" Michel's curse was loud enough that the other detectives in the bureau looked up from their work. He stared them down, then bent over his notes again.

He would, however, have to inform Rambert of his mistake.

Michel had done what he told himself he must not. He'd looked for evidence to implicate his chief suspect, fitted fact to theory. In doing that, he had overlooked a lead—the cocky young fiacre driver who had seen Averill Charron in Montmartre cemetery early in the morning. Zacharie Corbeau had been so obliging. So pleased to become part of the drama.

Was this Corbeau instead tweaking the tails of the police? Had he seized upon the chance to push an innocent man further into the spotlight? Could the driver possibly be working with Charron? If so, why not provide a better alibi?

"*Débile.*" Stupid. This time his mutter was low enough that no one else heard.

Why had he been so neglectful? He had solved cases in the past following just such oblique leads as this driver. But he had spent most of his time brooding over the Revenants. Why? The image of Theodora Faraday came to mind. Michel pushed it away. He did not like that a spirited young woman was endangering herself, but it was her choice, not the urging of her decadent poet friends. Then he realized it was exactly because his suspects were poets that he found them more intriguing as killers. Ridiculous. There was nothing poetic in the slaughter of Alicia.

Late in the afternoon, Hugh Rambert entered the dim, wood-paneled office. Michel beckoned him over. "*Zut!*" was Rambert's mild expletive after hearing the explanation. "It's like the warning Monsieur Bertillon has written on the wall upstairs, that the eye sees only what it is looking for."

"And looks for the idea already in the mind."

"Yes." He gave his pleasant, diffident smile. "I've been investigating the stables all day, working outward from Montmartre. It's good you have found a specific lead."

Michel could give only a bland description. "He looked a little less than thirty. Undistinguished—brown eyes, dark brown hair, light olive skin. Face and features a bit on the narrow side. Very animated. I think he wore a black coat but that means almost nothing."

"He could be the man I saw or one of a thousand others," Rambert agreed.

Michel handed him the interview. "The first step will be to find out if he was who he claimed to be. He gave his name as Zacharie Corbeau."

"Corbeau?" Rambert repeated, then began flipping through his notebook.

Michel leaned forward. "What?"

"He's here," Rambert announced with satisfaction. His smile took on a grim edge. "I felt that anyone who'd tortured Alicia so cruelly must enjoy inflicting pain, so at each stable I asked if they'd fired anyone because he was a bully or cruel to the animals."

"That was good thinking," Michel told him. "It did not occur to me."

Rambert stood straighter at the praise, then added apologetically, "I have a dog...sir."

Touched and amused, Michel confessed, "I feed the cats behind the Palais, but it still did not occur to me."

Rambert smiled broadly now. Michel pointed to the notebook. Rambert cleared his throat and resumed a serious expression. "Two or three drivers were mentioned. One had been fired from two places. I spent the morning chasing him down, only to find out he'd been trampled to death a week ago."

"Justice?"

"I think so. There was no time to continue before meeting you, but this other man was next because he was closest in age."

"Zacharie Corbeau?"

"I didn't learn his Christian name. One owner told me that Old Corbeau's grandson was an evil brute with the beasts." Anger sparked in Rambert's eyes.

"Go first thing tomorrow."

"I'll go now. The stables are near the Quai d'Orsay. That gives him river travel and train travel as well as the carriages."

Michel stayed him. "Aside from Blaise Dancier, you and I are the only ones who can recognize him. But he knows our faces as well. Work up some sort of disguise."

He eyed the other's thick mustache, but Rambert raised a protective hand. "More men have mustaches than not. Perhaps a fake beard?"

"Not too fake. At the very least wear worker's clothing and something different each day so you will be more difficult to spot."

"I can do it in an hour." Then he ran out of the building.

Michel waited till after nightfall. Just as he was about to leave, Rambert reappeared. His clothes were scruffy, his face bright with triumph. Michel stood to greet him. "Success?"

"It's him!"

Michel felt an answering surge of anticipation.

"I put on these workman's clothes and found a *café* on the corner across from the stables. I teased along a beer through the evening, had some bread and olives. There were checkered half-curtains to hide my face, but I could see over them. Just after sunset, Corbeau appeared and went into the stables. He's not so ordinary that I couldn't recognize him. The street lights were bright enough."

"You are sure he didn't notice you?"

"He didn't even glance at the *café*, but the owner's wife could tell I was watching the place. To win her over, I bought a nice dinner. Then I said this Zacharie owed me money, but I wondered if it might be more trouble than it was worth to try and collect it."

"Good. Did she offer information?"

"Oh yes. They don't like him there though he's done nothing in particular. The wife said he was arrogant and rude to her. Even worse, cheap. He's the grandson of the aging, ailing owner. The father's long dead. Our suspect lives in the house beside the stables and works when he pleases, sometimes day, sometimes night—sometimes both. For years there were other drivers, but the last few months there has been only the grandson."

Michel met Rambert's gaze. "That is suspicious."

"She even gave a little shiver when she talked about him," Rambert went on eagerly. "He hasn't murdered anyone on their doorstep, but something about him doesn't settle well. Maybe the other drivers quit because he was a brute to them as well as the animals."

"Or maybe he threw them out because he has something to hide."

Rambert nodded his accord. "Do you think this fiacre driver works alone?"

"A driver could, but we cannot discount a cohort. The driver captures the child and gives the other man an alibi. Perhaps they can even arrange the reverse."

"Does your instinct say Charron is this cohort? Or one of the others of his clique?"

"Nothing insists that any of the Revenants is guilty. They are simply the most probable suspects."

"We must hope we have the killer in our sights."

Michel agreed. "So far, our only other choice is Vipèrine."

"Once you mentioned Charron's vivisectionist father."

"He is still possible, but I thought the father dominated and perverted the son. With Corbeau that would make three. Also, the father is older, why wait so long to commit these crimes?"

"Who knows what might have set him off? What he does is cruel, but perhaps it was Corbeau who took him even further into the darkness."

"That is possible. And it is possible they are setting a frame on the son." Michel had Rambert pick four men to follow Corbeau while he was driving his carriage. Since Corbeau worked odd hours, two were to be in place at dawn and another two would come at noon. Michel and Rambert at sunset. Michel told them to follow very discreetly. "Stay on foot if he's meandering. Take a carriage if need be. It's better to lose him than have him spot you. If you can keep up with him, take note if he contacts anyone or goes anywhere suspicious."

After sunset, Michel and Rambert walked past the stables, noting one of their men loitering at the corner. They went into the *café* and joined the other watcher at the table by the window. Seeing Rambert again, the proprietor's wife grinned broadly and placed tankards of beer in front of them all. She was gleefully hoping that Corbeau was in deep trouble, swishing her skirts in anticipation. After a minute, the loiterer came in. He said Corbeau had gone out once in the afternoon for a few hours, then returned.

"You followed?"

"For a while he stopped often enough that I could keep up, but then he took a turn through the Bois de Boulogne. I couldn't match him, so I came back here."

"He turned up about an hour later," the second watcher said, then glanced at the first man uneasily.

"Did he spot you?" Michel asked.

The first man shrugged. "I don't know. I don't think so."

Which meant he thought so but hoped he was wrong. It made Michel uneasy. Just then, looking out over the checkered curtains, he saw Corbeau emerge on foot from the gates and lock them behind him. Rather than replace the afternoon watchers as planned, Michel sent the two men to follow Corbeau. When they were out of sight, he left the *café* with

Rambert and crossed to the stables. The street was sleepy. No one appeared to be watching except the *café* owner's wife peeping over the curtains. She counted herself part of the drama. Michel had Rambert hoist him to the top of the stone wall. He wanted an unofficial look around inside while Rambert waited to confront Corbeau if he returned unexpectedly.

Michel lowered himself on the other side of the wall and dropped down to a cobblestone courtyard thickly littered with straw and dung. Everything looked filthy. First he went to the front door of the house next to the stables. It was locked. Michel had his lockpicks but decided not to bend the rules that far. Instead he went to the stables, which were open. Inside were one carriage and an empty space for another. Three horses waited in the stalls. Both the carriage and the animals were better tended than the courtyard though the rest of the interior was shoddy. Corbeau was still keeping up appearances on the streets. Two of the horses were shy of him, perhaps because their owner was cruel, but one greeted him with a nicker and allowed its ears to be scratched. Looking around as he stroked the horse, Michel saw a wooden staircase rising on one side, leading up to a high hayloft. More bales of hay were piled up in a wall directly below it.

Michel thought he heard a rustle in the loft above. A rat in the straw? Most likely. But his uneasiness lingered. Drawing his gun, he moved quietly up the stairs. At the top he paused and quickly surveyed the loft. Nothing seemed awry, but there were hay bales everywhere, easy to hide behind, and storage cabinets were spaced out along the half-timbered walls. Michel moved as noiselessly as he could, but the hay crinkled and the floorboards creaked. He opened the three storage closets on the side wall, all filled with stable paraphernalia, extra tack and grooming tools, medicines for the animals. He turned and began to search along the back wall.

There was a sudden sharp creak and a surge of movement behind him. Michel had time to half turn before the cord looped over his head. He caught it with a hand in front of his throat and took a swift breath as Corbeau yanked it tight. Michel twisted against the pull. Reaching back, he managed to get his free hand around the base of Corbeau's skull, then lunged, trying to drag Corbeau over his back and onto the floor. Corbeau slid sideways, toppling onto a pile of bales and taking Michel with him. Michel scrabbled against him, unable to get any leverage. Rolling over, Corbeau landed on his feet, still holding tight. He yanked on the cord and rammed his knee into Michel's kidney.

Ignoring the clout of pain, Michel dropped to one knee, pulling Corbeau on top again, driving an elbow up into his solar plexus. Corbeau grunted but didn't let go of the cord. Michel twisted his hand, trying to get a better grip and only cutting his palm. He felt his own knuckles choking his windpipe. Corbeau pulled the cord tighter, lifting Michel to his feet and tightening his grip as they lurched back. Michel caught a glimpse of a trick door open between the timbers in the wall.

Swinging around, Corbeau flung Michel against the cabinet, thrusting his head against the wood. The panel cracked. Corbeau slammed him into it again and it splintered. Jagged wood cut his scalp. Tasting blood, Michel pivoted, braced a foot against the wall and shoved. They stumbled back together, but the pressure on the cord gave a little. Michel tightened his fist around the cord and pulled it forward. Taking a breath, he exhaled and jammed his elbow up into Corbeau's face.

Michel felt the grip on the cord slacken and seized the chance. He twisted free and spun around, cracking Corbeau's forehead with his own. Corbeau staggered. Michel grabbed him and landed a hard punch to the jaw. Corbeau reeled back, breaking his hold and lashing out with a nasty kick to the groin that Michel dodged. Regaining his balance, he sprang forward, but Corbeau twisted sideways, rolling across the flat top of the bales to land on his feet. A rope hung from the ceiling in the center of the hayloft. Corbeau leapt, catching hold of the rope and swinging to the far side. Michel raced toward him.

The floor cracked and dropped away. Michel fell straight down, catching the ragged edge of the floorboards. Splintered wood cut into his raw palm, layering new pain over the sliced line of the cord. Swaying, he looked down. The drop wasn't far at all, with inviting bales of hay piled up. More loose hay was scattered across the top. That seemed wrong. Then the dim lamplight picked up the glint of metal. Looking back up, he saw that some of the floorboards were splintered, others cut through. Corbeau had led him here, hoping he'd drop to his death. What was below?

There was a creak and a rush of sound above him. Corbeau swung back, landing on the still solid edge of the flooring. A booted foot lifted, threatening to crush his hands. Michel moved along the shattered edge. Corbeau grinned maliciously as it started to crack. Quickly, Michel reached for the far end of the break. Above him, Corbeau shifted, trying to drive him back toward the center. Was it only another ploy to fool him with deadly traps laid under all the bales? He could grab Corbeau and topple him, but then they would both be impaled on what lay below. Again, Corbeau lifted a booted foot, his body tensing to drive it down. Before his hands were smashed, Michel took the chance and swung forward, twisting in the air to try and land on his feet. One heel caught between the bales and he tripped and landed flat on his back. His breath was knocked out of him—but no metal pierced him.

He dragged in air. Exhaled in relief.

Overhead Corbeau cursed and ran across the loft. Michel guessed he was leaving through his secret entrance. He rose to his feet and looked up at the gaping hole eight feet above him, cursing in turn. Could he make the jump and haul himself up without falling back on the bales? It was quicker and less dangerous to take the stairs. But neither would be quick enough to catch his killer.

Heavy footsteps thundered across the cobbles. Michel rolled off the bales to see Rambert enter the stable. He must have heard the commotion and clambered over the wall. "You're bleeding. Are you hurt?"

"Just scraped." His voice sounded gritty. "Corbeau doubled back."

Rambert looked up at the cut floorboards. "He set a trap?"

Michel nodded. Together they circled behind the hay bales. Rambert reached out and pulled some down. Five pitchforks had been wedged into an improvised wooden stand between the bales. Michel had barely missed skewering his head on the last one.

"Nasty," Rambert said.

It had taken Corbeau a while to assemble this. Had the trap been set for them, or was he at odds with some partner in crime? Michel remembered the vacant space for the second fiacre and suspected Corbeau had it stored elsewhere.

Going upstairs, they found the cracked panel opened onto a landing with narrow stairs descending down to a door. Corbeau had jammed it, but they managed to shove it open. Outside was an overgrown backyard with a large but sickly apple tree and a multitude of weeds. There looked to be another door leading into the house, but Michel could not find the trigger to open it. Turning to Rambert, he said, "We have reason to search now that we've been attacked."

They entered the front door, moving carefully from room to room. Every one was filthy, thick with dust and debris, stinking of rotted food and waste. They found the grandfather alone in a room on the ground floor in the back. He was frail, crippled with arthritis, and almost deaf. When they asked about his grandson, he quivered with fear. He crossed his arms over his chest and pulled the bottom of his sleeves to cover his hands. Drawing the sleeves back Michel saw his hands and arms were covered with small round sores...cigarette burns.

Old Corbeau jerked his arms away and waved his hands at them. "Go away! Go away! He will kill me. Worse."

"He won't kill you," Michel promised.

"What? What?"

Michel spoke loudly and slowly. "We have men to guard you. One during the day, one at night."

The old man stared at him uncertainly. "You will protect me?"

"But you must tell us what you know."

"I don't know anything!" he cried.

"What you suspect," Michel challenged.

The old man looked away, looked back furtively. At last, he whispered, "The hideaway."

"What is that?"

"Under the stables." He began to recount what must be an old family story. "When the Catholic kings were helping kill off the Protestants, our family smuggled them from Paris to Dieppe. We had another stable there and were allied with a shipping company. The Protestants paid us well to escape Paris and sail to a friendlier place. It made us rich, yes, but it was dangerous. It was heroic."

"What is under the stables?" Michel asked again.

"A priest hole." The old man giggled. "A priest hole, but for Protestants."

"Where?"

"In the corner of the back stall, hidden under the feeding trough."

Rambert was eager to go search, but first Michel asked the old man, "Did your grandson come here with any friends?"

The old man shook his head but looked uncertain. At last he looked up and said, "Sometimes the floor shook, as if there were two people upstairs. Two people walking back and forth in his room."

Michel turned to Rambert. "First we look in his room, then the stables."

Rambert glanced at him uncertainly. "The grandson may try to return, either for something he has left or to silence any witnesses."

"I did just promise," Michel said wryly. "See if the other men have come back from their search and set them to watch here. And we need to find a relative, however distant."

Michel talked to old Corbeau while Rambert went on his errand. He managed to gather a few tales of wretched torment before Rambert reappeared with the first watcher. He'd left a note at the *café* for the other. The watcher scowled, unhappy with this new assignment that would last all night. It was the man that Michel was certain had clumsily alerted Corbeau earlier. He had no sympathy. "You had best stay awake, or you'll find yourself skewered by a pitchfork. There may be other escape routes hidden in these buildings."

With the grandfather guarded, Michel took Rambert up the stairs and down the corridor to the room that would be over the old man's. It overlooked the apple tree in the back yard. There was a stuffed raven on the table—Corbeau's namesake. Its glass eye caught the lamplight and winked at him. There were drawings and torn pictures of ravens on the walls. There were no books in the room, but there were clippings from the newspapers about the fire at the bazaar and others about Alicia being displayed at the morgue. There were also articles about some of the other missing children, the girls in particular, he noted. All that had been reported, Michel imagined. There were some older clippings, grisly murders that must have intrigued him. Michel had a sinking feeling. He had said to Averill Charron that in Paris even chimneysweeps read Baudelaire. Carriage drivers could read Huysmans. Corbeau was not illiterate, but there were only the clippings, no books. Whoever had created the Gilles persona was well read, to have ferreted out oddments from research. This man showed no sign of that sort of effort. He might have taken the story as it was and dressed himself in its trappings. Could someone else have given him the flourishes? Michel could not discount the possibility.

Seeing his frown, Rambert asked what was wrong. Michel went over his theory.

"Perhaps the books were elsewhere. Perhaps he has not kept them," Rambert argued.

"They would be his Bible."

"He might know the important bits by heart?"

Michel shook his head. "He's claimed the raven as his symbol, not the swan."

Rambert drew breath to argue, then paused, sighed. "I'm afraid you are right."

Michel nodded glumly. "Let us find this hidden room."

They went back to the stables, to the stall in the far corner that the old man had told them about. No horse was kept there, but there were extra bales piled up in the corner. Corbeau was not overly imaginative. When they pulled away the bales, they saw nothing. Probing the floorboards, Michel felt the slightly deeper seams of a door. In its time, it had been well designed to escape detection. The door slid back under the wall, perhaps into one of the storage sheds outside. Opened, it revealed a staircase leading underneath the stables.

Already, Michel caught the rotten scent of old blood rising from below. He and Rambert exchanged glances. "Stay here," Michel said.

"I must see it." Rambert's voice was bleak but determined.

"I understand, but we don't want to risk being trapped."

"Ah. He might come back."

Michel went and took one of the lanterns that lit the stable. "I haven't seen anything so precious he might return for it—unless he wants his stuffed raven—but neither do I want to risk being interred below."

Rambert smiled grimly. "If he killed off the others, there'd be no one to say where we were."

"Exactly." With Rambert keeping watch, Michel descended the ancient steps. The old man called it a hidey-hole, but he arrived in a large storage room. The reek of blood was overpowering. He leaned against the wall, nauseated. He had a strong stomach, but a voice in his mind whispered, *Alicia's blood*. The lantern showed a wooden table in the center of the room. Approaching it, he saw its surface was totally stained, though the edges were darker, silhouetting the shape of a small body. There were dark patterns on the stone floor and piles of soiled straw. He saw blood spatters on the wall. How many children had died here?

Corbeau had felt invulnerable. Little cleaning had been done. It could not be laziness alone, the killer must revel in the smell, adding the bright metallic scent of new blood to contrast with this foul decay. Piled in one corner were burlap bags and lengths of oilcloth along with coiled rope and balls of twine. He saw a sock, a shoe, a pink ribbon carelessly left behind from his disposal of the bodies. His whole body suddenly clenched when he saw a striped pinafore lying to one side. His memories of the fire were sometimes chaotic, sometimes searing in their clarity. He remembered now a little girl in a striped pinafore whom he'd held for a moment in his arms.

Overwhelmed, Michel left it all in place to be photographed tomorrow and went back up the stairs. To Rambert, he only said, "It is difficult."

The other man took the lantern and descended. He did not stay as long as Michel, though more than long enough. When he heard Rambert's heavy tread on the stairs, Michel found himself hoping he'd not seen the small clothes on the far side of the room. Rambert emerged whey-faced, walked a few steps into the straw, and vomited. Michel left the stable, fearing the sick aroma might trigger the nausea he'd fought off. After a moment, Rambert came out. "Sorry."

Michel shook his head. "I felt the same." He looked out into the night. Clouds were gathering, blocking out the stars. The moon was still visible, like the thick rind of some moldy half-devoured cheese. He felt his anger growing, the cold fury he feared most. "He escaped."

"He tried to kill us and failed," Rambert answered. "We know who he is."

"Who he was. Now he is free to become someone else." Knowing they would be on the watch for him here, Corbeau could run to another city. But if he was emotionally attached to Paris, perhaps he could not bear to leave. Or if he had a partner who shared his depravity, he might be loath to abandon their shared lust. Much depended on just how insane Corbeau was. Michel doubted he loved anything but mayhem. If he could no longer resist displaying his kills, he would be caught—eventually. But if he could control that urge, he might indulge his blood lusts for years.

"He will never be free," Rambert said seriously. "He is doomed to repeat these crimes. They are all he is now."

"But that is what I'm afraid of," Michel said. "We let him escape to kill again."

Chapter Thirty~Two

*No shining candelabra has prevented us from
looking into the darkness, and when one looks into
the darkness, there is always something there.*

William Butler Yeats

Carmine sent a note begging off the trip to the Mathers. Her father
needed help to finish a print run. Theo could hear her voice in the
brisk encouragement. "They are expecting you, so go by yourself. They
will not bite!"

Friday's weather was beautiful. Theo wheeled her bicycle down to
the flat boulevards and rode it across Paris. She passed three other women
in bloomers en route. They all smiled and returned her wave. Susan B.
Anthony said that the bicycle had done more for the emancipation of
women than anything else in the world. Theo loved her outfit—azure
Turkish trousers topped by an embroidered knee-length coat in iridescent
peacock. Scandalized, Uncle Urbain had threatened to burn it. Such
garments, such activities, led to indecent feelings. And feelings to actions,
Theo supposed. For the moment at least, she felt indecently free, the
sprightly breeze flowing around her all the way to the Mathers' abode.

When she knocked, it was MacGregor who opened the door. "Ah
yes, the young artist who is embroiled in darkness." He scrutinized Theo
intently. She looked down to hide her dismay. It was true enough, but his
manner was so theatrical it exasperated her. He gestured her into the
foyer where Moina waited, wearing one of the draped gowns that made
her look like a Grecian oracle, a necklace of heavy amber glowing golden
around her throat. Theo wanted to talk only with Moina, but MacGregor
obviously wanted to rule the situation. Gesturing to his wife, he said,
"Moina has dreamed of you, not once, but twice since we saw you. She is
very sensitive, very intuitive. It is certainly significant."

Theo looked to Moina, stunned. "Truly?"

"Truly," Moina affirmed. "It was as if the Tarot cards came alive and
I was wandering with you in the landscape of the moon."

Doubt settled around Theo like a murky grey cloak. For a second, she clung to it eagerly. But why bother coming here if she could not believe? Moina's dream was not that odd, given Theo's dramatic reading. Nonetheless, it felt darkly prophetic. Carmine was not a fool and she trusted Moina. MacGregor might be self-aggrandizing, but there was a ferocious intentness about him.

Theo let the doubt fall away. "Did you find some message for me in your dream?"

Moina shook her head, smiling sadly. "No. I felt I must warn you of something, but I never discovered just what it was. It may only be that the layout Carmine did was so troubling, but I have learned to trust such dreams."

MacGregor moved closer, his intentness demanding attention. "And you, Miss Faraday, have you had any dreams of import?"

"They have been troubled and I was happy to forget them quickly. I wasn't looking for import—my waking life seems overly full of it."

"When you dream," MacGregor said to her, "you should look for Moina."

Was that possible? What a fascinating idea. The Revenants always talked of the power of dreams. For a time Theo had written hers down, searching for inspiration for her art. But even the most vivid Moulin Rouge extravaganzas of her dreaming life never seemed to translate onto canvas for her. The waking world offered far more inspiration, even if her imagination then turned the image into something resembling a dream.

Theo followed the Mathers into the salon, where a china tea service was set out. The brew was an herbal tisane, for the fresh, pure fragrance of mint perfumed the air. Moina poured cups and handed them round. There were also a few simple sweets on a tray. Theo felt too nervous to eat so much as a biscuit, but she sipped her tea and felt the hot liquid flow through her. Unexpectedly, the brew gave her a new calmness and her mind felt clearer. She smiled at Moina, who gave her a warm smile in return. It seemed a good moment to begin, but just as Theo took out her notebook, a knock sounded at the door.

"I will send whoever it is away." Moina went into the hall. Theo heard her open the door and then the low sound of voices. After a moment, she returned, but not alone. A tall, slender man came with her. Theo recognized William Butler Yeats, an Irish poet she had first met at Verlaine's funeral. His poems were often mystical. Since he knew the Mathers, his interest in the occult must run deep. They exchanged greetings, then Moina said, "Mr. Yeats dropped by to bid us adieu, for he is returning to Ireland. His arrival seems fortuitous for, like us, he is a student of the occult. I have asked him to stay."

"But only if you feel comfortable with my presence. I will understand if you do not." There was a hint of Irish lilt in his voice and his paced speech differed little from the way he chanted his poetry.

Impulsively, Theo replied, "Yes, please join us." The poet's presence was like an omen that her friends were innocent. Theo knew her response was anything but rational, but she felt happier with him there.

Yeats settled himself in a chair beside her. She guessed him to be about thirty. The oval glasses he wore did not obscure the intense yet dreamy expression of his deep brown eyes. His lips were full and sensitive, but a strong nose gave his face character. He had lovely floppy hair rather like Averill's. She remembered them sitting side by side, murmuring over a poem, their hair falling over their foreheads.

Although Yeats spent most of his time with his Irish compatriots, he had come to some of the Revenants' *café* gatherings. Averill had coaxed him to submit a poem to the first issue of the magazine, Yeats' English version printed beside Averill's translation into French. Theo had suggested some alternate words, even a rhyme or two, for her vocabulary was wider than Averill's. But she did not have a poet's unique sense of rhythm, any more than Averill could draw a landscape as easily as he could critique one. She thought the translation a great success and Yeats had seemed pleased.

Moina set down her tea and looked at Theo. "Carmine said that you needed our help. She said that the Tarot reading we did for you had come true."

Theo nodded. "Yes, I believe it has."

"Which cards did you draw?" Yeats asked. When she told him, he frowned. "Most difficult."

"Yes," Moina said. "The forbidding landscape of The Moon and The Devil hovering over all."

"And Death at the end." Theo felt bleak.

Yeats looked directly at her. "Do you know who this Devil might be?"

"I am trying to identify him," Theo answered, then turned to the Mathers. "That is why I am here. I hope you can help me do that."

"Of course. But how?" Moina asked.

"First, I must ask you all for a promise. Please don't discuss what I tell you with anyone, not until the case is solved." It was a small precaution in respect for Inspecteur Devaux. He would be displeased at her coming here and even more at her showing them evidence.

"I promise," Moina said solemnly. Seated around the table, the others nodded as well.

Theo could not know that they would keep their promise, but people who practiced magic must be good at keeping secrets. Theo laid down the sketch she had done of the winged cross in her alley. She waited a heartbeat, then realized she'd been hoping for a gasp of recognition. She looked at Moina and Macgregor in turn. "This means nothing to you?"

"No, nothing," Moina answered.

Yeats asked, "Are they bird's wings?"

"I thought so," Theo answered.

"Perhaps an angel?" MacGregor stared at the image intently, but Theo saw no light of recognition in his eyes. He turned the paper this way and that. "It is an emblem of some sort, I believe."

"Of what sort?" she prompted.

"That I cannot say." His forehead creased in thought as he groped for the memory. "The concept does seem somewhat familiar, perhaps something which I encountered in passing."

Theo fought down a surge of frustration. How foolish to hope for an instant solution, some arcane bit of knowledge that would explain everything and point to the killer.

"A cross." Yeats tilted his head, considering the drawing as MacGregor turned it toward him. "Wings…ascension. Perhaps transformation."

Moina leaned toward Theo. "Why is it important?"

Meeting that warm, searching gaze, Theo went to the ghastly heart. "Children are being murdered. Only one body has been discovered—a little girl I knew. But there have been many mysterious disappearances and the police think the same man killed the others."

"And left this mark behind?" As if it were contaminated, MacGregor pushed the sketch back toward Theo.

She did not pick it up. Perhaps it might yet spark a memory. "Yes. The same symbol has appeared several times."

"This is terrible," Moina said. "Do you want me to do another Tarot layout for you? Even if it does not reveal your Devil, perhaps it will point in some new direction."

Theo shook her head. She needed substance, not mystical vision, however compelling that vision might be. "You believe magic should be used for good…."

"White magic, not black," Moina said softly.

"But you may know others who want to control those darker forces." Theo hesitated.

"And that we might know such a despicable person?"

MacGregor sounded as offended as Theo had feared. Yet the children's lives were more important. If he didn't see that, the others must. Theo appealed to them. "Haven't you at least heard of someone like that—a black magician who would attempt some sort of ritual sacrifice?"

"Symbolic sacrifice is an old and powerful form of magic," Yeats said.

Theo flared. "The murder of these children is not symbolic. It is horrible."

"However horrifying, it may still be a symbol," Yeats said quietly. "I am only saying that sacrifice is a powerful element, one that can be used for good or for ill."

MacGregor was seething. "Fools and charlatans abound in the occult—as they do in the mundane world. But a villain such as this, who would pervert the ancient wisdom, we would shun absolutely. Such black energy can infect the minds of others."

Theo decided to ask directly about Vipèrine, but before she could, Yeats intervened. "Macgregor, do you remember when I brought my friend to visit you in England?"

"The skeptic who yearned to believe?"

"The very one."

"Would you perform a similar ritual for Miss Faraday? This symbol may be significant."

Macgregor frowned. "I do not know that it is appropriate."

"My friend was no more an initiate than she," Yeats countered.

"Miss Faraday's path has crossed ours for a reason," Moina said. "Forces gather around her to which we should pay heed. We should help her in any way that we can."

Suddenly full of purpose, Macgregor stood. "I will prepare."

Theo swallowed her urge to protest. She had come for information, not rituals and incantations. Yet her trepidations about the Tarot were because the reading had been all too true, if all too ambiguous.

Macgregor withdrew to a far corner of the room, while Moina directed Theo and Yeats to move some of the lighter pieces of furniture aside, making the central space much longer. Macgregor opened a chest and withdrew a few objects and folded pieces of cloth. One of these, richly embroidered in jeweled hues, he lay over the chest to form a kind of dais. Atop it, he placed a small mace of golden polished wood, then propped up a tablet filled with squares of many colors. Each had a number on it. Macgregor unfolded an deep indigo robe that he donned. He picked up the mace and studied the tablet, moving a few of the squares to new positions. Then he turned to face them.

It seemed both strange and strangely simple to Theo, looking at the box with its numbered squares. The robe was painted with runes of some kind, but it was not particularly theatrical. The robe of a workaday wizard, she thought, biting back the smile that surfaced unbidden. She did sense a new concentration in MacGregor. His expression was intense but inward, absorbed in private thought or visions. Moina gestured for Theo and Yeats to stand together, facing her husband, then placed herself halfway between them, her gaze on him as well. She kept the drawing, studying it for a moment, then holding it so that Macgregor could look at it. He began to speak, a low chanting, which Moina echoed. Their resonant voices had a quiet power, but Theo did not recognize the language. It was not Latin. Was it an invocation in Greek—or perhaps in something more ancient still?

Not understanding, Theo felt ill at ease but knew she must make an effort to be more receptive. Closing her eyes, she drew a calming breath, and another, pacing her breathing to the exotic sounds. Slowly the unknown words become a kind of poetry, music, evoking images from pure sound. The soft intonations slowly created a quivering vibration in the room. The very air seemed to hum. Behind the darkness of her closed lids, Theo pictured the black cross with its upswept wings. What did it mean?

Suddenly, the lines quivered and moved, taking on dimension. The white of the paper condensed within them, forming a great, gleaming swan, fantastical and vividly alive. The wings flashed out, fire soaring from the tips of the quills. A corona of crimson light surrounded the bird and bled across the pale feathers. The wings closed, shadow and smoke pouring down.

"I see a swan," Moina said.

And MacGregor replied, "A swan in flames."

Theo gasped. The image vanished. She opened her eyes, staring at Moina, who had not moved but continued to commune with her husband.

Beside her, Yeats counseled softly, "Do not question now. Open yourself."

Shivers drizzled over Theo's back, fear and excitement mingled. She closed her eyes again, recalling the swan, but she could summon only a pale memory of the vibrant image that had blazed in her mind.

"He comes. He rides a black horse in the center of a procession," MacGregor said. Theo clasped her hands tightly and bit her lip in frustration. She did not see a man on a black horse.

"There is a great pageant, a performance." Moina said. "He has spent a fortune on the costumes, the livery. Even the beggars' rags are made of shredded silk."

Then, as if she were a hovering bird, Theo did see a vast procession winding slowly through a medieval city. Was it only because Moina evoked it? The images wavered, vanished, reappeared. Theo heard singing and found herself standing in the crowd, watching as the procession passed.

Passing pageboys sang hymns in their exquisite voices. Young women flung handfuls of rose petals in the street. And finally, there in the midst of the others, was a knight in silver armor. On the crest of his helmet, a bird lifted its shimmering wings.

"The swan crowns his head," Moina said, again echoing Theo's vision. "He bears the cross on his shield."

With the certainty of a dream, Theo knew the identity of the knight. *Gilles de Rais*. No—she had read about the pageant in the book. But she had not talked about *Là Bas* with Moina or MacGregor. With her denial the images wavered, faded, but this time they did not vanish. She watched the knight pass by her.

"*Le Mistère du Siège d'Orléans*," Moina said. "It is the tenth anniversary of the Maid's victory. They will perform the play he has written in her honor."

A young woman rode a white horse, her banner rippling in the wind. Theo knew that she saw Jeanne of Arc, not the Jeanne portrayed in the pageant but the real Jeanne, her cropped hair whipped by the same sharp wind, black and shining. Her face glowed with the fierce certainty of victory as she rode—not to Orléans, but to Paris. Her soldiers, her lieutenants turned to her, faith alight in their eyes as they approached devastation. Like transparent scrims, the images overlapped in Theo's mind. The staged triumph mingled with the blood and sweat of ruin.

Then, even more strangely, Theo saw the black horse Gilles had ridden led into a dimly lit stable. It was all very furtive. She watched as the black horse and eight others were sold along with their lavish trappings—sold for a pittance.

"Casse-noissette was his favorite," Moina said. "He is bankrupt."

"Like his coffers, his soul is empty," MacGregor intoned. "There is no alchemy that can transform his sin."

Theo saw Gilles kneeling, hands squeezing his temples as if he could crush the images there. He screamed silently as demons battled in his mind. Behind a locked door, a necromancer beat a mattress and screamed aloud as if he were being murdered. "He seeks to rule the Devil but is already his servant," MacGregor said.

"His faith was burned." Moina's voice was almost a sob.

Her armor stripped away, Jeanne walked forward, dressed in penitent's garb. She asked for a cross. An English soldier broke his lance and bound the pieces together, then handed her his gift. She clasped the cross to her. Theo saw her chained to the stake, the oiled wood lit beneath her. The fire ignited, the smoke billowed. The flames leaped higher and higher, terror mounting as the blaze soared. Theo could no longer see Jeanne, only a wall of flame.

The wall became the wall of a room, burning. A house, burning. A girl with long black hair ran through it, barefoot, her white nightdress catching flame. She stumbled. Fell.

Theo sobbed aloud, memories of Mélanie igniting in her mind.

Like an echo came other sobs. Weeping, endless weeping—a child crying, alone in the dark. The fault is his. His hatred has brought her death. Love has been incinerated with her.

"Jeanne!" Moina's cry is full of grief.

Theo sees the square where Jeanne was burned, the blackened stake. An image drifts over it on a cloud of smoke, a twisted, charred corpse pinned under a fallen timber. Everywhere the reek of ashes, reek of despair. Gilles wants to buy Jeanne's heart, but they have thrown it in the Seine.

The weeping goes on and on, sobs of the grieving child weave with Gilles' choir of innocents singing of salvation.

Then another fire, a furnace with a great fiery maw. Two men appear, lieutenants who had ridden beside Gilles in the parade. They carry a blood-stained canvas and lay it down before the furnace. Pulling back the canvas, they reveal the body of a child, his curling hair matted with blood, his eyes staring into nothingness. With small axes and knives, they hack the boy into pieces and throw him into the flames.

"They destroy the evidence of the murder." Moina faltered.

Theo knew it was not the first body fed to the flames and would not be the last.

"So many—" Moina's voice broke. She pitched forward but MacGregor caught her. "I cannot watch this!"

Theo opened her eyes to see MacGregor looking at her over his wife's shoulder. "We can do no more."

They were all visibly shaken. Theo did not doubt that they had shared a vision, however piecemeal the images. Moina turned to her. "Do you know who we saw?"

Theo spoke the name aloud. "It was Gilles de Rais."

"Yes." Macgregor handed her back the drawing. "The cross was his, and the swan, but this mark you found is only a symbol, an evocation. Did you learn the identity of the man who uses it?"

Theo sat on the divan, swept by a wave of frustration. She had learned a horrible truth, but how could it help her solve the murders? "No. I think perhaps I glimpsed him. Not everything I saw was from the medieval era. But it was too vague, too quick."

Moina sat beside her. "Your Devil has fused Gilles de Rais' identity with his own."

The shivers returned, slithering along Theo's nerves. Almost from the first, Gilles de Rais had become her own symbol of the killer. It was too bizarre to find the killer had chosen him as well. The chill of horror was quickly followed by a thrill of triumph. She had come full circle—back to the question she meant to ask before the Mathers had allowed her into their strange ceremony. "Do you know a man called Vipèrine?"

Yeats only looked curious, but the Mathers glanced at each other with expressions of disgust. MacGregor expounded. "Not a fool, but undeniably a charlatan. A villain who builds his power on seductive parlor tricks and tainted charisma. He is not interested in knowledge, only in power and manipulation."

"Do you think he is involved in these terrible crimes?" Moina asked.

"He plays at being sinister, but I believe it is more than an act," Theo said with growing certainty. She remembered Vipèrine's cold, lustful stare and cruel smile. "When I first saw him, he had a blue beard in imitation of Gilles de Rais."

"That is extraordinary," Moina said.

"Yet *Là Bas* may have tempted others to play with such malevolence." Yeats voiced her hidden fear. The Revenants all knew of Gilles de Rais.

"Vipèrine has appeared at the wrong place at the wrong time—but so have others," Theo admitted. She wanted it to be Vipèrine. It could not be Averill. It must not be one of her poets. But she hoped the killer was someone the police already suspected. If they were watching him, then he might be caught before he killed again. Was there anything in today's strange events that provided a clue for Inspecteur Devaux? She turned to MacGregor. "Have you seen a historical depiction of the shield, or the swan?"

"Little survives from that era," MacGregor answered. "Perhaps the concept seemed familiar because I read of it in heraldry. Gilles de Rais was not someone I studied extensively. His crimes were horrific, but he was not a powerful magician or even a serious alchemist."

Moina gestured to the drawing. "The choice of the swan is so perverse. They are the symbol of purity."

"But also of lust—remember Zeus took the form of a swan to ravish Leda," Yeats said. "In many ways they are creatures of contrast. Their movements embody the grace of the feminine, their necks the virile thrust of the masculine. In that union, they also represent the hermaphrodite."

"In medieval times, they were called hypocritical creatures, vain and deceitful, for the black flesh hidden beneath their white down," MacGregor argued. "Just so, this killer hides his corruption."

"Death," Theo said, thinking of the children. "Don't swans symbolize death?"

Moina nodded. "The myth says that mute swans sing only at their deaths."

Yeats leaned forward, intense and earnest. His slender hands were clasped together, almost in prayer, as he spoke directly to her. "There is great danger here, Miss Faraday. There are elemental forces, entities which shape our art and our lives. To imitate them is to summon them. The imagination is a more potent force than most realize."

"Such forces can inhabit us. We are always at risk." Once again, MacGregor gazed inward. Theo felt unnerved by the glassy intensity of his eyes. Moina touched his arm lightly and he looked round at them. "Such evil must be exorcised, or it will destroy whomever it inhabits. It will swallow them whole and take them into the abyss."

All the Revenants believed in looking into the abyss. No coward, Theo too believed in looking—but not in flinging stones into the darkness to see what demons could be stirred. "You think Vipèrine might be inhabited by such a spirit?"

Yeats said, "Perhaps the killer who now stalks Paris and Gilles de Rais were both inhabited by the same darkness."

There was a brooding pause. They were all still disturbed by the vision. Theo did not think she would find any more clarity, and she was too perturbed to sit and drink mint tea. "If you hear news of Vipèrine or of anyone else suspicious, can you let me know?" she asked the Mathers.

"You will take this information to the police?" MacGregor frowned.

"I know a detective who is discreet."

"Such persons are discreet at their own discretion," MacGregor said. "They cannot understand our purpose and so distrust us all. It may serve their purposes to discredit us as well as capture this villain."

"There is no way to prevent the ignorant from throwing us all in the same stewpot," Yeats said. "We should do what is right."

"Such darkness shadows the light of those like us, who seek wisdom rather than power," Moina said.

MacGregor hesitated then gave a sharp nod. Turning to Theo, he said, "We do not tolerate evil. If we hear of anything suspicious, we will inform you."

"Thank you." His answer filled Theo with both new hope and new trepidation.

Theo rode her bicycle to the foot of the Butte Montmartre and dismounted near the Moulin Rouge. Dusk was falling as she wheeled it up the steep incline of the rue Lepic, still mulling over what she had learned. She understood even more clearly the fascination Carmine felt with the occult world, but she knew her own path was different. Despite being brushed by the power of that world, Theo was an artist, not a seer. Whatever talent she possessed for understanding people came from reading their faces, observing their body movements, and listening to the shifts in their tone of voice, not because she could read minds or see into souls.

Theo stopped abruptly when she reached the first plateau. There were several gendarmes and groups of people talking. Farther up the street, even more people were gathered. She went to the nearest gendarme and asked what had happened. "A young girl has been kidnapped," he said, "the daughter of the bakers on rue…."

"Ninette?"

The gendarme nodded solemnly.

Lovely, innocent Ninette with her rosy cheeks and the scent of bread and sugar perfuming her skin.

Theo ran up the street but was stopped outside the shop by another officer. Instinctively, Theo looked through the window for Inspecteur Devaux. Just as she chastised herself for presuming him to be everywhere, she saw him. Beyond him, Madame Pommier wept on her husband's shoulder. Theo felt an awful twisting in her stomach, as if her innards were knotting themselves. Suddenly, vividly, Theo remembered Casimir and Averill joking about Paul's attraction to Ninette.

Paul. Not Averill. Paul. Theo felt a rush of relief, followed by a rush of shame. All the doubts she had shoved away had not vanished, but lurked, waiting to sink their claws in her. If Paul had seemed overly attentive to Ninette, that didn't mean he had kidnapped her. But it was yet another child that the Revenants knew. Like Denis, and Dondre, and Alicia….

Unbidden, Theo remembered Alicia sitting on her little chair in the morgue as all of Paris filed by to gawk at her. Again her stomach twisted and acid bile rose in her throat. She leaned against the nearest wall, fighting her nausea. A narrow street ran behind the bakery. Memory was a physical thrust, pushing her into the gloom to hunt frantically for the winged cross. It was nowhere to be seen. Where had Ninette been going? How many streets must be searched? Theo looked up and saw Inspecteur Devaux approaching. Silently, he shook his head, his expression grim. He had already hunted here just as she was hunting now. "There is no mark here," he told her. "She didn't return after school. We are exploring that area as well. It is more likely to be there."

"It may not be Alicia's killer."

"True. There are other unpleasant things that can have happened," he answered.

Theo knew that pretty young girls like Ninette were sometimes drugged and seduced, or forced into brothels. "If some seducer has taken her, there is a chance of rescue."

"Do not hope too much, mademoiselle," Inspecteur Devaux said. "There are too many coincidences."

He thought it was one of the Revenants. She still hoped to prove him wrong. "I know the meaning of the winged cross now."

He looked only mildly curious. "You have visited your occult scholars?"

She gave a brief nod, stunned that he didn't show more curiosity. She could not tell him of the vision she had shared, but she had already told him that the Mathers were knowledgeable about the occult. Defiantly, Theo said, "The wings are not an angel but a swan. They said it was the coat of arms of Gilles de Rais."

His gaze was level. Not a flicker of surprise. "My source said the same."

"And you don't find it the least bit strange?"

"Extremely strange," he acknowledged.

Theo wondered how long he had known. Would he even have told her? She battled down a surge of anger. "Surely it makes Vipèrine a stronger suspect?"

"Fractionally."

Sometimes Theo wanted to grab hold of him, to shake him free of that cold calm. "I won't bother to ask what fraction you calculated."

Ignoring her sarcasm, he gestured back toward the bakery. "What can you tell me about this missing girl?"

"She was—she is—very beautiful. Sweet and shy. Naïve." When she paused, he just looked at her. Theo knew what he was really asking. She told him the truth as she knew it. "Paul seemed especially fond of her, but most of the Revenants knew her."

"The Hyphens?" he asked, adopting their term.

"I don't know. I've never seen them in the bakery, but we've said that Monsieur Pommier makes the best croissants...." Her voice quavered and she pressed her hand to her lips. Why was she talking about croissants? "They prefer the Left Bank."

The streetlights came on, shining into the alley. Then a dark shadow as someone stepped into the entrance. Inspector Devaux turned instantly, then said, "Inspector Rambert, this is Mlle. Faraday, whose help has been so valuable already."

"Mademoiselle," the younger man acknowledged. Then to Inspector Devaux he said, "Sir, we have searched along the route that Mademoiselle Ninette takes home from school."

There was a long pause, then Inspector Devaux asked, "What have you discovered?"

Theo was grateful that he was allowing her to remain. She knew that the news was not good.

Rambert stood rigidly, his hands curled into fists. "We have found a winged cross."

Chapter Thirty~Three

*Lord, may your divine glory illuminate this
fiendish hothouse....*

Maurice Maeterlinck

Theo finished cleaning her Colt. She loaded it, set it snug in its holster, wrapped the gun belt around them, and put both on the table. Beside the gun, weighted with her copy of *Là Bas*, was the note from the Mathers. As promised, they had sent news of Vipèrine. Rumor said he was conducting a Black Mass tonight at Midnight. Some said there was to be a virgin sacrifice. She should inform the police. And so she would—after she was en route herself. Theo was certain Ninette was the intended victim. It was too much of a coincidence for the mass to be held the day after she was taken.

Her gaze was drawn back to the gleaming gun, beautiful in the way deadly things could be. Or ugly. Tonight it looked like a coiled rattlesnake. Theo was a good shot, though she hadn't practiced since she left California. She'd gotten the Colt when she lived alone above the stables, out back of the Louvre bar in Jagtown. The owner of the bar had daughters her age and let it be known Theo was under his protection, too. The regulars had come to regard her as one of their own, but once or twice a drunk had decided to try his luck. The door was locked, but sometimes they wouldn't stop pounding. Twice she'd fired out the window, scaring them off. One was crazy enough to smash through the door. She shot him in the thigh. Word got around, and she'd had no more unwanted visitors.

Midnight was not long off. She must hurry—but she must not forget to warn Michel. She picked up pen and paper. Writing quickly, she copied what was needed from the Mathers' note, giving him the location of the townhouse and chapel on the Left Bank, and the password.

"*Luxure*," she muttered under her breath. Lust. Rather blatant, but Theo doubted she'd observe any subtlety in tonight's evil drama. Would she make herself too conspicuous by refusing to blaspheme and dance naked? There must always be curiosity seekers skulking in corners at such events, voyeurs who only wanted to glimpse the darkness. That was what Averill wanted, wasn't it—to look into the abyss but not leap?

Theo sealed the note in an envelope, wrote Inspecteur Devaux's name on it and printed *Urgent* boldly across the top. It was very late. He must be home asleep, but someone would be on duty. She wrote 'Send for him at once' across the bottom. That looked serious enough to have him awakened.

Tonight she wore the scruffy clothes she used for sketching around the stables and other rough areas, breeches and boots, a man's shirt. They would let her run. Let her kick. Let her fight. After strapping on the Colt, Theo covered it with a long, loose jacket. She was tall and lanky with not much bust. Dressed like this, she should be able to pass for a youth if no one looked too closely or groped in the wrong places. She braided her hair and shoved it under a cap, then glared at her image in the mirror, unconvinced. Grabbing some charcoal, she smudged her face to suggest a beard and mustache. Finally, she crossed to a trunk and removed a black, hooded cape. It was velvet and too feminine, but she suspected that many of the attendees would be wearing such things. The hood would shadow her face and add to the illusion.

And Ninette might need something to cover her.

Theo felt feverish, her stomach roiling with apprehension, her senses painfully sharp. It was foolish to go alone, but there was no one she could ask. She thought of Ninette's father, but he was too distressed to behave rationally. Carmine might think it a wonderfully bizarre adventure, but Theo would not put her friend in danger. Rape was the centerpiece of tonight's entertainment—perhaps even murder? If Vipèrine believed himself the reincarnation of Gilles de Rais, he was insane but not so insane as to kill before a crowd. So far he had killed in secret. Theo prayed that his audience could not be so depraved.

She prayed, too, that none of her poets was conspiring with the Satanist. Paul seemed to despise Vipèrine. Could that be a blind to arrange the kidnapping of the exquisite Ninette? Jules had gazed on Vipèrine worshipfully, but did he have the courage to commit a crime? Casimir had seemed utterly scornful of Vipèrine's theatrics and was supposed to be on his way to meet Oscar Wilde in Dieppe. Was that only a ruse so he could indulge this secret lust? Theo screamed silently. She didn't want to believe any of them capable of rape, of murder—but she could not risk Ninette's life on her badly shaken faith. A Revenant was the obvious choice to help her, but innocent or guilty, they would all try to stop her going.

And Theo must go, even if it meant going alone. Averill might be there—not as Ninette's kidnapper, but because he had told Vipèrine he wanted to witness a Black Mass. She did not want him to be arrested for playing out some decadent fantasy. But if he was there and saw poor Ninette about to be ravaged, surely he would stop it?

So much the better—they would rescue her together. They might have to, if Inspecteur Devaux did not arrive in time—if he even came at all.

It was time to go. First, she hurried to the battered old coffee tin where she kept her savings. She would have to hire a fiacre. After calculating the cost as well as she was able, the ride across the Seine and back again, plus waiting time, she took it all. She had not bought paint and canvas yet this month—nor would she now. But the carriage was a necessity if Ninette must be spirited away.

Donning the cloak, Theo set out into the night.

A carriage was easy to find at the foot of the butte, but the ride seemed endless. Theo twitched with impatience while her driver delivered the note to the police station, fearful they would hold him there. But he returned quickly enough, and they crossed the island to the Left Bank, riding through the still noisy streets of the Latin Quarter and on into sleepy residential areas. At last, they arrived in a secluded area of Saint-Germain-des-Prés, filled with ancient walled homes of the aristocratic rich. Passing by the decaying mansion that was her destination, Theo glimpsed the gatekeeper move furtively behind the wall. She had her driver park not far away and walked back along the deserted…or almost deserted avenue. Other carriages waited on side streets. Approaching, Theo saw another group of cloaked figures admitted through the gates. She pulled the hood forward to increase her anonymity.

"*Luxure.*" Her voice sounded hoarse when she whispered the password. The gatekeeper pointed across the courtyard to a side path thickly framed with trees. She saw votive candles set to light the way. Reaching the path, Theo moved swiftly along, passing the ivy-shrouded house to reach the little chapel beyond. It was built in the Gothic style, tall and narrow, the stone ornately carved, though she could not make out the design in the gloom. The long stained glass windows gleamed darkly in the night, their intricate leading like thick black spider webs. Overhead, the waning moon looked oddly menacing amid gathering rain clouds. Its thin sickle of light curved around the bottom edge like an evil grin. *Cheshire cat,* Theo thought—but she was following not a white rabbit, but a black-souled viper.

Entering the chapel, Theo saw the building was dilapidated, the columns splotched with mildew and peeling paint. Near the door was a basin of what should have been holy water, but it reeked like urine. Under its sharpness, the anteroom smelled of dust and mold. Inside the nave, hundreds more votives burned, adding their waxy odor to the air. Their smell, the glimmering flames, took Theo back to the night of the catacombs concert. Even from the back of the chapel, she felt the frantic excitement that simmered in the two dozen people gathered within. But under the daring, the defiance, she sensed a festering shame.

Theo entered the nave, keeping to the shadows as much as she could. But it was impossible to dodge the four men who walked continuously up and down the aisles. They were dressed in mockery of choirboys. Their rouged lips smiled lasciviously, and their robes of transparent organdy displayed their arousal. As they paced, they swung heavy censers that gave off thick clouds of incense and musky herbs. Her nostrils quivered, trying to place a vaguely familiar smell. Hashish. She'd found Averill smoking it once, but he would not let her have any. "You may know everything," he'd said, "but I will not help you do everything!"

But he had not told her everything. He had not told her about Casimir.

The memory of the kiss she'd witnessed filled her mind. Her heart twisted and jerked, as if trying to escape her body.

Thrusting away the excruciating image, Theo forced her attention back to her surroundings. She could not afford to be careless. The smirking choirboys passed her again, swaying their fuming censers. Smoke rose and twisted into predatory shapes like winged snakes. Her head was starting to spin, but she kept circling round the church in search of Averill and the other Revenants. Many were masked, but she would recognize their stance. She did not see anyone with Paul's tall insectile figure, or Casimir's insouciant elegance. Jules moved tentatively—he could disguise himself in the crowd more easily than the others. She had not seen Vipèrine either. Even masked, he would draw his worshippers like a magnet.

Theo reached the front of the chapel, where a large altar was draped with a pure white sheet. The better to show off a virgin's blood... The image made her queasy, and the clinging smoke of the narcotic incense didn't help. Her head was throbbing now. She wanted desperately to go outside, just for a moment, and breathe fresh air, but she must search the other side of the room. Everywhere she looked the candle flames throbbed, tiny daggers of light. Color became exaggerated. The people she passed shimmered darkly, each surrounded by a strange warped halo—murky scarlet, indigo, dusky purple, sickly yellow. Their whispering voices seemed to echo inside the chapel, or inside her mind, hissing obscenities.

She heard a moan behind her. Turning, Theo saw a ménage à trois in a back corner, two men and a woman who had not waited for the ceremony to begin their orgy. They were embracing, their arms slithering over each other. The woman was naked under her robe and gripped the erect penises of the men on either side of her. They poured wine over her breasts and lapped it off. It trickled down over her belly. One of the men knelt before her. Theo stared shocked as he buried his head between her thighs. She thought of Averill touching her so, and a pulse of heat flashed through her. Flustered, embarrassed, a little frightened, Theo hurried on, searching the faces she passed.

At last she reached the doors through which she'd entered. Her quest had yielded no one she knew, and Theo was sure she had looked at everyone. Averill was not here. Relief rushed through her, more intoxicating than hashish. Then she heard a sound and turned. Obscured in shadow, a stone staircase descended…somewhere. A crypt? Was Ninette imprisoned there?

Just then the sound repeated—footsteps as someone climbed up from below. Shielding her face with her hood, Theo retreated to an obscure corner as a man in a helmet appeared. The gilded paper mache sported obscene crimson horns protruding out each side. The man's face was hidden, but the garish blue beard proved it was Vipèrine. He paused at the top of the aisle. His gaze swept her, and Theo's hand slid to the Colt, but he was not truly looking. He was summoning.

When all his followers had turned to him, he began to chant. "*In nomine Magni Dei Nostri Satanus introibo ad altare Domini Inferi.*"

Theo had almost no Latin, but she could understand that Vipèrine was evoking Satan.

"*In nomine Dei nostri Satanas Luciferi Excelsi,*" he intoned.

Now he beckoned to the choirboys. They swerved into line in front of him, their faces avid, smoke flowing from the swaying censers.

"*Ave Satanas.*"

They moved forward and Vipèrine followed in procession down the center aisle. The Satanist wore a satin chasuble, the purple so dark it was almost black. The gleaming color blurred with the quivering darkness that surrounded him like tainted smoke. As he walked past, she saw the back was painted with a rampant goat. When Vipèrine turned to face the congregation, he raised his arms and opened them wide. The robe had been split up the center to the waist. His gesture spread it apart, exposing his erection. He had painted or powdered his body to make it paler and stained his member to match the crimson horns thrusting from his helmet.

"*Rege Satanas!*"

The choirboys resumed their circling, dispensing plumes of smoke among the crowd.

Speaking now in French, Vipèrine began chanting curses that were praises of Satan, calling him Master of Slanders, Treasurer of Hatred, Dispenser of Sins. Theo felt like she'd fallen into the pages of *Là Bas*. Was this the usual sacrilege, or had Vipèrine just memorized the scene from the novel? The ugly words fell from his mouth, clanking like iron chains. As he spoke, the avid audience moved ever closer, willing slaves wrapping those chains around themselves. He must be the evil Devil of her Tarot.

The choirboys brought wine and wafers to the altar. The crowd surged forward in a black wave. The air billowed with the smoke of the incense and the manic fumes of color emanating from the participants. Fetid green, grim purple, and sullied red swirled and mingled in a gruesome storm cloud. Theo's head was splitting as she backed away from the nave—but here was a chance to find Ninette and escape with her. She could not wait for Michel to rescue them. She moved back toward the entrance and the stairwell that Vipèrine had ascended. Now there was a guardian standing beside it, watching Vipèrine until her movement had caught his eye. He was watching her now. Frustrated, Theo turned back toward the altar. Vipèrine was brandishing himself to the onlookers as the choirboys lifted up a plate of the wafers. He took handfuls of the host and wiped them over his flaunted sex, then reaching back and rubbed more between the cheeks of his buttocks. He tossed both handfuls into the crowd who gave a howling cry and descended on them.

The guardian moved forward—then stepped back to stand watch over the stairs. Ninette must be below. Perhaps there was another way into the chamber? Another entrance would make an easier escape. Theo's head was swimming from the fumes of the hashish and whatever weird herbs Vipèrine had added. Belladonna? Henbane? It was almost impossible to think. Going outside would clear her head. If there were no other entrance, she would come back and force her way down the stairs at gunpoint. The guardian gave her the briefest glance when she went out through the doors.

The rain had started, pattering softly on the leaves. Theo took a deep breath of the moist air, clearing her lungs, her brain. Luscious relief. But there was no time to spare, so she moved quickly down the steps and set off around the side of the chapel.

But as soon as she turned the corner, someone lunged out from the trees behind her. Shock took her breath as a hard arm closed around her ribs and yanked her backwards. A calloused hand closed roughly over her mouth, smothering her cry.

Chapter Thirty-Four

O we so worthy of these torments...
They promised to bury us in shadow
The shadow of the tree of good and evil.
                                    Arthur Rimbaud

ichel struck a match, shielding the tiny light to glance at his watch. "Midnight."

He and his men had gathered a street over from the estate. They had come in carriages like the participants of this satanic charade. The Black Marias would have been a warning. They would arrive by the time the raid was finished.

Walking alone, Michel approached the gate cautiously. He had not thought to wear a cloak, but his clothes were anonymous black. *"Luxure."* He gave the gatekeeper the password Lilias had sent. The man unlocked the gate. Once inside the walls, Michel subdued him without a sound and quickly motioned his men through. One of his officers stripped off the guardian's robe and took his place. Another Michel stationed behind the wall, the unconscious guardian bound and gagged beside him. Latecomers would be admitted, fleeing suspects captured. Michel signaled the rest of his men to follow the lighted pathway with its candles flickering and sputtering in the rain that filled the night like congealed mist.

Old as the Ancien Régime, the house they passed seemed to sag in slovenly disrepair. Ivy crawled over its crumbling stone. Cardboard patched broken windows. But for centuries this house had been noble. Had its owners worshipped the devil before? Had they been involved with the Black Masses arranged by Madame Du Barry and her coterie? The poisonings? Satanism and murder had gone hand in bloody hand for centuries in France—Gilles de Rais being its most notorious example.

As he walked silently toward his goal, Michel's mind swarmed with questions, their endless buzzing impossible to ignore. If not for the winged cross behind the bakery, he might think Ninette's abduction an exercise in perversity unrelated to the murders. The case made less sense to him now than before. Apparently, Vipèrine and Corbeau had conspired in the killings, with or without a Revenant. Was tonight's Black Mass simply part of some historical reenactment? Were the other murders only a prelude to a grisly public display, or would the participants see only the rape, with murder saved for later? Had Corbeau brought Ninette here? Did he keep another coach concealed in someone else's stable? Or had Ninette been lured by a familiar face, by Averill Charron or Paul Noret?

Perhaps tonight was only some sort of satanic circus act, and the virgin sacrifice was not Ninette, just a girl from the brothels tricked out with a fake hymen for the show. Perhaps she was some poor child sold by her family for a few francs. Michel shook his head. With luck, the girl would be spared, the killer captured and all his questions resolved.

He wished he believed more in the blessings of luck.

As they slowly circled the chapel, Michel gestured to a few men to stay in position beneath the canopy of the surrounding oaks. Turning the far corner, Michel saw stone steps descending the side of the chapel. Moving closer, he glimpsed a door below. A crypt most likely. An excellent place for murder following rape. He beckoned Rambert and another young officer, Rogier, to investigate—but then he heard a muffled cry. Quietly, he summoned Ganet, his senior officer. Keeping his voice low, he said, "I'll go down as well. You take the rest of the men to the front. Wait three minutes for my order, then begin the raid. If we don't reappear soon, we may need rescuing." Ganet nodded and set off for the front of the chapel. With the two men behind him, Michel silently went down the steps to the bottom. He tested the handle of the door and found it unlocked. It opened with a barely audible click. Michel and the others entered the crypt, the slight sounds of their footsteps muted by the chanting coming from the chapel.

Directly across from him, a man in a hooded cape held a weakly struggling girl in his arms. Ninette—he recognized her from the portrait her parents had shown him of Theo's painting. She wore only a transparent shift that revealed her budding breasts and the dark curls of her mons. Her hair spilled loose in an inky cascade. She was beautiful. The horde upstairs would descend on her like wolves if the leader of the pack offered her to them. Her wrists were bound in front of her, and she thumped helplessly at her captor's chest. Her feet were bare, delicate, and somehow more pathetic than all the rest. She gave small cries as she twisted and squirmed. The man put his hand over her mouth and shushed her. At first Michel could not see the man's face, but then the girl struck at him and the hood fell back.

It was Averill Charron.

Michel felt a surge of pure, cold-blooded satisfaction. Raising his gun, he pointed it at Charron's head and cocked it.

Hearing the sound, Charron turned and stared at him. Stared at the gun. He swallowed. "You don't understand."

Michel smiled a little. "I understand perfectly."

"No—"

"I am in no mood for games." Michel nodded to Rogier. "Tell Ganet to begin the raid." The officer ran out the door. Ganet could handle Vipèrine. Michel had what he wanted, Ninette safe and the killer captured. Michel cocked his weapon. "Lay her down. Carefully."

Now Charron looked frightened. His grip on Ninette tightened and she whimpered. "I was trying to save her."

"Of course you were," Michel said. "That's why she's struggling against you."

"She didn't recognize me."

"She recognized you all too well."

"She's been drugged."

"That I believe." Even in the dim light, the girl's eyes were glazed, unfocused.

Michel made a sharp gesture with the gun and repeated, "Put her down. Gently."

"She will be all right when the effects wear off," Charron said. "Her pulse is good." He lowered her feet to the floor, but she could not stand on her own and sank to her knees. Kneeling slowly, Charron laid her back against a pillar. He glanced up as the muted noise of pounding feet filtered down, along with cries of fear and outrage.

Holding the weapon on Charron, Michel ordered Rambert to put on the *ligote*. Instantly, he barreled past Michel and thrust Charron away from Ninette. Charron staggered, but Rambert kept moving, shoving Charron against the side wall and yanking his hands behind him to fasten the *ligote*. Charron cried out sharply as Rambert tightened the wire. When their prisoner was secured, Michel put away his gun and went to check on Ninette. She did not seem injured or in danger otherwise. Midway along the wall was a cot where she must have laid, a tattered blanket bunched at its foot. Michel grabbed it and covered her. He'd already asked the prison physician to come with the Black Marias. Looking over his shoulder, Charron met Michel's gaze. "I was rescuing her," he insisted. "They were going to rape her."

Michel stood and faced him. "Only rape? Perhaps some disembowelment for the supreme amusement, then a midnight excursion to the closest cemetery?"

His prisoner looked stunned, then suddenly terrified. But there was no guilt, no slyness in his expression. Was he innocent as he claimed? The hero of the drama and not the villain? Michel was inclined to think

Charron was an excellent actor. His killer had had much practice pretending to be human.

"I did not kidnap her, or mean to rape her," Charron repeated. "I did not intend to kill her."

"Liar!" Rambert struck him.

"Stop," Michel ordered instantly.

"I've seen his handiwork," Rambert snarled.

"Then do not imitate his brutality." Michel loathed crude violence and loathed himself when he felt compelled to use it. "He will stand trial. At the least, abduction and intended rape will get him five years at hard labor. Most do not survive it."

"Not enough." Rambert shook his head.

Michel knew he was thinking of the blood-stained cell below the stable and of Alicia propped against the gravestone. The images haunted him as well. Charron was silent, watching them both. Blood trickled from the corner of his mouth. Rambert's hands curled into fists. Michel said, "If we can prove he murdered Alicia, he will go to the guillotine."

"Unless your killer goes to an insane asylum," Charron said.

Michel held very still. Had Charron already plotted his defense? Would it work? His family was wealthy enough that he might be incarcerated someplace tolerable. Michel wanted the blade of the guillotine to finish his murderous career. You could escape from an asylum.

He walked closer, looked directly in Charron's eyes. "It's a pity they won't burn you at the stake—like Gilles de Rais." Charron looked startled, but only as he had when Michel had quoted Rimbaud in the cemetery. Michel would expect more reaction at having his other persona thrown in his face.

"Gilles de Rais was an aristocrat and was mercifully strangled before he was burned," Charron retorted with more of his old sarcasm. He gestured toward the staircase that led up to the chapel. "Why prate of medieval villains with Vipèrine parading himself upstairs?"

"Vipèrine?" Michel repeated, hoping Charron would let something slip.

"I was curious to see a Black Mass." Charron glared at him. "That does not make me a killer. Vipèrine told me there was to be one, then… nothing. But there were rumors and he was evading me. When I heard that Ninette was kidnapped, I suspected he had taken her."

"And why was that?"

"Because there was talk of a virgin sacrifice. Once he asked me if I knew any virgins."

"You did not find that…."

"Suspicious? Appalling?" Charron smiled sardonically. "If I had taken it seriously, yes, but I only joked that such a thing was impossible. Now I think he was searching out victims."

"Wouldn't someone seeking out a Black Mass expect a virgin sacrifice?" He didn't glance up, but overhead he could hear the noise of the raid dying down.

"I presumed whoever joined in these things did it because they wanted to."

"Then why bother to come at all? Surely the Grand Guignol offers as much. Or was it just the excuse for a picturesque orgy?"

Charron looked haughty. "I thought it would inspire a poem. That was reason enough."

"If you were not involved, how did you know where to come?" Michel asked.

"When Vipèrine first told me about his plans, he mentioned this church."

"And the password?"

"I used a more clandestine approach," Charron said. "I climbed the wall using an overhanging branch."

"Inspired."

"After that it was easy. There were no guards, except at the gate, and no real expectation of intruders. I thought I would have to knock out the guard that Vipèrine left, but he went to watch Vipèrine perform the mass. Ninette was too confused to escape."

"Did you plan to carry her back to Montmartre?"

"I had a carriage waiting."

"Your cohort?"

Charron's expression was blank. "Cohort? No, just a man I promised to pay well."

A gunshot cracked in the night. Another.

Michel pulled his weapon, as did Rambert. Were his men firing at a fleeing Vipèrine? No one else was worth the ammunition. Was Vipèrine shooting at his men? Michel had warned them of his penchant for smoke bombs and razors in his shoes. But Michel did not expect a gun. Not daring to leave Ninette alone in the crypt, he lifted her up, light as a thistle in his arms then handed her to Rambert. "Follow me."

Then he ran up the stairs into the drizzling air of the tree-shrouded garden.

Chapter Thirty~Five

And when Night across the air
Shall her solemn shadow fling,
Touching voice of our despair,
Long the nightingale shall sing.
                                    Paul Verlaine

Kicking, biting, Theo struggled fiercely against the man dragging her away from the chapel. He gave a cry as she got her teeth into his hand, but didn't let go. Gripping her with bruising strength, he pulled her into the dense darkness of the oaks.

"The whelp bites," he said as another figure emerged from the thick shadows. The second man grabbed her arm, slid a thick wire over her wrist and jerked it tight. She gasped at the searing pain.

"You are under arrest." His voice was low and thick with disgust. "Do not raise the alarm and you will not be harmed."

The police. Sagging with relief, she nodded agreement. The first man opened his smothering grip. Drawing a quick breath, she whispered hurriedly, "You're wrong about me. I'm Theodora Faraday. I sent Inspecteur Devaux the warning that this Black Mass was happening."

"*Merde!* A woman!" the man who'd grabbed her hissed.

"You sent a warning?" the second man asked. "Then why are you here?"

"In case you didn't get it."

She could almost hear him thinking in the silence. "When did you send it?"

"An hour ago, I think." Her sense of time was warped. "You got here very quickly."

"We were already here an hour ago. We were only waiting for it to be midnight."

"Oh." Theo felt foolish. Michel had his own sources, as he had often pointed out. "I thought Vipèrine kidnapped Ninette. I wanted to save her. I could not leave it to chance."

"But you're a woman," the first man said, flummoxed. "What could you do?"

Theo seethed with exasperation. "I thought France celebrated the brave heroines of the revolution. Surely you know we aren't all helpless?"

He tilted his head back to look down his nose at her. "You are a silly, reckless creature."

She glared at him. He had not discovered her Colt and she wasn't about to reveal his mistake. To the other officer, she said, "I didn't see Ninette inside the chapel. She may be down the stairs that are near the doors when you enter."

"Inspecteur Devaux has found her already."

"Oh!" Theo lit with joy. "Is she safe?"

"Alive and not obviously injured." He held up a hand, stopping her questions, but he did release her wrist from the *ligote*. "I am Inspecteur Ganet. I remember you did the painting of the girl in the bakery. But now we are going to raid the church. Stand over there and stay out of trouble, please."

"Yes, I will," she promised, rubbing her stinging wrist.

"Wait, mademoiselle. Can you tell me how many people are inside?"

"Thirty or less."

He nodded as if that was what he expected. "And their leader?"

"When I left, Vipèrine was standing by the altar."

"Thank you." He nodded curtly, then moved forward and gestured to his men to move out from their hiding places. At his command, they swarmed into the chapel. Keeping her promise, Theo stayed under the oak as the clamor broke loose inside. Her whole body tingled with relief, with elation, blood fizzing through her veins like fine champagne. The strange effects of the drugged smoke were waning, but her senses remained heightened. The night smelled of wet grass and damp earth. Rain pattered lightly on the leaves, an elusive music. She heard the sound of carriage wheels and horses' hooves clattering on cobblestones. Looking back toward the house, she glimpsed a Black Maria pulling up in the courtyard. Moving forward a little, she looked around for Ninette but didn't see anyone keeping watch over her. Theo needed to make sure Ninette was all right before she left. She needed to see Vipèrine in custody.

Soon enough the police emerged from the chapel, dragging the participants down the path toward the waiting Black Marias. Some were cursing or screeching, some weeping. Others were mute, their faces desolate. Turning back toward the chapel, Theo saw someone under a tree, watching the ongoing drama. It was too dark to make out his face, but from his height, his build, she thought it might be Paul Noret. She could not have missed him inside. Had he come late and was now hiding, watching, afraid to be noticed? He must have sensed her gaze, for he turned and looked directly at her. Pale hair gleamed in the night and she knew it was Paul. He glowered as if she were scum. Confused, a little frightened, Theo wrestled with her questions.

"*Va te faire foutre! Fils de pute. Bouffe ta merde, flic!*" Fuck you. Son of a whore. Eat shit. The raw curses erupted from Vipèrine as Inspecteur Ganet dragged him from the chapel, his wrists locked in *menottes*. He raised his arms and rattled the handcuffs. "*Brûle en enfer, salaud!*"

You're the one who'll burn in hell, Theo thought as he came past her. A streak of movement caught her eye, and she saw Paul walk forward from his hiding place. Why was he coming forward now? And then she saw the gun in his hand. She saw the hatred in his eyes as he raised it to point at his target.

"Vipèrine!" he cried. Startled, Ganet and the Satanist turned toward him.

"Paul, stop!" She had her own gun in her hand then, without thought, pointing it at him. He spared her a glance of loathing but did not stop. His weapon was aimed at Vipèrine's heart. Shooting an unarmed man would be murder. In the sudden quiet following her shout, she heard the hammer click on his weapon.

She shot him in the leg.

Paul screamed. His gun fired harmlessly into the air and he dropped to the ground. Theo ran toward him, crying out as he lifted the gun to fire again. The police pulled Vipèrine out of sight behind a Black Maria. She dropped to her knees beside him, yanking the gun from his hand and tossing it aside.

"Are you one of them?" Paul yelled at her, flinging his arm toward the prisoners being shoved into the police carriages. "One of those creatures?"

"No, no, I came to try and rescue Ninette."

"My daughter!" He began to sob. "My daughter."

Theo was stunned. She didn't resist when the police seized her, dragging her away from Paul. They picked up the gun she had tossed aside and took her Colt away, too. Paul was not courting the delicate Ninette, he was her father. He needed to know she was safe, so she cried out, "Paul, they found her! They found Ninette!"

He turned to her, hope lighting his face. "Unharmed?"

"I think she is safe. Inspecteur Devaux knows." Theo looked up to see if Ninette had been brought up from below. "Ninette is his daughter," she repeated to the *flic* holding her, in case he had not heard. "Please let him see her."

"That is not Monsieur Pommier," the man said stupidly.

"Perhaps not, but I believe Ninette is his child," Theo said, still finding it hard to fathom. He must have still been a student himself...seduced by the voluptuous Madame Pommier amid the yeasty aroma of baking bread. Ninette had her mother's dark eyes, but she was slim as a fawn.

"I must see her!" Paul struggled to rise, but the police held him down. A doctor carrying a bag came forward and bent down to exam his leg. He took a pad of gauze from the bag and pressed it to the wound. Paul stopped resisting and began to weep again. "I've been out searching the brothels."

"What's happening?"

Theo recognized Michel's voice and started toward it, but one of the *flics* gripped her tightly. "I know him!" she snapped.

She saw Michel then, handing a weak but alive Ninette to Inspecteur Ganet. The surge of relief was so intense she felt giddy, her knees weak. She almost laughed as the *flic's* grip tightened more, keeping her on her feet. She saw Ganet point to Paul and then to her. As she watched, Ganet carried Ninette toward Paul, bundled in a blanket. The poor girl didn't seem very aware, which was probably better if her parentage was to remain a secret. But Paul would know she was uninjured.

If Ninette discovered the truth, would she feel as betrayed as Theo had?

Michel stalked over to her, fury blazing in his eyes. "What the hell are you doing here?"

"Trying to find proof against Vipèrine!" Theo glared back, defiant. If she hadn't come, the police might have killed Paul.

"You are ridiculously reckless." Michel stared at her balefully. His voice grew colder, tighter. "How did you find out about this? Why didn't you inform me?"

"I sent you a warning."

"I didn't get it."

"Then you will find it on your return. I can hardly lie about it." Looking at the officers holding her, she asked, "Are you going to arrest me?"

"Release her," Michel said. The man did so instantly.

"Load the prisoners into the wagons," he ordered.

"Theo! Theo, don't believe them." It was Averill's voice calling out to her. "I swear I tried to rescue her."

"Averill!" Theo spun around, staring in disbelief as Rambert dragged Averill forward, his wrist bound with a *ligote*. He was leading him to the Black Maria. She felt blasted by shock. "No!"

She rushed past Michel, only to be grabbed again by one of his men. "Let me go!" She twisted in his grip, but his hands tightened. She stamped hard on his foot and broke free, rushing toward Averill. Another one of the guards grabbed her and slapped her face.

"Don't hurt her! She's not one of them."

Averill's cry overlapped Michel's barked order. "Stop that!"

Stricken, the guard obeyed at once. But when Michel took hold of her, his grip was just as hard. "You should not be here."

Averill said something to Paul as he was led past. Paul turned, still holding Ninette tightly and spat at his feet. Averill turned back toward Theo, his eyes full of desolation. The police dragged him forward and shoved him into the Black Maria.

She turned on Michel. "He's innocent! It was Vipèrine."

"We found him about to bring the girl upstairs for the ceremony. They are in league together."

"No!" Tears ran down her face, grief and fury mixed. "No. He was trying to save her."

"Perhaps," Michel allowed but his face was hard. He summoned Inspecteur Ganet who'd been standing beside Paul and Ninette. "You will have one of the happier duties, returning Ninette to her parents."

Ganet smiled at that. "It will good to bring her home."

Glancing at Theo, Michel added, "She lives near the Pommiers. Escort her home on the way there. Rogier can accompany you. Have him take her to a carriage now."

Theo started to protest but subsided. She would not be allowed to go with Averill, or to speak to him tonight. Trembling with frustration, she watched Ganet go to get the other officer. She must think of some way to help. As if reading her mind, Michel said, "Please, do not tell the Pommiers what you believe or even what you know. Not until we have had an opportunity to question them. I cannot stop you if you are bent upon it, but it will do more harm than good. The situation is too ambiguous."

Anger flashed, bright scarlet that seemed to scream in her blood. Theo fought to control her raging temper. "Won't you slant your questions to prove what you believe?"

"No, we will not. Too much is at stake." Meeting her accusing glare, he asked, "Will you give me your word?"

Which meant he would trust her to keep it. Quashing the struggle within, Theo finally agreed. "I will not go see the Pommiers for a day." No matter what Michel said, she was still afraid the police would imply Averill's guilt, subtly or blatantly. But her own explanation could slant their view of events in unpredictable ways. Trying to convince them of Averill's innocence might do the opposite. And Theo had a more important mission to accomplish tomorrow—she must go to Averill's parents.

Inspecteur Ganet came back with a young officer. He bowed stiffly. "I am Inspecteur Rogier, mademoiselle. Please follow me. We have carriages waiting beyond the gate."

"I have one." It came out a croak. She had to clear her throat and repeat the words. "It's not far."

"It may have left when the Black Marias appeared," Ganet said to her.

"Perhaps." Theo gave a helpless gesture. What did it matter?

Michel laid a hand on her arm. "One of the carriages will be there, yours or ours. But you must leave now, Mlle. Faraday."

She pulled away from him and watched, despairing, as the Black Maria holding Averill drove off into the night. Was he guilty after all?

No! She could not believe it. Would not believe it.

Was she wrong to listen to her heart?

Overhead the moon mocked her with its evil smile.

Chapter Thirty-Six

*Ah! What an infamous thing is prison! It
exudes a poison that assails all within its
pestilential reach.*

Victor Hugo

ichel watched as Rogier led Theo Faraday toward the carriages.
Pausing at the gate, she turned and looked back. The faint
candlelight caught the gleam of tears on her face. Her pain fed his anger
against Charron. Michel forced himself to rein it in. Turning back to Ganet,
he said. "After their joy at Ninette's return subsides, you will need to
question the parents. See if you can confirm Monsieur Noret's claim with
Madame Pommier—discreetly. I doubt it's a ruse, but it must be checked."

"It will take some time. Little Ninette will be all they're thinking
about. They're sure to summon a doctor to tend her."

"Undoubtedly," Michel agreed. "Aside from being drugged, I don't
believe she was hurt or molested, but they will need to assure themselves."

"And the fearful memory may work its own evil on Mlle. Ninette,"
Ganet said.

"Yes," Michel agreed. "If she recovers her senses while you are
there, find out what you can from her—gently. She may be too frightened
to talk, but the fresher her memories are, the better for gathering
evidence."

"How much can I reveal about tonight?"

Michel frowned. "Be ambiguous for the moment. You can say that
some of the Revenants organized their own rescue effort. Those who went
in disguise to the Black Mass have been arrested with the others but will
probably be released."

"But first they must be cleared of any suspicion."

"Exactly."

Rogier had returned with a carriage and was beckoning the other
passengers. Michel sent Ganet to gather Ninette. Noret looked devastated
to part with her but relinquished her to Ganet's arms. Noret's presence
seemed to have calmed her, for she had fallen asleep. Ganet murmured

to her anyway, comforting her as he carried her to the carriage that would take her home to Montmartre, along with Theo Faraday. Michel hoped she would heed his wishes and stay out of trouble for a day.

Rambert came up to him. "Corbeau is not among the prisoners."

"He might have been waiting in a carriage he borrowed or stole."

"To take the girl away after—for worse than this spectacle." Fuming, Rambert returned to help the final loading of the prisoners.

Michel was confused by all the scattered pieces that did not fit the puzzle. Had Corbeau fled Paris, or was he still here? Had he stolen the children for Averill? For Vipèrine? For both?

Michel shifted the pieces about as he finished securing the scene. Three men would remain on guard until morning when more evidence would be collected and the chapel and crypt photographed. Rambert was still agitated, so Michel sent him off in the last Black Maria. He got in the remaining carriage, where the prison doctor waited with Paul Noret. Dr. Foquet had agreed to remove the bullet in the prison infirmary. Michel didn't plan to arrest Noret, but it would do no harm to let him assume so.

The driver took off at a brisk pace. Noret winced with pain whenever the carriage joggled. "You're lucky Mlle. Faraday shot you in the leg," Michel said. "My men might have put a bullet through your heart."

"At the time, I did not care," Noret replied. "But I shall thank Miss Faraday when next I see her."

"How did you know where to come?"

"Jules Loisel told me."

Were all the Revenants dabblers in evil? So it seemed. But which one drank the dark liquor to the dregs? "And how did Monsieur Loisel know?"

"He was an acolyte of the foul serpent I tried to shoot. Jules wanted to be involved in the Black Mass."

"As Monsieur Charron did, to inspire a poem?" Sarcasm drenched the question.

Noret grew agitated. "I should not have spit on Averill. If he was trying to rescue Ninette…."

"If," Michel repeated.

Noret looked at him intently. "You doubt him?"

"It is my business to doubt." They rode in silence for a moment, the murkiness of the night like a funeral pall over the carriage. "Tell me more about Jules Loisel's connection."

"It was not just for his poetry. He has a rejected lover's longing and hatred for the Catholic Church. Vipèrine asked him to conduct the Black Mass. Such a violation was irresistible."

"But he did not carry through with the plan," Michel noted.

"Not when he saw Ninette." Noret adjusted the pad absorbing the blood of his wound, giving a low hiss at the pain.

"Yet Vipèrine dared to choose a girl Loisel knew. Why did he risk it?" Michel asked.

"Vipèrine thought Jules was jealous—that he wanted Ninette for himself," Noret answered. "Lately I'd begged off critiquing Jules' poems for the chance to visit her. He complained of my neglect to Vipèrine, who misinterpreted his anger."

"Did Vipèrine have anything against you in particular?"

"He thinks he is the new Rimbaud because he spews garbage from his filthy brain without censure. But he has no rhythm, no image that is not stolen from a better poet, no unique thoughts. I refused everything he submitted to the first *Le Revenant*. He did not try again, but whenever I see him, he regards me with hatred."

"He would kidnap your child because you refused his poems?"

"You underestimate his ego, Inspecteur, and his malice."

"Apparently." Michel was stunned, but revenge was always a motive, even such a bizarre revenge. Vipèrine had proved he could indulge in obscene cruelty whether or not he was playing at Gilles de Rais.

Noret shifted and winced with pain. He sucked in a breath, then went on. "At first, Jules thought I was smitten, that I had seduced Ninette or was trying to do so. I was furious and made some comment about not seducing innocent virgins. Jules said that women are all daughters of Eve, often most wicked when they appear most innocent. That he knew better than I the deceptions of which they were capable."

Noret stopped, struggling with his anger at the memory. Michel remembered a piece of his interview with Loisel in the morgue. "He admitted that he was dismissed from the seminary because of a woman."

"Yes. Guilty or not, he blames the woman for his fall," Noret said.

"Did you tell him that Ninette was your daughter?"

Noret shook his head. "Not then. Jules railed about our argument to Vipèrine. The creature was on the hunt for a virgin to despoil. He thought that Jules would relish the corrupt ceremony even more if it was mutual revenge. But he did not warn him of the plan before he brought her to the chapel. Even Jules could not accuse a kidnapped child of being a seductress worthy of such defilement. Instead, he rebelled and came to me."

"But not to the police?"

"He was frightened to have stumbled so far down the path of evil," Noret said.

Michel remembered their previous confrontation. "It seems no one is beyond good and evil when it comes to your child."

"Tonight I am only a father. Perhaps tomorrow you can question the anarchist poet."

Michel much preferred the father. "Jules came to warn you," he prompted.

"I told him then she was my daughter. He was horrified at what he'd done."

As with Charron, perhaps Loisel's tale was the truth, perhaps only the disguise for the ultimate lie. Gilles de Rais had been fervent in his love and hatred of God. Jules Loisel was a tormented religious reject. Could that rejection have set him on this murderous trail? Was his confession only some complicated subterfuge? Implicated in the slaughter of innocents, Loisel might have seen a way out. Knowing Noret loved the girl, for whatever reason, Jules might suspect Noret would commit a vengeful murder. If it had worked it would have been very tidy. Vipèrine would be both implicated and silenced. If that was the plan, was Jules Loisel only Vipèrine's accomplice, or was he the mastermind?

"Did Jules know you owned a gun?" he asked Noret.

Noret hesitated. "Yes."

Michel frowned. Even if Loisel possessed that crucial knowledge, the theory was flawed. The outcome could not be predicted. He might never have found Noret, who had been searching for Ninette. Was Loisel that desperate? Why not do as Averill Charron claimed and pretend to rescue the girl? If he had summoned the police, he could have killed Vipèrine himself and played the hero.

And Vipèrine—was he playing puppet master to the Revenants? Was he grasping as many strings as he could lay hold to and dancing them about, just to sweeten his revenge on Noret? He did not need to be the killer to play such a game, only the snake he was.

The Black Marias had a head start, but the carriage was swift and pulled into the Dépôt while they were still unloading the prisoners. Michel and the doctor helped Noret descend. "I will need to confirm what you've told me with Jules Loisel. I will not place you under arrest—unless you attempt to leave before that happens."

"I am in Limbo? Very well." Noret gave him a sardonic smile, followed by another wince. "Jules talked of making his way back to Normandy and begging the seminary for forgiveness. Frankly, I never wanted to see him again and gave him enough for train fare."

"We will find him."

"I hope you do so swiftly," Noret said. He was able to walk, albeit painfully, and Michel watched him make his way toward the infirmary with Dr. Foquet. He would have to confirm this latest piece of the story. He remembered Noret's hesitation when he mentioned the gun. Could Jules be dead and buried already? Given Noret's rage, it was possible—but not probable. Looking around, he picked out an officer to send to Loisel's pathetic hovel in Montparnasse. "Bring him in for questioning. If he is not there, try the Gare Saint-Lazare."

After the man was on his way, Michel took a deep breath. His brain was swarming with conjecture. He needed to choose a path and follow it. He went into the Dépôt, its anteroom crammed with his prisoners. This late at night they would be searched, then held in a gloomy waiting room until morning. Before he left for the raid, Michel had spoken to the officer on duty and made sure that there would be enough cells available to question the prisoners. His prime suspects were still waiting to be searched, so he had them moved forward. When Vipèrine went behind the curtain, Michel looked around for Rambert. He and some of his other men were bragging about the raid with the prison guards, justly proud of their success. Briefly, Michel considered changing the interrogation, as there was no question that Vipèrine was involved in the abduction. But despite the emblematic blue beard, Michel doubted Vipèrine was Gilles. He puzzled over why and decided that it was the man's attachment to the serpentine character he'd created. There was no particular logic to his belief—such a flamboyant persona could be chosen to cover an even more profane identity—but Michel had at least clarified his misgivings.

Along with that, Michel felt Rambert was too blunt to interrogate Charron effectively whereas Vipèrine was sly but not subtle. And the blow Rambert had inflicted earlier was as likely to silence Charron as to make him talk. But Charron was already used to engaging Michel verbally. With luck his prisoner would be unable to resist explaining himself. Revealing himself. His decision made, Michel took Rambert aside and conveyed the information that had been gleaned on the carriage ride. "Vipèrine may refuse to speak. If he does, take care not to lead him. He's not to be trusted. He will try to play to what you want to hear—either for or against. But do see what he says about his relationship to the Revenants."

"I'll ask about Loisel." Rambert hesitated. "But you do think Charron is our man? Charron and the viper did it together?"

Michel frowned. He suspected Rambert wanted justification for having struck Charron. He wanted to answer honestly, but it was always unwise to commit before all the facts had been gathered. And even facts had been known to deceive. "I think he is the most likely suspect but certainly not the only one."

"We have him *en flagrant délit* for kidnapping," Rambert protested.

"Or for rescue, as he says."

Rambert growled. "He was taking her up to be ravished, then they would murder her—as a public spectacle."

"Perhaps." He thought for a moment. "Question Vipèrine about the kidnapping, but do not mention the cross or the murders yet. Let him think he's not suspected."

"And if he confesses?"

Michel smiled. "So much the better."

Just then, Vipèrine emerged from the curtained alcove and the warders took Charron inside. There he would be stripped, his body and clothes examined. Despite such precautions, weapons still managed to be smuggled inside. Vipèrine was barefoot, as his shoes had been confiscated. When the guard led him off to the interrogation room, Rambert followed.

Most of the prisoners would be kept at the Dépôt two or three days before being formally charged and transferred to one of the other holding prisons to await trail. In special cases *l'inculpé*, the accused, would remain here. Particularly dangerous suspects could be kept at the Dépôt indefinitely. Michel would make certain Charron and Vipèrine were incarcerated.

Hearing weeping, Michel looked over the sorry lot of Satanists they had collected. Some were furious but most, like the sobbing woman, were totally abashed. When they went behind the curtain, many would only need to drop the cloaks they clutched to their bodies to stand naked. Questioning them could wait till after they were officially processed tomorrow. There were only two rooms and two significant suspects. If Charron could be believed, some were guilty of nothing more than trying to fulfill a dark fantasy. They believed the Black Mass to be a bit of decadent theatre, the debauch staged. For them he felt a mingled disgust and pity. Those who came hoping for a real rape, he loathed utterly. One or two among them had probably helped with Ninette's abduction and imprisonment. He perused the men and made note of those the most likely to be in league with Vipèrine. Any of them could possess some key piece of information, something to clarify this murk of fact and fantasy.

Remembering Lilias' information, Michel scanned the crowd for Minister Williquette but did not see him anywhere. Perhaps he'd proved too squeamish to attend the Black Mass, though it was possible that someone in the police, even Cochefert, had seen fit to warn him off. Government scandals were to be avoided at all cost. Michel doubted he would reach out a hand to free Vipèrine from these charges—he would not succeed.

When Charron emerged from behind the curtain, Michel came forward to escort him to the cell that had been set aside. One of the guards accompanied them, jingling the keys as he walked. Two stories high, the men's quarters were a grim gallery overlooked by a network of iron bridges and access stairways. In the faint glow of the lowered gaslight, it resembled the skeleton of some church—one far more demonic than the fake Gothic chapel of tonight's satanic debacle. The guard led them up along the second tier. Charron's cell was at the far end. As he unlocked the door, the guard winked at Michel and sniggered, "A perfect cell for spontaneous confession."

Michel said nothing in reply though Charron looked at them both askance as he stepped inside. Inside the barred door, the tiny cell was bare as a monk's. There was a table and chair, a rude toilet. Leaning against the wall were a plank bed and mattress that could be lowered for sleeping. Charron turned wearily, his pale eyes gleaming from the dark circles surrounding them. His skin showed stress easily. Despite Michel's warning off Rambert, Charron probably expected to be beaten. Michel did not believe in brutal interrogation except in the most dire circumstances. But when he thought of the dead children, he felt like reducing Charron to a pulp. Almost as evil was the poet's deception of his friends, his betrayal of the loyal Theo Faraday.

Except that he might be innocent of it all—

Charron chose the offensive. "Vipèrine is your kidnapper. Perhaps if you spent your time questioning him, the crime would become clear."

"You would prefer answering to Rambert?"

Charron regarded him sullenly. "Would he bother with questions?"

"In your case, he might find questions bothersome. I do not."

They went over the whole thing again, with the same answers. This time Michel asked what he knew of Vipèrine's relationship to Noret.

"Hostile," Charron replied. "They despise each other."

"And to Jules Loisel?"

"Master and servant—Jules worships Vipèrine."

"What is the appeal?"

"It is not just the flamboyance." Charron thought a moment. "I think Jules wishes he too had no conscience—so he could wallow in sin."

Was that psychological insight or an attempt to deflect suspicion?

"And what of Corbeau?" A fellow bird of prey?"

Charron stilled. Something flickered in his eyes, but so briefly Michel could not be certain. "A raven?" Sitting back, he gave a breathless laugh. "Nevermore?"

Coldly, Michel replied. "Don't condescend to me. I've read everything Baudelaire wrote, including his translations."

Charron's face became a mask. "I am tired. I am frightened. Interpret it as you will."

Michel pressed on. "How exactly did you choose your driver tonight?"

Charron repeated Michel's words. "How exactly did I choose my driver? I picked someone poor enough to wait for the other half of the money I promised."

Michel held his gaze, searching for another flicker of unease. But Charron bent forward, running his hands through his hair. Hiding his face as he muttered, "I should save my voice for the juge d'instruction. Perhaps he will consider the possibility of my innocence."

"I am considering it."

"With overwhelming skepticism."

"Yes."

"There is no point in talking to you." He looked around the cell. The oppression was growing on him already.

"We can keep you here indefinitely," Michel said, taking advantage of that unease. "The juge d'instruction has made it clear he does not want the killer to go free. There have been cases when the prisoner was simply forgotten, sometimes deliberately, sometimes not."

"*Une mise au secret?*"

"Exactly." He'd already conferred with the assigned juge d'instruction. They agreed that this case would be investigated in secret. It was sensational and it was vicious. Far better to gather the evidence and solidify the case before the press got hold of it.

"Those laws are medieval," Charron said angrily.

"Not quite. In the Middle Ages you could have called for holy combat to prove your innocence."

"And I would have been tortured as a matter of course. Now I will only have to survive the occasional beating."

Michel was annoyed with Rambert, but he did not want to show Charron any sympathy. He said nothing.

Charron gave a humorless laugh. "Secrecy might prove difficult. While my father would prefer if I vanish rather than besmirch the family name, Theo will organize a demonstration in front of the jail."

"To defend a murderer of children? She might find herself faced with a brutal mob looking for a scapegoat." Michel paused, seeing Charron's defiance turn fearful. "Secrecy has its benefits. If you are innocent, you do not want your name sullied with suspicion."

Charron managed a shrug. "It might add a certain *élan* to my reputation as a poet."

Michel regarded him stonily. "Do you remember the boy Denis?"

The poet's face grew shuttered. "You know I do. His mother was sometimes my laundress, and he often accompanied her."

"Or was sent on errands alone. Did you hold him in your apartment in Montmartre? You were there the day he vanished."

Now Charron looked white. "I was writing poetry. I was alone."

"So there is no one to say otherwise?"

Charron sighed heavily. "For whatever reason, you have decided I am the killer. I thought you wanted the right man, not just any man."

"I do not want more slaughtered innocents."

Charron sagged with weariness. Carefully, he repeated, "I did not abduct Ninette. Or Denis. I did not murder Alicia."

"The crimes are linked," Michel insisted. "We will find the truth."

"You cannot find the truth when you are searching for lies."

"I will find the truth hiding in the lies."

"Will you recognize it when you do?" After that Charron refused to say another word.

Michel prodded him verbally, expecting he would be unable to resist the duel, but was met with stony silence. He had hoped to achieve more. In a few hours, the official process would begin. After Charron went through Bertillon's measuring, the juge d'instruction would question him for hours. In the afternoon, Michel would take over again. There would be no problem getting the juge d'instruction to issue search warrants. He wanted one for Charron's home, another for the apartment in Montmartre that he shared with the baron.

Michel wanted to go back to his apartment and sleep for a couple of hours. Letting Charron brood alone in his cell might work where intimidation had not. Michel was also feeling uncertain. He needed to approach the next round of questioning with a clear head. Charron's story seemed preposterous at first, but he told it with weary conviction. Was Rambert having any better luck with Vipèrine?

Michel summoned the guard, who let him out and locked the cell behind him.

The anteroom was cleared of prisoners when he went through. Two guards sat playing cards but glanced up quickly as Michel passed. He nodded to them on his way out. Once he reached the street, he paused and looked around, feeling restless and uneasy. He walked over to the quai and watched the Seine flow under the hard gleam of the arc lamps. It was close to five in the morning. Perhaps he should have coffee instead of sleep. On the Left Bank, he could find a *café* open all night. But he would only chase the same thoughts in the same circles. Sleep might show him a different path. Still reluctant, he watched the river for a moment more, then set off for home.

Michel was almost to the bridge when he stopped, remembering the two guards playing cards. Impressions flashed in his mind—their tense posture and the shifty look thrown at him as he left. Something was wrong. Michel turned and began to walk back. With each step, his uneasiness increased until he was running back to the Dépôt. He flung open the door to the anteroom. The officers who had watched him—waited for him—were gone. Michel pulled his pistol. Then he was racing again, back through the ancient corridors. Near the entrance to the cells, he collared a patrolling guard and demanded he follow. He ran on ahead, hearing the other man lumbering behind him.

Turning the last corner, he almost collided with the card players. One took hold of him. The grip was tight, as if to prevent a fall, but it blocked his passage. Michel kicked the man's legs out from under him. He swiveled to get them both in his sight and pointed his pistol at them. "Don't move."

Burning with frustration, he waited for the trailing guard to catch up and told him to hold the other two. He wasted a few seconds seizing their weapons, then ran up to the level where they'd locked away Charron.

The last yards to the cell seemed endless, retreating before Michel like a nightmare. He reached the cell. Charron was hanging from the high grill of the bars. His shirt and linen had been ripped to make a noose. His chest was bare, bare and scarred. Strange. Michel lifted him up, pulling out his army knife to cut the cloth. Charron collapsed onto him and Michel lowered him to the floor. Kneeling beside him, he checked for his pulse.

Nothing.

Then he felt a vibration under his fingertips. Unconscious, not dead. The next quiver felt even weaker. Taking no chances, he bent over and covered Charron's mouth with his own. He gave him the kiss of life, breathing air into his lungs and withdrawing to let them deflate. Three breaths, four, and Charron gasped, dragging in air. His hands flew to his throat and he stared at Michel in terror.

"You are alive. You are safe," Michel said. "I will bring Dr. Foquet. Do not move."

He waited to see comprehension in Charron's eyes, then left. He made his way back to the culprits and their guard. Two other warders had joined them. He sent one for Dr. Fouquet. "Tell him the prisoner has been hanged in his cell."

"So he strung himself up rather than go to the guillotine," one of the card players scoffed.

The second took up the theme. "We were just telling him what was waiting for him. He took the coward's way out."

"You tried to kill him," Michel said. "He could not have lifted himself up."

"You don't have proof." The second man was starting to sweat. The first would swear it was all a mistake if he'd been found throttling Charron with his own hands.

"I have enough to get you cashiered."

The first man just sneered. "Over a bit of conversation with a child murderer? No one cares if he dies now or later."

"Is that what Rambert told you, that he was the child killer? Did he bother to mention he may have tried to rescue the young girl tonight, not kill her?"

They stared at him, jaws dropping. Then the first snarled at him, "Liar!"

"You bungled your assignment. Do you think Blaise Dancier will reclaim you when we toss you out on the street?" It was an intuitive leap, but it struck home. The first man flushed, the second paled. There were others who might have paid to have Charron murdered, but Blaise had informants already in place and the money to tempt them to worse treachery. "Dancier may pay well for betrayal, but he can't afford it in his own ranks. And you won't be paid for failure. If Charron is innocent, Blaise may kill you himself."

"You can't prove any of this." The second man was whining now. The cohort kicked him and told him to shut up.

When the doctor came, Michel helped Charron from the cell, then had the two guards locked inside. Then he took Charron to the infirmary. The doctor examined him briefly. "There may be no permanent damage. Perhaps his voice will suffer."

Michel summoned Rambert to watch over the prisoner for a time. Rambert might be in sympathy with the other men's goals, but he was not a killer. He was stricken that his bragging had led to the attempted murder. "I'll do a better job here. The viper just hisses at me."

By then it was early morning and Cochefert had arrived. Michel informed him of what had happened. Together they decided on the most trustworthy guards for the duration of Charron's imprisonment. Michel sent a second man to back up Rambert. No one was to go in or out of the infirmary except the doctor and his patients.

He should have known Dancier would want his own personal vengeance. He had been fond of at least one of the boys who had vanished from his territory. But Michel didn't think Dancier would have offered the case if he planned to subvert it. The attempted kidnapping of Lalou's little girl had put him into a fury. Did Dancier love Lalou, or was it only pride? Pride, Michel thought. Dancier was furious that anyone had even attempted to abduct someone under his personal protection.

And when you set off searching for vengeance? he asked himself. Pride. Yes. Love. And guilt. Guilt more than anything else.

Chapter Thirty~Seven

A man may drown, dreaming as he descends….
Arthur Rimbaud

rrested!" Casimir stared at Theo in disbelief. "How is that possible?" "He was trying to save Ninette from Vipèrine." Theo began the whole story over again, as she had told it to Averill's mother and sister two hours ago.

"Vipèrine is a charlatan," Casimir's voice dripped disdain, "but one quite capable of criminal excesses."

"Yes…yes…this diabolical creature must be the guilty one," her aunt whispered.

Theo deliberately left out that Averill had wanted to attend a Black Mass and hoped Casimir would not reveal it. She would have told him more details, but not with the others here. Theo glanced at Francine, who stood by the window staring at the heavy velvet drapes. They'd been drawn when Theo brought the unhappy news, as if the house were in mourning. *Grand-mère* had been told and was taking consolation with her poodle. A note had been dispatched to Uncle Urbain, who still had not appeared. Probably he'd not even bothered to read such a niggling trifle from his irksome wife.

At first Aunt Marguerite had closed herself in a fragile shell of calm. When her husband still had not appeared after an hour, she went upstairs to fetch a shawl—or so she said. Whatever drug she took while she was alone did not help. Her walk was unsteady, her eyes glassy. When Theo described to Casimir how the Black Maria drove off with Averill inside, her aunt gave a quavering sob. "They must not hurt him. He cannot endure being locked in prison."

"Averill has great strength of spirit," Casimir assured them all. "These accusations are ludicrous. Of course he was trying to rescue the girl."

"You know him best," Francine retorted, still studying the nap of the drapes.

Did Francine know about Casimir and Averill? The searing memory of their kiss pulsated in Theo's mind. Closing her eyes, she tried to will away the wretched headache. She'd spent the night in her chair by the window. Despite the worry that plagued her, she did fall asleep and woke to bright sunshine burning through her eyelids. The effects of the fumes she'd inhaled last night lingered and all her senses felt feverishly heightened.

"It is unfortunate he didn't accompany you to…" Aunt Marguerite trailed off, unable to remember where Casimir had been going.

"To Dieppe," he finished.

To see Oscar Wilde after his release after two years of hard labor in prison. Theo trembled. If convicted of this crime, Averill might receive an even harsher sentence.

"You are back quickly." Again, Francine made the simple statement into an accusation. Her anger made a jumble of Theo's already confused thoughts. Francine might be angry at the specter of scandal. She might be jealous. It was apparent that her parents hoped to snare an aristocrat for her husband. Infidelity was accepted in Paris society, expected even. But surely Francine would be appalled Casimir was her brother's lover?

"The friend I went to visit was in ill health," Casimir said. "He was much subdued. It seemed best to depart early."

"Oh…would you like an herbal tea? Chamomile perhaps?" Her aunt's voice quivered as she tried to carry on. The trivialities kept hysteria at bay. "You must not get ill yourself."

"I do not believe it is contagious." Casimir glanced at Theo, impatience simmering. "I thought to catch Averill outside his anatomy class, to tell him about my trip over lunch. I came here when I found he was absent."

"He has been doing very well…" Aunt Marguerite collapsed on the sofa, weeping helplessly. Francine stalked over and handed her a handkerchief. Crushing it in her hand, her aunt pleaded, "Where is your father? Why hasn't he come?"

"He will be furious." Francine smirked. "Perhaps he has gone to the police station."

"Or to his lawyer to have Averill disinherited," Casimir muttered under his breath.

Theo caught that and they exchanged a rueful glance.

"What will happen?" her aunt sobbed.

"I don't know," Francine snapped, then collected herself. "Perhaps Father will arrange to have Averill released."

Theo doubted that. Michel believed he was responsible for the murders as well as Ninette's kidnapping. She hadn't revealed that, but Casimir knew it all too well. He hid his concern, but Theo could see tension in his stance and the hard set of his jaw.

"I will go to the Dépôt. Perhaps the police will let me speak to him," Casimir offered.

"Yes, please," her aunt said. "You are most kind."

"Thank you." Theo hoped he could at least get a shred of new information.

As soon as Casimir left, Francine turned on her. "How dare Averill do this? The shame is unsupportable."

Theo was outraged. "What shame? He rescued a girl in danger!"

"This girl...this baker's daughter...surely she will clear his name?"

Theo hoped so. "I don't know what she remembers. She was drugged."

"These people—it's all so despicable." Francine's disdain encompassed Ninette and her parents as well as Vipèrine.

"Yes, it was despicable," Theo responded. "Think how terrified you would have been."

Francine looked at her blankly. Such a thing happening to her was incomprehensible. Theo turned back to her aunt. If Ninette didn't remember what had happened, would there be any way to disprove Averill's involvement? "We must get Averill a lawyer at once. He must consult with him, see what information they have...."

"Father will do that in due course," Francine said haughtily.

"Surely he will be cleared before the trial!" her aunt broke in with a cry.

Theo was bewildered. "But he needs a lawyer now. They need to go over the evidence, plan their defense."

Aunt Marguerite frowned at her, puzzled. "But he will not be permitted a lawyer before the trial."

"No lawyer?" Theo was flabbergasted. She knew French law was different, but she had never tested it beyond silly misdemeanors—wearing pants or sneaking into the catacombs with a hundred other gleefully guilty Parisians.

"The innocent need only cooperate with the juge d'instruction," her aunt recited the words like a catechism, but her lips trembled and new tears slid down her cheeks.

Theo trusted Michel to search for the truth, but that did not mean he would find it. With so many pieces that fit his theory, he could easily discard anything that did not. There would be no way to prove Averill was innocent until the killer struck again. And if the killer loathed the Revenants for some reason, he might wait till Averill was executed.

Guillotined.

She had refused to think of it till now. Losing your head seemed more horrible than hanging—so much bloodier. Was it truly more merciful?

There was a knock at the door. Theo exchanged apprehensive glances with her aunt. Outside in the hallway, the maid's tentative footsteps approached the door. When she opened it, Theo could hear muffled voices. Curiosity cracked through the brittle shell of fear and Theo hurried out, the others trailing behind. Inspecteur Devaux was there, accompanied by two younger officers. And with them was Averill, utterly haggard. Shadows lay under his eyes and huge bruises marred his cheek and forehead, their mottled colors of purple and green stark against his pale skin. He wore a shirt that was too big for him, and a red cotton handkerchief was knotted around his throat. They had him in handcuffs.

His mother went forward unsteadily, tears streaming. Michel nodded for the guards to stand back and allow her to embrace Averill. She clasped his face and kissed his cheeks again and again. Francine hung back, staring over their heads at the paintings on the walls. When Averill tried to catch her eye, she examined the pink rosettes on her shoes. Turning back to his mother, Averill spoke to her in a low voice. Theo could not hear all of what he said but she heard the most important word, "innocent."

She stepped forward, and Michel nodded that she could speak to Averill. She didn't dare embrace him but laid her hand over his heart, feeling it beat.

"Thank you for trying to help." His voice was strange, a rough croak. Had they been interrogating him all night? Then she saw the bruises around his throat. She gasped, her hand flying instinctively to her own throat. Averill shook his head infinitesimally. His mother had been too distraught to notice.

Stunned, Theo didn't know what to say, what to think. Had he tried to kill himself? Why, if he was innocent? No, the interrogators must have throttled him, hoping to squeeze a confession from him. She pivoted around and glared at Inspecteur Devaux. He looked away. It was the first time he had not met her gaze. Anger poured through Theo, filling her to the brim. Speechless with fury, she started toward him. Averill whispered her name, halting her. He glanced at Michel and shook his head. Michel was not responsible then? Theo stood where she was, wrapping her arms around herself to contain her raging emotions. She must not make it more difficult for Averill.

Michel nodded to the guards, who again stepped in front of Averill. "We will be searching the house," Michel told her aunt, who gaped in disbelief. "Perhaps you would like to retire to your own rooms. We will need to search everywhere, but we will do them last."

"Monstrous." Francine turned and stalked to the foot of the stairs, her back rigid. She'd still said nothing to Averill. Pausing, her back to them, she said only, "Mother."

It was unlike her to assume command, but suddenly she seemed very much her father's daughter. Marguerite looked confused but murmured, "Please, Inspecteur…" She trailed off, not knowing what to say. Lifting the lace hem of her skirt, she walked slowly over to join her daughter. Her elegance looked frail beside Francine's new-found authority. Together they went up the stairs.

"I'm staying," Theo announced.

Michel looked about to protest, but only said, "You will not interfere in any way."

Grateful he hadn't thwarted her challenge, Theo nodded. Did he permit her presence because she'd been part of Ninette's rescue? Or perhaps he thought to discover definitive proof of Averill's guilt, something she could in no way deny?

"Show us your room, Monsieur Charron," Michel said, beckoning to his men. Theo followed them up the stairs and along the hallway. Michel opened the door to Averill's room and they all went inside. To her the dusky purple room was sweetly familiar, with books scattered everywhere. Inspecteur Devaux ordered his men to search Averill's clothes while he stood by the entrance, watching the process and Averill's reaction.

Theo walked over to him. "What of Vipèrine?"

"He is being interrogated," Michel replied tersely.

"Why are you subjecting the family to this if you don't know whether Averill is guilty?"

"How do you think we discover if someone is guilty, mademoiselle? A very few are overcome by remorse and confess. Most continue to deny their crime even after you heap the evidence in front of them."

He was right, of course. She felt like a fool but her anger didn't abate.

Michel crossed the room to Averill's desk and began to examine the books there. Theo supposed the medical textbooks would be suspicious to a policeman. He continued searching while his men rummaged through the bureaus and stripped off the bed linens. Watching them, Averill looked as if he might be ill. Theo bit the inside of her lip, tasting blood. If she felt violated, how much worse it must be for Averill.

Michel began pulling open the desk drawers, searching in and under them, hunting for hidden spaces. Reaching the bottom drawer, he took out several folders. Averill took a step forward, only to be stopped by the guards. Michel looked at him. "Works in progress?"

"Yes," Averill replied, barely audible. "My poems."

Michel glanced up at Averill now and again as he read the poems silently. Finally he walked over to stand face to face with him. Lifting a sheet of paper, he quoted, "*She invites you to explore death.* Is this your poem about Alicia?"

Averill shut his eyes. Opening them, they looked haunted. "That is a different poem. I'd thought to make them a pair. Aesthetic horror and true horror, if you will." He smiled grimly. "But of course, you will not."

"Will not?"

"Believe me."

"I believe the evidence." Michel held up the poem and read.

> *Tes doigts cherchent dans le doux abîme.*
> *Des aveux furtifs qui t'entraînent,*
> *En éveillant un plaisir impie!*
> *Savoure cette obsession malsaine.*

Your fingers search in the sweet abyss. Furtive revelations pull you in, awakening a blasphemous pleasure! Savor the corrupt obsession. Theo forced herself to stand straighter, fighting the caving in her stomach.

"Do you often write of despoiling bodies, Monsieur Charron?" Michel asked.

"I write about death. What poet does not?"

"About Alicia?"

Averill hesitated. "I started to write a poem about Alicia…to exorcise the memory if I could."

"To exorcise it or to dramatize it?" Michel asked.

"I chose the word I wanted, Inspecteur." His voice was weary but adamant. "I destroyed the poem about Alicia because it distressed Theo."

Michel looked at each of them in turn. "She asked you to destroy it?"

"I would never ask that!" Theo was horrified.

She could hear the clink of the metal handcuffs as Averill buried his hands in his hair. "It lives on in my mind. It still wants to be written."

"Write it," she urged him. Averill cared enough about her pain to have destroyed the poem. The killer would revel in watching her misery. Theo wanted to shout Averill's innocence, but Michel would just say his delight was secret—the blasphemous delight of the poem. Instead, she struggled to think like a detective. "If Averill wrote this poem about Alicia, Inspecteur Devaux, then what about the others? Why just one of them? Wouldn't a killer poet commemorate each victim?"

"Perhaps he has, and the poems are well hidden."

"You found this one easily enough."

"Because he was still writing it. The others may be buried with the bodies."

She had no counter to that—but it didn't matter. The poem was not about Alicia. "Averill told you the truth. The woman in that poem is not even real."

"Not real?" Michel frowned at her.

Moving forward, Averill said, "No—she is wax."

"Wax?"

"She is an anatomical Venus that my father owns." Averill made a helpless gesture with his hands. "You can open her body to study the placement of the organs."

"She belongs to your father?"

"His most extravagant and adored possession." Averill smiled a challenge. "Perhaps he is your killer, Inspecteur Devaux. He is certainly a most monstrous murderer of souls."

"He is also one of the few with a legitimate alibi for one of the kidnappings, being away for a week at a physician's conference."

"Another fabulous hope shattered on the crags of reality," Averill said with bitter drama. But then he thought for a moment and said, "Vipèrine could have hidden the child and waited."

"For a week?"

Averill looked ill at the thought. "I'd hope the child's suffering ended more quickly."

"I want to see this anatomical Venus."

"That is easily done, she's downstairs in my father's library." Averill gave a twist of a smile. "You would have stumbled over her eventually."

Michel signaled his men to keep searching, then gathered up Averill's papers. He read from the Venus poem again, his voice cold and taunting.

Des aveux furtifs t'entraînent
Là où t'attendent des énigmes menaçantes.
Savoure cette obsession malsaine :
Cette peau rosée cache des horreurs ondulantes.

Furtive revelations pull you in, where menacing enigmas await. Savor the corrupt obsession: This rosy skin hides twisting horrors. Theo had to ball her hands into fists to stop herself snatching the poem from Michel's hands.

The Inspecteur nodded toward the door. "Show me your corrupt obsession."

They retraced their steps and Theo followed. She had to clutch the banister as memory again scorched her mind—Averill looking at her before he kissed Casimir—only a few hours after he'd embraced her with passion and desperation. When they walked along the hall to the library, she remembered the wrench of terror she'd felt when she saw the opened body of the anatomical Venus.

Once again, the room was in shadow. Michel lit the lamps. The wax sculpture was closed within her case like Snow White in her glass coffin, only far less chaste. Her nude body gleamed softly, her angelic face was turned toward them, watching their approach through half-closed eyes of blue glass.

"Her gaze is beseeching, don't you think?" Averill asked Michel. "It's as if she wants to be opened."

Theo's queasiness intensified. That was the same provoking tone Averill used to talk to his father. He was angry. When he was angry, he was reckless. She watched as Michel stared him down. Averill flushed and looked away.

She walked over to the glass case, nodded down at the figure. "You see, Inspecteur, Averill is not eviscerating people."

Michel's voice was flat. "This wax figure proves nothing for good or ill."

"But she's not real," Theo protested. "She belongs to his father."

"He chose her for the subject of his poem. She may long ago have inspired him to *explore death*."

As they argued, Urbain Charron marched through the door and stood in the middle of the room. He seemed to swell with outrage as he surveyed them one by one, then fixed on Inspecteur Devaux. "How dare you disturb my household!"

Michel's response to the pompous exclamation was a slight narrowing of his eyes. "The juge d'instruction gave me permission to search. Your son is present. That is all that is required."

Her uncle stared closely at Averill, then suddenly surged forward, grabbing the scarf and yanking it off to reveal the bruise circling his neck. "You tried to kill yourself." He scrutinized Averill, lips quivering with disgust. "It's a pity you didn't do a better job of it."

Theo wanted to claw his eyes out.

"Is that what you think?" Averill asked.

"Have you committed these obscene crimes? If you have, you are mad. You carry the same taint as your mother and your—" He broke off suddenly, his eyes darting nervously

"And my sister?" Averill finished his sentence, his voice dripping venom.

"Be quiet!" his father cried, truly furious now. "Don't speak of her."

"You thought I wouldn't find out—but I did! I found you'd shut her away in the asylum." Averill was white with fury, but patches of red flushed his cheeks, lurid bloodstains under the skin. "This killer has your sort of madness. Your sadism. Your love of degradation.

"Silence!" his father roared.

Averill's voice hardened. "My mother's spirit is trampled. My sister is lunatic. It is all your doing. Your oppression crushes and deforms us."

"Be quiet." A hiss now. A vein quivered on his father's forehead like a worm crawling under his skin.

Thoughts tangled inside Theo's mind but she couldn't pause to sort them out, not with the vicious family drama erupting in front of her. Michel was watching both men tensely, ready to intervene, but hoping some vital clue would tumble out.

"We are a degenerate family, a perfect case study. I will have to write a monograph about us, won't I, Father?" Averill laughed and lifted his cuffed hands. "Rather difficult to do in manacles. Do you want them to keep them on? Do you want them to take off my head? Will you pickle it in a jar and keep it beside your anatomical Venus?"

Urbain backed away. He extended his arm dramatically, pointing at Averill. "You are mad! You are as mad as Jeanette. They will lock you away."

Averill gave a choked cry and lunged at him, chained hands closing around his throat. His father pounded at him with his fists, but Averill's rage gave him strength. Michel leaped forward and pulled Averill away, gripping him tightly until he stopped struggling. Her uncle looked terrified, his fingers pawing at his throat. Slowly, he regained his composure. Glaring at Averill, he proclaimed hoarsely, "Patricide!"

"Unfortunately not," Averill sneered. He jerked away from Michel, who let him go. "What do you think, Inspecteur, have you found your killer—the degenerate son of degenerate stock? Perhaps the whole family is mad."

"Perhaps." He stood watching Averill and his father.

Averill face was stark with hatred. "Jeanette wasn't mad before but she is now, isn't she? That is your doing."

His father moved closer, his voice low and intimate. "I know you tried to visit her. You will never find where I've moved her—your whore of a sister."

Averill lunged for him again, but Michel seized him and pushed him down into a chair. Abruptly, Averill doubled over with a sob. The sound spurred Theo forward. She knelt beside the chair and laid her hand on his shoulder. At her touch, a shudder ran through him. She did not move, only waited, acutely aware of him and of Michel, weighing and measuring each movement, marking it in the innocent or guilty columns of his mind. Silently, Theo wished him to hell.

A long moment passed, then Averill lifted his head to face her. Tear tracks glistened on his cheeks but his gaze held a storm of fury as much as sorrow. His voice accused her. "I told you, there is too much darkness."

"Averill," she whispered his name, only wanting him to know she loved him.

He turned away from her. His manacled hands wrapped together, first a gesture of prayer, then a fist that he struck against his forehead. "A sea of darkness—inside and out. If I can go deep enough, submerge myself, I will find peace."

Theo did not know what to say. Silence settled like a pall. Averill was wretched. His father glared at them, his face warping from triumph to fury to fear and back again. At last Michel spoke. "How long have you known your sister did not die in the accident?"

"Sometime after Christmas…."

When he began drinking absinthe with such fervor, Theo realized. When he began acquiescing to his father.

Urbain Charron glowered at him. "My efforts to prevent her shame from destroying us were futile. You have brought far worse scandal crashing down on us."

"He is innocent!" Theo exclaimed.

"Is Averill innocent?" Her uncle asked Michel with a sneer.

Michel gave him a cold smile. "I have not totally discounted the possibility."

But Theo did not believe him.

Chapter Thirty~Eight

I dread sleep as one dreads a looming hole,
Brimming with nameless horrors,
A mouth opening to the unknown....
                                   Charles Baudelaire

White hot, the sun burned down. Michel staggered forward as rays like hot knives peeled away skin with each step. Ahead, the Sahara stretched endlessly, a vast dry sea that crunched beneath his feet. Blood dripped from his hands onto the sand. Not his own blood. Slowly the grains turned an ugly, clotted crimson. That darkness spread until the desert became an evil quagmire, sucking at his feet with every step. He began to sink.

Michel saw his father—saw Guillame Devaux—walking toward him and reached out. He could still be saved. His father looked at him sadly, but would not give Michel his hand. He shimmered, vanished, a mirage of redemption. Slowly, Michel sank into the stinking morass that smelled like decomposing flesh.

He woke with a cry. Throwing off the covers, he swung his legs around to sit on the edge of the bed. His breath came in gasps. He swallowed air greedily, like water. The dream returned over and over—that blood-soaked desert. He hated the terror. Hated the guilt that choked him. Suffocated him. Taut as vibrating wire, Michel went to the front room and stared blindly out the window, still locked in his own night. There was no point in trying to sleep. After Charron almost died, Michel knew the nightmares would return, as they had after the carnage of the bomber's arrest. But he did not need these wretched dreams to summon the memory of Guillame Devaux's death. Memory sank its teeth in his brain and shook him like prey.

A tour in the Foreign Legion was five years. It took him four to find Luc. In Algiers, Michel forced himself to live solely by the Legion code of *Valeur et Discipline*. Both his fathers had taught him discipline. Valor was easy when he did not care if he lived or died. He volunteered for the disastrous campaign in Madagascar because Luc had named it as part of his travels. It was a pestilential hellhole. Early on Michel was shot, a head wound that he miraculously survived on the trip back to Algiers. He saw its crenelated walls, its domes and minarets again with thanksgiving. Most of the men he'd served with in Madagascar died, wasted with malaria.

Recuperating from his wound, his Parisian French and clear hand got him an offer to work as secretary to a colonel. He took it, not for safety, or for the promotion that went with it, but for the chance to search through the intelligence. And so he found Luc outside Algiers—supplying arms to the dissidents. Freedom fighters he would have said, given the chance. But Michel gave him no chance.

He followed him to a desert meeting. When the others were gone, he knocked out Luc's bodyguard then faced his cousin at last. Luc could see words were of no use. They fought ruthlessly, a struggle of pouring sweat and blood, the grit of sand in mouth and eyes, brutal kicks and vicious knife cuts. The end came quickly, for it only took one misstep. Michel hooked his arms around Luc and broke his neck.

Michel had expected—what? Release. Finality. A sense of justice.

He looked down at his dead cousin, now about the age his first father had been when shot by the Versailles firing squad. Luc looked almost exactly like him. Michel felt he had murdered his father twice over.

He had nothing. There was only the vast desert within that matched the desert stretching out before him, blank and dry and relentless. He stood under its pitiless eye. He would wish it undone if he could, yet he knew that his own unyielding nature would not have rested until he found his vengeance.

Guillame Devaux would not have approved. For the first time, Michel understood why, not only in his brain, but in body and soul. He had sought darkness, found it, become it. He could feel the abyss calling. Having killed, nothing would be easier than to go on killing until someone killed him. Rough justice. It was only the memory of Guillame Devaux that made him turn away.

Back in France, with the influence of his adoptive father's friends, he was permitted to complete his required army service without reprisal. Ironically, he was sent back to Algiers. Finally, he returned to Paris and joined the police. There had never been any question that he would be accepted. His father had been liked and respected by all but the most corrupt. His son was welcomed back. Michel swore then that he would work within the law. It would be his ongoing penance to Guillame Devaux, who had made Michel his son and died for it. His adoptive mother had waited for that final step. She never accused him in words, but her eyes did, when she could bear to look at him. One day, he returned to find she'd moved back to her parents' home. They did not speak again.

Michel worked hard and found he had a talent for investigation. Some guessed that he had joined the Legion to hunt down the killer and asked if he'd found what he was looking for there.

"No."

It was still his answer.

Michel stood at his window, watching the flow of the Seine, a glitter of gold and black through the shadowy net of the leaves.

He did not want to see Averill Charron's head rolling across the dream sands of the Sahara.

He did not dare be wrong about the killer.

For the first time in years Michel had been tempted to betray his oath. It had been the glimmer of temptation only, when Charron had said the killer would be declared insane. But a glimmer could become a blinding glare. For five years in the Legion everything he saw was ignited by a white blaze of hatred. He must not allow it to happen again.

Michel was almost grateful to Blaise Dancier for the attempt on Charron's life. Seeing others violate that trust had pulled him back into the world of law, however flawed it might be.

Could such a detestable murderer of children be set free? Someone as clever as this faux Gilles de Rais might contrive to be declared insane. But however mad his motives, this killer had plotted his crimes with a cold and calculating sanity. He sought out suffering, not only the suffering of the children he tortured and murdered, but the suffering of their families and of his own friends. He ruled a kingdom of pain. Whoever he was, he deserved the guillotine. But was it Charron? The evidence said so. Michel believed that his killer was an excellent actor, wearing his ordinary persona like a costume over the evil within. In the Legion they called the identity you assumed the *anonymat*—the myth you created for yourself.

Michel had seen the butchery of battle. He had seen terrible murders—an old lady hacked to bits with an axe, a woman's body broken to fit inside a trunk. He had seen children brutally killed by their own parents for no other reason than they had cried when beaten. But this insidious evil was unlike anything he had experienced. Even the cruelty, the barbaric prejudice he had witnessed in the Legion was more comprehensible.

With a sigh, Michel sat at his table and lit the lamp. If he could not sleep, he would review the evidence. He had brought the folders home with him and now he set them out, looking through the photographs first. He examined the list of possible kidnapped victims he had complied with the help of Cochefert and Dancier. A few he had since dismissed as too young, or old enough to be runaways. The parents he'd suspected had been arrested when their child's body was found buried in the back yard. One child had returned unharmed. There were still a dozen cases that were possible, at least half of which felt like his killer's work.

Sitting on the table were Michel's copy of *Là Bas* and the biography he'd bought of Gilles de Rais. He laid a hand on each book, recalling what he'd read. Neither had said anything about the winged cross, but Huysmans had come across the knowledge somewhere in his research. If need be, he could be called upon to testify at the trial. The killer didn't need to have the literary leanings of the Revenants to have discovered it— he needed only to have been told it by someone who did. Even Corbeau could have overheard it. Perhaps one of the Revenants had fleshed out the fantasy for him. But instinct insisted Corbeau had claimed the raven as his emblem, as Vipèrine had the snake.

The killer would know Gilles' history. But perhaps he had become Gilles because of some similarity. Michel had brought home the research he and his men had gathered on the Revenants' backgrounds. He set aside the Hyphens, who felt peripheral to the inner circle. He did the same with Paul Noret, who seemed far too stricken about Ninette to be able to torture someone else's child. He topped the pile with Urbain Charron, who had an alibi with witnesses for an entire week surrounding one abduction. He could not afford to dismiss them, but he would begin with his chief suspects, Averill Charron, Jules Loisel, and Casimir Estarlian.

Michel laid out Charron's poems. Having rescued the poet, Michel had turned him into an innocent victim in his mind. A purely emotional reaction he was unaware of until the discovery of the poems revealed his mistake. He'd been furious with himself. Lifting the pantoum, he read the last stanza aloud.

> *Là où t'attendent des énigmes menaçantes,*
> *Son corps s'ouvre comme une porte.*
> *Cette peau rosée cache des horreurs ondulantes.*
> *Elle t'invite à sonder la mort.*

Where menacing enigmas await, her body opens like a door. This rosy skin hides twisting horrors. She invites you to explore death. The words evoked Alicia's appalling torture but they fit the anatomical Venus as well. Was the wax figure simply a macabre creation which haunted the poet's mind, or was it an inspiration for the murders?

Charron said he'd destroyed the poem about Alicia because of Theo. Was that true, or did Charron see that some phrase implicated him? Then why not also destroy the suggestive poem about the Venus?

Leafing through the rest, Michel read one about madness—was it about Averill's sister, or himself? The next visited the secret chambers of the catacombs. Was Dondre's body hidden within them? He found another, half-finished, about Gilles de Rais, but it depicted the fairy tale Bluebeard who had murdered his wives. That seemed odd. If he was Gilles, wouldn't Charron write about the medieval baron rather than the later imaginary killer?

Michel shook his head. These poems might be just as Charron described them, a poet's quest to exorcise haunting evils—but coupled with his having discovered the body and dragged his friends to see the corpse at the morgue, the pendulum was again swinging towards guilt. The attack on his father proved he was capable of violence. And anyone who had grown up with Urbain Charron for a father would have their spirit twisted, one way or another.

Even if Charron was telling the truth about his attempted rescue, he might still be Gilles, working on his own murderous agenda. If he'd succeeded in rescuing Ninette, he would indeed have been a hero and deflected suspicion.

Michel had all but discounted Vipèrine. One of the interrogators had discovered the brothel keeper from Rouen among the revelers at the Black Mass. This was l'Anguille, the same slippery Eel that Lilias had mentioned. The madam made a deal and talked. Ninette was to be hers after the ceremony. The girl would have vanished into a brothel in another city. An equivalent innocent would have been gifted to her sister, who kept a house here. Michel did not think the modern Gilles would surrender his chosen prey.

The madam had known Vipèrine's mother, a lesser courtesan who'd formed an alliance with a cut-rate spiritualist, seducing the unwary in one form or another. Their son, then inaptly named Percival, had worked with them as a child and as an adolescent. Approaching twenty, he struck out on his own, pimping for L'Anguille and playing pornographic games in her brothel. After a chance meeting with the Abbé Boullan, he realized that Satanism would get him both sex and perverted adoration. Vipèrine was born.

The snake refused to talk until Michel confronted him with L'Anguille's confession. Already shaken, he'd been terrified when accused of the murders. "The child in Montmartre cemetery, the one you showed in the morgue?"

"Exactly," Michel answered. "You must have known you were a suspect."

"No. No! I thought you had men following me for…other things." His gaze darted about the room, searching for somewhere to hide.

"Perhaps an abortive poisoning attempt?"

"I don't know what you mean!" Terror flared in the black eyes, then transformed into defiance. "I thought it was only your animosity after I was released from jail."

Michel was anything but convinced. "You left a cross by the bakery."

"Jules told me the police were asking about a cross with big wings," he said. Words began to tumble, an obvious rush of relief. "I thought it would be clever to put it nearby and deflect suspicion from my Black Mass onto this madman. Why not have the police chasing after him while I had the girl safe in my church?"

"Why not indeed?" Michel asked coldly.

"I am not this baby killer!" the snake screeched at him.

"Ninette is scarcely older than Alicia."

Vipèrine clenched his jaw. "Jules said Alicia was a child."

Michel tried another approach. "What did you tell Charron about the Black Mass?"

"Nothing once I decided Ninette would be the centerpiece. Averill is that weasel Noret's pet. I could not afford to tell him or the baron. They would have betrayed the secret."

Michel would rather not have believed him, but he did. Instead, he followed this new thread. "Estarlian wanted to attend?"

"He is an aristocrat. His presence would add elegance." Vipèrine shrugged. "Years ago, I saw him at a Black Mass that the Abbé Boullan conducted. But he was no longer interested."

Or perhaps the baron only scorned Vipèrine's offering? Either way, this was interesting. "How many years ago?"

"A year before the Abbé's death."

So *Là Bas* had been published and Gilles awakened. When Ninette was abducted, the baron was supposed to be in Dieppe consorting with the scandalous English writer just released from prison. Michel had dismissed him. But if the girl was taken only for the Black Mass and not for darker, deadlier games, then Estarlian remained a suspect.

Michel paused. He had put the baron aside too soon, just as he had failed to suspect the cab driver. What other mistake could he be making? His men had located Jules Loisel. He had been hiding out in Noret's apartment, supposedly waiting to beg forgiveness. When they searched

Loisel's own pathetic room, they discovered it filled with religious and sacrilegious objects and scribblings. But its centerpiece was an inverted pentagram, not a winged cross. Rambert had questioned him and believed his fear and regret to be genuine.

But Loisel had told Vipèrine about the winged cross. He had told Vipèrine that Ninette was Noret's daughter. Loisel and Corbeau might have constructed the whole drama and lingered to see it play out—their own Grand Guignol.

There was a knock. It was after midnight, but his light was on. Was Rambert also finding sleep impossible? But when Michel opened the door, he found Blaise Dancier instead. Michel had gone hunting for him this morning. He'd been coldly furious then. Now he was too tired, too miserable, to lacerate him. He stood aside, gestured to a chair. Going to his cupboard, he took out his brandy. Michel bought the best he could reasonably afford but it didn't approach the quality Dancier possessed. He poured two glasses. Sat. Waited. Neither of them drank.

After a moment, Dancier said, "I'm here to apologize."

"Not to bribe me to let you murder my prisoner?" Michel was still angry but he felt hypocritical too. He held up a hand. "You betrayed my trust."

He could feel Dancier gather breath to argue. He was not used to being challenged. Nor was he used to apologizing. Michel did not care. "He invaded my territory," Dancier snapped. "He tried to kill someone under my protection."

"I know why you attempted it." Michel drank a swallow of the brandy, letting it burn. "You invaded my territory to try."

"I apologized."

"So you did." Michel waited another breath. "I accept your apology, provided—"

"It won't happen again," Dancier finished for him.

Michel nodded. It was, after all, a rather extraordinary gesture, but he did not feel appeased. "Charron may not have killed the children."

Dancier looked aside, so his hirelings must have visited him. Better to have failed if Charron was innocent. Facing him, Dancier asked, "Then who did?"

"I will hardly tell you that."

"You know I'll find out."

"I'm sure you can, so the question returns. What will you do about it?"

Dancier sulked. Finally, he said, "Nothing—unless he wiggles free."

"He must be insane, but perhaps not insane in a fashion that will allow him to escape the guillotine."

"You hope?"

"I hope," Michel acknowledged. He took a sip of the brandy.

"If this poet isn't the killer, I'll make it up to him," Dancier announced.

Michel stared at him in disbelief.

"One way or another?" Dancier shrugged. "I can always publish his poems."

Michel gave a bark of laughter. "I find that truly perverse."

"I can be perverse." Dancier winked.

The man was incorrigible, but the confrontation, the banter had pulled Michel from the worst of his bleakness. He was grateful. He smiled and drank another swallow of brandy.

Dancier finished his in one jolt. He got up and went to the door, turned. "If you ever think we're even, let me know."

Michel locked the door, then sat down again with the evidence—the books, the photos, the histories. Somewhere there was a key.

Chapter Thirty-Nine

*The desolate marshes of these pages, full of black
poison, will soak into his soul.*

Comte de Lautréamont

Zigzagging through the streets of Paris, Theo pedaled furiously, swerving at last onto the Quai de l'Horloge and into the Dépôt. Dismounting, she leaned the bicycle against the wall then rushed through the door of the police station, only to be stopped by a glaring detective.

"Let me by!" Theo said, but he stood in her way, pointing at her legs in outrage. She was still wearing her riding breeches, not the wisest choice. Most police overlooked the pointless law, but this one disliked such rebellion flouted in his face. She felt like screaming at him, but that was more likely to get her arrested.

"Out!" He pointed at the door now, wrinkling his nose with disdain. Theo knew she smelled of sweat and horses. "Out!"

"I must find Inspecteur Devaux," Theo insisted, her eyes searching the station. Michel had heard the argument, for he stood up. The officer glared but turned to look at Michel, who gestured to admit her. The man stepped aside and Theo strode to Michel's desk.

His gaze was guarded. "Mademoiselle, if you are here about Monsieur Charron—"

"No." She shook her head, then blurted, "Matthieu has disappeared."

"Another child?" His expression did not change but his eyes were bleak.

"My landlady's son," she said. "There is a new winged cross in the alleyway."

"When did he disappear?"

"Four hours ago. I was out riding when he went missing."

"How much does she know?"

"After Denis disappeared, she was always wary. But she didn't think Matthieu would be taken in broad daylight..." Theo fought down panic. "She doesn't know that Denis and Alicia were taken by the same man."

"It is better she does not. Her fear will be terrible enough." He looked down at the folders on his desk.

Theo knew they held photos he had never shown her. "Averill could not have done this."

He looked at her directly. "But his accomplice could have."

Theo clenched her fists but kept her voice even. "You have Vipèrine in prison, too."

"I no longer think Vipèrine is the killer."

A wave of fear swept through Theo. She swayed under its force. Michel reached out and steadied her, but she took a breath and pulled away. "Then who took Matthieu?"

"There is another man involved, a fiacre driver."

"What?" How long had he known about this other man?

He paused. "There is a chance it is not him. Some friend might...."

Shock gave way to anger. Her voice dripped disdain. "Kidnap a child? Commit murder?"

"Stage a ruse," he countered. "If the friend believes him innocent, perhaps the child is only being held till the real killer is found. Noret might feel guilty enough."

"Not guilty enough to kidnap someone else's child."

He frowned. "I know it is unlikely. Would the baron be so ruthless?"

Theo froze. What might Casimir risk for Averill? "If it's true, so much the better. Matthieu would be safe. But neither of us believes that."

Michel got to his feet and reached for the jacket hung over the back of his chair, then hesitated.

"Whoever it is will torture Matthieu, murder him. We must search!"

"And where are we to search? Every attempt to find the other children failed."

Fear and terror battered her. "I don't know!"

He met her gaze, acknowledging her turmoil, then sat and gestured to the chair across from him. "I want you to go over some of the evidence with me. If we uncover the killer, we may know where to look for him."

Muscle and nerve screamed for action, but Theo sat down. It didn't matter how repellent the evidence was if it would help find Matthieu. "Who is this fiacre driver?"

"His name is Corbeau." He waited.

The name meant nothing to her. "Why not this Corbeau and Vipèrine?"

"Ninette was taken for the Black Mass to be ravished, not murdered. Afterwards, Vipèrine meant to sell her to a madam who lives in Rouen."

"Sell her?"

"Yes. He is vile, he is mercenary. He is even capable of murder, but I do not believe he is the killer we have been seeking."

"But Ninette's kidnapper left a winged cross."

"Jules Loisel told Vipèrine about the emblem."

"So now you know Vipèrine kidnapped Ninette. Averill is telling the truth!"

"It is entirely possible Averill thought to snatch her for himself. It is even possible he thought to play the hero and deflect suspicion for his other crimes."

"That would be a crazy risk."

"Our killer is crazy, Mlle. Faraday. But he is crazily clever too." Michel took two books from the side of his desk. She recognized one and knew why he had it with him. "*Là Bas.*"

"We both discovered the killer thinks of himself as Gilles de Rais. I have looked for similarities in their history to create this strange union."

Theo forced a calm question. "What have you found?"

"Loisel is devious, but apart from his fascination with sacrilege, I see nothing to connect him to the medieval baron. He fears and perhaps hates women, but would not see an innocent young girl ravished. If my theory is correct, it must be either Averill Charron or Casimir Estarlian."

Theo closed her eyes, then made herself open them. Blindness was cowardice. She could not bear for the killer to be Averill. But Casimir had never been anything but charming and kind to her. Except in helping to break her heart. Even then, it was Averill who had shown her they were lovers. Casimir had never hinted at such a thing. But whoever the killer was, he was skilled at pretense. Of all of them, Casimir presented the most polished façade to the world, too bright to see behind.

"Tell me your theory." Her voice sounded hollow to her own ears.

"You know that Averill was deeply affected by all that happened to his sister, both the false events and the true."

"Yes. Jeanette."

"Little Jeanne."

Theo felt a chill crawl along her spine, cold talons digging into her nerves. "Isn't that a gigantic leap of the imagination?"

"Our killer made some such leap, to enter into his vision of Gilles de Rais."

"But Jeanne is one of the most common French names."

"Do you believe it signifies nothing?"

She was arguing only because of Averill. "No. The killer believes he is Gilles de Rais, so Jeanne d'Arc will have immense importance to him. But perhaps only the historical Jeanne."

"Jeanne d'Arc gave the medieval baron de Rais a moment of glory. She gave faith and simple goodness to a life that was at its best utterly selfish, at its worst vile almost beyond comprehension."

"That is not Averill."

"Not the face that he shows you. He may have another."

Theo balled her hands into fists and kept silent. With Matthieu's life at stake, she must help Michel, not fight him.

Michel went on, "The killer may have felt that like the baron de Rais, he had betrayed his own Jeanne by not saving her."

"Yet she also betrayed him, by not being saved." Theo knew he was talking of Jeanette's madness, of Averill's quest, but some other memory was tugging at her mind. She groped for the words. "Greater even than betrayal by a lover."

Who had said that? Was it Casimir or Averill? Did it matter? They were both fascinated by Gilles de Rais.

Michel watched her attentively. "Yes, I can see it would seem so. He wanted a miracle. Yet it is also the fate of saints to be martyred."

"But why would that make our killer kidnap children?"

"We need only know that our Gilles found some reason to clothe himself in the other's history. Perhaps he only looked for the excuse to kill."

"So, Averill has a sister named for the saint, about whom he feels overwhelming guilt." When Michel nodded, she asked. "And what of Casimir?"

"Gilles de Rais had a grandfather who mistreated him. So did Estarlian. He was an orphan taken in by an old and perhaps cruel man. His grandfather died a little over a year ago, and the killings seem to have begun not long afterwards."

"A man most ancient and utterly corrupt..." Theo remembered.

"Yes, there is something like that in *Là Bas*."

"Not only the book. Casimir said that to me the first time I met him. We both wore mourning, but he did not pretend to love his grandfather."

"It sounds as if he hated him."

"But is that enough to create a killer—a Gilles de Rais who destroys children?"

"Fire invaded both their lives. Casimir lost his childhood home. Averill's country estate burned to the ground not long ago."

"And Jules?" she asked again.

"We've found no such parallel in his life, beyond the fascination with Satanism, which Charron and the baron both share."

"Casimir?"

"Vipèrine said the baron had been to a Black Mass conducted by the infamous Abbé Boullan."

Theo thought that strange. Casimir had chastised Averill for his interest in the mass but had been to one himself. But if Casimir had told him that, Averill would have been all the more determined to go.

"We have a room for questioning here as well as in the cells," Michel told her. "Inspecteur Rambert will bring Monsieur Charron there."

Michel escorted her inside the interrogation room. The claustrophobic walls were stained yellow and reeked from tobacco smoke but this could not be as terrible as the cells. There was a small rectangular table with two chairs on either side. Theo stood waiting until Averill was led into the room, once more in manacles. Michel directed Averill to sit on the far side of the table. Theo sat and Michel took the chair beside her. Inspecteur Rambert remained to guard the door.

Unexpectedly, Michel gave her the lead. "Tell him what has happened."

Theo swallowed hard. "Matthieu was kidnapped today, Averill."

Shock, horror, relief played across his face in quick succession. "Then…" he began.

"No." Theo broke in. "The killer has an accomplice."

"And so you would still be guilty," Michel finished.

Averill turned to look at him. "Because madness runs in my blood? Because I write poems about death?"

"Perhaps," Michel answered, then coldly, "Tell me about Corbeau."

Averill paled. Theo's heart seemed to drain of blood with that paleness.

"You know him," Michel said coldly. "When I questioned you the other night, you remembered the name."

Averill spoke very carefully. "A few times we had a driver named Zacharie. Once I remember Casimir calling him *le corbeau*—he wore a large black coat that night, loose and flapping. It might have been this Zacharie's last name or simply a poetic jest."

"No jest. His name is Zacharie Corbeau."

"He is involved in these murders?"

"Yes, very. But not alone."

"I knew him only as a guide. He had an extensive knowledge of the more unusual brothels." Averill realized the implication of that and scowled at Michel. "None with children—or none that we visited."

"You should not have lied."

"I did not lie!" Anger ignited in his eyes. "I was not sure he was the man you meant. I was not certain why you brought up his name. Why should I make myself look guiltier than I did already—or tangle someone else in your web?"

He had not wanted to tangle Casimir, Theo realized.

Averill slammed the desk with his fists. "I believed Vipèrine was the killer,"

"For a time," Michel said. "Then you only wished to believe it."

"You don't know my mind. I feel like a child given a jigsaw puzzle with half the pieces hidden."

"When did you last see Corbeau?"

"He was often our driver a year ago but not so much recently."

"Your driver—and Casimir's?"

"Anyone can hire a carriage."

"All the victims are known to at least one of the Revenants," Theo reminded him. Averill glared at her like an enemy, then looked away.

"Tell me any link you know to these missing children." Michel began to go through them in order, their names, their parents' occupations, where they'd lived.

As the names went by, Averill looked more horrified but still he battled. "Corbeau often drove us around Montmartre and many other places. But he did not clamber down and talk to children. Casimir did not halt the fiacre and point them out."

"Dondre," Theo broke in. When Averill turned to her, she said. "Dondre was the boy who guided us through the catacombs."

Averill closed his eyes. He shuddered. "The catacombs."

"It must be Casimir," Theo whispered, not wanting to believe it, except that it meant Averill was innocent.

He shook his head vehemently, refusing to look at her. "No."

Theo reached out and took his hands, grateful that Michel did not stop her. "Matthieu will be tortured and murdered. Help us."

He raised his head and met her gaze, hiding nothing. "How can I accuse him?"

"Did Casimir give you *Là Bas*?" Michel asked.

"Yes. But that was years ago. He even researched the archives," Averill paused, totally puzzled. He turned to Michel again. "Why do you keep battering me with Gilles de Rais?"

"Why do you think?"

Averill looked faintly sick. "He kidnapped and murdered little children—but that was centuries ago."

"And the winged cross?" Michel asked.

"The one you showed me on the gravestone?" Averill paused. "And there was the other one by the Seine."

Michel only watched him, looking for some crack in the façade. So Theo told him, "Both Inspecteur Devaux and I discovered that the killer is signing his work with Gilles de Rais' emblem."

Averill looked back at Michel. "I thought the name was only a metaphor for evil—but you were trying to provoke me."

"Yes, I was trying to provoke you. The name has taken on new life."

Hesitantly, Averill said, "Once or twice, he asked if I'd ever been tempted to kill."

"And you answered?"

"Only my father." Averill's voice was caustic. "It was *café* conversation. Nietzsche's concept of the superman. Rimbaud's disordering of the senses to achieve deeper knowledge."

"Didn't you ask if he'd been tempted to kill?" Michel asked.

"Yes." Again Averill paused. "He said he hated his grandfather as much as I do my father."

"Before his death?" Michel asked.

"Do you think—?" Theo broke off. As terrible as such a murder would have been, the children were worse.

"He was an old man…he fell down the stairs and broke his neck," Averill said.

"Did Casimir ask why you did not surrender to temptation?" Michel asked.

"I said the sin would bury my soul alive," Averill replied stiffly.

Theo sensed there was more. "And what did Casimir answer?"

"He said sin was the way to enter the furthest reaches of darkness." Averill had stopped naming Casimir. "He said that only in utter darkness could you find your way to the pure and burning light, the holy fire that transfigures the soul."

Michel leaned forward, intent. "There was a fire at Casimir's estate when he was a child."

"Yes. He said more than once that he should have died in that fire and instead…" Averill stopped abruptly.

"Someone else died there?" Michel asked at once.

"A servant girl who took care of him. He loved her. She was good to him—took terrible beatings for him."

Theo's vision came to life in her mind. She saw the girl in the white nightgown running through the halls. She heard the child weeping. "Jeanne. Her name was Jeanne."

Averill looked at her, desolation on his face. "Yes," he whispered. "She burned to death in the fire. Casimir could hear her screams. He had nightmares about her sometimes."

"Casimir is the killer." Theo had no doubt now. She remembered him watching the Bazar de la Charité burn, tears streaming down his face. *Fire is a terrible way to die.*

Averill leaned toward her. "I remember now—Casimir said Jeanne called him her Dauphin, her little prince. He told her he would rather ride to war by her side, her soldier, defending her as she defended him."

"Her Gilles de Rais," Theo whispered, sick with pity and terror.

There was a silence. Then Michel stood. "I believe it, but it is not proven. Monsieur Charron, you will be escorted back to the infirmary while we search for him."

Averill nodded, his face blank.

Theo had known betrayal but nothing like Casimir's betrayal of him. Years of precious memories transformed into a quagmire of horror.

Michel went to the door, then turned back to Averill. "The baron has a small townhouse off the Champs Élysées and shares an apartment with you in Montmartre. Is there anywhere else he might hide a child?"

Averill looked dazed, as if he did not understand the question. Theo answered instead. "He could have gone to his country estate."

"The chateau in La Veillée sur Oise? I thought it was destroyed."

"There is a gardener's cottage of sorts. And a room or two of the chateau stills stands." A tremor coursed through her. "He took us there to show us the picturesque ruins. I sketched it."

"It was right after the dog washer's child disappeared. A beautiful autumn day—leaves like a sea of blood—" Averill's voice cracked. He pressed his forehead to his clasped hands, his knuckles white. Theo felt as if she were back in the catacombs, drowning in darkness. She reached out and covered his hands with her own. Michel made no move to stop her. Averill lifted his head and gave her a twisted smile. "Well, I keep my head, at least. My mind is another matter."

"We may save Matthieu," she said.

"Yes." Averill nodded, but his eyes were desolate.

Michel turned to the detective guarding the door. "Inspecteur Rambert, have someone else return Monsieur Charron to the infirmary." Rambert opened the door and summoned the officer who had chastised Theo. "Monsieur Charron, you will follow this officer."

Averill rose and leaned across the table. His eyes met hers, still full of pain but also gratitude. He kissed her lightly on each cheek, as much a salute as an endearment. "*Au revoir.*"

Then he was gone out the door. Theo turned to Michel. "Now we search?"

"Yes," he answered. "Corbeau would have wanted to hide outside of Paris, so the chateau is the most likely place. We already have men watching Corbeau's stables. Matthieu is not there. I will send men to search the baron's Paris house and the apartment in Montmartre, but Rambert and I will go to the baron's estate."

"Do we notify the local police?" Rambert asked.

"It is only a hunch," Michel answered cautiously, then added bluntly, "We cannot trust either their competence or their honesty."

Rambert grinned at him and went to get his jacket. Theo guessed they wanted to keep possession of their case. Michel called after him, "The chief has a phone in his office. I will call for the train schedule."

"La Veillée sur Oise is a remnant of a village," Theo told him. "There is no direct train. The closest station is a half an hour beyond it. It will be faster to ride."

"How long?"

"Riding hard? Less than two hours, changing horses once."

He considered that. "We have horses stabled here. We could switch mounts at Argenteuil."

"Then we ride," Theo said, including herself.

"No," Michel replied, as if his refusal would stop her. Sensing her determination, he glanced toward the cells. Would he dare lock her up? Of course he would dare. He could arrest her for wearing trousers or something else absurd.

"I know where the chateau is," Theo said. "I know Matthieu. And I know Casimir—if not Gilles. Perhaps he will surrender Matthieu to me. I doubt he would give him to you."

He met her gaze. "You cannot know that. You may only increase the risk."

"Perhaps—but is the best chance we have?"

He stood for a moment, weighing his choices. "We ride."

Chapter Forty

And yet, as much as my victim, I suffered! Forgive me, child.
Once we are freed from this transient life, I want us to be entwined
forevermore, becoming but one being, my mouth fused to your mouth.
                                        Comte de Lautréamont

Matthieu was perfection. Looking at him, Gilles swelled with longing—the curling light brown hair, the hazel eyes. Rough ropes bound him, contrasting exquisitely with the silken skin, their abrasions a provocative scarlet against its fairness. His nude body swayed, the ropes linked to the hook overhead.

"Don't be afraid," Gilles whispered. He so loved the look of hope that shone in Matthieu's imploring gaze. The bright gleam of it was trapped inside the tears that spilled along the downy cheek. He caught one on his fingertip and sipped the salty liquid morsel, savoring its flavor like the finest wine. The hope was sweet, elusive, passing swiftly like flowers crushed in a storm. Terror gave it a bitter depth that lingered on the palate. A taste of eternity.

Gilles knew ruined hope as well. He had hoped Averill would become his Poitou, his servant through the centuries. He'd hoped that they would seek out the sacrifices together. His lover's fascination with pain had seemed a lure, but Averill had no desire to inflict it, only to be transformed by it. He played seductive games with darkness, with death, but it was flirtation only, not a true amour. No fool, Gilles had abandoned his hope without ever voicing it.

Although he held less power, this epoch had its recompenses. At first, Gilles' new courtiers had been so oblivious he'd hoped his rituals might go on indefinitely. Even in this later century, the children of peasants had their equivalent. Few had noticed when he took his chosen ones. Few—but enough. Now Gilles no longer expected to escape. After all, he had not escaped before. Death had claimed him, but not Heaven or Hell. For centuries he had been imprisoned in the oblivion of Limbo. He had not learned enough from his crimes, else he would not have been returned.

Once again, Gilles had lost himself in the ecstasy of sin. The greater ecstasy of redemption waited. This time he would not fail.

There was a rustle of sound. Gilles turned toward Matthieu. The boy watched him attentively but could not keep his eyes from darting to the corner where Corbeau sat.

"Do not pay him any heed, he can't hurt you," Gilles assured him. The boy's eyes widened as Gilles approached. "The Raven swooped down and carried you off to my castle, but he has no power now."

Corbeau slumped in the corner, staring blindly, watching but not seeing. Gilles had no intention of sharing Matthieu with him. He had slit his throat, then gutted him. It had always been a possibility that he would kill Corbeau. Certainly, Gilles knew that Corbeau might attempt to kill him. Their collaboration had worked so well at first, but Corbeau had grown both cruder and more reckless with time, wanting more and more kills. Then he had dared to display Alicia and leave Gilles' own mark on the grave.

"He won't hurt you." Gilles smiled at Matthieu.

The boy watched him warily. He was not a dreamer like sweet Denis had been. For all his pretty looks, he was a sharp child, like Dondre. Inspiration flamed, golden bright. Gilles wondered if he could begin again, make this boy his Poitou, teach him the art....

But, after all, the art was but a means to attain glory.

The flame guttered, leaving a lingering melancholy. Gilles held fast to one last hope. He prayed that they would not be discovered before the dark of the moon. That fool Vipèrine was no sorcerer if he had not awaited the perfect moment for his sacrifice. Nor had Corbeau understood the subtleties when he tried to seize Darline.

No matter. Matthieu was the best of all Gilles' sacraments. He would offer the boy at midnight when the utter blackness of night would match the utter blackness of deed. His last, his most perfect offering.

The thought had him pulsing with the promise of ultimate ecstasy. He released his member, pulling Matthieu to him and rubbing on the delicate skin of his belly. Shock and horror filled the boy's eyes. So exquisite. Gilles gripped him harder, thrust harder, lunging toward a rapture that evaded him. They should be closer, more intimate still in this ancient dance of death. He had the knife. It was a monumental effort not to kill him, not to cut his throat so that the blood poured over them both as he climaxed. For a moment, he thought that the image alone would not suffice, that only the deed would release him. But now, the boy gave a sob, a small sound that exploded inside of Gilles. His seed poured out, anointing the sacrifice.

The ritual usually ended so, with the dreadful glory of death completing the bliss. But no—not now. Gilles was determined to wait. He allowed himself only one long, tender kiss. A benediction. Yet the need pulsed, darker and heavier with each beat of his heart. The boy knew, the answering darkness filled his eyes. Terror. Wrath. Despair.

He must not stay, or he would succumb. Leaving the boy suspended, Gilles climbed the steps out of the wine cellar to the remains of the kitchen. It was better preserved than the rest of the rooms. The roof had not totally collapsed here. He sauntered to what had been the grand foyer. The worst of the debris had been cleared two decades ago. He went to the sacred spot. She had died here, his Jeanne. She had carried the old devil this far and tripped and broken her ankle. His grandfather had crawled over her, crawled out the door and lived. She tried to follow after, despite her pain, but the flaming beams had fallen and trapped her. Burned her alive. Her screams of agony still shredded his soul.

Once again, Jeanne had left him alone. Once again, he had failed to save her.

Gilles went outside to the edge of the hill. From here he could see the forest on one side, rolling hills with Paris waiting to the south. The rest was cultivated, vineyards and the golden sway of wheat fields. Below lay the glimmering ribbon of the river and beyond a glimpse of the town nestled on its banks. Remnants of his vast domains, the heritage his grandfather had squandered.

He was not so lost in daydream as to miss the riders turning at the last curve in the road. In a few minutes they would be here. His wish had not been granted. His final ritual would not be in the dark of the moon.

The last time, he had died at dawn.

Chapter Forty~One

It is the tomb, I am off to the worms, oh horror of horrors!
Satan, you buffoon, you want me to waste away with your
spells. I implore! I implore! A stab of the fork, a splash of fire.
                                                      Arthur Rimbaud

Rescue Matthieu. Rescue Matthieu. Rescue Matthieu.
The words drummed in Theo's head, echoing the galloping beat of
the horses' hooves. At last they turned off the highway onto the country
road approaching Casimir's domain. They were lucky, first with the strong
police mounts, then with the choice animals they'd rented at their one
stop. Long shadows stretched across the dirt as the sun slowly lowered.
Their pace was good, but it seemed forever before Theo recognized the
crumbled remnants of the monks' dwellings on the outskirts of La Veillée
sur Oise. Just past them, Theo pointed to the neglected road that led to
the chateau. They'd barely turned onto it when Rambert's mount stumbled
in an obscured pothole and wrenched off a shoe. Michel and Rambert
dismounted to look at the horse's hoof. Theo stayed on her mare. She
had no trouble guessing the outcome of this twist of events. She'd be
expected to give up her mount and walk Rambert's into town while the
men went on ahead.

"My horse can't go on," Rambert said. "He could bruise the foot
irreparably."

Michel frowned at the upturned hoof, then turned to look at Theo.
She instantly wheeled around and sent her mare running toward the
chateau.

"Theo!" She heard Michel call after her. Had he ever called her
Theo before? She kept riding, listening to hear if he was pursuing her.
The docile mare had some speed, but not as much as Michel's solid
gelding. After a moment, she heard his horse closing in on her. She spared
one glance over her shoulder and Michel yelled again, "Theo, stop!"

Instead she urged her new horse to higher speed, searching the
uneven road for rocks and hidden holes. A quarter mile and she crossed
a bridge over the River Oise and began to travel up the hill. The mare was

flagging, so halfway up Theo slowed, letting Michel catch up to her at last. His glare spoke volumes, but he said nothing. Together they continued to climb the winding, rutted road. At the pinnacle, the road curved round a stand of trees. Between the tall trunks and rich spring growth, they glimpsed the derelict estate. Then they were riding on the overgrown gravel drive that led to the burned-out hulk of Casimir's chateau. Fresh wheel tracks cut a pathway through the spring growth of grass and weeds. Vines crawled over the shabby caretaker's cottage. Half-hidden behind it stood a black fiacre. Freed from its traces, the horse that had drawn it wandered under the apple trees of the small orchard. They rode over to the nearest tree, dismounted, and tied their mounts.

"Stand back." Michel drew his gun. Motioning her back, he kicked open the door of the cottage. There was no one within. If there had been a caretaker, Casimir had dismissed him when he started bringing his victims here.

Together they walked to the burned ruins of the chateau. Theo led him through the ravaged foyer with its skeletal staircase leading nowhere. Beyond it were the remnants of a grand hallway flanked by elegant rooms opening to the sky. The back was in slightly better condition. Here they found the kitchen, with an old stone fireplace standing, three walls, a bit of roof. And a door of charred oak. Theo expected to find the door locked, that Michel would have to force it, but it opened smoothly. Below, faint light glimmered. The smell of corruption wafted upward, sweetly rotten.

A chill iced Theo's spine. She wondered if Casimir had killed Matthieu and buried him. Burned him? She tried to thrust her fear to the back of her mind. It would only cripple her.

Stepping forward, Michel descended first. The stone steps were worn in the center from centuries of use. They reached a small passage where an iron gateway stood open. Looking inside, Theo fought back a cry. Votive candles formed a circle in the center of the room. Above them, a man hung from a hook in the rafters. His throat gaped and dried blood covered his clothing. His belly was gutted, the exposed entrails looping down from the wound. The reek of blood and excrement saturated the room.

"Corbeau. He was killed before he was hung there." Michel glanced towards the far corner, bloodier than the floor beneath the body.

Theo saw the flagstones beneath the corpse were darkened with old bloodstains. The flash of pity she'd felt for what had once been a living man was squelched by the knowledge of his crimes. This was the man who had helped murder Alicia and the others. Denis and Dondre might have hung from this same hook. Had Matthieu?

"He is staging this for us like some obscene spectacle," Michel said in a low voice.

"Then Matthieu must be alive, or he would be hanging there."

"Perhaps," Michel said.

That horror might still await them. Theo went forward and picked up one of the glass votives. Michel did as well. Looking around the brick-walled room, she saw some dilapidated wine shelves and a few broken bottles. There was a faint sound behind them. Michel heard it too, and they both turned at the same time. Was it nothing more than a rat lurking in this cellar, or was it a summons? They walked toward the back of the room. Obscured in shadows a scrolled metal gate stood open. An invitation. Theo followed Michel through into a long corridor. At its end was another door, ominous, strapped with leather and studded. Theo's heart thudded, heavy and dull as an iron clapper pounding the wall of her chest. With every step the stench of death thickened, falling over them like murky veils. Death. Death and some other strident, sickening odor.

"Petrol," Michel said. "Put the candles out."

They extinguished the votives and went forward along the darkened corridor, led by the rim of light beneath the door. When they reached the end, Michel turned to her. Theo met his gaze and nodded, her mouth too dry for speech. Then he pushed open the door.

Swaying slightly, a hanging lantern with yellow glass panels illuminated the center of the room. Beneath its sulphurous light was a row of four tall wooden stakes. A cry choked Theo's throat. On each stake was a head…the small head of a child. They faced her, their eyes glazed, their rotting lips exposing little white teeth in false leers. Revulsion clutched her with icy claws that twisted into her belly. Theo shut her eyes, fighting the quaking that swept her. She should have known that an imitator of Gilles de Rais would display this grotesque beauty pageant. Michel gathered her to him, blocking the sight. Theo felt the burn of rising tears. She fought back a sob, swallowing a breath of the putrid air. There was no escape from this horror. She pulled away from Michel and forced herself to turn. Her tears blurred the grisly display, but she could see now there was another lantern on the side of the table beyond. She went forward, forcing herself to look at the ghastly decomposed faces. She must know if Matthieu was displayed there. But no—these poor children had been dead for weeks—or months. Light gleamed at the corner of her vision and she turned to see Casimir step forward from the darkest corner, pushing Matthieu in front of him.

"You've come at last—my witnesses." Casimir smiled, the golden, boyish smile Theo had always found so lovely. Even in the flickering candlelight, he looked radiant. A terrible sadness mingled with her abhorrence. Did a sliver of that Casimir exist? Did it matter, after what he'd done?

She looked to Matthieu and saw a noose looped around his throat. It trailed down and tied to Casimir's waist. Wet streaks glistened on their clothing and the reek of gasoline floated around them. Casimir carried another lantern, its thin glass walls all that kept the flame from igniting the fumes. Tears stained Matthieu's face, but he was not crying now. His eyes were wide with fear, but Theo saw courage and hope in them too. He searched their faces, watching for some clue to his salvation.

"Drop the gun, Inspecteur," Casimir said as he walked Matthieu to a table behind the staked heads. "If you shoot me, the lamp shatters and we both die."

"Let the boy go," Michel said. "You cannot believe you will escape."

"I did not escape before. This time I must achieve my goal. Drop the gun and kick it here." He lifted the lantern he held aloft.

Theo cursed silently. She had not thought to bring her colt—but even if she had, it would be too dangerous to use.

Michel dropped the gun.

"Here," Casimir said, his voice, his face growing hard.

"Not to you." Michel kicked the gun toward the back corner. It skittered on across the stones.

Casimir laughed. "Theo, fetch the gun and put it on the table."

Theo glanced at Michel, then did as Casimir bade her. She would not defy him when there was still a chance to save Matthieu. She laid the gun down, watching the lantern light dance over the horrible array of knives and pincers, a hammer, a saw. She shuddered. Beneath the table was a streaked jug that must hold the gasoline. Casimir nodded for her to back away, then pulled Matthieu with him as he went to pick up the gun. He checked it, then trained it on Michel. "I will not go back to Paris, Inspecteur. I will not go to the guillotine."

Casimir yanked Matthieu back to the gruesome display. Matthieu flinched away, but Casimir gripped his hair and held him still. Nodding toward the heads, Casimir asked, "Which is the most beautiful, Theodora?"

"They are all hideous."

"Do you think so? I do not." He tilted his head, a smile teasing the corner of his lips. "Do you think Averill would see their beauty, the implacable lure of Death?"

"No!"

Keeping Matthieu close, Casimir went to the head on the far end. "You must remember Dondre?" Theo had all she could do not to be sick as he bent slightly, watching her as he kissed the curling hair. Disgust, fury, terror were a pack of vicious rats clawing over each other inside her belly.

"Six boys—but you killed more," Michel said.

"Only the prettiest are here."

"Did you kill your grandfather, too?" Michel asked.

"I tried twice—but I only succeeded once." Casimir smirked, but then his expression warped into a mask of loathing.

"What did he do, that you hated him so much?" Theo asked.

"What do you think?" His voice was scornful. "I endured every form of abuse at his hands—and from whatever other part of his anatomy that he chose."

"So you set the fire that burned this chateau?" Michel asked.

"I wanted him dead, but she died instead—" Casimir broke off suddenly. "It was the judgment of God on my sin, taking the only one I loved, the only one who loved me."

"We know about your Jeanne," Theo said softly. At least once he had been able to love.

"You know nothing," he accused, hatred igniting in his eyes. "I lived with him, year after year, afraid to try again, afraid some greater calamity would befall me. I suffered every atrocity he wanted to inflict. I waited for God to take him—but he lived on and on and on."

"But you did succeed in killing him," Michel said.

"The fire at Averill's country house was a portent. My grandfather was the cause of Jeanne's death as much as I. He had to die. It did not matter what happened to me after. I pushed him down the stairs. I was free of him at last."

No, Theo thought, not free. More trapped than ever.

"When I returned to Montmartre, *Là Bas* was sitting on the table, waiting for me. Averill had left it out. Another portent. I saw who I must become. Jeanne was good, but I was never good except with her. Goodness needs miraculous courage. God punishes the good, like poor mawkish Job, seeing if they will succumb. But God, like the Devil, is intoxicated by evil. I had only to be wicked enough, and I would be gathered up with love. Forgiven. Blessed. I would be taken into her presence again, she who protected me though I was not worthy of it."

"You were going to frame Averill for your crimes?" Michel said. "Was that another offering of evil?"

"Averill could not have taken Matthieu." Casimir looked at him as if he were the madman. "I ordered Corbeau to take him for me."

"You kidnapped Matthieu while Averill was in prison. You never wanted to hurt him." Theo prayed it was true.

"Oh, I wanted to hurt Averill, but only as he wanted to be hurt. He showed me that pain can lead to freedom." Casimir laughed. "You'll never win him, *chère Amazone*. Unless it hurts, it can't be love. He needs the darkness. Your bright sunlight will only push him deeper into the shadows."

Theo's heart twisted. Averill had spoken almost the same words. But her pain, her love for him was only a distraction Casimir used to goad her. Saving Matthieu was all that mattered now, but she choked on her words.

Michel spoke for her. "You will not be forgiven if you take Matthieu with you. Your repentance will only have meaning if you surrender him."

"He belongs to me." Casimir said it as if were indisputable.

Seeing them together, Theo thought Matthieu might be Casimir himself as a boy. Denis and Dondre resembled him as well, but Matthieu most of all, with his large eyes and curling mop of hair. Casimir gazed at her, his eyes so guileless now, utterly enraptured with this evil fairy tale of his own creation. In it he destroyed his image again and again. Only his own death would end it.

"He is not you," Theo said, fighting her rage. "He only looks like you. He has a mother who loves him."

"And his own Jeanne d'Arc who will fight to protect him." Casimir's voice was condescending, but myriad emotions flickered over his face, sadness, envy, hatred.

Theo saw Michel move toward her protectively. Casimir smiled at him. "Do you think I would consign her to the flames?"

"I think you would burn the world down if you could," Michel answered.

"Ah, you are wrong. Jeanne d'Arc was sent to redeem me. She failed and I failed. I must achieve my own redemption. She is beyond pain, yet the path to her is through pain. Centuries ago they offered me the chance to follow her into the flames, but I was too proud, too fearful, and I let the executioner strangle me on the pyre. Jeanne came again when I was a child here, and died again, right above us. I should have burned with her."

He knelt, the tug of the rope pulling Matthieu to his knees beside him. He lowered his head, as if in prayer, but kept the gun trained on Michel. "I am your brother in Christ. You must pray for me and forgive me freely, as you desire God to forgive you and have mercy on your souls. I have lacerated your hearts, yet I beg you to pity me."

Gilles de Rais' words, before he died. Theo answered, "I will pray for you, but only if you release Matthieu."

He gazed up at her. "He is my sacrifice. The greater the sin, the greater the forgiveness. I need only feel profound regret and contrition."

Theo did not dare look at Michel. She sensed his presence like a wire taut between them, but did not dare turn her eyes away from Casimir. "I do not see regret and contrition. I see pride, indulgence, defiance. Do not heap another sin on your soul. Matthieu is indeed your sacrifice, not burned upon the altar of your sin but freed, whole and innocent."

"Not quite innocent. He is anointed with my sin."

Matthieu gave a low sob, tears running down his cheeks now.

She was desperate. He had an answer for everything. "No, you are the last sacrifice, Gilles. You and you alone."

He smiled at her, his most charming, boyish smile. "You are valiant, but you are not Jeanne. You cannot make that claim."

"But I am Jeanne," she said to him. "Jeanne Theodora Faraday. When I came to France, I thought that my other name would be more unusual. I wanted to be a great artist and I chose it out of pride. I too sinned."

"No," he said, rising, staring at her. Fury rippled through the muscles of his face, distorting it. "Do not dare!"

She went on, heedless of his wrath. "Jeanne's spirit came to me. When I was little, I would ride my horse through the meadows, dreaming I was leading her armies. I could almost hear my valiant companions— almost hear you—but I thought it was only the wind."

"Liar!" He searched her face, still angry and disbelieving.

She defied both. "What more proof do you need than that I am here, now, when you must come face to face with God?"

"You wear men's clothes. You have the heart of a warrior," he murmured, trying now to convince himself. Then he glared at her, "You are Averill's lover."

"No, I am a virgin."

He stared at her, wonder and fear in his eyes. His lips trembled. "Her spirit came to you?"

"Jeanne!" Matthieu called to her. He was not too young to understand some of this bizarre drama. "Save me, Jeanne!"

Theo knelt and held out her arms, imploring Casimir. "Give him to me."

"I did not die alone," Casimir said.

"Those who died with you were your servants in evil."

"My servants but not my true companions," Casimir agreed, watching her intently. "If you are Jeanne, return to me. Join with me, as it was meant to be, and I will let him go."

Theo walked back to the table. Ignoring Michel's gasp, she picked up the jar of gasoline. Shaking, she poured the vile liquid over her shoulders, feeling it run down her body and soak her clothing. Beside her, the lantern blazed ominously.

"More." The fervor of a fanatic glowed in Casimir's eyes.

She poured more over her arms, her legs, then put the jug on the table with its flaunted implements of torture. Terror and hope twisted every nerve and muscle, but she kept her voice clear, commanding. "Release him."

"Come to me."

She moved closer, held out her hand, almost but not quite within reach. "You cannot have us both. You must choose."

He hesitated, then said to Matthieu, "You can untie the rope." Matthieu turned, his hands fumbling with the knot. She watched, praying silently as he jerked and tugged. Then suddenly Matthieu was running—though he seemed barely to move through the yellow air thick as poisoned honey. The rope flapped as he ran past the gasoline pooled on the floor, beyond the line of staked heads, beyond Michel. As he passed, Michel's eyes met hers and he cried out, "Theo, jump!"

She jumped, her shaking legs seeming to give way even as she flung herself sideways. Her dive carried her as far as the stakes, the yellow light swaying above them. She rolled and kept rolling. Glimpses of terror and hope flashed with every turn. Casimir hurled his lantern at her. It crashed against a stake in a crackle of glass but its spurting flames did not reach her. Still rolling toward the door, she saw Michel rush the table. Casimir fired the gun at his hurtling body. Michel gave a harsh cry and spun with the impact. Then he whirled and kicked out, a long hard kick that hit Casimir and sent him flying back to crash against the table. The jolt of his body set the lantern rocking. Michel staggered back toward the door then collapsed. The lantern toppled, the glass shattering on the floor. With a hissing rush, the pool of gasoline became a pool of fire. Greedy fingers of flame reached out and seized Casimir, rushing up his legs, his body, licking over his face. She watched in horror as he leapt up, a human candle, screaming and screaming and screaming as the fire engulfed him. He stared back at her from the center of that agony—and then he was running toward her, his hands outstretched.

"Don't let him touch you!" Michel cried.

Theo sensed the miasma of fumes hovering all around her, thicker now than when she first poured the gasoline. She leapt to her feet and raced through the door. Matthieu stood in the hall, watching the horrific end unfold. Theo grabbed his hand, pulled him with her, running down the hall and through the wine cellar, past the gruesome dangling body of Corbeau. Another shot sounded behind her as she ran with Matthieu out the door and up the steps to the demolished kitchen. At the top she turned, waiting for any glimpse of fire below, waiting for the evil spirit of Gilles de Rais to seek her out. No light showed except the dim flicker of candlelight through the open door. They were safe. But what of Michel? Casimir's first shot had wounded him. Had Michel ended Casimir's agony with the second? Had Casimir somehow managed to kill him?

Matthieu pressed against her, trembling as she was still trembling. She held him close, needing the same comfort he did, needing to feel him alive. He looked up at her. "Is your name Jeanne, mademoiselle, like Jeanne d'Arc? Did she speak to you?"

"No, my name is just Theo. And if she spoke to me, it was to tell me to save you."

"You did not burn," Matthieu whispered. "It is a miracle."

"No. It is not the gasoline that ignites, it's the fumes. I was lucky," she told him.

"A miracle," he said again. Theo thought it was too, whatever the scientific explanation. She was alive. But she must go back down. "You stay here, Matthieu. I must go see if Inspecteur Devaux is hurt."

"No need." They both swiveled round to stare down the stairs. Michel stood at the bottom, his face white with strain. "He's dead."

"You shot him?" Matthieu asked.

Michel gave a sharp nod.

Theo drew a long breath. "I'm glad you ended his suffering."

"Mercy is better than vengeance." His gaze was dark, and his voice sounded as uncertain as she felt. She went down the stairs to him, looked at the bloodstained hand pressed to his side. "Rib," he said.

"There's the carriage," Theo said. "I can drive us back to town."

He nodded, then set himself to climb the stairs, refusing her help. There was a working pump by the abandoned cottage, so Theo began to wash the gasoline off herself and Matthieu. Suddenly she had the image of Casimir standing here, washing away his victims' blood. How many children had perished here?

She led Matthieu off as soon as she felt they would not burst into flames at the slightest friction. He helped her put the carriage horse back in his traces. Gingerly, Michel got into the carriage. Matthieu beside her, she drove slowly down to the bottom of the hill where the river Oise flowed by, water gleaming in the sun.

Impulsively, Theo stopped so she and Matthieu could wash again. And again....

The cold water swept away more of the petrol, more of the stench of death.

But the memories were burned into them forever.

Chapter Forty~Two

Let us go, then, my poor heart. Let us go, my old accomplice.
Repair and paint anew all your triumphal arcs. Burn bitter incense
On your pinchbeck altars. Scatter with flowers the cliff's gaping brink.
Let us go then, my poor heart. Let us go, my old accomplice.

Paul Verlaine

Theo walked up the rue Lepic toward home, her damp hair drying in the bright June afternoon. The compulsion to wash hadn't waned. She'd been to the baths once or twice a day for a week, scrubbing with vinegar, with ground coffee, with whatever remedy anyone could suggest. The clothes she had thrown away. The stench of death and dying was gone from her skin but not from her mind. Rotting corpses. Burning flesh. Gasoline. The smell clung to her hair and she almost hacked it off—then thought of Jeanne d'Arc and her shorn hair. Theo kept hers long and returned to the vinegar. Lifting some strands to her nose now, she sniffed only dampness and sunshine and felt a swell of relief.

A week....

A week, and still Averill had not come to see her. Had he not forgiven her? Did he think she despised him? She had told herself to wait until he was ready to speak to her. A week was not so terribly long, not after what they had all endured. Averill was grieving—and he had other worries. His sister was still hidden away in some asylum.

Michel had let her tell Averill of Casimir's death. He heard her out, every hideous detail. He did not wish to be spared. But then he wanted to be alone. In mourning for a dream. But as she left he reached out his hand and clasped hers. "I still love you," he whispered. A voice from the bottom of a well.

"I love you too," she'd answered, but she'd felt only wretchedness.

After his release, his mother had come to thank her, trembling and almost incoherent with joy. Francine had been with her, tense and acidic. Had she hoped Casimir would propose? Was her lost chance at being a baroness more important than her misconception of who he was? A misconception they had all shared. Theo remembered how strangely perfect Casimir had seemed. Too perfect—because he was always playing a part. Not knowing what tales her uncle might spin, Theo had written her father so he would have an honest, if expurgated, version of what had happened. Yesterday, a telegram came, pleading with her to travel with him in Italy. It lay on her table, unanswered.

Theo approached the door of her home, for home it still was. Matthieu's mother had mixed feelings, her heartfelt gratitude for Theo's rescue tainted with blame for her knowing such a monster. At first Madame Masson wanted Casimir's guilt shouted from the rooftops. Then Michel warned that the newspaper reporters would descend upon her and Matthieu like jackals. The story had been covered up by the Paris police with the help of the locals. Corbeau took the blame and few knew the full truth. The Revenants did and disbanded. None of them wanted to be associated with a killer.

Casimir had been the true revenant, possessed by Gilles de Rais. Possessed by the idea, perhaps by the spirit, as Yeats had suggested.

Theo paused as she entered the courtyard, closed her eyes and breathed deeply. It had rained earlier. The fragrance of the pink tea roses mingled with the rich aromas of bark and soil, the glimmering greens of leaves and damp grass. The air smelled sweetly alive, idyllic, peaceful. She inhaled again, the sweet, living scents keeping the ugly memories at bay for a few more seconds. When she opened her eyes again, she saw Averill rise from where he'd been sitting beneath the shadow of the rose tree—reading while he waited, for he carried a book in his hand.

She walked forward, going to meet him under the cool shade of the overhanging branches. Close to, he looked exhausted, a rim of the bruise still faintly visible on his throat, his eyes hollowed. But he smelled lovely, the scent of warm woods and lavender. Yet now that he was here, her emotions were an awkward tangle and she did not know what to say. She glanced down at the book. "Baudelaire?"

"I have stopped drinking absinthe," Averill said, "but I still drink the darkness. You would think that Casimir's death would have cured me of that addiction, yet it is more potent than ever, the mystery deeper."

So they were at the heart of things already. Casimir stood between them, a dreadful burning brightness that obliterated everything else. She stared at Averill, words knotted in her throat.

He met her gaze. Pale as his eyes were, his gaze seemed bottomless. "I never came back for the portrait. You can paint it now if you want. I have nothing more to hide from you."

A flare of anger gave her back her voice. "Then we can be truly honest at last?"

"I told myself I was honest," he answered, "that it was only a lie of omission. I did not tell you about the women I bedded, why should I tell you about Casimir?"

"I did not know them."

"We were lovers only occasionally." His voice was hesitant. "I kept thinking it might be over, but it never was, quite." He paused. "If you had asked, I would have told you—but I did not want you to ask."

Theo still felt betrayed. "You implied there were such adventures—but only as a schoolboy experiment."

"I was sixteen when Casimir saved me from some bullies who were beating me for reading poetry." He frowned. "I was small for my age and looked much younger. Now I wonder now if that drew him. He took me home with him. It was my first time."

Her heart ached. Averill had told her once that was how they met, but spoke only of the valiant rescue, not the seduction.

He smiled a little. "That year I shot up inches. It seemed like magic, as if he had worked some miracle on me."

"You were in love with him."

It was an accusation, not a question, but Averill answered it quietly. "In love—and always a little afraid. Casimir was tender with me, but he also led me to the darkness. Then he showed me that darkness can lead to light."

Theo almost choked on the words, but she gave them to him. "He said the same of you."

"Did he?" Averill asked, puzzled. "Knowing what he did, that seems abominable."

Unable to stop herself, she repeated Casimir's mysterious words. "He said unless it hurts you, it couldn't be love."

Averill flinched as if slapped, but continued to answer her quietly. "Yes. I am a masochistic…at least on occasion. Nothing else is as…transfiguring. It is more like worship than sex. I discovered that secret with Casimir, that first time. Hurt lingered from the bullies beating. I wanted him so much the hurt did not matter. Pain and pleasure dissolved together. Dissolved me—body and soul."

Theo shivered a little. "And that made you love the pain?"

"At first it was a transformation, a joy. Later—the more I hated myself, the more I craved it." He closed his eyes, then opened them to face her again. "I needed the obliteration."

"But why did you hate yourself?"

"Why do I hate myself? For not fighting my father—then for trying to kill him. For abandoning my mother and sister to my father's viciousness. For returning to the same prison that destroyed them. There is no escape."

She put her hands on his shoulders. He leaned forward, resting his forehead against hers with a sigh. His hands rose to rest on her arms. She ached inside, filled with yearning and a terrible sadness. Impulsively, she kissed him. His lips were warm and full against her own. They trembled slightly. She felt him tense. His hands tightened fiercely but did not push her away or pull her closer. She felt no more than before, a yearning, an aching emptiness. She felt him waiting—as she was waiting. There was no rush of desire, no urge to melt into him.

Confused, Theo drew back. Meeting her gaze, he smiled bitterly. "So he has murdered that as well."

It was true. She did not even know when it had happened. Was it when she saw Averill kiss Casimir? No, it had not ended then. But perhaps that had been the mortal wound that let desire bleed away and die, a husk on Casimir's funeral pyre. "I wanted to marry you," she whispered, stricken.

Averill shook his head. "I will never marry. My family's blood is degenerate."

"No!" she said fiercely.

"Still defending me?"

"I still love you," she said, as he had said to her in the prison. She did.

"But you are not in love with me anymore?"

She did not answer. The pain in his eyes revealed he was still in love with her, which made it far more terrible. She ached all over, a pain in her heart that spread outward to every limb.

A shaft of sunlight slanted across his face. He shielded his eyes. "Can we go inside? It is so bright here."

Theo was aware of the garden again, after seeing only him. The sunshine was a balm, one of the few she'd found, but he was always sensitive to its brightness. She led the way upstairs. In her apartment, the windows were open, vases filled with flowers. Underneath the fresh air and fragrant blossoms lingered the fumes of turpentine—something a painter with her own studio must live with. It was faint now, with the bottles sealed and paints put away, but still it made her queasy. It was a thinner, sharper smell than gasoline, but near enough to turn her stomach. It had not stopped her work at the easel. Painting was her exorcism. There would always be reminders. Would fire ever be friendly again?

Averill looked over at the empty easel. "Have you been able to work at all?"

He had been honest with her. Theo went to the corner, picked up the portrait that faced the wall and placed it on the easel. Turning back to him, she said, "I haven't been drinking the darkness. I have been drowning in it."

Averill stared at the portrait. At last he said, "It's horrific—horrific and magnificent."

"I hate it."

He nodded. "But you had to paint it."

Matthieu stared out from the canvas. The light falling across half his face was warm, but Theo revealed the grim shadow haunting his memory. She painted it, blackness bleeding scarlet and breathing sulphurous yellow. An acidic green oozed forth like a sickness of the soul. Not his sickness, yet he was stained by it. *Anointed.* The colors reached out from the background, wove through his hair and spilled over his shoulders.

"Does the boy hate it too?"

She shook her head. "He seems oddly comforted."

"He feels the presence. He is grateful you can see it too."

"Perhaps." Theo did not know why Matthieu found comfort in her company, but he did. Perhaps because he did not want his mother to know how horrible it had been, but Theo knew already. There was no need to pretend.

Going back to the wall, she took out a study of Mélanie with her skirt on fire, the image she had been too frightened, too ashamed to paint before. "I don't want to show them."

He nodded, then glanced at the other canvases against the wall. Understanding, she said, "There are no pictures of Casimir. That's strange isn't it? Images of him blaze quickly, like a match, but then there is only utter darkness. With all the terrible memories haunting me, you think he would too."

Averill rested a hand on the easel. "You are not only painting Matthieu—you are painting yourself."

She nodded. It was not only the stench of the physical horrors that clung to her. It was the metaphysical horror as well.

"But it has not corrupted you," Averill said. "I do not know if you will ever lose your innocence. It is an innocence of the heart, of the spirit."

"I do not feel innocent. Not after what has happened. I feel swallowed by the darkness."

"Inside it for now, but never a part of it. Even lost in it as you feel you are now, you give off light. You are a beacon."

Theo thought how Averill shied from the sunlight and how Casimir had said she drove him deeper into the shadow. She glanced at the telegram sitting on the table. "My father wants to take me to Italy."

"Go. See all the beauty that you can. I will be going to Vienna this summer for a convention on the new methods in psychiatry." He paused. "And there is a chance my father has hidden Jeanette there."

Theo had spared little thought for Jeanette these last days, but she knew his sister was precious to Averill. "You will keep searching for her?"

"Yes, though I think it is hopeless. Father will have given her another name whether she is still in France or in some other country. He will have hidden the records far better. She may be well tended, or abused. I do not know. But I must look."

"I will help."

He shook his head. "Perhaps later."

She nodded, feeling as hopeless as he did. Averill came to her and kissed each cheek in a formal salute. "It may be months before we see each other again."

He needed those months, she realized. But surely this wound would heal. He smiled sadly then turned and left her alone.

Theo cried after he left, but only briefly. Averill's loss was greater, and she felt a sham indulging hers. Going to the table, she started to compose a telegram of acceptance to her father. There was a knock. When she went to the door, it was Matthieu. He looked at her closely, but didn't question her red-rimmed eyes, any more than she ever questioned his. "Maman is making *bouillabaisse*, mademoiselle, with many fish. You are invited."

Theo wanted to be alone, but alone she would be miserable. "Thank you, I love *bouillabaisse*."

"The Inspecteur is coming."

"Is he? That will be nice." Michel had come by once already this week to make sure they were doing all right.

"He promised to bring his guitar."

That was hard to picture, Michel strumming a guitar. Would he let her sketch him while he played? "I'll bring bread and wine."

"At seven tonight, so we can hear some songs first."

"At seven, then."

After Matthieu left, Theo washed her face and walked down to the Pommiers to buy bread and bring news. But Averill had been by earlier, so instead she listened to their praise and agreed that he was the kindest of gentlemen and brave as a lion.

"He rescued my Ninette from that evil Satanist—a vile, slithering snake who should go to the guillotine," Madame Pommier declared. "But they may only send him to Devil's Island like that traitor, Dreyfus."

"It has been a terrible time," Theo said. They agreed most earnestly.

Baguette in hand, she made her way to the vintner's shop and chose a rich, silky red from Margaux for the shared dinner. Back home, she still felt at odds and ends. Going to the wardrobe, she began to lay out clothes that she might take to Italy. The decision made, she wanted to leave as soon as possible. But before she left, she had two favors to ask Michel.

When Theo went downstairs, he was already there, sitting on a chair tuning his guitar. It looked old but carefully tended. She greeted Matthieu's mother, who was chopping parsley and thyme for the soup. Theo handed over the bread and wine, and made her usual offer to help. But Madame Masson was possessive of her kitchen and shooed her away. Matthieu was in his room, finishing his schoolwork before dinner. Theo went to sit beside Michel.

Looking up, he asked in the careful English he'd begun practicing with her now that he was more friend than *flic*, "How are you this evening, Miss Faraday?"

She shrugged off that unhappy answer and said, "I will be going to Italy. My guardian is taking me to see the museums and artists' workshops."

Surprise flickered in his eyes but he only said, "I understand why you wish to leave."

"Yes, for a time. But I'll worry about Matthieu. Could you come by sometime?"

"I will come at least once a week," he said.

"Thank you." She felt both grateful and puzzled that he would promise to visit so often. "Are you always so kind?"

"No."

She waited but he said nothing more. Feeling awkward, she added, "I'm sorry if that sounded insulting."

He returned to French. "Someone helped me when I was a boy. I think perhaps it is time for me to help this boy in return."

Again Theo waited for Michel to explain, but he resumed tuning his guitar. Quietly, she said, "I have another favor to beg."

Her choice of phrase made him look at her sharply. "If I can help, I will."

"You remember that Averill's father told him Jeanette was hidden away?"

He understood instantly. "If she is in France, I might be able to find some record. But his father is also in a position to circumvent such rules."

"I know."

"Monsieur Cochefert, the chief of the Sûrêté, will be sympathetic to the situation," Michel said, "since Monsieur Charron was falsely accused."

"Thank you." Theo was glad he made the acknowledgement himself.

He frowned, then said hesitantly. "I know a man of many resources who may offer assistance."

Theo waited for more, but Michel only asked, "Does Averill have any clues?"

"He told me he is going to look in Vienna, but he believes she may still be here in France." Theo's sense of hopelessness returned. When Matthieu emerged from his room, paper in hand, she welcomed the distraction to look over his work. "Only one mistake."

He gave her a smile, then began to set things on the table.

Michel finished tuning the guitar and turned to Madame Masson. "I am happy to sing for my supper, Madame. Do you have any requests?"

"Can you play *Le Temps des cerises*?" she asked. "They are no longer singing it in the streets, but I keep hearing it in my mind."

Last week was the anniversary of the death of the Commune, Theo remembered. They called it *La semaine sanglante*—the bloody week. Appropriate in more ways than one.

Michel frowned, and Matthieu's mother looked disconcerted. Michel was a policeman after all, Theo thought, and probably no friend to Communards and their sympathizers.

Giving him an excuse, Madame Masson said, "Perhaps you don't know it?"

He gave her a small smile. "I think everyone knows it, Madame."

Theo listened as his fingers plucked the melody from the strings. Then he began to sing the poignant song that was the emblem of the Commune. His voice was lovely, deeper than she'd have expected. Matthieu and his mother joined in.

Unexpectedly Theo felt the tears she'd conquered earlier return, stinging her eyes. Only two months ago, she'd been riding beneath the blossoming cherry trees, the same pink as the tea roses in the courtyard below. Two months ago, she realized she was in love with Averill. That same day she met Michel and discovered something malevolent haunted the streets of her beloved Montmartre. Two months and all of it was gone. The evil destroyed. Love destroyed. The beauty of the cherry blossoms had conjured an idyllic future—a future as much a pipedream as the aspirations of the Commune.

Her heart ached, but Theo swallowed back the tears and joined in the last verse.

I'll always cherish cherry season
a time I keep within my heart
an open wound
and Lady Luck, afflicting me
can never ease my pain
I'll always cherish cherry season
and keep the memory in my heart.

Acknowledgments

Floats The Dark Shadow was carefully researched in Paris and in dozens of fascinating books. But somewhere in these pages an error must lurk. I hope the reader will accept this world as a slightly alternate universe in which the discrepancy is true.

Michel Colson's marvelous Fog On Montmartre is our cover photo. Visit his website at: www.photoinparis.com

Fax Sinclair did my cover portrait. You can see her gorgeous nature photography at: www.fax-sinclair.com

The uniquely talented Juan Casco designed our marvelous text font, Refugiatta: www.juancasco.net

David Rakowski kindly gave permission for us to use his beautiful font, Horst, for our drop capitals.

Special thanks to Captain Jay Jorgensen of the Albany, CA. fire department, for his expert advice.

A toast to the critique partners who offered advice on the full text: Mary Eichbauer, Tashery Shannon, Judith Stanton: www.catcrossing.com, Nancy Adams: nancyadamsfiction.com, nancyadamsediting.com, Barb Schlichting: www.barbschlichting.com, and my husband, Richard Anderson.

Quotes from J. K. Huysman's *Là Bas* are from the public domain translation by Keene Wallace.

Jon McKenny provided the moving translation of Cherry Time. The epigrams for Chapters 3, 6, 7, 16, 18, 24, 30, 41 and 42 are his. Contact him at: jonmckenney@juno.com

Sonja Elen Kisa did the Maldodor translation: kisa.ca

A.S. Kline gave permission for me to use his wonderful Verlaine translation for Chapter 13: www.poetryintranslation.com

Mary Eichbauer did the translations of Anna, Comtesse de Noailles, and together we fashioned the poem about the Anatomical Venus.

Charles Sturm's beautiful translation inspired the title. His work is also used for the epigrams of Chapters 1 & 27. Other public domain epigrams are the work of M.D. Calvocoressi in Chapter 4, Gertrude Hall in Chapters 18 and 35. The mysterious Eugenia de B translated Victor Hugo's prose for Chapter 36.

The remaining epigrams, the Danse Macabre and Anarchists' Song translations are mine: www.YvesFey.com

About the Author

Photo by Fax Sinclair

Yves Fey has an MFA in Creative Writing from Eugene Oregon, and a BA in Pictorial Arts from UCLA. She has read, written, and created art from childhood. A chocolate connoisseur, she's won prizes for her desserts. Her current fascination is creating perfumes, including fragrances inspired by her novel. She's traveled to many countries in Europe and lived for two years in Indonesia. She currently lives in the San Francisco area with her husband and three cats. Writing as Gayle Feyrer and Taylor Chase, she previously published unusually dark and mysterious historical romances.

CPSIA information can be obtained
at www.ICGtesting.com
Printed in the USA
BVOW08*1523050717
488391BV00004B/39/P